OLD
CREOLE
DAYS

OLD CREOLE DAYS

BY GEORGE WASHINGTON CABLE

together with

THE SCENES OF CABLE'S ROMANCES

BY LAFCADIO HEARN

A PROLOGUE

BY EDWARD LAROCQUE TINKER

and

ILLUSTRATIONS IN COLOR

BY JOHN O'HARA COSGRAVE II

THE HERITAGE PRESS
NEW YORK

THE CONTENTS

(*v*)

CABLE
AND THE CREOLES
A PROLOGUE BY EDWARD LAROCQUE TINKER

GEORGE WASHINGTON CABLE was as much a misfit in New Orleans as a parson in a crap game, and for this discongruity his mother was, in a great measure, responsible.

When he was born in 1844, the city's reputation for gilded vice was known the length of the Mississippi River and even reached across the Alleghanies to New York and Boston. Bull-baiting was still practiced and cock-fighting and gambling were rampant. Alluring *café-au-lait* colored girls, tricked out in ribbons, were exposed for sale in the windows of the Royal Street slave-pens, where their physical charms rather than their ability to work were touted. Dissipation was provided for all classes; the aristocrats had their elaborate octoroon balls, while the rawboned flatboatmen, with their coonskin caps at a rakish angle, and a bowie knife in their belts, had their nightly debauches in "the swamps," and were often rooked of the money they made from the sale of their "broad-horns" and the produce they had floated down the river from Kentucky. Gentlemen settled quarrels by duels conducted under rigid codes, and wastrels by stabbing in the back or fighting bloody battles in which every form of mayhem, from gouging out eyes to biting off noses was tried. Indeed one notorious character had his teeth filed sharp to more easily accomplish his diabolical designs. Never a night passed that the watch did not stumble over the corpse of one or more victims of foul play.

New Orleans had other and more praiseworthy facets, for it was a city of outstanding culture and luxury, with a brilliant social life.

(*vii*)

Opera was given there for the first time in this country; while many of the rich Creoles owed their educations to Parisian universities and had acquired well-chosen libraries of French classics. It was the hot-blooded, pleasure-loving Franco-Americans, proud, haughty and high-strung, who dictated the tone and character of the city.

In this exotic, sensuous, impulsive and aristocratic atmosphere, where slavery was considered as sanctioned by Holy Writ, George Cable's mother brought him up as austerely Presbyterian and as ardently abolitionist as though he had been born in Boston. With her background and experience this was inevitable, for she had inherited the grim, indefatigable religious principles of her Puritan ancestors. Her husband's fortunes had gone from bad to worse after they had settled in New Orleans, and when, very much against her will, he opened a "saloon and wine store," her distress reached its climax. He became a notary after he failed as a purveyor of spirituous liquors, then a deputy constable, and finally died leaving as his only legacy the four children his wife had practically supported. With the memory of her husband's shortcomings constantly before her, she determined they should never follow his example, so she saw to it that they were raised in the strictest Presbyterian orthodoxy to believe that industry was a duty, indolence a depravity, honesty a necessity, drink a curse, and that the theatre and dancing were but devils' traps to damn their souls to eternity.

It was a training that George Cable never forgot, one that influenced his whole life, and made him as alien as an Eskimo in the pleasure-loving Catholic city of his birth. He left school at his father's death, when he was fourteen, to help support the family, and labored at various humble jobs until, five years later, he joined the Confederate cavalry. He showed courage as a soldier and acquitted himself with honor. When the war was over he returned to a ruined New Orleans. After a hard experience of surveying in the swamps, he got work as a bookkeeper in a cotton broker's office. When he was twenty-five, in spite of a meagre salary, shared with his mother, he took upon himself the duties of a married man.

Although in those days clerks worked terribly long hours, from "cain see to caint see," as the Negroes said, Cable found time to write a Sunday column for the *Picayune*, which he signed with the sanguinary *nom de guerre* of "Drop Shot"—a strange conceit for a delicate, slight young man, whose sharp brown eyes, peeping over a long drooping mustache and luxuriant beard, suggested a mouse hiding in the grass. The coy, chaste attempts at humor of his rather labored and verbose contributions must have caused much levity among his fellow journalists, the majority of whom fought as a pastime, drank as a serious vocation, and swore like a bucko mate.

The *Picayune* editor, Richard Rhett, boisterous, hair-trigger tempered and a notorious duelist, was typical of the breed, and kept in practice by firing at a target on the farther wall of the newsroom, over the heads of his reporters at their copy desk. Cable called him surreptitiously "Duelsome Dick" and, inspired by one of his angry fits, gravely discussed in his column the number of accidents in sawmills, factories, and steamboats, ending with the statement: "We only wish we could give the casualties resulting from the explosions of fighting editors."

As a journalist Cable's career blossomed only to fade, for he was fired when he refused to report an "ungodly" theatrical performance. Years later he accused his "somewhat vexatious scrupulosity" of being the stumbling block, but this was only after a dramatization of his own novel, *The Cavalier*, had mellowed his opinion of the theatre.

Nothing could swerve him from his ambition to become an author; and he got up at four o'clock every morning for a few hours' writing before he was due at his desk in the cotton broker's office. The stories he heard about the Creoles he began to set down in detail; for, to this slow, prudish and plodding clerk, these exotic people had all the charm of the dissimilar. While he felt in duty bound to disapprove of many of their characteristics, some of their failings and foibles endeared them to him. The even uneventful monotony of his inhibited, laborious existence made him look with envy at the gay, impulsive Creoles, with their debonair, insouciant courage, their lily-of-the-field philosophy and their instinctive clutch at immediate pleasure, with little regard for future costs. Possibly the mere description of their volatile emotions and their impetuous love affairs may have given him a vicarious sense of adventure.

His manner of recounting these fascinating tales was entirely individual, for he was following no pattern. Until well past middle age he thought it was sinful to read novels, and while this probably deprived him of the inspiration of much good literature, his narrow point of view did a great deal to give freshness and originality to his style. His isolation had saved him from acquiring the outworn clichés and the grandiose ideology of most of the popular Southern writers of his day, who completely disregarded Emerson's admonition to write of the "near, the low and the common." Instead, most of the authors of that section and time painted ornate, stilted portraits of the ruling aristocrats, women of glacial virtue and fainting refinement, and men invariably chivalrous and continent. Only one character was permitted to fall below this unattainable high standard—the villain, with his drooping black mustache, whose presence was necessary to enhance by contrast the impeccable nobility of his victims. Few words of social criticism were published for, even if the Southern writer noticed inconsistencies in the mode of life below the Mason-Dixon line, it was ill-bred to mention them, and people were loath to risk the ostracism, and even the challenges to duels, that were the almost inevitable aftermath of any censure.

Saved from this stultifying influence, Cable's stories had a new flavor that Edward King, on a visit to New Orleans to obtain material for a book on the South, was quick to recognize. He encouraged the little bookkeeper and took some of his manuscripts to New York to submit to *Scribner's Monthly*. "'Sieur George" was bought for fifty dollars and appeared in 1873. In the next few years they printed the other stories (except "Posson Jone'," which came out in *Appleton's*) that were included in Cable's first book, *Old Creole Days*, published in 1879. This small volume was received with immediate enthusiasm, not only because its tales described an exotic, quaint and colorful life hitherto unknown in New England, but also because the sympathy shown toward the Negro was a popular viewpoint in the North. War rancors were still bitter, so it was natural for the abolitionist Yankees to applaud implied criticism—especially if made by a Southerner—of the treatment of Negro slaves. They were particularly interested in Cable's exposition of the tragic consequences of miscegenation as typified in his character, "'Tite Poulette," whose octoroon mother made a gallant but pathetic fight to preserve her daughter's virtue in defiance of a social order that doomed her to a practically inevitable concubinage.

Old Creole Days did not have to rely for its success upon a conditioned public, for these sentimental stories were sufficiently vivid and interesting in themselves to stand on their own merits, and perhaps nothing since *Uncle Tom's Cabin* had become so quickly popular. They were immediately hailed as masterpieces in England, and one Britisher, after reading them, said that if the octoroon mothers were half as alluring and virtuous as Cable depicted them, he, for one, regretted the abolition of a social order that produced such unusual characters. That it made a lasting impression in the English-speaking countries was evidenced by Stephen Leacock who, more than half a century after it appeared, wrote that it would not readily be forgotten and said of its author: "In George W. Cable the South produced a humanist in the highest sense of the word, and one whose works reached two continents. His was the humor of that high type that does not excite the loud laughter, exploding over single strokes of comicality and single incongruities of words, but that is interwoven as a golden thread in the texture of depicted life."

Some of the causes that went to make Cable famous in the North made him equally infamous in the South. Fiction below the Mason-Dixon line had never treated the Negro except as a black-faced buffoon or a loyal, humble, family retainer. As a flesh and blood problem in adjustment the Negro was too sore a subject, so by tacit agreement the South ignored the question inherent in his existence and, on pain of ostracism, forbade any public discussion. The excesses of Reconstruction had persuaded these people that their safety and survival depended upon the ruthless disciplining of the freed blacks, and anyone who advocated their rights—especially one of their own countrymen—or even stirred up sympathy in their behalf was, in their eyes, a renegade scalawag, more loathsome than a Carpetbagger.

The Creoles felt they had additional and special reasons to be incensed, for Cable, not content with describing the quadroon balls of the Rue d'Orléans and saying they were attended by Creole gentlemen, went even further. In "Belles Demoiselles Plantation," whose prototype was the old Zeringue place on the other side of the Mississippi River, he made a well-born Creole chaffer, none too honestly, for a piece of ancestral real estate owned by an illegitimate relative with a strain of mixed Indian and Negro blood. It only made matters worse that he added: "One thing I never knew a Creole to do. He will not utterly go back on the ties of blood, no matter what sort of knots those ties may be. For one reason he is never ashamed of his or his father's sins; and for another—he will tell you he is 'all heart.' "

It was more than they could endure, inheriting, as they did, a sensitive, thin-skinned pride from their Old World ancestors; particularly as they feared that these stories would give the impression in other parts of the country that the Creole race was not of unsullied white descent. Their acute sense of personal dignity was further offended because Cable made his Franco-American characters speak a quaint lacerated lingo. Although George Cable was always careful to render the dialogue in correct English, when the principals in his stories were speaking French, the Creoles remained convinced that he was holding them up to ridicule and advertising them to the world as crude and unlettered. They complained too of his ignorance of the French language and of the Negro patois, and one of his detractors insisted that his entire knowledge of these subjects "would not overload the back of a mouse." But whether or not his notation of their peculiarities of pronunciation was philologically correct, there is no doubt that many well-bred Creoles of his day spoke with a decided accent and were guilty of many quaint solecisms. Nevertheless, the whole *Vieux Carré* boiled with rage and, when Cable's name was mentioned, many people spat upon the banquette with rage.

His first long novel, *The Grandissimes*, published in 1880, further inflamed their passionate resentment, although he described one of the Grandissime family by saying, "his whole appearance was a dazzling contradiction that a Creole is a person of mixed blood." Feeling ran so high that a delegation of Creole ladies waited on Sir James Barrie when he went South, in spite of his remark that to see New Orleans a long journey was quite unnecessary; all one had to do was to sit in a steam laundry and read *The Grandissimes*. His indignant visitors warned him that Cable had misrepresented them; and it is reported Sir James replied ungallantly: "I'm sure that's so, for no real people could be half so charming."

In *Old Creole Days*, Cable was an enthusiastic writer, fascinated by his material, and entirely absorbed in telling his story; but in *The Grandissimes*, although it was an immediate success, he displayed the first evidence of the struggle which was to destroy him as a literary man—the first proofs that the propagandist was beginning to strangle the creative artist. This was increasingly apparent in his next book, *Dr. Sevier*, a formless, discursive story, full of trite "preachy" morality.

As time went on he became more and more the controversial pamphleteer. He attacked in print and speech the convict lease system of the Southern states, the management of penitentiaries and lunatic asylums, and the political and social treatment of the freedman: philippics that were published in a small volume called *The Silent South.*

He was both honest and eloquent in his arguments for ameliorating the status of the colored race, but he might as well have tried to extinguish a forest fire with a syringe as attempt the reforms he advocated, especially as, by that time, he had become the target for active vilification. The Creoles would not understand that he was driven by a fanatic evangelism, directly inherited from his witch-burning ancestors. They believed his attitude on the Negro question was due solely to a mercenary desire to sell more books to the Northerners.

When he left for a widely heralded lecture tour with Mark Twain, they could hardly contain themselves, for Cable, as his share of the entertainment, sang "Gombo" songs and gave dialect readings from *Old Creole Days* and *The Grandissimes*. The show always opened in the same way; shock-headed Mark Twain led his tiny, bearded partner down to the footlights and introduced him as "my little brother." Off stage their relations were sometimes strained, for experience in the world had not softened Cable's puritanical severity. He was emphatic in his refusal to have food cooked in his house on Sunday, and once, wishing to hear Henry Ward Beecher preach, he went to Brooklyn Saturday night and did not return until Monday, because he thought it sinful to cross the ferry on the Sabbath. This punctilious observance of the Seventh Day led him to introduce a clause in his contract with Mark Twain against traveling on Sunday, and it often proved a source of annoyance, especially when their performance finished one Saturday night in a jerkwater town with an atrocious hotel. Mark Twain begged and implored Cable to go on to Chicago to spend the week-end in comfort, but Cable pointed stubbornly to the letter of his agreement, until irrepressible irritation caused the Mississippi River ex-pilot to call him "a Christ-besprinkled, psalm-singing Presbyterian." This almost ended the tour.

The reaction in the South to this successful barn-storming was exactly what might have been expected, and one Southern periodical summarized it by saying: "The last catch-penny enterprize of this literary tradesman was going around the country singing Creole and negro songs. His piping voice sounded like the buzzing of a mosquito. No doubt this public exhibition of himself added to his bank account, but who can calculate the injury of such a display upon the honor and dignity of American literature? It may seem quite the proper thing for Mr. Cable to make money in such a way, for he has been raised from the stool of a cotton broker's office to the desk of the author, therefore, he is not expected to possess a very high and delicate sense of literary propriety."

Since the publication of *The Grandissimes,* violent attacks had been aimed at Cable in the Creole press and were followed by a rain of bitter pamphlets. The most curious was by the venerable Abbé Rouquette, last of the Black Robe Fathers to the Indians, called a *Critical Dialogue between Aboo and Caboo,* published under the pseudonym of E. Junius. A senile, heavy-footed satire, it was filled with the most turgidly fantastic and floriated vituperation.

"What would you feel, what would you say," its author asked, "were you to see a buzzard, glutted with carrion, lighting heavily upon a desecrated shrine? You would shudder and recoil! What would you feel, what would you say, were you to behold a jackal disinter a cherished corpse, drag it away, tear it to pieces, and devour its lacerated flesh? You would stand mute and awe-struck. Say, then, has not this heartless and grim-humored dwarf done something like the foul buzzard, has he not done something like the hideous jackal?"

The Rouquette booklet ended with a mean, obscene little poem in the Creole dialect, in which the Reverend Abbé so far forgot his cloth as to accuse Cable of joining in voudoo dances with Marie

Laveau, and other even more reprehensible practices—charges that were quite without foundation.

Judge Charles Gayarré, the Louisiana historian, hired a hall to denounce the author of *The Grandissimes* before a large and enthusiastic audience, and in the course of his remarks accused Cable of advocating in his *Freedman's Case in Equity* a universal panacea labeled on the bottle, "Social and conjugal fusion of the blacks and the whites."

All these manifestations whipped up the tinder-temper of the Creoles until the more inflammable decided to wipe out the insults to their race by challenging Cable to a duel. Some of the cooler heads rebuked the ringleaders and said all they could accomplish by the move would be to horse-whip a very small and frail person who would absolutely refuse to defend himself. The idea was abandoned, but the hate that inspired it still burns in Louisiana, and with few exceptions the present generation of Creoles, though they have never read his books, have inherited a garbled version of the reasons for their indignation. One of them was heard to explain that Madame Lalaurie refused to receive Cable because he was not all white, so in order to get even he had written "The Haunted House in Royal Street," in which he described how the mob, learning of the brutal treatment her slaves received, had sacked her house. There are only two inaccuracies in this statement: there never was any doubt that George W. Cable was white; and he could never have seen Mme. Lalaurie, because she sailed for France in 1834, ten years before he was born.

A contemporary Creole writer, M. John L. Peytavin, was much more fair-minded in his judgment of Cable. He explained that he called him "a hawker of Creole caricatures" because: *"M. Cable prend invariablement les exceptions et les donne comme régles générales. Il prend les Créoles du dernier degré de l'échelle sociale et les presente aux gens du Nord comme l'élite de la société néo-orléaniste. Créole, Cadien, mulâtre, sont pour M. Cable synonymes."*

In spite of many idiosyncrasies, Cable was a kind man who craved approbation and affection, and it pained him to live in an atmosphere of such decorticating hate. Many times he must have wished to escape from the city of his birth, but his chance did not come until

1886, when his success as a writer became sufficiently assured to warrant moving his numerous family. Making the excuse that he wished to be nearer his publishers, he left New Orleans. His arrival in New York suggested a Mardi Gras parade, for he wore a strange, planter-like hat on his head, and his flowing mustache and brown beard streamed luxuriantly over a long yellow duster, buttoned up to his chin and falling almost to his heels, that made him look like a small boy masquerading in his father's clothes. A child clung to each hand, and Mrs. Cable trailed behind with the other children.

His publisher, Charles Scribner, invited them to dinner, and was surprised that Cable would neither drink nor smoke, and when Scribner announced he had tickets for the theatre, his guest refused to go. When Sunday came the difficulties faded into thin air, for the publisher took the whole family to church. He said later he had never felt so important in his life as when he sat at the end of the pew with Cable next, and the long line of children, graded as to size, extending to a seeming infinity.

After this visit, Cable moved his family to a home in Northampton, Massachusetts, where a change, that was destined to militate against his literary career, finally came to a head. Cable the creative artist had always been at war with Cable the Sunday school teacher, and now, in this new congenial atmosphere, his evangelistic predisposition gained the upper hand, and he indulged in an orgy of proselyting, teaching a Bible class of two thousand at Tremont Temple in Boston on Saturday afternoons and another in Northampton on Sundays. He reinforced his preaching by publishing two small books on the twin objects of his zealous propaganda—*The Busy Man's Bible* and *The Negro Question;* and he founded The People's Institute, Culture and Garden Clubs for working families, and even became a member of the Simplified Spelling Board. These pedagogic excesses and manifold activities aimed at social reform sapped his strength and murdered any imaginative ability. Renan declared that saints are usually dull people, and he might have added propagandists as well. Cable lost the brilliant freshness of his early stories, and became a dull writer, his novels prosy, platitudinous, and hamshackled by trite moralizing.

Still another important factor contributed to Cable's literary degeneration. Like Lafcadio Hearn, he did not have a positive creative type of mind. His inspiration had to be nourished by continuous impressions of the life around him. These he could fashion into books with the meticulous care of a Swiss watchmaker; but, after leaving the South, he still tried to write of it, though cut off from the new turns of phrase and accretions of picturesque incident to which he had been accustomed by daily contacts. His mind was not sufficiently fertile nor his imagination vivid enough to supply this lack, so only two of the books published after his hegira have serious merit— *Bonaventure*, because its three tales were written before he forsook his native state; and *Strange True Stories of Louisiana*, because it was based on the manuscripts of others. The rest, pale shadows of his early successes, were negligible, commonplace, run-of-the-mill romances.

In spite of this, Cable's services to Southern literature were of primary importance. He was the first Southerner to write objectively and realistically of the life he saw around him, the first to break the taboo against discussing the Negro as a human being rather than as a chattel. It was his courage that freed the authors who followed him from the necessity of fulsome praise for all things sectional; taught them their right and duty to analyze and portray truthfully, to criticize if necessary, the social conditions under which they and those around them lived. He was the Moses who led them out of the bondage to "magnolia and mocking-bird," the legitimate father of the literary movement that is producing such splendid fruit in the South today. This he accomplished at the cost of practical ostracism by his own people. He may well be called the first martyr to literary freedom in the South.

Two of Cable's books have achieved a permanent place in American literature—*The Grandissimes* and *Old Creole Days*. The latter's delicate, pathetic and subtly humorous resurrections of the exotic and prismatic past of New Orleans make it one of our most appealing pieces of regional writing. It should be stated that "Madame Delphine" was not in the first edition of *Old Creole Days*, 1879, but was added later; and that "Père Raphaël" has never before been numbered in the collection. It was written years after the other stories, as a companion piece to "Posson Jone'," and finds a place in this volume because Cable insisted that the two tales were inseparable.

It seemed fitting also to include in this edition Lafcadio Hearn's "Scenes of Cable's Romances," that appeared in the *Century Magazine* in 1883. It was written in the heyday of their friendship (later wrecked by Hearn's moody suspicions), and his iridescent verbal palette has added the charm and vividness of a different angle of vision to Cable's delightful architectural portraits of the *Vieux Carré.*

THE SCENES
OF CABLE'S ROMANCES
BY LAFCADIO HEARN

W HEN I first viewed New Orleans from the deck of the great steamboat that had carried me from gray northwestern mists into the tepid and orange-scented air of the South, my impressions of the city, drowsing under the violet and gold of a November morning, were oddly connected with memories of "Jean-ah Poquelin." That strange little tale had appeared previously in the *Century;* and its exotic picturesqueness had considerably influenced my anticipations of the Southern metropolis, and prepared me to idealize everything peculiar and semi-tropical that I might see. Even before I had left the steamboat my imagination had already flown beyond the wilderness of cotton-bales, the sierra-shaped roofs of the sugar-sheds, the massive fronts of refineries and store-houses, to wander in search of the old slave-trader's mansion, or at least of something resembling it—"built of heavy cypress, lifted up on pillars, grim, solid, and spiritless." I did not even abandon my search for the house after I had learned that Tchoupitoulas "Road" was now a great business street, fringed not by villas but by warehouses; that the river had receded from it considerably since the period of the story; and that where marsh lands used to swelter under the sun, pavements of block-stone had been laid, enduring as Roman causeways, though they will tremble a little under the passing of cotton-floats. At one time, I tried to connect the narrative with a peculiar residence near the Bayou road—a silent wooden mansion with vast verandas, surrounded by shrubbery which had become fantastic by long neglect. Indeed, there are several old houses in the more ancient quarters of the city which might have served as models for the description of "Jean-ah Poquelin's" dwelling, but none of them is situated in his original neighborhood—old plantation homes whose broad lands have long since been cut up and devoured by the growing streets. In reconstructing the New Orleans of 1810, Mr. Cable might have selected any of these to draw from, and I may have found his model without knowing it. Not, however, until the *Century* appeared, with its curious article upon the "Great South Gate," did I learn that in the early years of the nineteenth century such a house existed precisely in the location described by Mr. Cable. Readers of "The Great South Gate" must have been impressed by the description therein given of "Doctor" Gravier's home, upon the bank of the long-vanished Poydras canal—a picture of desolation more than justified by the testimony of early municipal chronicles; and the true history of that eccentric "Doctor" Gravier no doubt inspired the creator of "Jean-ah Poquelin." An ancient city map informs us that the deserted indigo fields, with their wriggling amphibious population, extended a few blocks north of the present Charity Hospital; and that the plantation house itself must have stood near the juncture of Poydras and Freret Streets—a region now very closely built and very thickly peopled.

The sharp originality of Mr. Cable's description should have convinced the readers of *Old Creole Days* that the scenes of his stories are in no sense fanciful; and the strict perfection of his Creole architecture is readily recognized by all who have resided in New Orleans. Each one of those charming pictures of places—veritable pastels—was painted after some carefully selected model of French or Franco-Spanish origin, typifying fashions of building which prevailed in colonial days. Greatly as the city has changed since the eras in which Mr. Cable's stories are laid, the old Creole quarter still contains antiquities enough to enable the artist to restore almost all that has vanished. Through those narrow, multicolored and dilapidated streets one may still wander at random with the certainty of encountering eccentric façades and suggestive Latin appellations at every turn; and the author of "Madame Delphine" must have made many a pilgrimage into the quaint district, to study the wrinkled faces of the houses, or perhaps to read the queer names upon the signs—as Balzac loved to do in old-fashioned Paris. Exceptionally rich in curiosities is the Rue Royale, and it best represents, no doubt, the general physiognomy of the colonial city. It appears to be Mr. Cable's favorite street, as there are few of his stories which do not contain references to it; even the scenery of incidents laid elsewhere has occasionally been borrowed from that "region of architectural decrepitude," which is yet peopled by an "ancient and foreign-seeming domestic life." For Louisiana dreamers, Mr. Cable has peopled it also with many delightful phantoms; and the ghosts of Madame Délicieuse, of Delphine Carraze, of 'Sieur George, will surely continue to haunt it until of all the dear old buildings there shall not be left a stone upon a stone.

From the corner of Canal Street at Royal—ever perfumed by the baskets of the flower-sellers—to the junction of Royal with Bienville, one observes with regret numerous evidences of modernization. American life is invading the thoroughfare—uprearing concert-halls, with insufferably pompous names, multiplying flashy saloons and cheap restaurants, cigar-stores and oyster-rooms. Gambling indeed survives, but only through metamorphosis—it is certainly not of that aristocratic kind wherein Colonel De Charleu, owner of "Belles Demoiselles Plantation," could have been wont to indulge. Already a line of electric lights mocks the rusty superannuation of those long disused wrought-iron lamp frames set into the walls of various Creole buildings. But from the corner of Conti Street—where Jules St.-Ange idled one summer morning "some seventy years ago"—Rue Royale begins to display a picturesqueness almost unadulterated by innovation, and opens a perspective of roof lines astonishingly irregular, that jag and cut into the blue strip of intervening sky at every conceivable angle, with gables, eaves, dormers, triangular peaks of slate, projecting corners of balconies or verandas—overtopping or jutting out from houses of every imaginable tint: canary, chocolate, slate-blue, speckled gray, ultramarine, cinnamon red, and even pale rose. All have sap-green batten shutters; most possess balconies balustraded with elegant arabesque work in wrought iron—graceful tendrils and curling leaves of metal, framing some monogram of which the meaning is forgotten. Much lattice-work also will be observed about verandas, or veiling the ends of galleries, or suspended like green cage-work at the angle formed by a window-balcony with some lofty court-wall. And far down the street, the erratic superimposition of wire-hung signs, advertising the presence of many quiet, shadowy little shops that hide their faces from the sun behind slanting canvas awnings, makes a spidery confusion of lines and angles in the very centre of the vista.

I think that only by a series of instantaneous photographs, tinted after the manner of Goupil, could the physiognomy of the street be accurately reproduced, such is the confusion of projecting show-windows, the kaleidoscopic medley of color, the jumble of infinitesimal stores. The characteristics of almost any American street may usually be taken in at one glance; but you might traverse this Creole thoroughfare a hundred times without being able to ordinate the puzzling details of its perspective.

But when the curious pilgrim reaches the corner of Royal and St. Peter Streets (Rue Saint Pierre), he finds himself confronted by an edifice whose oddity and massiveness compel special examination—a four-story brick tenement house, with walls deep as those of a mediæval abbey, and with large square windows having singular balconies, the ironwork of which is wrought into scrolls and initials. Unlike any other building in the quarter, its form is that of an irregular pentagon, the smallest side of which looks down Royal and up St. Peter Streets at once, and commands through its windows, in a single view, three street angles. This is the house where 'Sieur George so long dwelt. It is said to have been the first four-story building erected in New Orleans; and it certainly affords a singular example of the fact that some very old buildings obstinately rebel against innovations of fashion, just as many old men do. Despite a desperate effort recently made to compel its acceptance of a new suit of paint and whitewash, the venerable structure persisted in remaining almost precisely as Mr. Cable first described it. The cornices are still dropping plaster; the stucco has not ceased to peel off; the rotten staircases, "hugging the sides of the court," still seem "trying to climb up out of the rubbish"; the court itself is always "hung with many lines of wet clothes"; and the rooms are now, as ever, occupied by folk "who dwell there simply for lack of activity to find better and cheaper quarters elsewhere." Cheaper it would surely be easy to find, inasmuch as 'Sieur George's single-windowed room rents unfurnished at ten dollars per month. There is something unique in the spectacle of this ponderous, dilapidated edifice, with its host of petty shops on the *rez-de-chaussée*—something which recalls an engraving I once saw in some archæological folio, picturing a swarm of Italian fruit-booths seeking shelter under the crumbling arches of a Roman theatre.

Upon the east side of Rue Royale, half a square farther up, the eye is refreshed by a delicious burst of bright green—a garden inclosed on three sides by spiked railings, above which bananas fling out the watered-satin of their splendid leaves, and bounded at its eastern extremity by the broad, blanched, sloping-shouldered silhouette of the Cathedral. Here linger memories of Padre Antonio de Sedella (Père Antoine), first sent to Louisiana as a commissary of the Holy Inquisition, immediately shipped home again by sensible Governor Miro. But Padre Antonio returned to Louisiana, not as an inquisitor, but as a secular priest, to win the affection of the whole Creole population, by whom he was venerated as a saint even before his death. Somewhere near this little garden, the padre used to live in a curious wooden hut; and the narrow, flagged alley on the southern side of the Cathedral and its garden still bears the appellation, Passage Saint Antoine, in honor of the old priest's patron. The name is legibly inscribed above the show-windows of the Roman Catholic shop on the corner, where porcelain angels appear to be perpetually ascending and descending a Jacob's-ladder formed of long communion candles. The "Pères Jeromes" of our own day reside in the dismal brick houses bordering the alley farther toward Chartres Street—buildings which protrude, above the heads of passers-by, a line of jealous-looking balconies, screened with latticework, in which wicket lookouts have been contrived. On the northern side of garden and Cathedral runs another flagged alley, which affects to be a continuation of Orleans Street. Like its companion passage, it opens into Chartres Street; but on the way it forks into a grotesque fissure in the St. Peter Street block—into a marvelous mediæval-looking by-way, craggy with balconies and peaked with dormers. As this picturesque opening is still called Exchange Alley, we must suppose it to have once formed part of the much more familiar passage of that name, though now widely separated therefrom by architectural reforms effected in Rue Saint Louis and other streets intervening. The northern side-entrance of the Cathedral commands it—a tall, dark, ecclesiastically severe archway, in whose shadowed recess Madame Delphine might safely have intrusted her anxieties to "God's own banker"; and Catholic quadroon women on their daily morning way to market habitually enter it with their baskets, to murmur a prayer in patois before the shrine of Notre Dame de Lourdes. Jackson Square, with its rococo flower-beds and clipped shrubbery, might be reached in a moment by either of the flagged alleys above described; but it retains none of its colonial features, and has rightly been deprived of the military titles it once bore: Place d'Armes, or Plaza de Armas.

There stands, at the corner of St. Anne and Royal Streets, a one-story structure with Spanish tile roof, a building that has become absolutely shapeless with age, and may be torn away at any moment. It is now a mere hollow carcass—a shattered brick skeleton to which plaster and laths cling in patches only, like shrunken hide upon the bones of some creature left to die and to mummify under the sun. An obsolete directory, printed in 1845, assures us that the construction was considered immemorially old even then; but a remarkable engraving of it, which accompanies the above remark, shows it to have at that time possessed distinct Spanish features and two neat entrances with semicircular stone steps. In 1835 it was Café des Réfugiés, frequented by fugitives from the Antilles, West Indian strangers, filibusters, *révolutionnaires*—all that singular class of Latin-Americans so strongly portrayed in Mr. Cable's "Café des Exilés."

At the next block, if you turn down Dumaine Street from Royal, you will notice, about halfway toward Chartres, a very peculiar house, half brick, half timber. It creates the impression that its builder commenced it with the intention of erecting a three-story brick, but changed his mind before the first story had been completed, and finished the edifice with second-hand lumber—supporting the gallery with wooden posts that resemble monstrous balusters. This is the house bequeathed by "Mr. John," of the Good Children Social Club, to the beautiful quadroon Zalli and her more beautiful reputed daughter, 'Tite Poulette. As Mr. Cable tells us, and as one glance can verify, it has now become "a den of Italians, who sell fuel by day, and by night are up to no telling what extent of deviltry." On the same side of Dumaine, but on the western side of Royal Street, is another remarkable building, more imposing, larger—"whose big, round-arched windows in the second story were walled up, to have smaller windows let into them again with odd little latticed peep-holes in their batten shutters." It was to this house that Zalli and 'Tite Poulette removed their worldly goods, after the failure of the bank; and it was from the most westerly of those curious windows in the second story that Kristian Koppig saw the row of cigar-boxes empty their load of earth and flowers upon the head of the manager of the Salle de Condé. Right opposite you may see the good Dutchman's one-story Creole cottage. The resemblance of 'Tite Poulette's second dwelling-place to the old Spanish barracks in architectural peculiarity has been prettily commented upon by Mr. Cable; and, in fact, those barracks, which could shelter six thousand troops in O'Reilly's time, and must, therefore, have covered a considerable area, were situated not very far from this spot. But the only fragments of the barrack buildings that are still positively recognizable are the arched structures at Nos. 270 and 272 Royal Street, occupied now, alas! by a prosaic seltzer factory. The spacious cavalry stables now shelter vulgar mules, and factory wagons protrude their shafts from the mouths of low, broad archways, under which once glimmered the brazen artillery of the King of Spain.

A square west of Royal, at the corner of Bourbon and St. Philip Streets, formerly stood the famed smithy of the brothers Lafitte; but it were now useless to seek for a vestige of that workshop, whose chimes of iron were rung by African muscle. Passing St. Philip Street, therefore, the visitor who follows the east side of Royal might notice upon the opposite side an elegant and lofty red brick mansion, with a deep archway piercing its *rez-de-chaussée* to the courtyard, which offers a glimpse of rich foliage whenever the portecochère is left ajar. This is No. 253 Royal Street, the residence of "Madame Délicieuse"; and worthy of that honor, it seems, with its superb tiara of green verandas. A minute two-story cottage squats down beside it—a miniature shop having tiny show-windows that project like eyes. The cottage is a modern affair; but it covers the site of Dr. Mossy's office, which, you know, was a lemon-yellow Creole construction, roofed with red tiles. What used to be the "Café de Poésie" on the corner, is now a hat store. Further on, at the intersection of Royal and Hospital Streets (Rue d'Hôpital, famous in Creole ballads), one cannot fail to admire a dwelling solid and elegant as a Venetian *palazzo*. It has already been celebrated in one foreign novel; and did I not feel confident that Mr. Cable will tell us all about it one of these days, I should be tempted to delay the reader on this corner, although Madame Delphine's residence is already within sight.

No one can readily forget Mr. Cable's description of "the small, low, brick house of a story and a half, set out upon the sidewalk, as weather-beaten and mute as an aged beggar fallen asleep." It stands near Barracks Street, on Royal; the number, I think, is 294. Still are its solid wooden shutters "shut with a grip that makes one's nails and knuckles feel lacerated"; and its coat of decaying plaster, patched with all varieties of neutral tints, still suggests the raggedness of mendicancy. Even the condition of the garden gate, through which Monsieur Vignevielle first caught a glimpse of Olive's maiden beauty, might be perceived to-day as readily as ever by "an eye that had been in the blacksmithing business." But the picturesqueness of the upper part of the cottage has been greatly diminished by architectural additions made with a view to render the building habitable. Over the way may still be seen that once pretentious three-story residence "from whose front door hard times have removed all vestiges of paint," a door shaped like old European hall doors, and furnished with an iron knocker. It has not been repainted since Mr. Cable wrote his story, nor does it seem likely to be.

Only a few paces farther on yawns the dreamy magnificence of aristocratic Esplanade Street, with its broad, central band of grass all shadow-flecked by double lines of trees. There Royal Street terminates, Esplanade forming the southern boundary line of the old French Quarter.

If the reader could now follow me westwardly along one of the narrow ways leading to the great Rue des Remparts, he would soon find himself in that quadroon quarter, whose denizens still "drag their chairs down to the narrow gateways of their close-fenced gardens, and stare shrinkingly at you as you pass, like a nest of yellow kittens." He would be at once charmed and astonished by the irregularity of the perspective and the eccentricity of the houses: houses whose foreheads are fantastically encircled by wooden parapets, striped like the foulards of the Negresses; houses yellow-faced and sphinx-featured, like certain mulatto women; houses which present their profiles to the fence, so that as you approach they seem to turn away their faces with studied prudery like young Creole girls; houses that appear felinely watchful, in spite of closed windows and doors, gazing sleepily at the passer-by through the chinks of their green shutters, as through vertical pupils. Five minutes' walk over banquettes of disjointed brick-work, through which knots of tough grass are fighting their upward way, brings one to Rampart Street, where Mr. Cable found the model for his "Café des Exilés." It was situated on the west side, No. 219, and the artist has sketched it under a summersglow that brought out every odd detail in strong relief. But hereafter, alas! the visitor to New Orleans must vainly look for the window of Pauline, "well up in the angle of the broad side-gable, shaded by its rude awning of clapboards, as the eyes of an old dame are shaded by her wrinkled hand." Scarcely a week ago, from the time at which I write, the antiquated cottage that used to "squat right down upon the sidewalk, as do those Choctaw squaws who sell bay and sassafras and life-everlasting," was ruthlessly torn away, together with its oleanders, and palmettoes, and pomegranates, to make room, no doubt, for some modern architectural platitude.

A minute's walk from the vacant site of the Café des Exilés will bring you to Congo Square, the last green remnant of those famous Congo Plains, where the Negro slaves once held their bamboulas. Until within a few years ago, the strange African dances were still danced, and the African songs still sung by Negroes and Negresses who had been slaves. Every Sunday afternoon the bamboula dancers were summoned to a wood-yard on Dumaine Street by a sort of drum-roll, made by rattling the ends of two great bones upon the head of an empty cask; and I remember that the male dancers fastened bits of tinkling metal or tin rattles about their ankles, like those strings of copper gris-gris worn by the Negroes of the Soudan. Those whom I saw taking part in those curious and convulsive performances—subsequently suppressed by the police—were either old or beyond middle age. The veritable Congo dance, with its extraordinary rhythmic chant, will soon have become as completely forgotten in Louisiana as the signification of those African words which formed the hieratic vocabulary of the Voudoos.

It was where Congo Square now extends that Bras-Coupé was

lassoed while taking part in such a dance; it was in the same neighborhood that Captain Jean Grandissime, of the Attakapas, lay hiding—secure in his white man's skin—"as if cased in steel"—to foil the witchcraft of Clemence; and it was there, also, that a crowd of rowdy American flatboatmen, headed by "Posson Jone'," of Bethesdy Church, stormed the circus and slew the tiger and the buffalo. Now, "Cayetano's circus" was not a fiction of Mr. Cable's imagining. Such a show actually visited New Orleans in 1816 or thereabouts, and remained a popular "fixture" for several seasons. The Creole-speaking Negroes of that day celebrated its arrival in one of their singular ditties.* And whosoever cares to consult certain musty newspaper files which are treasured up among the city archives may find therein the quaint advertisement of Señor Gaëtano's circus and the story of its violent disruption.

But Congo Square has been wholly transformed within a twelvemonth. The high railings and gateways have been removed; the weeds that used to climb over the moldering benches have been

---

* Some years ago, when I was endeavoring to make a collection of patois songs and other curiosities of the oral literature of the Louisiana colored folk, Mr. Cable kindly lent me his own collection, with permission to make selections for my private use, and I copied therefrom this *chanson créole:*

> C'est Michié Cayétane
> Qui sorti la Havane
> Avec so chouals et so macacs!
> Li gagnin ein homme qui dansé dans sac;
> Li gagnin qui dansé si yé la main;
> Li gagnin zaut' à choual qui boi' di vin;
> Li gagnin oussi ein zeine zolie mamzelle
> Qui monté choual sans bride et sans selle;—
> Pou di tou' ça mo pas capabe,—
> Mais mo souvien ein qui valé sab'.
> Yé n'en oussi tout sort bétail:
> Yé pas montré pou' la négrail
> Qui ya pou' dochans—dos-brulés
> Qui fé tapaze—et pou' birlé
> Ces gros mesdames et gros michiés
> Qui ménein là tous p'tis yé
>   'Oir Michié Cayétane
>   Qui vivé la Havane
>   Avec so chouals et so macacs.

(*xxviii*)

plucked up; new-graveled walks have been made; the grass, mown smooth, is now refreshing to look at; the trunks of the shade-trees are freshly whitewashed; and, before long, a great fountain will murmur in the midst. Two blocks westward, the sombre, sinister, Spanish façade of the Parish Prison towers above a huddling flock of dingy frame dwellings, and exhales far around it the heavy, sickly, musky scent that betrays the presence of innumerable bats. At sundown, they circle in immense flocks above it, and squeak like ghosts about its naked sentry towers. I have been told that this grim building will soon be numbered among those antiquities of New Orleans forming the scenery of Mr. Cable's romances.

The scene of, perhaps, the most singular tale in *Old Creole Days*—"Belles Demoiselles Plantation"—remains to be visited; but if the reader recollects the observation made in the very first paragraph of the story, that "the old Creoles never forgive a public mention," he will doubtless pardon me for leaving the precise location of "Belles Demoiselles" a mystery, authentic though it is, and for keeping secret its real and ancient name. I can only tell him that to reach it he must journey far from the Creole faubourg and beyond the limits of New Orleans to a certain unfamiliar point on the river's bank, whence a ferryman, swarthy and silent as Charon, will

     'Tis Monsieur Gaëtano
     Who comes out from Havana
     With his horses and his monkeys!
He has a man who dances in a sack;
He has one who dances on his hands;
He has another who drinks wine on horseback;
He has also a pretty young lady
Who rides a horse without bridle or saddle:
To tell you all about it I am not able,—
But I remember one who swallowed a sword.
There are all sorts of animals, too;—
They did not show to nigger-folk
What they showed to the trash—the burnt-backs (*poor whites*)
Who make so much noise—nor what they had to amuse
All those fine ladies and gentlemen,
Who take all their little children along with them
     To see Monsieur Gaëtano
     Who lives in Havana
     With his horses and his monkeys.

row him to the farther side of the Mississippi, and aid him to land upon a crumbling levee erected to prevent the very catastrophe anticipated in Mr. Cable's tale. Parallel with this levee curves a wagon-road whose farther side is bounded by a narrow and weed-masked ditch, where all kinds of marvelous wild things are growing, and where one may feel assured that serpents hide. Beyond this little ditch is a wooden fence, now overgrown and rendered superfluous by a grand natural barrier of trees and shrubs, all chained together by interlacements of wild vines and thorny creepers. This forms the boundary of the private grounds surrounding the "Belles Demoiselles" residence; and the breeze comes to you heavily sweet with blossom-scents, and shrill with vibrant music of cicadas and of birds.

Fancy the wreck of a vast garden created by princely expenditure —a garden once filled with all varieties of exotic trees, with all species of fantastic shrubs, with the rarest floral products of both hemispheres, but left utterly uncared-for during a generation, so that the groves have been made weird with hanging moss, and the costly vines have degenerated into parasites, and richly cultured plants returned to their primitive wild forms. The alley-walks are soft and sable with dead leaves; and all is so profoundly beshadowed by huge trees that a strange twilight prevails there even under a noonday sun. The lofty hedge is becrimsoned with savage roses, in whose degenerate petals still linger traces of former high cultivation. By a little gate set into that hedge, you can enter the opulent wilderness within, and pursue a winding path between mighty trunks that lean at a multitude of angles, like columns of a decaying cathedral about to fall. Crackling of twigs under foot, leaf whispers, calls of birds and cries of tree-frogs are the only sounds; the soft gloom deepens as you advance under the swaying moss and snaky festoons of creepers; there is a dimness and calm, as of a place consecrated to prayer. But for their tropical and elfish drapery, one might dream those oaks were of Dodona. And even with the passing of the fancy, lo! at a sudden turn of the narrow way, in a grand glow of light, *even the Temple appears,* with splendid peripteral of fluted columns rising boldly from the soil. Four pillared façades—east, west, north, and south—four superb porches, with tiers of galleries suspended in their recesses; and two sides of the antique vision ivory-tinted by the sun. Impossible to verbally describe the effect of this matchless relic of Louisiana's feudal splendors, that seems trying to hide itself from the new era amid its neglected gardens and groves. It creates such astonishment as some learned traveler might feel, were he suddenly to come upon the unknown ruins of a Greek temple in the very heart of an equatorial forest; it is so grand, so strangely at variance with its surroundings! True, the four ranks of columns are not of chiseled marble, and the stucco has broken away from them in places, and the severe laws of architecture have not been strictly obeyed; but these things are forgotten in admiration of the building's majesty. I suspect it to be the noblest old plantation-house in Louisiana; I am sure there is none more quaintly beautiful. When I last beheld the grand old mansion, the evening sun was resting upon it in a Turneresque column of yellow glory, and the oaks reaching out to it their vast arms through ragged sleeves of moss, and beyond, upon either side, the crepuscular dimness of the woods, with rare golden luminosities spattering down through the serpent knot-work of lianas, and the heavy mourning of mosses, and the great drooping and clinging of multitudinous disheveled things. And all this subsists only because the old Creole estate has never changed hands, because no speculating utilitarian could buy up the plantation to remove or remodel its proud homestead and condemn its odorous groves to the saw-mill. The river is the sole enemy to be dreaded, but a terrible one; it is ever gnawing the levee to get at the fat canefields; it is devouring the roadway; it is burrowing nearer and nearer to the groves and the gardens; and while gazing at its ravages, I could not encourage myself to doubt that, although his romantic anticipation may not be realized for years to come, Mr. Cable has rightly predicted the ghastly destiny of "Belles Demoiselles Plantation."

JEAN-AH POQUELIN

$\mathcal{I}$N THE first decade of the present century, when the newly established American Government was the most hateful thing in Louisiana—when the Creoles were still kicking at such vile innovations as the trial by jury, American dances, anti-smuggling laws, and the printing of the Governor's proclamation in English—when the Anglo-American flood that was presently to burst in a crevasse of immigration upon the delta had thus far been felt only as slippery seepage which made the Creole tremble for his footing—there stood, a short distance above what is now Canal Street, and considerably back from the line of villas which fringed the river-bank on Tchoupitoulas Road, an old colonial plantation-house half in ruin.

It stood aloof from civilization, the tracts that had once been its indigo fields given over to their first noxious wildness, and grown up into one of the horridest marshes within a circuit of fifty miles.

The house was of heavy cypress, lifted up on pillars, grim, solid, and spiritless, its massive build a strong reminder of days still earlier, when every man had been his own peace officer and the insurrection of the blacks a daily contingency. Its dark, weather-beaten roof and sides were hoisted up above the jungly plain in a distracted way, like a gigantic ammunition-wagon stuck in the mud and abandoned by some retreating army. Around it was a dense growth of low water willows, with half a hundred sorts of thorny or fetid

(*1*)

bushes, savage strangers alike to the "language of flowers" and to the botanist's Greek. They were hung with countless strands of discolored and prickly smilax, and the impassable mud below bristled with *chevaux de frise* of the dwarf palmetto. Two lone forest-trees, dead cypresses, stood in the centre of the marsh, dotted with roosting vultures. The shallow strips of water were hid by myriads of aquatic plants, under whose coarse and spiritless flowers, could one have seen it, was a harbor of reptiles, great and small, to make one shudder to the end of his days.

The house was on a slightly raised spot, the levee of a draining canal. The waters of this canal did not run; they crawled, and were full of big, ravening fish and alligators, that held it against all comers.

Such was the home of old Jean Marie Poquelin, once an opulent indigo planter, standing high in the esteem of his small, proud circle of exclusively male acquaintances in the old city; now a hermit, alike shunned by and shunning all who had ever known him. "The last of his line," said the gossips. His father lies under the floor of the St. Louis Cathedral, with the wife of his youth on one side, and the wife of his old age on the other. Old Jean visits the spot daily. His half-brother—alas! there was a mystery; no one knew what had become of the gentle, young half-brother, more than thirty years his junior, whom once he seemed so fondly to love, but who, seven years ago, had disappeared suddenly, once for all, and left no clew of his fate.

They had seemed to live so happily in each other's love. No father, mother, wife to either, no kindred upon earth. The elder a bold, frank, impetuous, chivalric adventurer; the younger a gentle, studious, book-loving recluse; they lived upon the ancestral estate like mated birds, one always on the wing, the other always in the nest.

There was no trait in Jean Marie Poquelin, said the old gossips, for which he was so well known among his few friends as his apparent fondness for his "little brother." "Jacques said this," and "Jacques said that"; he "would leave this or that, or any thing to Jacques," for "Jacques was a scholar," and "Jacques was good," or "wise," or "just," or "far-sighted," as the nature of the case required; and "he should ask Jacques as soon as he got home," since Jacques was never elsewhere to be seen.

(*2*)

It was between the roving character of the one brother, and the bookishness of the other, that the estate fell into decay. Jean Marie, generous gentleman, gambled the slaves away one by one, until none was left, man or woman, but one old African mute.

The indigo fields and vats of Louisiana had been generally abandoned as unremunerative. Certain enterprising men had substituted the culture of sugar; but while the recluse was too apathetic to take so active a course, the other saw larger, and, at that time, equally respectable profits, first in smuggling, and later in the African slave-trade. What harm could he see in it? The whole people said it was vitally necessary, and to minister to a vital public necessity—good enough, certainly, and so he laid up many a doubloon, that made him none the worse in the public regard.

One day old Jean Marie was about to start upon a voyage that was to be longer, much longer, than any that he had yet made. Jacques had begged him hard for many days not to go, but he laughed him off, and finally said, kissing him:

"*Adieu, 'tit frère.*"

"No," said Jacques, "I shall go with you."

They left the old hulk of a house in the sole care of the African mute, and went away to the Guinea coast together.

Two years after, old Poquelin came home without his vessel. He must have arrived at his house by night. No one saw him come. No one saw "his little brother"; rumor whispered that he, too, had returned, but he had never been seen again.

A dark suspicion fell upon the old slave-trader. No matter that the few kept the many reminded of the tenderness that had ever marked his bearing to the missing man. The many shook their heads. "You know he has a quick and fearful temper"; and "Why does he cover his loss with mystery?" "Grief would out with the truth."

"But," said the charitable few, "look in his face; see that expression of true humanity." The many did look in his face, and, as he looked in theirs, he read the silent question: "Where is thy brother Abel?" The few were silenced, his former friends died off, and the name of Jean Marie Poquelin became a symbol of witchery, devilish crime, and hideous nursery fictions.

The man and his house were alike shunned. The snipe and duck hunters forsook the marsh, and the wood-cutters abandoned the canal. Sometimes the hardier boys who ventured out there snake-shooting heard a slow thumping of oar-locks on the canal. They would look at each other for a moment half in consternation, half in glee, then rush from their sport in wanton haste to assail with their gibes the unoffending, withered old man who, in rusty attire, sat in the stern of a skiff, rowed homeward by his white-headed African mute.

"O Jean-ah Poquelin! O Jean-ah! Jean-ah Poquelin!"

It was not necessary to utter more than that. No hint of wickedness, deformity, or any physical or moral demerit; merely the name and tone of mockery: "Oh, Jean-ah Poquelin!" and while they tumbled one over another in their needless haste to fly, he would rise carefully from his seat, while the aged mute, with downcast face, went on rowing, and rolling up his brown fist and extending it toward the urchins would pour forth such an unholy broadside of French imprecation and invective as would all but craze them with delight.

Among both blacks and whites the house was the object of a thousand superstitions. Every midnight, they affirmed, the *feu follet* came out of the marsh and ran in and out of the rooms, flashing from window to window. The story of some lads, whose word in ordinary statements was worthless, was generally credited, that the night they camped in the woods, rather than pass the place after dark, they saw, about sunset, every window blood-red, and on each of the four chimneys an owl sitting, which turned his head three times round, and moaned and laughed with a human voice. There was a bottomless well, everybody professed to know, beneath the sill of the big front door under the rotten veranda; whoever set his foot upon that threshold disappeared forever in the depth below.

What wonder the marsh grew as wild as Africa! Take all the Faubourg Ste. Marie, and half the ancient city, you would not find one graceless dare-devil reckless enough to pass within a hundred yards of the house after nightfall.

The alien races pouring into old New Orleans began to find the few streets named for the Bourbon princes too strait for them. The wheel of fortune, beginning to whirl, threw them off beyond the ancient corporation lines, and sowed civilization and even trade upon the lands of the Graviers and Girods. Fields became roads,

roads streets. Everywhere the leveler was peering through his glass, rodsmen were whacking their way through willow-brakes and rose-hedges, and the sweating Irishmen tossed the blue clay up with their long-handled shovels.

"Ha! that is all very well," quoth the Jean-Baptistes, feeling the reproach of an enterprise that asked neither co-operation nor advice of them, "but wait till they come yonder to Jean Poquelin's marsh; ha! ha! ha!" The supposed predicament so delighted them, that they put on a mock terror and whirled about in an assumed stampede, then caught their clasped hands between their knees in excess of mirth, and laughed till the tears ran; for whether the street-makers mired in the marsh, or contrived to cut through old "Jean-ah's" property, either event would be joyful. Meantime a line of tiny rods, with bits of white paper in their split tops, gradually extended its way straight through the haunted ground, and across the canal diagonally.

"We shall fill that ditch," said the men in mud-boots, and brushed close along the chained and padlocked gate of the haunted mansion. Ah, Jean-ah Poquelin, those were not Creole boys, to be stampeded with a little hard swearing.

He went to the Governor. That official scanned the odd figure with no slight interest. Jean Poquelin was of short, broad frame, with a bronzed leonine face. His brow was ample and deeply furrowed. His eye, large and black, was bold and open like that of a war-horse, and his jaws shut together with the firmness of iron. He was dressed in a suit of Attakapas cottonade, and his shirt unbuttoned and thrown back from the throat and bosom, sailor-wise, showed a herculean breast, hard and grizzled. There was no fierceness or defiance in his look, no harsh ungentleness, no symptom of his unlawful life or violent temper; but rather a peaceful and peaceable fearlessness. Across the whole face, not marked in one or another feature, but as it were laid softly upon the countenance like an almost imperceptible veil, was the imprint of some great grief. A careless eye might easily overlook it, but, once seen, there it hung—faint, but unmistakable.

The Governor bowed.

"*Parlez-vous français?*" asked the figure.

"I would rather talk English, if you can do so," said the Governor.

"My name, Jean Poquelin."

"How can I serve you, Mr. Poquelin?"

"My 'ouse is yond'; *dans le marais là-bas.*"

The Governor bowed.

"Dat *marais* billong to me."

"Yes, sir."

"To me; Jean Poquelin; I hown 'im meself."

"Well, sir?"

"He don't billong to you; I get him from me father."

"That is perfectly true, Mr. Poquelin, as far as I am aware."

"You want to make strit pass yond'?"

"I do not know, sir; it is quite probable; but the city will indemnify you for any loss you may suffer—you will get paid, you understand."

"Strit can't pass dare."

"You will have to see the municipal authorities about that, Mr. Poquelin."

A bitter smile came upon the old man's face:

"*Pardon, monsieur,* you is not *le Gouverneur?*"

"Yes."

"*Mais,* yes. You har *le Gouverneur*—yes. Vehwell. I come to you. I tell you, strit can't pass at me 'ouse."

"But you will have to see"—

"I come to you. You is *le Gouverneur.* I know not the new laws. I ham a Fr-r-rench-a-man! Fr-rench-a-man have something *aller au contraire*—he come at his *Gouverneur.* I come at you. If me not had been bought from me king like *bossals* in the hold time, ze king gof —France would-a-show *Monsieur le Gouverneur* to take care his men to make strit in right places. *Mais,* I know; we billong to *Monsieur le Président.* I want you do somesin for me, eh?"

"What is it?" asked the patient Governor.

"I want you tell *Monsieur le Président,* strit—can't—pass—at—me—'ouse."

"Have a chair, Mr. Poquelin"; but the old man did not stir. The Governor took a quill and wrote a line to a city official, introducing Mr. Poquelin, and asking for him every possible courtesy. He handed it to him, instructing him where to present it.

"Mr. Poquelin," he said, with a conciliatory smile, "tell me, is it your house that our Creole citizens tell such odd stories about?"

The old man glared sternly upon the speaker, and with immovable features said:

"You don't see me trade some Guinea nigga'?"

"Oh, no."

"You don't see me make some smugglin'?"

"No, sir; not at all."

"But, I am Jean Marie Poquelin. I mine me hown bizniss. Dat all right? Adieu."

He put his hat on and withdrew. By and by he stood, letter in hand, before the person to whom it was addressed. This person employed an interpreter.

"He says," said the interpreter to the officer, "he come to make you the fair warning how you muz not make the street pas' at his 'ouse."

The officer remarked that "such impudence was refreshing"; but the experienced interpreter translated freely.

"He says: 'Why you don't want?' " said the interpreter.

The old slave-trader answered at some length.

"He says," said the interpreter, again turning to the officer, "the marass is a too unhealth' for peopl' to live."

"But we expect to drain his old marsh; it's not going to be a marsh."

"*Il dit*"— The interpreter explained in French.

The old man answered tersely.

"He says the canal is a private," said the interpreter.

"Oh! *that* old ditch; that's to be filled up. Tell the old man we're going to fix him up nicely."

Translation being duly made, the man in power was amused to see a thunder-cloud gathering on the old man's face.

"Tell him," he added, "by the time we finish, there'll not be a ghost left in his shanty."

The interpreter began to translate, but—

"*J' comprends, j' comprends*," said the old man, with an impatient gesture, and burst forth, pouring curses upon the United States, the President, the Territory of Orleans, Congress, the Governor and all his subordinates, striding out of the apartment as he cursed, while the object of his maledictions roared with merriment and rammed the floor with his foot.

"Why, it will make his old place worth ten dollars to one," said the official to the interpreter.

" 'Tis not for de worse of de property," said the interpreter.

"I should guess not," said the other, whittling his chair—"seems to me as if some of these old Creoles would liever live in a crawfish hole than to have a neighbor."

"You know what make old Jean Poquelin make like that? I will tell you. You know"—

The interpreter was rolling a cigarette, and paused to light his tinder; then, as the smoke poured in a thick double stream from his nostrils, he said, in a solemn whisper:

"He is a witch."

"Ho, ho, ho!" laughed the other.

"You don't believe it? What you want to bet?" cried the interpreter, jerking himself half up and thrusting out one arm while he bared it of its coat-sleeve with the hand of the other. "What you want to bet?"

"How do you know?" asked the official.

"Dass what I goin' to tell you. You know, one evening I was shooting some *grosbec*. I killed three; but I had trouble to fine them, it was becoming so dark. When I have them I start' to come home; then I got to pas' at Jean Poquelin's house."

"Ho, ho, ho!" laughed the other, throwing his leg over the arm of his chair.

"Wait," said the interpreter. "I come along slow, not making some noises; still, still"—

"And scared," said the smiling one.

"*Mais*, wait. I get all pas' the 'ouse. 'Ah!' I say; 'all right!' Then I see two thing' before! Hah! I get as cold and humide, and shake like a leaf. You think it was nothing? There I see, so plain as can be (though it was making nearly dark), I see Jean—Marie—Po-que-lin walkin' right in front, and right there beside of him was something like a man—but not a man—white like paint!—I dropp' on the grass from scared—they pass'; so sure as I live 'twas the ghos' of Jacques Poquelin, his brother!"

(*8*)

"Pooh!" said the listener.

"I'll put my han' in the fire," said the interpreter.

"But did you never think," asked the other, "that that might be Jack Poquelin, as you call him, alive and well, and for some cause hid away by his brother?"

"Bᵤᵤ there har' no cause!" said the other, and the entrance of third parties changed the subject.

Some months passed and the street was opened. A canal was first dug through the marsh, the small one which passed so close to Jean Poquelin's house was filled, and the street, or rather a sunny road, just touched a corner of the old mansion's dooryard. The morass ran dry. Its venomous denizens slipped away through the bulrushes; the cattle roaming freely upon its hardened surface trampled the superabundant undergrowth. The bellowing frogs croaked to westward. Lilies and the flower-de-luce sprang up in the place of reeds; smilax and poison-oak gave way to the purple-plumed iron-weed and pink spiderwort; the bindweeds ran everywhere blooming as they ran, and on one of the dead cypresses a giant creeper hung its green burden of foliage and lifted its scarlet trumpets. Sparrows and red-birds flitted through the bushes, and dewberries grew ripe beneath. Over all these came a sweet, dry smell of salubrity which the place had not known since the sediments of the Mississippi first lifted it from the sea.

But its owner did not build. Over the willow-brakes, and down the vista of the open street, bright new houses, some singly, some by ranks, were prying in upon the old man's privacy. They even settled down toward his southern side. First a wood-cutter's hut or two, then a market gardener's shanty, then a painted cottage, and all at once the faubourg had flanked and half surrounded him and his dried-up marsh.

Ah! then the common people began to hate him. "The old tyrant!" "You don't mean an old *tyrant?*" "Well, then, why don't he build when the public need demands it? What does he live in that unneighborly way for?" "The old pirate!" "The old kidnapper!" How easily even the most ultra Louisianians put on the imported virtues of the North when they could be brought to bear against the hermit. "There he goes, with the boys after him! Ah! ha! ha! Jean-ah Poquelin! Ah! Jean-ah! Aha! aha! Jean-ah Marie! Jean-ah Poquelin!

(*9*)

The old villain!" How merrily the swarming *Américains* echo the spirit of persecution! "The old fraud," they say—"pretends to live in a haunted house, does he? We'll tar and feather him some day. Guess we can fix him."

He cannot be rowed home along the old canal now; he walks. He has broken sadly of late, and the street urchins are ever at his heels. It is like the days when they cried: "Go up, thou bald-head," and the old man now and then turns and delivers ineffectual curses.

To the Creoles—to the incoming lower class of superstitious Germans, Irish, Sicilians, and others—he became an omen and embodiment of public and private ill-fortune. Upon him all the vagaries of their superstitions gathered and grew. If a house caught fire, it was imputed to his machinations. Did a woman go off in a fit, he had bewitched her. Did a child stray off for an hour, the mother shivered with the apprehension that Jean Poquelin had offered him to strange gods. The house was the subject of every bad boy's invention who loved to contrive ghostly lies. "As long as that house stands we shall have bad luck. Do you not see our pease and beans dying, our cabbages and lettuce going to seed and our gardens turning to dust, while every day you can see it raining in the woods? The rain will never pass old Poquelin's house. He keeps a fetich. He has conjured the whole Faubourg Ste. Marie. And why, the old wretch? Simply because our playful and innocent children call after him as he passes."

A "Building and Improvement Company," which had not yet got its charter, "but was going to," and which had not, indeed, any tangible capital yet, but "was going to have some," joined the "Jean-ah Poquelin" war. The haunted property would be such a capital site for a market-house! They sent a deputation to the old mansion to ask its occupant to sell. The deputation never got beyond the chained gate and a very barren interview with the African mute. The President of the Board was then empowered (for he had studied French in Pennsylvania and was considered qualified) to call and persuade M. Poquelin to subscribe to the company's stock; but—

"Fact is, gentlemen," he said at the next meeting, "it would take us at least twelve months to make Mr. Pokaleen understand the rather original features of our system, and he wouldn't subscribe when we'd done; besides, the only way to see him is to stop him on the street."

There was a great laugh from the Board; they couldn't help it. "Better meet a bear robbed of her whelps," said one.

"You're mistaken as to that," said the President. "I did meet him, and stopped him, and found him quite polite. But I could get no satisfaction from him; the fellow wouldn't talk in French, and when I spoke in English he hoisted his old shoulders up, and gave the same answer to every thing I said."

"And that was—?" asked one or two, impatient of the pause.

"That it 'don't worse w'ile.' "

One of the Board said: "Mr. President, this market-house project, as I take it, is not altogether a selfish one; the community is to be benefited by it. We may feel that we are working in the public interest [the Board smiled knowingly], if we employ all possible means to oust this old nuisance from among us. You may know that at the time the street was cut through, this old Poquelann did all he could to prevent it. It was owing to a certain connection which I had with that affair that I heard a ghost story [smiles, followed by a sudden dignified check]—ghost story, which, of course, I am not going to relate; but I *may* say that my profound conviction, arising from a prolonged study of that story, is, that this old villain, John Poquelann, has his brother locked up in that old house. Now, if this is so, and we can fix it on him, I merely *suggest* that we can make the matter highly useful. I don't know," he added, beginning to sit down, "but that it is an action we owe to the community—hem!"

"How do you propose to handle the subject?" asked the President.

"I was thinking," said the speaker, "that, as a Board of Directors, it would be unadvisable for us to authorize any action involving trespass; but if you, for instance, Mr. President, should, as it were, for mere curiosity, *request* some one, as, for instance, our excellent Secretary, simply as a personal favor, to look into the matter—this is merely a suggestion."

The Secretary smiled sufficiently to be understood that, while he certainly did not consider such preposterous service a part of his duties as secretary, he might, notwithstanding, accede to the President's request; and the Board adjourned.

Little White, as the Secretary was called, was a mild, kind-hearted little man, who, nevertheless, had no fear of any thing, unless it was the fear of being unkind.

"I tell you frankly," he privately said to the President, "I go into this purely for reasons of my own."

The next day, a little after nightfall, one might have descried this little man slipping along the rear fence of the Poquelin place, preparatory to vaulting over into the rank, grass-grown yard, and bearing himself altogether more after the manner of a collector of rare chickens than according to the usage of secretaries.

The picture presented to his eye was not calculated to enliven his mind. The old mansion stood out against the western sky, black and silent. One long, lurid pencil-stroke along a sky of slate was all that was left of daylight. No sign of life was apparent; no light at any window, unless it might have been on the side of the house hidden from view. No owls were on the chimneys, no dogs were in the yard.

He entered the place, and ventured up behind a small cabin which stood apart from the house. Through one of its many crannies he easily detected the African mute crouched before a flickering pine-knot, his head on his knees, fast asleep.

He concluded to enter the mansion, and, with that view, stood and scanned it. The broad rear steps of the veranda would not serve him; he might meet some one midway. He was measuring, with his eye, the proportions of one of the pillars which supported it, and estimating the practicability of climbing it, when he heard a footstep. Some one dragged a chair out toward the railing, then seemed to change his mind and began to pace the veranda, his footfalls resounding on the dry boards with singular loudness. Little White drew a step backward, got the figure between himself and the sky, and at once recognized the short, broad-shouldered form of old Jean Poquelin.

He sat down upon a billet of wood, and, to escape the stings of a whining cloud of mosquitoes, shrouded his face and neck in his handkerchief, leaving his eyes uncovered.

He had sat there but a moment when he noticed a strange, sickening odor, faint, as if coming from a distance, but loathsome and horrid.

Whence could it come? Not from the cabin; not from the marsh, for it was as dry as powder. It was not in the air; it seemed to come from the ground.

Rising up, he noticed, for the first time, a few steps before him a narrow footpath leading toward the house. He glanced down it—ha! right there was some one coming—ghostly white!

Quick as thought, and as noiselessly, he lay down at full length against the cabin. It was bold strategy, and yet, there was no denying it, little White felt that he was frightened. "It is not a ghost," he said to himself. "I *know* it cannot be a ghost"; but the perspiration burst out at every pore, and the air seemed to thicken with heat. "It is a living man," he said in his thoughts. "I hear his footsteps, and I hear old Poquelin's footsteps, too, separately, over on the veranda. I am not discovered; the thing has passed; there is that odor again; what a smell of death! Is it coming back? Yes. It stops at the door of the cabin. Is it peering in at the sleeping mute? It moves away. It is in the path again. Now it is gone." He shuddered. "Now, if I dare venture, the mystery is solved." He rose cautiously, close against the cabin, and peered along the path.

The figure of a man, a presence if not a body—but whether clad in some white stuff or naked the darkness would not allow him to determine—had turned, and now, with a seeming painful gait, moved slowly from him. "Great Heaven! can it be that the dead do walk?" He withdrew again the hands which had gone to his eyes. The dreadful object passed between two pillars and under the house. He listened. There was a faint sound as of feet upon a staircase; then all was still except the measured tread of Jean Poquelin walking on the veranda, and the heavy respirations of the mute slumbering in the cabin.

The little Secretary was about to retreat; but as he looked once more toward the haunted house a dim light appeared in the crack of a closed window, and presently old Jean Poquelin came, dragging his chair, and sat down close against the shining cranny. He spoke in a low, tender tone in the French tongue, making some inquiry. An answer came from within. Was it the voice of a human? So unnatural was it—so hollow, so discordant, so unearthly—that the stealthy listener shuddered again from head to foot, and when something stirred in some bushes near by—though it may have been nothing more than a rat—and came scuttling through the grass, the little Secretary actually turned and fled. As he left the enclosure he moved with bolder leisure through the bushes; yet now and then he spoke aloud: "Oh, oh! I see, I understand!" and shut his eyes in his hands.

How strange that henceforth little White was the champion of Jean Poquelin! In season and out of season—wherever a word was uttered against him—the Secretary, with a quiet, aggressive force that instantly arrested gossip, demanded upon what authority the statement or conjecture was made; but as he did not condescend to explain his own remarkable attitude, it was not long before the dis-relish and suspicion which had followed Jean Poquelin so many years fell also upon him.

It was only the next evening but one after his adventure that he made himself a source of sullen amazement to one hundred and fifty boys, by ordering them to desist from their wanton hallooing. Old Jean Poquelin, standing and shaking his cane, rolling out his long-drawn maledictions, paused and stared, then gave the Secretary a courteous bow and started on. The boys, save one, from pure aston-ishment, ceased; but a ruffianly little Irish lad, more daring than any had yet been, threw a big hurtling clod, that struck old Po-quelin between the shoulders and burst like a shell. The enraged old man wheeled with uplifted staff to give chase to the scampering vagabond; and—he may have tripped, or he may not, but he fell full length. Little White hastened to help him up, but he waved him off with a fierce imprecation and staggering to his feet resumed his way homeward. His lips were reddened with blood.

Little White was on his way to the meeting of the Board. He would have given all he dared spend to have stayed away, for he felt both too fierce and too tremulous to brook the criticisms that were likely to be made.

"I can't help it, gentlemen; I can't help you to make a case against the old man, and I'm not going to."

"We did not expect this disappointment, Mr. White."

"I can't help that, sir. No, sir; you had better not appoint any more investigations. Somebody'll investigate himself into trouble. No, sir; it isn't a threat, it is only my advice, but I warn you that whoever takes the task in hand will rue it to his dying day—which may be hastened, too."

The President expressed himself "surprised."

"I don't care a rush," answered little White, wildly and foolishly. "I don't care a rush if you are, sir. No, my nerves are not disordered; my head's as clear as a bell. No, I'm *not* excited."

A director remarked that the Secretary looked as though he had waked from a nightmare.

"Well, sir, if you want to know the fact, I have; and if you choose to cultivate old Poquelin's society you can have one, too."

"White," called a facetious member, but White did not notice. "White," he called again.

"What?" demanded White, with a scowl.

"Did you see the ghost?"

"Yes, sir; I did," cried White, hitting the table, and handing the President a paper which brought the Board to other business.

The story got among the gossips that somebody (they were afraid to say little White) had been to the Poquelin mansion by night and beheld something appalling. The rumor was but a shadow of the truth, magnified and distorted as is the manner of shadows. He had seen skeletons walking, and had barely escaped the clutches of one by making the sign of the cross.

Some madcap boys with an appetite for the horrible plucked up courage to venture through the dried marsh by the cattle-path, and come before the house at a spectral hour when the air was full of bats. Something which they but half saw—half a sight was enough —sent them tearing back through the willow-brakes and acacia bushes to their homes, where they fairly dropped down, and cried:

"Was it white?" "No—yes—nearly so—we can't tell—but we saw it." And one could hardly doubt, to look at their ashen faces, that they had, whatever it was.

"If that old rascal lived in the country we come from," said certain *Américains*, "he'd have been tarred and feathered before now, wouldn't he, Sanders?"

"Well, now he just would."

"And we'd have rid him on a rail, wouldn't we?"

"That's what I allow."

"Tell you what you *could* do." They were talking to some rollicking Creoles who had assumed an absolute necessity for doing *something*. "What is it you call this thing where an old man marries a young girl, and you come out with horns and"—

"*Charivari?*" asked the Creoles.

"Yes, that's it. Why don't you shivaree him?" Felicitous suggested.

Little White, with his wife beside him, was sitting on their doorsteps on the sidewalk, as Creole custom had taught them, looking toward the sunset. They had moved into the lately opened street. The view was not attractive on the score of beauty. The houses were small and scattered, and across the flat commons, spite of the lofty tangle of weeds and bushes, and spite of the thickets of acacia, they needs must see the dismal old Poquelin mansion, tilted awry and

shutting out the declining sun. The moon, white and slender, was hanging the tip of its horn over one of the chimneys.

"And you say," said the Secretary, "the old black man has been going by here alone? Patty, suppose old Poquelin should be concocting some mischief; he don't lack provocation; the way that clod hit him the other day was enough to have killed him. Why, Patty, he dropped as quick as *that!* No wonder you haven't seen him. I wonder if they haven't heard something about him up at the drug-store. Suppose I go and see."

"Do," said his wife.

She sat alone for half an hour, watching that sudden going out of the day peculiar to the latitude.

"That moon is ghost enough for one house," she said, as her husband returned. "It has gone right down the chimney."

"Patty," said little White, "the drug-clerk says the boys are going to shivaree old Poquelin to-night. I'm going to try to stop it."

"Why, White," said his wife, "you'd better not. You'll get hurt."

"No, I'll not."

"Yes, you will."

"I'm going to sit out here until they come along. They're compelled to pass right by here."

"Why, White, it may be midnight before they start; you're not going to sit out here till then."

"Yes, I am."

"Well, you're very foolish," said Mrs. White in an undertone, looking anxious, and tapping one of the steps with her foot.

They sat a very long time talking over little family matters.

"What's that?" at last said Mrs. White.

"That's the nine-o'clock gun," said White, and they relapsed into a long-sustained, drowsy silence.

"Patty, you'd better go in and go to bed," said he at last.

"I'm not sleepy."

"Well, you're very foolish," quietly remarked little White, and again silence fell upon them.

"Patty, suppose I walk out to the old house and see if I can find out any thing."

"Suppose," said she, "you don't do any such—listen!"

Down the street arose a great hubbub. Dogs and boys were howling and barking; men were laughing, shouting, groaning, and blowing horns, whooping, and clanking cow-bells, whinnying, and howling, and rattling pots and pans.

"They are coming this way," said little White. "You had better go into the house, Patty."

"So had you."

"No. I'm going to see if I can't stop them."

"Why, White!"

"I'll be back in a minute," said White, and went toward the noise.

In a few moments the little Secretary met the mob. The pen hesitates on the word, for there is a respectable difference, measurable only on the scale of the half century, between a mob and a *charivari*. Little White lifted his ineffectual voice. He faced the head of the disorderly column, and cast himself about as if he were made of wood and moved by the jerk of a string. He rushed to one who seemed, from the size and clatter of his tin pan, to be a leader. *"Stop these fellows, Bienvenu, stop them just a minute, till I tell them something."* Bienvenu turned and brandished his instruments of discord in an imploring way to the crowd. They slackened their pace, two or three hushed their horns and joined the prayer of little White and Bienvenu for silence. The throng halted. The hush was delicious.

"Bienvenu," said little White, "don't shivaree old Poquelin to-night; he's"—

"My fwang," said the swaying Bienvenu, "who tail you I goin' to chahivahi somebody, eh? You sink bickause I make a little play-fool wiz zis tin pan zat I am *dhonk?*"

"Oh, no, Bienvenu, old fellow, you're all right. I was afraid you might not know that old Poquelin was sick, you know, but you're not going there, are you?"

"My fwang, I vay soy to tail you zat you ah dhonk as de dev'. I am *shem* of you. I ham ze servan' of ze *publique*. Zese *citoyens* goin' to wickwest Jean Poquelin to give to the Ursuline' two hondred fifty dolla' "—

"Hé quoi!" cried a listener, *"Cinq cent piastres, oui!"*

"Oui!" said Bienvenu, "and if he wiffuse we make him some lit' *musique;* ta-ra-ta!" He hoisted a merry hand and foot, then frowning, added: "Old Poquelin got no bizniz dhink s'much w'isky."

"But, gentlemen," said little White, around whom a circle had gathered, "the old man is very sick."

"My faith!" cried a tiny Creole, "we did not make him to be sick. W'en we have say we going make *le charivari*, do you want that we hall tell a lie? My faith! 'sfools!"

"But you can shivaree somebody else," said desperate little White.

"Oui!" cried Bienvenu, *"et chahivahi* Jean-ah Poquelin tomo'w!"

"Let us go to Madame Schneider!" cried two or three, and amid

huzzas and confused cries, among which was heard a stentorian
Celtic call for drinks, the crowd again began to move.

"*Cent piastres pour l'hôpital de charité!*"

"Hurrah!"

"One hongred dolla' for Charity Hospital!"

"Hurrah!"

"Whang!" went a tin pan, the crowd yelled, and Pandemonium
gaped again. They were off at a right angle.

Nodding, Mrs. White looked at the mantel-clock.

"Well, if it isn't away after midnight."

The hideous noise down street was passing beyond earshot. She
raised a sash and listened. For a moment there was silence. Some
one came to the door.

"Is that you, White?"

"Yes." He entered. "I succeeded, Patty."

"Did you?" said Patty, joyfully.

"Yes. They've gone down to shivaree the old Dutchwoman who
married her step-daughter's sweetheart. They say she has got to pay
a hundred dollars to the hospital before they stop."

The couple retired, and Mrs. White slumbered. She was awakened
by her husband snapping the lid of his watch.

"What time?" she asked.

"Half-past three. Patty, I haven't slept a wink. Those fellows
are out yet. Don't you hear them?"

"Why, White, they're coming this way!"

"I know they are," said White, sliding out of bed and drawing
on his clothes, "and they're coming fast. You'd better go away from
that window, Patty. My! what a clatter!"

"Here they are," said Mrs. White, but her husband was gone.
Two or three hundred men and boys pass the place at a rapid walk
straight down the broad, new street, toward the hated house of
ghosts. The din was terrific. She saw little White at the head of the
rabble brandishing his arms and trying in vain to make himself
heard; but they only shook their heads, laughing and hooting the
louder, and so passed, bearing him on before them.

Swiftly they pass out from among the houses, away from the dim
oil lamps of the street, out into the broad starlit commons, and enter

the willowy jungles of the haunted ground. Some hearts fail and their owners lag behind and turn back, suddenly remembering how near morning it is. But the most part push on, tearing the air with their clamor.

Down ahead of them in the long, thicket-darkened way there is— singularly enough—a faint, dancing light. It must be very near the old house; it is. It has stopped now. It is a lantern, and is under a well-known sapling which has grown up on the wayside since the canal was filled. Now it swings mysteriously to and fro. A goodly number of the more ghost-fearing give up the sport; but a full hundred move forward at a run, doubling their devilish howling and banging.

Yes; it is a lantern, and there are two persons under the tree. The crowd draws near—drops into a walk; one of the two is the old African mute; he lifts the lantern up so that it shines on the other; the crowd recoils; there is a hush of all clangor, and all at once, with a cry of mingled fright and horror from every throat, the whole throng rushes back, dropping everything, sweeping past little White and hurrying on, never stopping until the jungle is left behind, and then to find that not one in ten has seen the cause of the stampede, and not one of the tenth is certain what it was.

There is one huge fellow among them who looks capable of any villainy. He finds something to mount on, and, in the Creole patois, calls a general halt. Bienvenu sinks down, and, vainly trying to recline gracefully, resigns the leadership. The herd gather round the speaker; he assures them that they have been outraged. Their right peaceably to traverse the public streets has been trampled upon. Shall such encroachments be endured? It is now daybreak. Let them go now by the open light of day and force a free passage of the public highway!

A scattering consent was the response, and the crowd, thinned now and drowsy, straggled quietly down toward the old house. Some drifted ahead, others sauntered behind, but every one, as he again neared the tree, came to a stand-still. Little White sat upon a bank of turf on the opposite side of the way looking very stern and sad. To each newcomer he put the same question:

"Did you come here to go to old Poquelin's?"

"Yes."

"He's dead." And if the shocked hearer started away he would say: "Don't go away."

"Why not?"

"I want you to go to the funeral presently."

If some Louisianian, too loyal to dear France or Spain to understand English, looked bewildered, some one would interpret for him; and presently they went. Little White led the van, the crowd trooping after him down the middle of the way. The gate, that had never been seen before unchained, was open. Stern little White stopped a short distance from it; the rabble stopped behind him. Something was moving out from under the veranda. The many whisperers stretched upward to see. The African mute came very slowly toward the gate, leading by a cord in the nose a small brown bull, which was harnessed to a rude cart. On the flat body of the cart, under a black cloth, were seen the outlines of a long box.

"Hats off, gentlemen," said little White, as the box came in view, and the crowd silently uncovered.

"Gentlemen," said little White, "here come the last remains of Jean Marie Poquelin, a better man, I'm afraid, with all his sins—yes a better—a kinder man to his blood—a man of more self-forgetful goodness—than all of you put together will ever dare to be."

There was a profound hush as the vehicle came creaking through the gate; but when it turned away from them toward the forest, those in front started suddenly. There was a backward rush, then all stood still again staring one way; for there, behind the bier, with eyes cast down and labored step, walked the living remains—all that was left—of little Jacques Poquelin, the long-hidden brother—a leper, as white as snow.

Dumb with horror, the cringing crowd gazed upon the walking death. They watched, in silent awe, the slow cortege creep down the long, straight road and lessen on the view, until by and by it stopped where a wild, unfrequented path branched off into the undergrowth toward the rear of the ancient city.

"They are going to the *Terre aux Lépreux*," said one in the crowd. The rest watched them in silence.

The little bull was set free; the mute, with the strength of an ape, lifted the long box to his shoulder. For a moment more the mute and the leper stood in sight, while the former adjusted his heavy burden; then, without one backward glance upon the unkind human world, turning their faces toward the ridge in the depths of the swamp known as the Leper's Land, they stepped into the jungle, disappeared, and were never seen again.

'TITE POULETTE

KRISTIAN KOPPIG was a rosy-faced, beardless young Dutchman. He was one of that army of gentlemen who, after the purchase of Louisiana, swarmed from all parts of the commercial world, over the mountains of Franco-Spanish exclusiveness, like the Goths over the Pyrenees, and settled down in New Orleans to pick up their fortunes, with the diligence of hungry pigeons. He may have been a German; the distinction was too fine for Creole haste and disrelish.

He made his home in a room with one dormer window looking out, and somewhat down, upon a building opposite, which still stands, flush with the street, a century old. Its big, round-arched windows in a long, second-story row, are walled up, and two or three from time to time have had smaller windows let into them again, with odd little latticed peep-holes in their batten shutters. This had already been done when Kristian Koppig first began to look at them from his solitary dormer window.

All the features of the building lead me to guess that it is a remnant of the old Spanish Barracks, whose extensive structure fell by government sale into private hands a long time ago. At the end toward the swamp a great, oriental-looking passage is left, with an arched entrance, and a pair of ponderous wooden doors. You look at it, and almost see Count O'Reilly's artillery come bumping and trundling out, and dash around into the ancient Plaza to bang away at King St. Charles's birthday.

I do not know who lives there now. You might stand about on

the opposite banquette for weeks and never find out. I suppose it is a residence, for it does not look like one. That is the rule in that region.

In the good old times of duels, and bagatelle-clubs, and theatre-balls, and Cayetano's circus, Kristian Koppig rooming as described, there lived in the portion of this house, partly overhanging the archway, a palish handsome woman, by the name—or going by the name —of Madame John. You would hardly have thought of her being "colored." Though fading, she was still of very attractive countenance, fine, rather severe features, nearly straight hair carefully kept, and that vivid black eye so peculiar to her kind. Her smile,

which came and went with her talk, was sweet and exceedingly intelligent; and something told you, as you looked at her, that she was one who had had to learn a great deal in this troublesome life.

"But!"—the Creole lads in the street would say—"her daughter!" and there would be lifting of arms, wringing of fingers, rolling of eyes, rounding of mouths, gaspings and clasping of hands. "So beautiful, beautiful, beautiful! White?—white like a water lily! White—like a magnolia!"

Applause would follow, and invocation of all the saints to witness.

And she could sing.

"Sing?" (disdainfully)—"if a mocking-bird can *sing!* Ha!"

They could not tell just how old she was; they "would give her about seventeen."

Mother and daughter were very fond. The neighbors could hear them call each other pet names, and see them sitting together, sewing, talking happily to each other in the unceasing French way, and see them go out and come in together on their little tasks and errands. " 'Tite Poulette," the daughter was called; she never went out alone.

And who was this Madame John?

"Why, you know!—she was"—said the wig-maker at the corner to Kristian Koppig—"I'll tell you. You know?—she was"—and the rest atomized off in a rasping whisper. She was the best yellow-fever nurse in a thousand yards round; but that is not what the wig-maker said.

A block nearer the river stands a house altogether different from the remnant of old barracks. It is of frame, with a deep front gallery over which the roof extends. It has become a den of Italians, who sell fuel by daylight, and by night are up to no telling what extent of deviltry. This was once the home of a gay gentleman, whose first name happened to be John. He was a member of the Good Children Social Club. As his parents lived with him, his wife would, according to custom, have been called Madame John; but he had no wife. His father died, then his mother; last of all, himself. As he is about to be off, in comes Madame John, with 'Tite Poulette, then an infant, on her arm.

"Zalli," said he, "I am going."

She bowed her head, and wept.

"You have been very faithful to me, Zalli."

She wept on.

"Nobody to take care of you now, Zalli."

Zalli only went on weeping.

"I want to give you this house, Zalli; it is for you and the little one."

An hour after, amid the sobs of Madame John, she and the "little one" inherited the house, such as it was. With the fatal caution which characterizes ignorance, she sold the property and placed the proceeds in a bank, which made haste to fail. She put on widow's weeds, and wore them still when 'Tite Poulette "had seventeen," as the frantic lads would say.

How they did chatter over her. Quiet Kristian Koppig had never seen the like. He wrote to his mother, and told her so. A pretty fellow at the corner would suddenly double himself up with beckoning to a knot of chums; these would hasten up; recruits would come in from two or three other directions; as they reached the corner their countenances would quickly assume a genteel severity, and presently, with her mother, 'Tite Poulette would pass—tall, straight, lithe, her great black eyes made tender by their sweeping lashes, the faintest tint of color in her Southern cheek, her form all grace, her carriage a wonder of simple dignity.

The instant she was gone every tongue was let slip on the marvel of her beauty; but, though theirs were only the loose New Orleans morals of over fifty years ago, their unleashed tongues never had attempted any greater liberty than to take up the pet name, 'Tite Poulette. And yet the mother was soon to be, as we shall discover, a paid dancer at the Salle de Condé.

To Zalli, of course, as to all "quadroon ladies," the festivities of the Conde Street ball-room were familiar of old. There, in the happy days when dear Monsieur John was young, and the eighteenth century old, she had often repaired under guard of her mother—dead now, alas!—and Monsieur John would slip away from the dull play and dry society of Théâtre d'Orléans, and come around with his crowd of elegant friends; and through the long sweet hours of the ball she had danced, and laughed, and coquetted under her satin mask, even to the baffling and tormenting of that prince of gentlemen, dear Monsieur John himself. No man of questionable blood dare set his foot within the door. Many noble gentlemen were pleased to dance with her. Colonel De —— and General La ——: city councilmen and officers from the Government House. There were no paid dancers then. Every thing was decorously conducted indeed! Every girl's mother was there, and the more discreet always left before there was too much drinking. Yes, it was gay, gay!—but sometimes dangerous. Ha! more times than a few had Monsieur John knocked down some long-haired and long-knifed rowdy, and kicked the breath out of him for looking saucily at her; but that was like him, he was so brave and kind;—and he is gone!

There was no room for widow's weeds there. So when she put these on, her glittering eyes never again looked through her pink and white mask, and she was glad of it; for never, never in her life had they so looked for anybody but her dear Monsieur John, and now he was in heaven—so the priest said—and she was a sick-nurse.

Living was hard work; and, as Madame John had been brought up tenderly, and had done what she could to rear her daughter in the same mistaken way, with, of course, no more education than the ladies in society got, they knew nothing beyond a little music and embroidery. They struggled as they could, faintly; now giving a few private dancing lessons, now dressing hair, but ever beat back by the steady detestation of their imperious patronesses; and, by and by, for want of that priceless worldly grace known among the flippant as "money-sense," these two poor children, born of misfortune and the complacent badness of the times, began to be in want.

Kristian Koppig noticed from his dormer window one day a man standing at the big archway opposite, and clanking the brass knocker on the wicket that was in one of the doors. He was a smooth man, with his hair parted in the middle, and his cigarette poised on a tiny gold holder. He waited a moment, politely cursed the dust, knocked again, threw his slender sword-cane under his arm, and wiped the inside of his hat with his handkerchief.

Madame John held a parley with him at the wicket. 'Tite Poulette was nowhere seen. He stood at the gate while Madame John went upstairs. Kristian Koppig knew him. He knew him as one knows a snake. He was the manager of the Salle de Condé. Presently Madame John returned with a little bundle, and they hurried off together.

And now what did this mean? Why, by any one of ordinary acuteness the matter was easily understood, but, to tell the truth, Kristian Koppig was a trifle dull, and got the idea at once that some damage was being planned against 'Tite Poulette. It made the gentle Dutchman miserable not to be minding his own business, and yet—

"But the woman certainly will not attempt"—said he to himself— "no, no! she cannot." Not being able to guess what he meant, I cannot say whether she could or not. I know that next day Kristian Koppig, glancing eagerly over the "*Ami des Lois*," read an advertisement which he had always before skipped with a frown. It was

(27)

headed, *"Salle de Condé,"* and, being interpreted, signified that a
new dance was to be introduced, the *Danse de Chinois,* and that *a
young lady* would follow it with the famous *"Danse du Shawl."*

It was the Sabbath. The young man watched the opposite window steadily and painfully from early in the afternoon until the
moon shone bright; and from the time the moon shone bright until
Madame John!—joy!—Madame John! and not 'Tite Poulette,
stepped through the wicket, much dressed and well muffled, and hurried off toward the Rue Condé. Madame John was the "young lady";
and the young man's mind, glad to return to its own unimpassioned
affairs, relapsed into quietude.

Madame John danced beautifully. It had to be done. It brought

some pay, and pay was bread; and every Sunday evening, with a
touch here and there of paint and powder, the mother danced the
dance of the shawl, the daughter remaining at home alone.

Kristian Koppig, simple, slow-thinking young Dutchman, never
noticing that he stayed at home with his window darkened for the
very purpose, would see her come to her window and look out with a
little wild, alarmed look in her magnificent eyes, and go and come

again, and again, until the mother, like a storm-driven bird, came panting home.

Two or three months went by.

One night, on the mother's return, Kristian Koppig coming to his room nearly at the same moment, there was much earnest conversation, which he could see, but not hear.

" 'Tite Poulette," said Madame John, "you are seventeen."

"True, *maman*."

"Ah! my child, I see not how you are to meet the future." The voice trembled plaintively.

"But how, *maman?*"

"Ah! you are not like others; no fortune, no pleasure, no friend."

"*Maman!*"

"No, no;—I thank God for it; I am glad you are not; but you will be lonely, lonely, all your poor life long. There is no place in this world for us poor women. I wish that we were either white or black!"—and the tears, two "shining ones," stood in the poor quadroon's eyes.

The daughter stood up, her eyes flashing.

"God made us, *maman*," she said with a gentle, but stately smile.

"Ha!" said the mother, her keen glance darting through her tears, "Sin made *me*, yes."

"No," said 'Tite Poulette, "God made us. He made us just as we are; not more white, not more black."

"He made you, truly!" said Zalli. "You are so beautiful; I believe it well." She reached and drew the fair form to a kneeling posture. "My sweet, white daughter!"

Now the tears were in the girl's eyes. "And could I be whiter than I am?" she asked.

"Oh, no, no! 'Tite Poulette," cried the other; "but if we were only *real white!*—both of us; so that some gentleman might come to see me and say 'Madame John, I want your pretty little chick. She is so beautiful. I want to take her home. She is so good—I want her to be my wife.' Oh, my child, my child, to see that I would give my life— I would give my soul! Only you should take me along to be your servant. I walked behind two young men to-night; they were coming home from their office; presently they began to talk about you."

(*29*)

'Tite Poulette's eyes flashed fire.

"No, my child, they spoke only the best things. One laughed a little at times and kept saying 'Beware!' but the other—I prayed the Virgin to bless him, he spoke such kind and noble words. Such gentle pity; such a holy heart; 'May God defend her,' he said, *chérie;* he said, 'May God defend her, for I see no help for her.' The other one laughed and left him. He stopped in the door right across the street. Ah, my child, do you blush? Is that something to bring the rose to your cheek? Many fine gentlemen at the ball ask me often, 'How is your daughter, Madame John?' "

The daughter's face was thrown into the mother's lap, not so well satisfied, now, with God's handiwork. Ah, how she wept! Sob, sob, sob; gasps and sighs and stifled ejaculations, her small right hand clinched and beating on her mother's knee; and the mother weeping over her.

Kristian Koppig shut his window. Nothing but a generous heart and a Dutchman's phlegm could have done so at that moment. And even thou, Kristian Koppig!——for the window closed very slowly.

He wrote to his mother, thus:

"In this wicked city, I see none so fair as the poor girl who lives opposite me, and who, alas! though so fair, is one of those whom the taint of caste has cursed. She lives a lonely, innocent life in the midst of corruption, like the lilies I find here in the marshes, and I have great pity for her. 'God defend her,' I said to-night to a fellow clerk, 'I see no help for her.' I know there is a natural, and I think proper, horror of mixed blood (excuse the mention, sweet mother), and I feel it, too; and yet if she were in Holland to-day, not one of a hundred suitors would detect the hidden blemish."

In such strain this young man wrote on trying to demonstrate the utter impossibility of his ever loving the lovable unfortunate, until the midnight tolling of the cathedral clock sent him to bed.

About the same hour Zalli and 'Tite Poulette were kissing good-night.

" 'Tite Poulette, I want you to promise me one thing."

"Well, *maman?*"

"If any gentleman should ever love you and ask you to marry—not knowing, you know—promise me you will not tell him you are not white."

"It can never be," said 'Tite Poulette.

"But if it should," said Madame John pleadingly.

"And break the law?" asked 'Tite Poulette, impatiently.

"But the law is unjust," said the mother.

"But it is the law!"

"But you will not, dearie, will you?"

"I would surely tell him!" said the daughter.

When Zalli, for some cause, went next morning to the window, she started.

" 'Tite Poulette!"—she called softly without moving. The daughter came. The young man, whose idea of propriety had actuated him to this display, was sitting in the dormer window, reading. Mother and daughter bent a steady gaze at each other. It meant in French, "If he saw us last night!"—

"Ah! dear," said the mother, her face beaming with fun—

"What can it be, *maman?*"

"He speaks—oh! ha, ha!—he speaks—such miserable French!"

It came to pass one morning at early dawn that Zalli and 'Tite Poulette, going to mass, passed a café, just as—who should be coming out but Monsieur, the manager of the Salle de Condé. He had not yet gone to bed. Monsieur was astonished. He had a Frenchman's eye for the beautiful, and certainly there the beautiful was. He had heard of Madame John's daughter, and had hoped once to see her, but did not; but could this be she?

They disappeared within the cathedral. A sudden pang of piety moved him; he followed. 'Tite Poulette was already kneeling in the aisle. Zalli, still in the vestibule, was just taking her hand from the font of holy-water.

"Madame John," whispered the manager.

She courtesied.

"Madame John, that young lady—is she your daughter?"

"She—she—is my daughter," said Zalli, with somewhat of alarm in her face, which the manager misinterpreted.

"I think not, Madame John." He shook his head, smiling as one too wise to be fooled.

"Yes, monsieur, she is my daughter."

"Oh, no, Madame John, it is only make-believe, I think."

"I swear she is, Monsieur de la Rue."

"Is that possible?" pretending to waver, but convinced in his heart of hearts, by Zalli's alarm, that she was lying. "But how? Why does she not come to our ball-room with you?"

Zalli, trying to get away from him, shrugged and smiled. "Each to his taste, monsieur; it pleases her not."

She was escaping, but he followed one step more. "I shall come to see you, Madame John."

She whirled and attacked him with her eyes. "Monsieur must not give himself the trouble!" she said, the eyes at the same time adding, "Dare to come!" She turned again, and knelt to her devotions. The manager dipped in the font, crossed himself, and departed.

Several weeks went by, and M. de la Rue had not accepted the fierce challenge of Madame John's eyes. One or two Sunday nights she had succeeded in avoiding him, though fulfilling her engagement in the Salle; but by and by pay-day—a Saturday—came round, and though the pay was ready, she was loath to go up to Monsieur's little office.

It was an afternoon in May. Madame John came to her own room, and, with a sigh, sank into a chair. Her eyes were wet.

"Did you go to his office, dear mother?" asked 'Tite Poulette.

"I could not," she answered, dropping her face in her hands.

"*Maman*, he has seen me at the window!"

"While I was gone?" cried the mother.

"He passed on the other side of the street. He looked up purposely, and saw me." The speaker's cheeks were burning red.

Zalli wrung her hands.

"It is nothing, mother; do not go near him."

"But the pay, my child."

"The pay matters not."

"But he will bring it here; he wants the chance."

That was the trouble, sure enough.

About this time Kristian Koppig lost his position in the German importing house where, he had fondly told his mother, he was indispensable.

"Summer was coming on," the senior said, "and you see our young men are almost idle. Yes, our engagement *was* for a year, but ah— we could not foresee"—etc., etc., "besides" (attempting a parting flattery), "your father is a rich gentleman, and you can afford to take the summer easy. If we can ever be of any service to you," etc., etc.

So the young Dutchman spent the afternoons at his dormer window reading and glancing down at the little casement opposite, where a small, rude shelf had lately been put out, holding a row of cigar-boxes with wretched little botanical specimens in them trying to die. 'Tite Poulette was their gardener; and it was odd to see—dry weather or wet—how many waterings per day those plants could take. She never looked up from her task; but I know she performed it with that unacknowledged pleasure which all girls love and deny, that of being looked upon by noble eyes.

On this peculiar Saturday afternoon in May, Kristian Koppig had been witness of the distressful scene over the way. It occurred to 'Tite Poulette that such might be the case, and she stepped to the casement to shut it. As she did so, the marvelous delicacy of Kristian Koppig moved him to draw in one of his shutters. Both young heads came out at one moment, while at the same instant—

"Rap, rap, rap, rap, rap!" clanked the knocker on the wicket. The black eyes of the maiden and the blue over the way, from looking into each other for the first time in life, glanced down to the arched doorway upon monsieur the manager. Then the black eyes disappeared within, and Kristian Koppig thought again, and reopening his shutter, stood up at the window prepared to become a bold spectator of what might follow.

But for a moment nothing followed.

"Trouble over there," thought the rosy Dutchman, and waited. The manager waited too, rubbing his hat and brushing his clothes with the tips of his kidded fingers.

"They do not wish to see him," slowly concluded the spectator.

"Rap, rap, rap, rap, rap!" quoth the knocker, and M. de la Rue looked up around at the windows opposite and noticed the handsome young Dutchman looking at him.

"Dutch!" said the manager softly, between his teeth.

"He is staring at me," said Kristian Koppig to himself;—"but then I am staring at him, which accounts for it."

A long pause, and then another long rapping.

"They want him to go away," thought Koppig.

(*33*)

"Knock hard!" suggested a street youngster, standing by.

"Rap, rap"— The manager had no sooner recommenced than several neighbors looked out of doors and windows.

"Very bad," thought our Dutchman; "somebody should make him go off. I wonder what they will do."

The manager stepped into the street, looked up at the closed window, returned to the knocker, and stood with it in his hand.

"They are all gone out, monsieur," said the street youngster.

"You lie!" said the cynosure of neighboring eyes.

"Ah!" thought Kristian Koppig; "I will go down and ask him"— Here his thoughts lost outline; he was only convinced that he had somewhat to say to him, and turned to go down-stairs. In going he became a little vexed with himself because he could not help hurrying. He noticed, too, that his arm holding the stair-rail trembled in a silly way, whereas he was perfectly calm. Precisely as he reached the street-door the manager raised the knocker; but the latch clicked and the wicket was drawn slightly ajar.

Inside could just be descried Madame John. The manager bowed, smiled, talked, talked on, held money in his hand, bowed, smiled, talked on, flourished the money, smiled, bowed, talked on and plainly persisted in some intention to which Madame John was steadfastly opposed.

The window above, too—it was Kristian Koppig who noticed that—opened a wee bit, like the shell of a terrapin. Presently the manager lifted his foot and put forward an arm, as though he would enter the gate by pushing, but as quick as gunpowder it clapped— in his face!

You could hear the fleeing feet of Zalli pounding up the staircase.

As the panting mother re-entered her room, "See, *maman*," said 'Tite Poulette, peeping at the window, "the young gentleman from over the way has crossed!"

"Holy Mary bless him!" said the mother.

"I will go over," thought Kristian Koppig, "and ask him kindly if he is not making a mistake."

"What are they doing, dear?" asked the mother, with clasped hands.

"They are talking; the young man is tranquil, but 'Sieur de la Rue is very angry," whispered the daughter; and just then—pang!

came a sharp, keen sound rattling up the walls on either side of the narrow way, and "Aha!" and laughter and clapping of female hands from two or three windows.

"Oh! what a slap!" cried the girl, half in fright, half in glee, jerking herself back from the casement simultaneously with the report. But the "ahas" and laughter, and clapping of feminine hands, which still continued, came from another cause. 'Tite Poulette's rapid action had struck the slender cord that held up an end of her hanging garden, and the whole rank of cigar-boxes slid from their place, turned gracefully over as they shot through the air, and emptied themselves plump upon the head of the slapped manager. Breathless, dirty, pale as whitewash, he gasped a threat to be heard from again, and, getting round the corner as quick as he could walk, left Kristian Koppig, standing motionless, the most astonished man in that street.

"Kristian Koppig, Kristian Koppig," said Greatheart to himself, slowly dragging up-stairs, "what a mischief you have done. One poor woman certainly to be robbed of her bitter wages, and another —so lovely!—put to the burning shame of being the subject of a street brawl! What will this silly neighborhood say? 'Has the gentleman a heart as well as a hand?' 'Is it jealousy?' " There he paused, afraid himself to answer the supposed query; and then—"Oh! Kristian Koppig, you have been such a dunce!" "And I cannot apologize to them. Who in this street would carry my note, and not wink and grin over it with low surmises? I cannot even make restitution. Money? They would not dare receive it. Oh! Kristian Koppig, why *did* you not mind your own business? Is she any thing to you? Do you love her? *Of course not!* Oh!—such a dunce!"

The reader will eagerly admit that, however faulty this young man's course of reasoning, his conclusion was correct. For mark what he did.

He went to his room, which was already growing dark, shut his window, lighted his big Dutch lamp, and sat down to write. "Something *must* be done," said he aloud, taking up his pen; "I will be calm and cool; I will be distant and brief; but—I shall have to be kind or I may offend. Ah! I shall have to write in French; I forgot that; I write it so poorly, dunce that I am, when all my brothers and sisters speak it so well." He got out his French dictionary. Two hours slipped by. He made a new pen, washed and refilled his ink-stand, mended his "abominable!" chair, and after two hours more made another attempt, and another failure. "My head aches," said he, and lay down on his couch, the better to frame his phrases.

He was awakened by the Sabbath sunlight. The bells of the Cathedral and the Ursulines' chapel were ringing for high mass, and a mocking-bird, perching on a chimney-top above Madame John's rooms, was caroling, whistling, mewing, chirping, scream-ing, and trilling with the ecstasy of a whole May in his throat. "Oh! sleepy Kristian Koppig," was the young man's first thought, "—such a dunce!"

Madame John and daughter did not go to mass. The morning wore away, and their casement remained closed. "They are offended," said Kristian Koppig, leaving the house, and wandering up to the little Protestant affair known as Christ Church.

"No, possibly they are not," he said, returning and finding the shutters thrown back.

By a sad accident, which mortified him extremely, he happened to see, late in the afternoon—hardly conscious that he was looking across the street—that Madame John was—dressing. Could it be that she was going to the Salle de Condé? He rushed to his table, and began to write.

He had guessed aright. The wages were too precious to be lost. The manager had written her a note. He begged to assure her that he was a gentleman of the clearest cut. If he had made a mistake the previ-ous afternoon, he was glad no unfortunate result had followed ex-cept his having been assaulted by a ruffian; that the *Danse du Shawl* was promised in his advertisement, and he hoped Madame John (whose wages were in hand waiting for her) would not fail to assist as usual. Lastly, and delicately put, he expressed his conviction that mademoiselle was wise and discreet in declining to entertain gentle-men at her home.

So, against much beseeching on the part of 'Tite Poulette, Ma-dame John was going to the ball-room. "Maybe I can discover what 'Sieur de la Rue is planning against monsieur over the way," she said, knowing certainly the slap would not be forgiven; and the daughter, though tremblingly, at once withdrew her objections.

The heavy young Dutchman, now thoroughly electrified, was writing like mad. He wrote and tore up, wrote and tore up, lighted his lamp, started again, and at last signed his name. A letter by a Dutchman in French!—what can be made of it in English? We will see:

"Madame and Mademoiselle:

"A stranger, seeking not to be acquainted, but seeing and admiring all days the goodness and high honor, begs to be pardoned of them for the mistakes, alas! of yesterday, and to make reparation and satisfaction in destroying the ornaments of the window, as well as the loss of compensation from monsieur the manager, with the enclosed bill of the Banque de la Louisiane for fifty dollars ($50). And, hoping they will seeing what he is meaning, remains, respectfully,

"Kristian Koppig.

"P.S.—Madame must not go to the ball."

He must bear the missive himself. He must speak in French. What should the words be? A moment of study—he has it, and is off down the long three-story stairway. At the same moment Madame John stepped from the wicket, and glided off to the Salle de Condé, a trifle late.

"I shall see Madame John, of course," thought the young man, crushing a hope, and rattled the knocker. 'Tite Poulette sprang up from praying for her mother's safety. "What has she forgotten?" she asked herself, and hastened down. The wicket opened. The two innocents were stunned.

"Aw—aw"—said the pretty Dutchman, "aw"—blurted out something in virgin Dutch, . . . handed her the letter, and hurried down street.

"Alas! what have I done?" said the poor girl, bending over her candle, and bursting into tears that fell on the unopened letter. "And what shall I do? It may be wrong to open it—and worse not to." Like her sex, she took the benefit of the doubt, and intensified her perplexity and misery by reading and misconstruing the all but unintelligible contents. What then? Not only sobs and sighs, but moaning and beating of little fists together, and outcries of soul-felt agony stifled against the bedside, and temples pressed into knitted palms, because of one who "sought *not to be* acquainted," but

(37)

offered money—money!—in pity to a poor—shame on her for saying that!—a poor *nigresse*.

And now our self-confessed dolt turned back from a half-hour's walk, concluding there might be an answer to his note. "Surely Madame John will appear this time." He knocked. The shutter stirred above, and something white came fluttering wildly down like a shot dove. It was his own letter containing the fifty-dollar bill. He bounded to the wicket, and softly but eagerly knocked again.

"Go away," said a trembling voice from above.

"Madame John?" said he; but the window closed, and he heard a step, the same step on the stair. Step, step, every step one step deeper into his heart. 'Tite Poulette came to the closed door.

"What will you?" said the voice within.

"I—I—don't wish to see you. I wish to see Madame John."

"I must pray monsieur to go away. My mother is at the Salle de Condé."

"At the ball!" Kristian Koppig strayed off, repeating the words for want of definite thought. All at once it occurred to him that at the ball he could make Madame John's acquaintance with impunity. "Was it courting sin to go?" By no means; he should, most likely, save a woman from trouble, and help the poor in their distress.

Behold Kristian Koppig standing on the floor of the Salle de Condé. A large hall, a blaze of lamps, a bewildering flutter of fans and floating robes, strains of music, columns of gay promenaders, a long row of turbaned mothers lining either wall, gentlemen of the portlier sort filling the recesses of the windows, whirling waltzers gliding here and there—smiles and grace, smiles and grace; all fair, orderly, elegant, bewitching. A young Creole's laugh mayhap a little loud, and—truly there were many sword-canes. But neither grace nor foulness satisfied the eye of the zealous young Dutchman.

Suddenly a muffled woman passed him, leaning on a gentleman's arm. It looked like—it must be, Madame John. Speak quick, Kristian Koppig; do not stop to notice the man!

"Madame John"—bowing—"I am your neighbor, Kristian Koppig."

Madame John bows low, and smiles—a ball-room smile, but is frightened, and her escort—the manager—drops her hand and slips away.

"Ah! monsieur," she whispers excitedly, "you will be killed if you stay here a moment. Are you armed? No. Take this." She tried to slip a dirk into his hands, but he would not have it.

"Oh, my dear young man, go! Go quickly!" she pleaded, glancing furtively down the hall.

"I wish you not to dance," said the young man.

"I have danced already; I am going home. Come; be quick! we will go together." She thrust her arm through his, and they hastened into the street. When a square had been passed there came a sound of men running behind them.

"Run, monsieur, run!" she cried, trying to drag him; but Monsieur Dutchman would not.

"*Run*, monsieur! Oh, my God! it is 'Sieur"—

"*That* for yesterday!" cried the manager, striking fiercely with his cane. Kristian Koppig's fist rolled him in the dirt.

"*That* for 'Tite Poulette!" cried another man dealing the Dutchman a terrible blow from behind.

"And *that* for me!" hissed a third, thrusting at him with something bright.

"*That* for yesterday!" screamed the manager, bounding like a tiger; "That!" "THAT!" "Ha!"

Then Kristian Koppig knew that he was stabbed.

"That!" and "That!" and "That!" and the poor Dutchman struck wildly here and there, grasped the air, shut his eyes, staggered, reeled, fell, rose half up, fell again for good, and they were kicking him and jumping on him. All at once they scampered. Zalli had found the night-watch.

"Buz-z-z-z!" went a rattle. "Buz-z-z-z!" went another.

"Pick him up."

"Is he alive?"

"Can't tell; hold him steady; lead the way, misses."

"He's bleeding all over my breeches."

"This way—here—around this corner."

"This way now—only two squares more."

"Here we are."

"Rap-rap-rap!" on the old brass knocker. Curses on the narrow wicket, more on the dark archway, more still on the twisting stairs.

Up at last and into the room.

"Easy, easy, push this under his head! never mind his boots!"
So he lies—on 'Tite Poulette's own bed.

The watch are gone. They pause under the corner lamp to count
profits;—a single bill—Banque de la Louisiane, fifty dollars. Providence is kind—tolerably so. Break it at the Guillaume Tell. "But
did you ever hear any one scream like that girl did?"

And there lies the young Dutch neighbor. His money will not flutter back to him this time; nor will any voice behind a gate "beg
monsieur to go away." O, Woman!—that knows no enemy so terrible as man! Come nigh, poor Woman, you have nothing to fear.
Lay your strange, electric touch upon the chilly flesh; it strikes no
eager mischief along the fainting veins. Look your sweet looks upon
the grimy face, and tenderly lay back the locks from the congested
brows; no wicked misinterpretation lurks to bite your kindness. Be
motherly, be sisterly, fear nought. Go, watch him by night; you may
sleep at his feet and he will not stir. Yet he lives, and shall live—
may live to forget you, who knows? But for all that, be gentle and
watchful; be womanlike, we ask no more; and God reward you!

Even while it was taking all the two women's strength to hold the
door against Death, the sick man himself laid a grief upon them.

"Mother," he said to Madame John, quite a master of French in
his delirium, "dear mother, fear not; trust your boy; fear nothing.
I will not marry 'Tite Poulette; I cannot. She is fair, dear mother,
but ah! she is not—don't you know, mother? don't you know? The
race! the race! Don't you know that she is jet black. Isn't it?"

The poor nurse nodded "Yes," and gave a sleeping draught; but
before the patient quite slept he started once and stared.

"Take her away"—waving his hand—"take your beauty away.
She is jet white. Who could take a jet-white wife? O, no, no, no, no!"

Next morning his brain was right.

"Madame," he weakly whispered, "I was delirious last night?"

Zalli shrugged. "Only a very, very, wee, wee trifle of a bit."

"And did I say something wrong or—foolish?"

"O, no, no," she replied; "you only clasped your hands, so, and
prayed, prayed all the time to the dear Virgin."

"To the Virgin?" asked the Dutchman, smiling incredulously.

"And St. Joseph—yes, indeed," she insisted; "you may strike me
dead."

(*40*)

And so, for politeness' sake, he tried to credit the invention, but grew suspicious instead.

Hard was the battle against death. Nurses are sometimes Amazons, and such were these. Through the long, enervating summer, the contest lasted; but when at last the cool airs of October came stealing in at the bedside like long-banished little children, Kristian Koppig rose upon his elbow and smiled them a welcome.

The physician, blessed man, was kind beyond measure; but said some inexplicable things, which Zalli tried in vain to make him speak in an undertone. "If I knew Monsieur John?" he said, "certainly! Why, we were chums at school. And he left you so much as that, Madame John? Ah! my old friend John, always noble! And you had it all in that naughty bank? Ah, well, Madame John, it matters little. No, I shall not tell 'Tite Poulette. Adieu."

And another time:— "If I will let you tell me something? With pleasure, Madame John. No, and not tell anybody, Madame John. No, madame, not even 'Tite Poulette. What?"—a long whistle—"is that pos-si-ble?—and Monsieur John knew it?—encouraged it?— eh, well, eh, well!— But—can I believe you, Madame John? Oh! you have Monsieur John's sworn statement. Ah! very good, truly, but—you *say* you have it; but where is it? Ah! to-morrow!" a skeptical shrug. "Pardon me, Madame John, I think perhaps, *perhaps* you are telling the truth.

"If I think you did right? Certainly! What nature keeps back, accident sometimes gives, Madame John; either is God's will. Don't cry. 'Stealing from the dead?' No! It was giving, yes! They are thanking you in heaven, Madame John."

Kristian Koppig, lying awake, but motionless and with closed eyes, hears in part, and, fancying he understands, rejoices with silent intensity. When the doctor is gone he calls Zalli.

"I give you a great deal of trouble, eh, Madame John?"

"No, no; you are no trouble at all. Had you the yellow fever— ah! then!"

She rolled her eyes to signify the superlative character of the tribulations attending yellow fever.

"I had a lady and gentleman once—a Spanish lady and gentleman, just off the ship; both sick at once with the fever—delirious— could not tell their names. Nobody to help me but sometimes Monsieur John! I never had such a time—never before, never since—as that time. Four days and nights this head touched not a pillow."

"And they died!" said Kristian Koppig.

"The third night the gentleman went. Poor señor! 'Sieur John—he did not know the harm—gave him some coffee and toast! The fourth night it rained and turned cool, and just before day the poor lady"—

"Died!" said Koppig.

Zalli dropped her arms listlessly into her lap and her eyes ran brimful.

"And left an infant!" said the Dutchman, ready to shout with exultation.

"Ah! no, monsieur," said Zalli.

The invalid's heart sank like a stone.

"Madame John"—his voice was all in a tremor—"tell me the truth. Is 'Tite Poulette your own child?"

"Ah-h-h, ha! ha! what foolishness! Of course she is my child!" And madame gave vent to a true Frenchwoman's laugh.

It was too much for the sick man. In the pitiful weakness of his shattered nerves he turned his face into his pillow and wept like a child. Zalli passed into the next room to hide her emotion.

"*Maman,* dear *maman,*" said 'Tite Poulette, who had overheard nothing, but only saw the tears.

"Ah! my child, my child, my task—my task is too great—too great for me. Let me go now—another time. Go and watch at his bedside."

"But, *maman*"—for 'Tite Poulette was frightened—"he needs no care now."

"Nay, but go, my child; I wish to be alone."

The maiden stole in with averted eyes and tiptoed to the window —*that window.* The patient, already a man again, gazed at her till she could feel the gaze. He turned his eyes from her a moment to gather resolution. And now, stout heart, farewell; a word or two of friendly parting—nothing more.

" 'Tite Poulette."

The slender figure at the window turned and came to the bedside.

"I believe I owe my life to you," he said.

She looked down meekly, the color rising in her cheek.

"I must arrange to be moved across the street, to-morrow, on a litter."

She did not stir or speak.

"And I must now thank you, sweet nurse, for your care. Sweet nurse! Sweet nurse!"

She shook her head in protestation.

"Heaven bless you, 'Tite Poulette!"

Her face sank lower.

"God has made you very beautiful, 'Tite Poulette!"

She stirred not. He reached, and gently took her little hand, and as he drew her one step nearer, a tear fell from her long lashes. From the next room, Zalli, with a face of agonized suspense, gazed upon the pair, undiscovered. The young man lifted the hand to lay it upon his lips, when, with a mild, firm force, it was drawn away, yet still rested in his own upon the bedside, like some weak thing snared, that could only not get free.

"Thou wilt not have my love, 'Tite Poulette?"

No answer.

"Thou wilt not, beautiful?"

"Cannot!" was all that she could utter, and upon their clasped hands the tears ran down.

"Thou wrong'st me, 'Tite Poulette. Thou dost not trust me; thou fearest the kiss may loosen the hands. But I tell thee nay. I have struggled hard, even to this hour, against Love, but I yield me now; I yield; I am his unconditioned prisoner forever. God forbid that I ask aught but that you will be my wife."

Still the maiden moved not, looked not up, only rained down tears.

"Shall it not be, 'Tite Poulette?" He tried in vain to draw her.

" 'Tite Poulette?" So tenderly he called! And then she spoke.

"It is against the law."

"It is not!" cried Zalli, seizing her round the waist and dragging her forward. "Take her! she is thine. I have robbed God long enough. Here are the sworn papers—here! Take her; she is as white as snow—so! Take her, kiss her; Mary be praised! I never had a child—she is the Spaniard's daughter!"

«POSSON JONE'»

To Jules St.-Ange—elegant little heathen—there yet remained at manhood a remembrance of having been sent to school, and of having been taught by a stony-headed Capuchin that the world is round—for example, like a cheese. This round world is a cheese to be eaten through, and Jules had nibbled quite into his cheese-world already at twenty-two.

He realized this as he idled about one Sunday morning where the intersection of Royal and Conti Streets some seventy years ago formed a central corner of New Orleans. Yes, yes, the trouble was he had been wasteful and honest. He discussed the matter with that faithful friend and confidant, Baptiste, his yellow body-servant. They concluded that, papa's patience and *tante's* pin-money having been gnawed away quite to the rind, there were left open only these few easily enumerated resorts: to go to work—they shuddered; to join Major Innerarity's filibustering expedition; or else—why not? —to try some games of confidence. At twenty-two one must begin to be something. Nothing else tempted; could that avail? One could but try. It is noble to try; and, besides, they were hungry. If one could "make the friendship" of some person from the country, for instance, with money, not expert at cards or dice, but, as one would say, willing to learn, one might find cause to say some "Hail Marys."

The sun broke through a clearing sky, and Baptiste pronounced it good for luck. There had been a hurricane in the night. The weed-grown tile roofs were still dripping, and from lofty brick and low adobe walls a rising steam responded to the summer sunlight. Up street, and across the Rue du Canal, one could get glimpses of the gardens in Faubourg Ste. Marie standing in silent wretchedness, so many tearful Lucretias, tattered victims of the storm. Short remnants of the wind now and then came down the narrow street in erratic puffs heavily laden with odors of broken boughs and torn flowers, skimmed the little pools of rain-water in the deep ruts of the unpaved street, and suddenly went away to nothing, like a juggler's butterflies or a young man's money.

It was very picturesque, the Rue Royale. The rich and poor met together. The locksmith's swinging key creaked next door to the bank; across the way, crouching mendicant-like in the shadow of a great importing house, was the mud laboratory of the mender of broken combs. Light balconies overhung the rows of showy shops and stores open for trade this Sunday morning, and pretty Latin faces of the higher class glanced over their savagely pronged railings upon the passers below. At some windows hung lace curtains, flannel duds at some, and at others only the scraping and sighing one-hinged shutter groaning toward Paris after its neglectful master.

M. St.-Ange stood looking up and down the street for nearly an hour. But few ladies, only the inveterate mass-goers, were out. About the entrances of the frequent cafés the masculine gentility stood leaning on canes, with which now one and now another beckoned to Jules, some even adding pantomimic hints of the social cup.

M. St.-Ange remarked to his servant without turning his head that somehow he felt sure he should soon return those *bons* that the mulatto had lent him.

"What will you do with them?"

"Me!" said Baptiste, quickly; "I will go and see the bull-fight in the Place Congo."

"There is to be a bull-fight? But where is M. Cayetano?"

"Ah, got all his affairs wet in the tornado. Instead of his circus, they are to have a bull-fight—not an ordinary bull-fight with sick horses, but a buffalo-and-tiger fight. I would not miss it——"

Two or three persons ran to the opposite corner and began striking at something with their canes. Others followed. Can M. St.-Ange and servant, who hasten forward—can the Creoles, Cubans, Spaniards, St. Domingo refugees, and other loungers—can they hope it is a fight? They hurry forward. Is a man in a fit? The crowd pours in from the side-streets. Have they killed a so-long snake? Bareheaded shopmen leave their wives, who stand upon chairs. The crowd huddles and packs. Those on the outside make little leaps into the air, trying to be tall.

"What is the matter?"

"Have they caught a real live rat?"

"Who is hurt?" asks some one in English.

"*Personne,*" replies a shopkeeper; "a man's hat blow' in the gut-

ter; but he has it now. Jules pick it. See, that is the man, head and shoulders on top the res'."

"He in the homespun?" asks a second shopkeeper. "Humph! an *Américain*—a West-Floridian; bah!"

"But wait; 'st! he is speaking; listen!"

"To who' is he speak——?"

"Sh-sh-sh! to Jules."

"Jules who?"

"Silence, you! To Jules St.-Ange, what h-owe me a bill since long time. Sh-sh-sh!"

Then the voice was heard.

Its owner was a man of giant stature, with a slight stoop in his shoulders, as if he were making a constant, good-natured attempt to accommodate himself to ordinary doors and ceilings. His bones were those of an ox. His face was marked more by weather than age, and his narrow brow was bald and smooth. He had instantaneously formed an opinion of Jules St.-Ange, and the multitude of words, most of them lingual curiosities, with which he was rasping the wide-open ears of his listeners, signified, in short, that, as sure as his name was Parson Jones, the little Creole was a "plumb gentleman."

M. St.-Ange bowed and smiled, and was about to call attention, by both gesture and speech, to a singular object on top of the still uncovered head, when the nervous motion of the *Américain* antici-pated him, as, throwing up an immense hand, he drew down a large roll of bank-notes. The crowd laughed, the West-Floridian joining, and began to disperse.

"Why, that money belongs to Smyrny Church," said the giant.

"You are very dengerous to make your money expose like that, Misty Posson Jone'," said St.-Ange, counting it with his eyes.

The countryman gave a start and smile of surprise.

"How d'd you know my name was Jones?" he asked; but, with-out pausing for the Creole's answer, furnished in his reckless way some further specimens of West-Floridian English; and the con-ciseness with which he presented full intelligence of his home, fam-ily, calling, lodging-house, and present and future plans, might have passed for consummate art, had it not been the most run-wild nature. "And I've done been to Mobile, you know, on busi*ness* for Bethesdy Church. It's the on'yest time I ever been from home; now you wouldn't of believed that, would you? But I admire to have saw you, that's so. You've got to come and eat with me. Me and my boy ain't been fed yit. What might one call yo' name? Jools? Come on, Jools. Come on, Colossus. That's my niggah—his name's Colossus of Rhodes. Is that yo' yallah boy, Jools? Fetch him along, Colossus. It seems like a special provi*dence*.—Jools, do you believe in a special provi*dence*?"

Jules remembered the roll of bank-notes and said he did.

The new-made friends moved briskly off, followed by Baptiste and a short, square, old Negro, very black and grotesque, who had

(*47*)

introduced himself to the mulatto, with many glittering and cavernous smiles, as "d'body-sarvant of d'Rev'n' Mr. Jones."

Both pairs enlivened their walk with conversation. Parson Jones
descanted upon the doctrine he had mentioned, as illustrated in the
perplexities of cotton-growing, and concluded that there would always be "a special provi*dence* again' cotton untell folks quits a-
pressin' of it and haulin' of it on Sundays!"

"*Je dis*," said St.-Ange, in response, "I thing you is juz right.
I believe, me, strong-strong in the improvidence, yes. You know my
papa he h-own a sugah-plantation, you know. 'Jules, my son,' he
say one time to me, 'I goin' to make one baril sugah to fedge the
moze high price in New Orleans.' Well, he take his bez baril sugah—
I nevah see a so careful man like my papa always to make a so beautiful sugah *et sirop.* 'Jules, go at Father Pierre an' ged this lill
pitcher fill with holy-water, an' tell him sen' his tin bucket, and I will
make it fill with *quitte.*' I ged the holy-water; my papa sprinkle it
over the baril, an' make one cross on the 'ead of the baril."

"Why, Jools," said Parson Jones, "that didn't do no good."

"Din do no good! Id broughd the so great value! You can strike
me dead if thad baril sugah din fedge the more high cost than any
other in the city. *Parceque*, the man what buy that baril sugah he
make a mistake of one hundred pound' "—falling back—"*Mais* certainlee!"

"And you think that was growin' out of the holy-water?" asked
the parson.

"*Mais*, what could make it else? Id could not be the *quitte*, because
my papa keep the bucket, an' forget to sen' the *quitte* to Father
Pierre."

Parson Jones was disappointed.

"Well, now, Jools, you know, I don't think that was right. I
reckon you must be a plumb Catholic."

M. St.-Ange shrugged. He would not deny his faith.

"I am a *Catholique, mais*"—brightening as he hoped to recom-
mend himself anew—"not a good one."

"Well, you know," said Jones—"where's Colossus? Oh! all right.
Colossus strayed off a minute in Mobile, and I plumb lost him for
two days. Here's the place; come in. Colossus and this boy can go to
the kitchen.—Now, Colossus, what *air* you a-beckonin' at me faw?"

He let his servant draw him aside and address him in a whisper.

"Oh, go 'way!" said the parson with a jerk. "Who's goin' to throw me? What? Speak louder. Why, Colossus, you shayn't talk so, saw. 'Pon my soul, yo're the mightiest fool I ever taken up with. Jest you go down that alley-way with this yallah boy, and don't show yo' face untell yo' called!"

The Negro begged; the master wrathily insisted.

"Colossus, will you do ez I tell you, or shell I hev' to strike you, saw?"

"O Mahs Jimmy, I—I's gwine; but"—he ventured nearer—"don't on no account drink nothin', Mahs Jimmy."

Such was the Negro's earnestness that he put one foot in the gutter, and fell heavily against his master. The parson threw him off angrily.

"Thar, now! Why, Colossus, you most of been dosted with sumthin'; yo' plumb crazy.—Humph, come on, Jools, let's eat: Humph! to tell me that when I never taken a drop, exceptin' for chills, in my life—which he knows so as well as me!"

The two masters began to ascend a stair.

"*Mais*, he is a sassy; I would sell him, me," said the young Creole.

"No, I wouldn't do that," replied the parson; "though there is people in Bethesdy who says he is a roscal. He's a powerful smart fool. Why, that boy's got money, Jools; more money than religion, I reckon. I'm shore he fallen into mighty bad company"—they passed beyond earshot.

Baptiste and Colossus, instead of going to the tavern kitchen, went on to the next door and entered the dark rear corner of a low grocery, where, the law notwithstanding, liquor was covertly sold to slaves. There, in the quiet company of Baptiste and the grocer, the colloquial powers of Colossus, which were simply prodigious, began very soon to show themselves.

"For whilst," said he, "Mahs Jimmy has eddication, you know—whilst he has eddication, I has 'scretion. He has eddication and I has 'scretion, an' so we gits along."

He drew a black bottle down the counter, and, laying half his length upon the damp board, continued:

"As a p'inciple I discredits de imbimin' of awjus liquors. De imbimin' of awjus liquors, de wiolution of de Sabbaf, de playin' of de fiddle, and de usin' of by-words, dey is de fo' sins of de conscience; an' if any man sin de fo' sins of de conscience, de debble done sharp his fork fo' dat man.—Ain't dat so, boss?"

The grocer was sure it was so.

"Neberdeless, mind you"—here the orator brimmed his glass from the bottle and swallowed the contents with a dry eye—"mind you, a roytious man, sech as ministers of de gospel and deir body-sarvants, can take a *leetle* for de weak stomach."

But the fascinations of Colossus's eloquence must not mislead us; this is the story of a true Christian; to wit, Parson Jones.

The parson and his new friend ate. But the coffee M. St.-Ange declared he could not touch; it was too wretchedly bad. At the French Market, near by, there was some noble coffee. This, however, would have to be bought, and Parson Jones had scruples.

"You see, Jools, every man has his conscience to guide him, which it does so in——"

"Oh, yes!" cried St.-Ange, "conscien'; thad is the bez, Posson Jone'. Certainlee! I am a *Catholique*, you is a *schismatique;* you thing it is wrong to dring some coffee—well, then, it *is* wrong; you thing it is wrong to make the sugah to ged the so large price—well, then, it *is* wrong; I thing it is right—well, then it *is* right; it is all 'abit; *c'est tout.* What a man thing is right, *is right;* 'tis all 'abit. A man muz nod go again' his conscien'. My faith! do you thing I would go again' my conscien'? *Mais allons,* led us go and ged some coffee."

"Jools."

"W'at?"

"Jools, it ain't the drinkin' of coffee, but the buyin' of it on a Sabbath. You must really excuse me, Jools, it's again' conscience, you know."

"Ah!" said St.-Ange, "*c'est* very true. For you it would be a sin, *mais* for me it is only 'abit. Rilligion is a very strange; I know a man one time, he thing it was wrong to go to cock-fight Sunday evening. I thing it is all 'abit. *Mais,* come, Posson Jone'; I have got one friend, Miguel; led us go at his house and ged some coffee. Come; Miguel have no familie; only him and Joe—always like to see friend; *allons,* led us come yonder."

(*50*)

"Why, Jools, my dear friend, you know," said the shamefaced parson, "I never visit on Sundays."

"Never w'at?" asked the astounded Creole.

"No," said Jones, smiling awkwardly.

"Never visite?"

"Exceptin' sometimes amongst church-members," said Parson Jones.

"*Mais,*" said the seductive St.-Ange, "Miguel and Joe is church-member'—certainlee! They love to talk about rilligion. Come at Miguel and talk about some rilligion. I am nearly expire for my coffee."

Parson Jones took his hat from beneath his chair and rose up.

"Jools," said the weak giant, "I ought to be in church right now."

"*Mais,* the church is right yond' at Miguel, yes. Ah!" continued St.-Ange, as they descended the stairs, "I thing every man muz have the rilligion he like the bez—me, I like the *Catholique* rilligion the bez—for me it *is* the bez. Every man will sure go to heaven if he like his rilligion the bez."

"Jools," said the West-Floridian, laying his great hand tenderly upon the Creole's shoulder, as they stepped out upon the banquette, "do you think you have any shore hopes of heaven?"

"Yaas!" replied St.-Ange; "I am sure-sure. I thing everybody will go to heaven. I thing you will go, *et* I thing Miguel will go, *et* Joe—everybody, I thing—*mais,* h-of course, not if they not have been christen'. Even I thing some niggers will go."

"Jools," said the parson, stopping in his walk—"Jools, I *don't* want to lose my niggah."

"You will not loose him. With Baptiste he *cannot* ged loose."

But Colossus's master was not reassured.

"Now," said he, still tarrying, "this is jest the way; had I of gone to church——"

"Posson Jone'," said Jules.

"What?"

"I tell you. We goin' to church!"

"Will you?" asked Jones, joyously.

"*Allons,* come along," said Jules, taking his elbow.

They walked down the Rue Chartres, passed several corners, and by and by turned into a cross street. The parson stopped an instant as they were turning, and looked back up the street.

"W'at you lookin'?" asked his companion.

"I thought I saw Colossus," answered the parson, with an anxious face; "I reckon 'twa'n't him, though." And they went on.

The street they now entered was a very quiet one. The eye of any chance passer would have been at once drawn to a broad, heavy, white brick edifice on the lower side of the way, with a flag-pole standing out like a bowsprit from one of its great windows, and a pair of lamps hanging before a large closed entrance. It was a theatre, sub-let to gamblers. At this morning hour all was still, and the only sign of life was a knot of little barefoot girls gathered within its narrow shade and each carrying an infant relative. Into this place the parson and M. St.-Ange entered, the little nurses jumping up from the sills to let them pass in.

A half-hour may have passed. At the end of that time the whole juvenile company were laying alternate eyes and ears to the chinks, to gather what they could of an interesting quarrel going on within.

"I did not, saw! I given you no cause of offence, saw! It's not so, saw! Mister Jools simply mistaken the house, thinkin' it was a Sabbath-school! No such thing, saw; I *ain't* bound to bet! Yes, I kin git out! Yes, without bettin'! I hev a right to my opinion; I reckon I'm *a white man*, saw! No, saw! I on'y said I didn't think you could get the game on them cards. 'Sno such thing, saw! I do *not* know how to play! I wouldn't hev a roscal's money ef I should win it! Shoot, ef you dare! You can kill me, but you can't scare me! No, I shayn't bet! I'll die first! Yes, saw; Mr. Jools can bet for me if he admires to; I ain't his mostah."

Here the speaker seemed to direct his words to St.-Ange.

"Saw, I don't understand you, saw. I never said I'd loan you money to bet on me. I didn't suspicion this from you, saw. No, I won't take any mo' lemonade; it's the most notorious stuff I ever drank, saw!"

M. St.-Ange's replies were in falsetto and not without effect; for presently the parson's indignation and anger began to melt. "Don't ask me, Jools, I can't help you. It's no use; it's a matter of conscience with me, Jools."

"*Mais oui!* 'tis a matt' of conscien' wid me, the same."

"But, Jools, the money's none o' mine, nohow; it belongs to Smyrny, you know."

"If I could make juz *one* bet," said the persuasive St.-Ange, "I would leave this place, fas'-fas', yes. If I had thing—*mais* I did not soupspicion this from you, Posson Jone'——"

"Don't, Jools, don't!"

"No! Posson Jone'."

"You're bound to win?" said the parson, wavering.

"*Mais certainement!* But it is not to win that I want; 'tis my conscien'—my honor!"

"Well, Jools, I hope I'm not a-doin' no wrong. I'll loan you some of this money if you say you'll come right out 'thout takin' your winnin's."

All was still. The peeping children could see the parson as he lifted his hand to his breast pocket. There it paused a moment in bewilderment, then plunged to the bottom. It came back empty, and fell lifelessly at his side. His head dropped upon his breast, his eyes were for a moment closed, his broad palms were lifted and pressed against his forehead, a tremor seized him, and he fell all in a lump to the floor. The children ran off with their infant loads, leaving Jules St.-Ange swearing by all his deceased relatives, first to Miguel and Joe, and then to the lifted parson, that he did not know what had become of the money "except if" the black man had got it.

In the rear of ancient New Orleans, beyond the sites of the old rampart (a trio of Spanish forts) where the town has since sprung up and grown old, green with all the luxuriance of the wild Creole summer, lay the Congo Plains. Here stretched the canvas of the historic Cayetano, who Sunday after Sunday sowed the sawdust for his circus-ring.

But to-day the great showman had fallen short of his printed promise. The hurricane had come by night, and with one fell swash had made an irretrievable sop of everything. The circus trailed away its bedraggled magnificence, and the ring was cleared for the bull.

Then the sun seemed to come out and work for the people. "See," said the Spaniards, looking up at the glorious sky with its great white fleets drawn off upon the horizon—"see—heaven smiles upon the bull-fight!"

In the high upper seats of the rude amphitheatre sat the gayly decked wives and daughters of the Gascons, from the *métairies* along the Ridge, and the chattering Spanish women of the market, their shining hair unbonneted to the sun. Next below were their husbands and lovers in Sunday blouses, milkmen, butchers, bakers, black-bearded fishermen, Sicilian fruiterers, swarthy Portuguese sailors in little woollen caps, and strangers of the graver sort; mariners of England, Germany, and Holland. The lowest seats were full of trappers, smugglers, Canadian *voyageurs*, drinking and singing; *Américains*, too—more's the shame—from the upper rivers—who will not keep their seats, who ply the bottle, and who will get home by and by and tell how wicked Sodom is; broad-brimmed, silver-braided Mexicans, also, with their copper cheeks and bat's eyes, and their tinkling spurred heels. Yonder, in that quieter section, are the quadroon women in their black lace shawls—and there is Baptiste; and below them are the turbaned black women, and there is—but he vanishes—Colossus.

The afternoon is advancing, yet the sport, though loudly demanded, does not begin. The *Américains* grow derisive and find pastime in gibes and raillery. They mock the various Latins with their national inflections, and answer their scowls with laughter. Some of the more aggressive shout pretty French greetings to the women of Gascony, and one bargeman, amid peals of applause, stands on a seat and hurls a kiss to the quadroons. The mariners of England, Germany, and Holland, as spectators, like the fun, while the Spaniards look back and cast defiant imprecations upon their persecutors. Some Gascons, with ·timely caution, pick their women out and depart, running a terrible fire of gallantries.

In hope of truce, a new call is raised for the bull: "The bull, the bull!—hush!"

In a tier near the ground a man is standing and calling—standing head and shoulders above the rest—calling in the *Américaine* tongue. Another man, big and red, named Joe, and a handsome little Creole in elegant dress and full of laughter, wish to stop him, but the flatboatmen, ha-ha-ing and cheering, will not suffer it. Ah, through some shameful knavery of the men into whose hands he has fallen, he is drunk! Even the women can see that; and now he throws his arms wildly and raises his voice until the whole great circle hears it. He is preaching!

Ah! kind Lord, for a special providence now! The men of his own nation—men from the land of the open English Bible and temperance cup and song are cheering him on to mad disgrace. And now another call for the appointed sport is drowned by the flatboatmen singing the ancient tune of Mear. You can hear the words—

"Old Grimes is dead, that good old soul"

—from ribald lips and throats turned brazen with laughter, from singers who toss their hats aloft and roll in their seats the chorus swells to the accompaniment of a thousand brogans—

"He used to wear an old gray coat
All buttoned down before."

A ribboned man in the arena is trying to be heard, and the Latins raise one mighty cry for silence. The big red man gets a hand over the parson's mouth, and the ribboned man seizes his moment.

"They have been endeavoring for hours," he says, "to draw the terrible animals from their dens, but such is their strength and fierceness, that——"

His voice is drowned. Enough has been heard to warrant the inference that the beasts cannot be whipped out of the storm-drenched cages to which menagerie life and long starvation have attached them, and from the roar of indignation the man of ribbons flies. The noise increases. Men are standing up by hundreds, and women are imploring to be let out of the turmoil. All at once, like the bursting of a dam, the whole mass pours down into the ring. They sweep across the arena and over the showman's barriers. Miguel gets a frightful trampling. Who cares for gates or doors? They tear the beasts' houses bar from bar, and, laying hold of the gaunt buffalo, drag him forth by feet, ears, and tail; and in the midst of the *mêlée*, still head and shoulders above all, wilder, with the cup of the wicked, than any beast, is the man of God from the Florida parishes!

In his arms he bore—and all the people shouted at once when

(55)

they saw it—the tiger. He had lifted it high up with its back to his breast, his arms clasped under its shoulders; the wretched brute had curled up caterpillar-wise, with its long tail against its belly, and through its filed teeth grinned a fixed and impotent wrath. And Parson Jones was shouting:

"The tiger and the buffler *shell* lay down together! You dah to say they shayn't and I'll comb you with this varmint from head to foot! The tiger and the buffler *shell* lay down together. They *shell*. Now, you, Joe! Behold! I am here to see it done. The lion and the buffler *shell* lay down together!"

Mouthing these words again and again, the parson forced his way through the surge in the wake of the buffalo. This creature the Latins had secured by a lariat over his head, and were dragging across the old rampart and into a street of the city.

The northern races were trying to prevent, and there was pommeling and knocking down, cursing and knife drawing, until Jules St.-Ange was quite carried away with the fun, laughed, clapped his hands, and swore with delight, and ever kept close to the gallant parson.

Joe, contrariwise, counted all this child's play an interruption. He had come to find Colossus and the money. In an unlucky moment he made bold to lay hold of the parson, but a piece of the broken barriers in the hands of a flatboatman felled him to the sod, the terrible crowd swept over him, the lariat was cut, and the giant parson hurled the tiger upon the buffalo's back. In another instant both brutes were dead at the hands of the mob; Jones was lifted from his feet, and prating of Scripture and the millennium, of Paul at Ephesus and Daniel in the "buffler's" den, was borne aloft upon the shoulders of the huzzaing *Américains*. Half an hour later he was sleeping heavily on the floor of a cell in the *calaboza*.

When Parson Jones awoke, a bell was somewhere tolling for midnight. Somebody was at the door of his cell with a key. The lock grated, the door swung, the turnkey looked in and stepped back, and a ray of moonlight fell upon M. Jules St.-Ange. The prisoner sat upon the empty shackles and ring-bolt in the centre of the floor.

"Misty Posson Jone'," said the visitor, softly.

"O Jools!"

"*Mais*, w'at de matter, Posson Jone'?"

"My sins, Jools, my sins!"

"Ah! Posson Jone', is that something to cry, because a man get sometime a litt' bit intoxicate? *Mais*, if a man keep *all the time* intoxicate, I think that is again' the conscien'."

"Jools, Jools, your eyes is darkened—oh! Jools, where's my pore old niggah?"

"Posson Jone', never mine; he is wid Baptiste."

"Where?"

"I don' know w'ere—*mais* he is wid Baptiste. Baptiste is a beautiful to take care of somebody."

"Is he as good as you, Jools?" asked Parson Jones, sincerely.

Jules was slightly staggered.

"You know, Posson Jone', you know, a nigger cannot be good as a w'ite man—*mais* Baptiste is a good nigger."

The parson moaned and dropped his chin into his hands.

"I was to of left for home to-morrow, sun up, on the *Isabella* schooner. Pore Smyrny!" He sighed deeply.

"Posson Jone'," said Jules, leaning against the wall and smiling, "I swear you is the moz funny man what I never see. If I was you I would say, me, 'Ah! 'ow I am lucky! the money I los', it was not mine, anyhow!' My faith! shall a man make hisse'f to be the more sorry because the money he los' is not his? Me, I would say, 'it is a specious providence.'

"Ah! Misty Posson Jone'," he continued, "you make a so droll sermon ad the bull-ring. Ha! ha! I swear I thing you can make money to preach thad sermon many time ad the theatre St. Philippe. Hah! you is the moz brave dat I never see, *mais* ad the same time the moz rilligious man. Where I'm goin' to fin' one priest to make like dat? *Mais*, why you can't cheer up an' be 'appy? Me, if I should be miserabl' like dat I would kill meself."

The countryman only shook his head.

"*Bien*, Posson Jone', I have the so good news for you."

The prisoner looked up with eager inquiry.

"Laz' evening when they lock' you, I come right off at M. De Blanc's house to get you let out of the calaboose; M. De Blanc he is the judge. So soon I was entering—'Ah! Jules, my boy, juz the

man to make complete the game!' Posson Jone', it was a specious
providence! I win in t'ree hours more dan six hundred dollah'!
Look." He produced a mass of bank-notes, *bons*, and due-bills.

"And you got the pass?" asked the parson, regarding the money
with a strange sadness.

"It is here; it take the effect so soon the daylight."

"Jools, my friend, your kindness is in vain."

The Creole's face became a perfect blank.

"Because," said the parson, "for two reasons: firstly, I have
broken the laws, and ought to stand the penalty; and secondly—
you must really excuse me, Jools, you know, but the pass has been
got onfairly, I'm afeerd. You told the judge I was innocent; and in
neither case it don't become a Christian (which I hope I can still
say I am one) to 'do evil that good may come.' I muss stay."

M. St.-Ange stood up aghast, and for a moment speechless, at
this exhibition of moral heroism; but an artifice was presently hit
upon. "*Mais*, Posson Jone'!"—in his old falsetto—"de order—
you cannot read it, it is in French—compel you to go h-out, sir!"

"Is that so?" cried the parson, bounding up with radiant face—
"is that so, Jools?"

The young man nodded, smiling; but, though he smiled, the
fountain of his tenderness was opened. He made the sign of the
cross as the parson knelt in prayer, and even whispered "Hail
Mary," etc., quite through, twice over.

Morning broke in summer glory upon a cluster of villas behind
the city, nestled under live-oaks and magnolias on the banks of
a deep bayou, and known as Suburb St. Jean.

With the first beam came the West-Floridian and the Creole out
upon the bank below the village. Upon the parson's arm hung a pair
of antique saddle-bags. Baptiste limped wearily behind; both his
eyes were encircled with broad blue rings, and one cheek-bone bore
the official impress of every knuckle of Colossus's left hand. The
"beautiful to take care of somebody" had lost his charge. At mention of the Negro he became wild, and, half in English, half in the
"gumbo" dialect, said murderous things. Intimidated by Jules to
calmness, he became able to speak confidently on one point; he could,
would, and did swear that Colossus had gone home to the Florida
parishes; he was almost certain; in fact, he thought so.

There was a clicking of pulleys as the three appeared upon the bayou's margin, and Baptiste pointed out, in the deep shadow of a great oak, the *Isabella,* moored among the bulrushes, and just spreading her sails for departure. Moving down to where she lay, the parson and his friend paused on the bank, loath to say farewell.

"O Jools!" said the parson, "supposin' Colossus ain't gone home! O Jools, if you'll look him out for me, I'll never forget you—I'll never forget you, nohow, Jools. No, Jools, I never will believe he taken that money. Yes, I know all niggahs will steal"—he set foot upon the gang-plank—"but Colossus wouldn't steal from me. Good-by."

"Misty Posson Jone'," said St.-Ange, putting his hand on the parson's arm with genuine affection, "hol' on. You see dis money— w'at I win las' night? Well, I win it by a specious providence, ain't it?"

"There's no tellin'," said the humbled Jones. "Providence

'Moves in a mysterious way
His wonders to perform.' "

"Ah!" cried the Creole, "*c'est* very true. I ged dis money in the mysterieuze way. *Mais,* if I keep dis money, you know where it goin' be to-night?"

"I really can't say," replied the parson.

"Goin' to the dev'," said the sweetly smiling young man.

The schooner captain, leaning against the shrouds, and even Baptiste, laughed outright.

"O Jools, you mustn't!"

"Well, den, w'at I shall do wid *it?*"

"Anything!" answered the parson; "better donate it away to some poor man——"

"Ah! Misty Posson Jone', dat is w'at I want. You los' five hondred dollah'—'twas my fault."

"No, it wa'n't, Jools."

"*Mais,* it was!"

"No!"

"It *was* my fault! I *swear* it was my fault! *Mais,* here is five hondred dollah'; I wish you shall take it. Here! I don't got no use

(*59*)

for money.—Oh, my faith! Posson Jone', you must not begin to cry some more."

Parson Jones was choked with tears. When he found voice he said:

"O Jools, Jools, Jools! my pore, noble, dear, misguidened friend! ef you hed of hed a Christian raisin'! May the Lord show you your errors, better'n I kin, and bless you for your good intentions—oh, no! I cayn't touch that money with a ten-foot pole; it wa'n't rightly got; you must really excuse me, my dear friend, but I cayn't touch it."

St.-Ange was petrified.

"Good-by, dear Jools," continued the parson. "I'm in the Lord's haynds, and he's very merciful, which I hope and trust you'll find it out. Good-by!"—the schooner swung slowly off before the breeze —"good-by!"

St.-Ange roused himself.

"Posson Jone'! make me hany'ow *dis* promise: you never, never, *never* will come back to New Orleans."

"Ah, Jools, the Lord willin', I'll never leave home again!"

"All right!" cried the Creole; "I thing He's willin'. Adieu, Posson Jone'. My faith! you are the so fighting an' moz rilligious man as I never saw! Adieu! Adieu!"

Baptiste uttered a cry and presently ran by his master toward the schooner, his hands full of clods.

St.-Ange looked just in time to see the sable form of Colossus of Rhodes emerge from the vessel's hold, and the pastor of Smyrna and Bethesda seize him in his embrace.

"O Colossus! you outlandish old niggah! Thank the Lord! Thank the Lord!"

The little Creole almost wept. He ran down the tow-path, laughing and swearing, and making confused allusion to the entire personnel and furniture of the lower regions.

By odd fortune, at the moment that St.-Ange further demonstrated his delight by tripping his mulatto into a bog, the schooner came brushing along the reedy bank with a graceful curve, the sails flapped, and the crew fell to poling her slowly along.

Parson Jones was on the deck, kneeling once more in prayer. His hat had fallen before him; behind him knelt his slave. In thundering tones he was confessing himself "a plumb fool," from whom "the conceit had been jolted out," and who had been made to see that even his "nigger had the longest head of the two."

Colossus clasped his hands and groaned.

The parson prayed for a contrite heart.

"Oh, yes!" cried Colossus.

The master acknowledged countless mercies.

"Dat's so!" cried the slave.

The master prayed that they might still be "piled on."

"Glory!" cried the black man, clapping his hands; "pile on!"

"An' now," continued the parson, "bring this pore, backslidin' jackace of a parson and this pore ole fool niggah back to thar home in peace!"

"Pray fo' de money!" called Colossus.

But the parson prayed for Jules.

"Pray fo' de *money!*" repeated the Negro.

"And oh, give thy servant back that there lost money!"

Colossus rose stealthily, and tiptoed by his still shouting master. St.-Ange, the captain, the crew, gazed in silent wonder at the strategist. Pausing but an instant over the master's hat to grin an acknowledgment of his beholders' speechless interest, he softly placed in it the faithfully mourned and honestly prayed-for Smyrna fund; then, saluted by the gesticulative, silent applause of St.-Ange and the schooner men, he resumed his first attitude behind his roaring master.

"Amen!" cried Colossus, meaning to bring him to a close.

"Onworthy though I be——" cried Jones.

"*Amen!*" reiterated the Negro.

"A-a-amen!" said Parson Jones.

He rose to his feet, and, stooping to take up his hat, beheld the well-known roll. As one stunned he gazed for a moment upon his slave, who still knelt with clasped hands and rolling eyeballs; but when he became aware of the laughter and cheers that greeted him from both deck and shore, he lifted eyes and hands to heaven, and cried like the veriest babe. And when he looked at the roll again, and hugged and kissed it, St.-Ange tried to raise a second shout, but choked, and the crew fell to their poles.

And now up runs Baptiste, covered with slime, and prepares to cast his projectiles. The first one fell wide of the mark; the schooner swung round into a long reach of water, where the breeze was in her favor; another shout of laughter drowned the maledictions of the muddy man; the sails filled; Colossus of Rhodes, smiling and bowing as hero of the moment, ducked as the main boom swept round, and the schooner, leaning slightly to the pleasant influence, rustled a moment over the bulrushes, and then sped far away down the rippling bayou.

M. Jules St.-Ange stood long, gazing at the receding vessel as it now disappeared, now reappeared beyond the tops of the high undergrowth; but, when an arm of the forest hid it finally from sight, he turned townward, followed by that fagged-out spaniel, his servant, saying, as he turned, "Baptiste."

"Miché?"

"You know w'at I goin' do wid dis money?"

"*Non*, miché."

"Well, you can strike me dead if I don't goin' to pay hall my debts! *Allons!*"

He began a merry little song to the effect that his sweetheart was a wine-bottle, and master and man, leaving care behind, returned to the picturesque Rue Royale. The ways of Providence are indeed strange. In all Parson Jones's after life, amid the many painful reminiscences of his visit to the City of the Plain, the sweet knowledge was withheld from him that by the light of the Christian virtue that shone from him even in his great fall, Jules St.-Ange arose, and went to his father an honest man.

PÈRE RAPHAËL

WHEN Jules St.-Ange said to Parson Jones in the cala-boose, "M. De Blanc, he is the judge," he—abridged. The judge was M. Réné De Blanc St.-Ange—his father.

The St.-Ange house stood on the swamp side of the Rue Royale, next to a corner of that very intersection with Conti Street where Jones and Jules first met. It opened on the sidewalk and had at its ground floor, extending from the street-door steps on its right to the porte-cochère on the left, a narrow, hooded balcony masked by a lattice along its sidewalk face and across its porte-cochère end. In the great batten gate of the porte-cochère was the usual small one for servants, and close to it, in the balcony lattice, a very small hinged window. Into this balcony let also the long French windows of the drawing-room. Its unlatticed end, by the front door, was fair with potted flowers, and through the railing there one might pass to the steps and the street.

The adjoining edifice on the right, at the corner, was a prim affair of whose sort one was a great plenty—a gambling-house. Happily its main entrance was on its broader face, around in Conti Street, where it called itself a theatre. Let us not be intolerant; in the judge's own house there was lively card-playing every evening, and few could surpass the brilliancy of his own betting.

"What harm is that betting," asked the judge, "if the game is fair? In one's own domiceel, with fran'," (friends) "ah! think! out of what mischieve it may keeb them—on Sunday evenings!" The judge, his family of three, and even the servants were more or less addicted to what they believed was the English tongue. "Lang-uage of the law and those court'," he affably apologized, "and sinze appointed on the bench 'tis biccome one of my bad 'abit'."

He had long been a widower, the executive head of his house was his maiden sister, and both facts may, in part, explain the further one that his son was already a bitter disappointment. This very afternoon father and son had quarreled and the son had been forbidden the house. Florestine, youngest of the household, was really not a relative, but the orphan of the judge's old law partner. She was as beautiful and intelligent as she was high-spirited, and the judge doted on high spirit. His last hope for his son lay in the young man's invincible mettle.

Within an hour after the rupture there came to the house those "only two really dear and good *Américaines* in the worl'—although Protestan', alas!"—the widow Merrifield and her mild blue-eyed daughter Abigail. Mrs. Merrifield's call was not merely social; she had a matter in hand which she could not with comfort carry directly to the widower judge, albeit he was an old friend and her lawyer; yet it was a matter in which, through his sister, she *must* seek his kind offices. For it was one in which only a Creole gentleman could know how to intervene, and she had already made bold to refer to him M. Dimitry Davezac, another and much younger Creole gentleman. Had he called? No? She was glad. Yes, the matter was about Abby, and when the mother had stated it to Mademoiselle St.-Ange—while Florestine had led Abigail up-stairs to a conversation quite as private and far more intense—and the judge's sister came back from the judge's part of the house and from telling him the Davezac case, the widow's heart was lighter.

And now she and Abby must fly, night was so near. But a coming storm thundered No! and mademoiselle calmed them with the assurance that after the rain Florestine's maid Caroline, with one of the men-servants, should conduct them home, since the judge could not.

"On account those sore h-eye'," he explained with gallant regret, touching the green pasteboard shade which overhung his brows. "But, any'ow," he said, "that pain of the light is now nearly pass'. Thangs be to God, those sigs week' to wear me that accursed thing, they finizh on the day after to-morrow; then 'tis my 'ope to 'ave the more smooth tamper."

The five were yet standing together when the rain began to fall, and Caroline ushered in kind old Father Pierre, taking refuge from the weather. Good company he was, and an hour passed brightly while all tongues ran nimbly, and five hearts, not counting his, hid each its own distress. A second hour followed, and then, in a lull of the tremendous rain, the good priest, laughing away the judge's protest, rose to go. The Merrifields openly admired his masculine ability to pooh-pooh the "must not" of a friend.

As the two men stepped out into the sheltered balcony the judge had new wrenchings of secret torture to think of his son out in this tempest with no better comfort than the companionship of that mulatto scamp Baptiste—Caroline's lover, by the way. All at once, hardly knowing what he did, he told the bare fact of the quarrel and then as abruptly changed the subject. "But, my faith! how that Florestine has been to me an angel those sigs week' of those sore h-eye'! Had it not 'ave been for that Florestine I muz' 'ave suffer' those sigs week' without one game of card'."

Caroline stood at close earshot just there in the porte-cochère wicket, where she had come to catch any stray news there might be of her momselle Florestine's beloved Jules and her own "triflin'" Baptiste, and she heard even Father Pierre's soft words.

"My fran'," said he after a moment of meditation, "you muz' not priv-ent yo' son to make that h-angel yo' daughter."

Caroline, in a wild gladness, listened on. "Ah!" exclaimed the judge, "my son *he* muz' not priv-ent *me* to make her my daughter. You know well I have swear that to her father; but also I have swear him that my son shall not know that till he get her, and he shall not have her till he is fit!"

"Fit? Ah, well, when tha' 'z going to be?"

"Father Pierre, you preach againz' those seven sin, eh? You are a pries', you got to do that. Me, I preach only againz' one; that is —debt! When my son pay h-all his debt' he can have Florestine; but biffo'? he shall not even h-ask for her."

"Ah! but ad the same time, so soon he *say*——"

"No; only so soon he *pay!*"

"Yes; but I thing if you let me *tell* him he can have her so soon he pay——"

"No-o! When he have *pay*—that laz' dolla'—*I* will tell him *if* he can have her or no. But he—you know what he say? He tell me—when I be ready to say he can have her, *then* he let me know if he goin' pay *any* of those debt'."

"But if he 'ave no money———"

"Let him go to work, *sacré* tonn'—pardon! He shall not one dollah risceive from me till he pay his debt', not to save the life! Well, good-night—biffo' it rain hard some mo'—Father Pierre, a moment! I am no miser, me—no! That *hour* my son is finizh' to pay those debt', I swear you, I give him back aggain two dollah for one, every dollah he have pay. Only tha' 'z another thing he muz' not know biffo'. Well, good-night!"

The judge watched his friend hurry away through the wet lamplight. The skies poured again, and he from the balcony—Caroline from the wicket—fled into the house. There the Merrifields were bowing to the decree of mademoiselle and Florestine that they must stay all night. Who could argue against such a pair backed by such a sky? While they asked the door-bell rang, and with their hostess they started for their rooms; but Florestine untwined her arms from Abigail, laid them on her guardian's neck, and offered to stay with him and once more be his eyes. The other three hurried on up-stairs and M. Davezac entered.

How the storm-delayed suitor had contrived, after all, to arrive so nearly dry was remarkable, only his feet being wet enough to justify his neglect of an invitation to be seated. Manifestly he was from the country—the sugar country—and as haughty as he was handsome. His dress was odd, even for New Orleans. He wore buckskin breeches above his exquisite top-boots, and a fawnskin vest under his voluminous coat, giving an effect half pioneer, half Incroyable. To Florestine, as she sat close to her guardian's ear, he seemed, save Jules, as fair a youth as she had ever looked upon. The judge explained her presence and his disfiguring green shade, and at once came to business.

"Madame Merrifiel' she say you come tell her you every day passin' at Place Congo, by her house, see her daughter up on balconie, and fall in love to her till you cann' stan' that no mo', and you want madame let you come make visite."

The youth bowed grandly: "Tha' 'z w'at I want."

"Yes. Well, tha' 'z maybee h-all right, if you got some fran' want to speak good word for you."

"No, m'sieu'." The lover stiffened up till he could but just peer down over his lower lashes: "H-all those fran' livin' on plantation'."

But the judge, still wrung with the pain of having parted two lovers, had no inclination to part another two. "Tha' 'z an unfortunate," he said. "Any'ow, me, I bil-ieve you one gen'leman, though I'm not ab'e to see you, bic-ause those sore h-eye'. That be pretty good, if you get fran' on plantation' send sairtifi-*cate*."

The young man stood with chin lifted and eyes dropped. "M'sieu', I bet you w'at you want; I swear you w'at you want; I fight you who you want; but sairtifi-*cate?*—bah!"

"But sit down. I bil-ieve I like you pretty good. Me, I don' want you to bet, neither to fight; only I like you to swear me one thing the truth."

The petitioner somewhat relaxed: "Verie well, m'sieu'; I swear you the truth, I don' care w'at it is."

"Verie well. You h-owe some debt', I sue-pose; 'ow much you h-owe?"

The youth showed a faint smile of scorn. "Not one dollah," he said, and hardened his neck as he added, "even to my papa." Catching signs of approval from Florestine, he condescended further: " 'Tis to ezcape that that I am from home. I could 'ave res' yond' so long I want. I am a Davezac!" He curved back until he had to lean on his cane. Florestine whispered some suggestion to the judge, who murmured his approval of it.

" 'Sieur Davezac," he said, "you don't got one father *con*-fessor?"

"Yes," replied the suitor; but when he discerned Florestine's wish that he would show himself more compliant, he added: "Yes, m'sieu', tha' 'z Père Raphaël. I shall send you Père Raphaël?"

"Père—eh—Raphaël—eh?" mused the judge. "Ah, I dunno; I thing I'm maybee not verie well acquain'd with that father. He's a verie h-old, that Père Raphaël?"

The young man darkened; he suspected a sly attempt at cross-examination. "No, m'sieu'; that Père Raphaël he's a verie yo'ng."

"Ah, yes; a verie yo'ng, yes; but is he not a verie large fat?"

M. Davezac bridled. "No, m'sieu'; he's a verie small thin."

The judge seemed all at once to remember: "Ah, yes! But—exceb' the hand' and feet, eh?"

The reply came with a smile as sweet as Florestine's, yet distinctly threatening: "No, m'sieu'; hand' and feet same size my ear', and I 'ope my inquisitor he don't find those the ear' of a jack-*ass?*"

Florestine colored in protest, but the judge laughed outright. "Ah, no-o! Send me that Père Raphaël. If I like him so well I like you, that be h-all right."

At a pause in the storm the visitor bowed himself out. The judge went to his room, Florestine mounted to hers. There she learned from Caroline the glorious things overheard at the porte-cochère wicket, and between her distress for the storm-beaten Jules and her vivid and highly practical plannings to make use of her dear guardian's incautious revelations, she slept as little, all night, as the judge or his sister or Madame Merrifield.

The Sabbath began to dawn, the rain-spent clouds to break, and Florestine, for the hundredth time, looked down into the drenched and still lamplighted street. Her mind revolved an astounding plot she had laid while others slept. She was seeking its moral justification.

"To the gayest endurance," thought she, "there is a limit. People have no right to forget that. The judge has no right. No more has dear Tante"—as she called Mademoiselle St.-Ange. "Yet only Caroline remembers—ah, faithful Caroline! But where is *she* presently, that frightful laggard?" The sufferer tearfully smiled.

She lingered at the open casement, taking comfort in the triumphant re-arising of the storm-swept city. Remotely she could hear the shock-headed Gascons of the French Market whistling and singing and making its vaults resound with the ring of their busy cleavers.

"How happy," she sighed, "is the lot of the butcher!"

A watchman, with lantern and leather helmet, came up the street and gave three slowly swung taps of his iron-shod club on the corner curbstone as a signal to his fellows. "What a care-free life is that of the watchman!—as, likewise"—her contemplation taking in a two-wheeled milk-cart and a two-wheeled bread-cart wildly tilted in the mire, stalled and abandoned—"as likewise the life of the milk-man and the baker!"

The carts stood under a lamp which, from a great crane, over-hung the two ways. An hour earlier she had seen them crash to-gether, and it had been balm to her soul's wounds to hear their drivers exchange the compliments customary on such occasions. "What splendid liberties are to the milkman, the bread man—while to the gayest and moz girlish enduranze there is a limit!"

A lamplighter passed, quenching the lamps: " 'Ow 'appy is the lot of the lamplighter!"

Day broadened; one could read a distant poster that promised amazing things for Cayetano's Circus on the Place Congo. The shops began to open, yonder pawnship down street on the farther side not excepted. Men and women, white, black, yellow, passed with market-baskets on arm, and here came a slave maid as straight as an Egyptian and as black as Creole coffee, with a huge basket, heap-ing full, on her head. At the porte-cochère a milkman sent in his usual catcall, and the wicket latch clinked. That was Caroline with her pitcher.

Florestine saw the departing milkman turn the upper street cor-ner, but heard no wicket reclosed: "Ah, Caroline, murderess!" she inwardly cried, "do you want to bring yo' miztrezz ad the door of death, standing idle, doubtlezz, down there in the 'alf-open wicket?"

She did not guess that Baptiste had come upon the scene, nor could she hear any note of Caroline's wary speech: "No, suh! no milk fo' you tell you go an' come ag'in; an' no mo' sweet-sweetenin' o' dis yeh gal tell she know who gwine marry her missy! By de law I goes wid my missy, thaynk Gawd! an' I don' go sweetheartenin' wid no French yalleh niggah to-day to be his grass-widdeh to-morrow! No, suh; you go ten times fasteh'n you come, an' fetch me yo' mawsteh!"

A bread man filled the maid's arms with loaves and hurried on. She gave one to the mulatto. "Here, pig; now fo' de Lawd's sake, run on an'——"

"Yass, yass; but, Caroline, y' ought to see! All behine Rue Bour-gogne h-overflow'!"

"Lawd 'a' massy! man, I wants to see Miché Jules! I got dat news fo' Miché Jules, what——"

The messenger went, but Abigail Merrifield, slipping down through the drawing-room and out into the latticed balcony, heard

Caroline moan after him, to see him stop and share his loaf with a very black and rustic old Negro who presently moved on with him out of sight. With the wicket shut Abigail breathed easier, though still in a tremor of hope, longing, and self-blame.

She was just in time. Dimitry Davezac came up the far side of the street with the high-minded air of a man who could always be counted on. As he passed, as he glanced across at all the upper balconies of the house, and as he looked back while he turned riverward into the Rue Conti, Abigail, in the lattice, as badly frightened as she was well hid, stood as still as a stone. Her heart pounded like a ship on a reef—it was a ship on a reef! Oh, what would her mother say if she knew her child had not the self-command, the moral force, even to retreat into the house? The question gave her strength to start, but at that moment some one entered the drawing-room and she could only stand petrified again.

Around in the Rue Conti the young man's steps flagged—flagged —ceased. He laid the head of his cane to his lips. Then he pressed smartly on again. This was but for a moment, however, and his trim feet went slowly once more. He stopped, turned half round, looked back, consulted his watch, frowned. All pure stage-play; he was recollecting nothing which he had left behind and must return for; yet now he went back. At the same time Abigail was having great relief from her fears. Whoever had come into the drawing-room, she thought, must have gone out again, it was so still. Here at hand offered itself, moreover, a plausible task, and with healing caresses she began to reanimate the storm-torn flowers at the open end of the balcony. Now she soothed this one and now that, and this, and this, and this; reaching, bending, drawing back, half straightening, and bending again, a languid flower herself, while Dimitry came once more into view and moved down the farther sidewalk.

"What odd chimneys and dormer windows!" his manner implied, and she saw him even when he had got entirely at her back. Ah, but she should have seen more! The very flowers, laughing through their grateful tears, tried to cry, "Look behind you, benefactress! Look, Abigail, behind you in the balcony!" For who had unlawfully slipped into this show and was seeing the whole performance free but Florestine!

Davezac was gone, yet Abby's touch lingered among the flowers, and not until a voice as soft as their perfume called her name did she flash round to stare and gasp. Suddenly her tears shone and she clung to the arm of her friend. "I couldn't sleep. I *couldn't* keep my room."

"Ah, tha' 'z not the fault of you. Tha' 'z the fault of Tante to give you that room behine yo' mama, and withoud balconie-e!"

"Oh, Florestine, this is the first time in my life I ever——"

"Did anything! Ah, ha, ha! I billieve you, Abbee; I billieve that, my faith!"

"Oh, oh! If you could only have told me last night what took place between the judge and—and *him*, I might now be honestly asleep."

"Ah, I cou'n' he'p *that*. I had to keep me with the judge till the en', biccause those sore h-eye'. Then, after, I cou'n' come to you in that room behine. I can tell you now, but I don't want tell you if that goin' put you as-leep."

But Abigail begged and Florestine told.

As she finished—"Oh, Florestine, Florestine," cried her listener, "you've made his heart's fortune—his and mine together!"

"*Attendez*—wait; tha' 'z not sure yet. We dunno if that Père Raphaël—of the so small han' an' feet, ha, ha!—be willing to come. And even if he come we dunno if the judge goin' be please' with Père Raphaël."

"Oh, but he will, he will. Ah, darling, how can I ever repay you?"

"You want to know? Come! Come inside! You can pay in advanze." They hastened to Florestine's chamber, where Florestine explained. "You shall make 'Sieur Davezac take me this letter to Jules." She showed one. "Ah, Abbee, 'ow glad the good God muz' be, now, that he led them teach me to write! But firz' I'll tell you w'at Caroline fine out laz' night from the judge."

While she recounted the entrancing story, Jules St.-Ange, with Baptiste at his back, stood on the sidewalk close by his lost home. To this outcast pair the inundation had made the shape of the earth newly problematical. Baptiste was perplexed, but his master, as ever, remained cheerful and unbiased. "Me, I dunno," he said, "but I thing it is roun', *mais* ad the same time flat—like a plate. Because, me, if I was making that worl' I would try to suit every-*bodie*, and I thing that muz' be the way 'tis make. You fine it flat; well, then, it is flat: Father Pierre fine it roun'; well, then, it is roun'—*mais* that Caroline!—wanting to see me so bad—w'ere she is hide?"

"Ah, I dunno; laz' time she was righd there. I shall knock?"

"Knock? ad the porte-cochère of my papa? Baptiste, 'f you knock there I sell you to-day, h-auction! Knock if you want; that h-auction raise me some money for the bread and coffee, else, me, I dunno 'ow I'm goin' raise that."

While he spoke M. St.-Ange noted with mingled amusement and regard, on the other side of the way, a strikingly dressed stranger. It was Davezac, passing again, and the two gave each other stare for stare. The spying maidens, from Florestine's high chamber, could see Dimitry, though not Jules.

"*Sacré!*" murmured the lover of Abigail between his perfect teeth, "any plaze but there, and with her perchanze looking, I would crozz all that mud and make you to elucidade that stare; but I'll see you aggain."

He scanned him sidewise, carefully; so much too carefully that, to Florestine's exquisite entertainment, he ran into a towering backwoodsman, who affectionately apologized, while street observers and even the frightened Abigail laughed; but Jules so courteously refrained that M. Davezac forgave his earlier offence.

Up on the next square Dimitry looked back. At the corner opposite the front of the judge's house people were running together from all directions. Bareheaded in the midst of the press towered the backwoodsman, Parson Jones. Presently he was talking to Jules, who had crossed to his side. However, two or three onlookers from upper balconies said it was all a false alarm, and as they spoke Dimitry espied Caroline slip from her wicket and hurry his way, though with the street between them. Now she sidled into an arch, openly smiled at him, and slyly showed Florestine's letter. He went to her swiftly enough, read and parleyed; parleyed twice as long as he would have done had he known that Abigail was once more in the lattice.

"But, oh, Florestine," said the overmatched Abby—for Florestine was with her and had revealed her whole mad plot, proposing to make it a round conspiracy of five, including Caroline—"that would be to steal! to steal, Florestine! How can I—can I—ask him to help me steal?"

"Ste-eal! Ah, ha, ha, Abbee, you dunno bittween to steal and to borrow?"

"Oh, but to strip the house like a gang of thieves—ah, me, me! It's tearing my poor conscience in two!"

"Abbee, look!" Florestine counted off on her fingers: "Firs', we take all those bric-à-brac; segond, 'Sieur Davezac he pawn them yondeh and give the money to Jules; three, Jules he pay with it all his debt'; four, the judge he give aggain to Jules the double all he pay; five, we riddeem those bric-à-brac, and the fortune of the 'eart is made for every-*bodie*. Ah, Abbee, if you don't help me to make that, you tear my poor conscien' in fi-i-ive!"

"Oh, sweet, I am such an awful coward!"

"Ah, yes, but sometime' they are very uzeful, those coward'."

"But you spoke of difficulties——"

"Yes, ah, yes! Firz' place, I dunno can we make Jules take those money, he is a so proud of his honor! And, segond place, ev'n if he do that, I dunno if he h-use those money to pay those debt'—ha, ha, ha! *Than* w'at we goin' do, w'en Tante and the judge big-in to mizz those candelabra, those vase', those spoo-oon'?"

Abigail gasped and moaned, but Florestine clutched her arm and they peered through the lattice. Up their own sidewalk came Parson Jones, and at his elbow tripped Jules St.-Ange. The parson was making reckless show of his bank-notes, which Jules regarded with lively desire while he warned their holder of his folly. Behind the two were Baptiste and Colossus, with the loaf they had shared stowed safely inside them. The four passed close by the lattice. Florestine, gathering some hint of Jules's design, sent him a soft call of distress, but Parson Jones drowned it unaware with the re-echoing voice in which he explained that the fund belonged to his church in the wilderness, and invited Jules to breakfast.

"Abbee, Abbee," she gasped, "I shall follow them!"

But Abby seized her as if the pair were drowning together, and in panting suspense Florestine lingered and gazed. The gambling-house! the gambling-house at the corner! Would Jules lead the stranger into it? For there the two masters and servants had halted. But the maidens took courage when they heard the parson set forth his theory of a special Providence, and Jules profess a like conviction. And now grateful tears sprang into Florestine's eyes as the men turned away, picked their steps across the mire of the Rue Royale, and disappeared toward the Rue Chartres.

"Wait, darling, wait!" whispered the clinging Abigail. "There's hope yet; let me think a moment!"

"Ah!" cried the more daring one, "sinze all night I have wait and think. Watch you there; I goin' fedge those bric-à-brac!" She darted in.

Abigail wrung her hands. "I cannot do this!" she cried, "I cannot, I cannot!" Yet where courage failed, friendship held fast, and her act was stouter than her word. She flinched with affright, for Caroline, who had returned unnoticed, softly called in through the lattice from the angle by the porte-cochère.

"I foun' him, Miss Abbie, yass 'm. But, well, eh, he say Père Raphaël ain't comin'. Don't give no reason, he say, 'cep' dat Miché Dabzac he stay away too much f'om confession."

"W'at, w'at, w'at?" exclaimed Florestine, as she reappeared with a small heavy burden wrapped in a large woollen garment.

"Oh, Lawdy, missy," said the maid, "Père Raphaël refuse' to come!"

"Caroline!" The mistress snatched open the lattice window. "Assassin, you! 'Sieur Davezac—*he* riffuse to come, al-*so?*"

"Lawd, no! He waitin' dess round de cawneh; but he 'fraid nobody gwine trus' him now sence Père Raphaël 'fuse to come."

"Go, Caroline, slow torture, you! fly! Tell him come! Tell him Père Raphaël he 'ave change' his mind!"

"Florestine!" gasped Abigail.

"*Mais certainement!* Caroline, tell him Père Raphaël sen' the judge word he comin' speak well-well for him. *Allez! va!*"

The maid glided away. Her mistress set down her burden and, drawing the wrapper from it, whispered, "Hun'rade-dolla' clock to big-in!"

Abigail gulped. "In the judge's own cloak!" she moaned.

"Ah, no," replied her smiling friend; "and, any'ow, we don't goin' to pawnbreak *that*. But you, Abbee; you di'n' prayed laz' night for Père Raphaël to come?"

"I had never heard of Père Raphaël!"

"Ah, yes; you never hear'; and yet ad the same time you di'n' billieve he's coming! Ah, Abbee, I dunno 'ow you can be a so wicked like that! *Mais* wait there whiles I fedge some more of those thing'."

The next moment Abigail, left alone, saw Dimitry reappear at the corner. Caroline was with him, but they parted; she came, he went in search of Jules. He turned the corner St.-Ange and the parson had turned; but unluckily he had not seen them enter the parson's lodging-house, and thinking they had passed on into and down the Rue Chartres, he hastened that way.

"Oh, yass 'm," said Caroline, again at the lattice window, "he be right back. He on'y gwine tell Miché Jules fo' Gawd's sake don't go gitt'n' money in no scan'lous way whiles we a-raisin' it faw him squah and clean."

"Abbee!" cried Florestine, returning with fresh booty, " 'ow you are fine, to be a so brave like that, an' same time withoud a tea-spoon of courage!"

"I think so, myself!" was the flashing reply.

When the breakfast-bell tinkled and Florestine, busy as a bird with nestlings, caught her breath and hearkened, fortune was kind. Mrs. Merrifield, Tante, and the judge, worn with the cares of a sleepless night, sent excuses for their non-appearance. So prospered the reckless scheme, and presently, while Abigail, alone, and always the better nerved in Florestine's absence, watched in the balcony for her lover's return, there came instead, without their servants and unfound by Davezac, Jules St.-Ange and Parson Jones. Through what a maze the prodigal was leading his victim! They passed again down street and out of sight.

Laden with her final spoils Florestine stepped into the balcony once more and Abigail told of the two men. "And there's hope yet, dear," she said with spirit, "for they're on their way to church; I heard them say so. At any rate we can wait and see!"

"Wait!" replied Florestine, "for Jules to go to church? Ah, no!"

Caroline emerged from the porte-cochère and passed up through the lattice the family's biggest market-basket, and while Florestine filled it Dimitry arrived.

"Now, Miss Abby," said the maid, "please han' me dat ah big dud fo' to kyiver de load. Thank you, ma'am. Lead off, Miché Dabzac, and de Lawd have mussy on ow souls!"

"Stop! stop!" commanded Abigail, with sudden authority, "let us—oh, let us—oh, wait, wait!"

"Mademoiselle," put in her lover—he tried to show the tenderest worship, but it was the first word he had ever spoken to her and he burst into a blaze—"I break any law you want! Even I *keep* any law you want. But to wait? My God! Mademoiselle, sinze five hun'rade year' di'n' no Davezac wait for no-*body! Allons*, Caroline!"

By his aid the great load had risen to the slave girl's head, and as they went it rested there as jauntily as a flowered hat. The two maidens watched them go in at the pawnbroker's door, and were looking for them to come forth again, when all at once Florestine dragged Abigail from the balcony, and from a drawing-room window showed her Tante and Mrs. Merrifield issuing into the street by the front door. "Tsh-sh! they thing we are there in my room asleep together; Caroline tole that to them w'en yo' mama di'n' fine you in yo' bed. Ah, yo' mama she 'ave her li'l' sicret, too. She want to go and riturn withoud you finding that out—ha, ha, ha!—that she have been *there*."

"Where?"

"Ah, only to mass. She don't want riffuse that to Tante, an' same time she dunno if tha' 'z maybee a li'l' bit wrong, and of course, you know, the only way to fine that out 't is to try it. Then if you fine it wrong you be sorrie, and that make it right." The pair came out again into the balcony and after much anxious waiting Davezac and Caroline reappeared.

"W'at! Caroline, you 'ave the sick stomach—to smile like that?"

"Momselle, 'cept dis yeh old dud what you tell me be sho' to fetch back, do whole kit an' bilin' brung dess half what we bound to raise."

"Ah, *mon Dieu!* and if Tante fine those thing' gone!"

"Mesdemoiselles," interposed Dimitry, "look! I shall go at my room—bring h'all my thing'—raise that balanze in half an hour!"

"Whiles they are at mass!" broke in the delighted Florestine. "Yass! 'Tis the h-only way, Abbee. Go, 'Sieur Davezac, go. God will pay you for that! Go, make quick biffo' Père Raphaël come fine uz all here together. Go! and same time send me that Jules St.-Ange, while me I make Père Raphaël tell the judge you makin' yo' possible to bring him back his son."

A half-hour was all that remained of the Sabbath forenoon, and Judge St.-Ange had not yet left his bedchamber, when the front-door bell rang and Caroline went up-stairs to announce Père Raphaël.

"Yass, suh, an' he got"—she made a distressed effort not to smile at thought of the two figures meeting—"he got a green shade ove' his eyes biggeh 'n yone."

Père Raphaël paced the drawing-room alone, truly "a verie small thin." The house was still. Now and again as the scant form, trim even in the rude draping of rope-tied gown and unlifted cowl, came to the balcony windows, the deeply hooded eyes looked out, first down the street and then up. Thus they were presently drawn to a number of unwashed little girls near the next door, a door of the gambling-house. The flock were listening against it, giggling, trying to peep under it, starting away, wringing hands, and stealing back to listen again. Père Raphaël stepped out upon the open end of the balcony.

" 'Tis Miché Jules," said a brazen youngster, her eyes on the green shade, her apron in her teeth. "Yass, he pass in yondeh wid a so beeg man, by front way, round cawneh, and beeg man he don't want play card', and he yell so loud dey scared of him."

The visitor returned to the drawing-room, wearily chose a chair and knelt beside it, but instantly stood upright again at sound of a footfall.

Judge St.-Ange came slowly in and paused. "Caroline!" he called. The maid came. "Mademoiselle Florestine," he asked, "where she is?"

"Miché, she say Miss Abby got sich a pow'ful migraine she feel bound to stay wid her ef you kin escuse her; yass, suh."

The judge waved out the servant and turned to his visitor. Père Raphaël's eyes remained downcast behind their ugly screen until the two were seated.

"Is that a fact, indeed," asked the judge, "that we 'ave the one maladie?"

"Ah," replied the little father, in a thin obstructed voice, "with me 'tis but a cold, and in the throat like-*wise*, till I was nearly privvent the honor to come."

"They privvent many thing', those sore h-eye'," agreed the judge.

"Yes," rejoined the caller, "I cannot read me those prayer', cannot wride me those sermon'. Almoze they stop me playing those domino'—those card'."

"Ha-a-ah! you are fon' of those card'?"

"Yes, I am verie, verie fon' to play them. *Mais,* w'en I cann' play, that save me money. Biccause those hoss-raze—those cock-*fight*— I never bet on *those.* Tha' 'z only thing I ever bet, me—those card'."

"And me the same," said the judge. A business silence ensued. Then—"Père Raphaël, that young man—he is one of those Davezac', I sue-pose, of the Côte d'Or, eh? You can speak good word for him?"

"Ah, that dippan'. Me, I h-am a pries'; you, you h-are a judge. I dunno w'at goin' be good word to *you.* 'Sieur Davezac he got, h-any'ow, all the bad 'abit' *nécessaire* to a perfec' Creole gen'leman."

"Aha! Well, tha' 'z mighty good word. For one pries' tha'd be verie bad; but for one Creole gen'leman, you know——"

"Hmm. *Mais,* same time, there is one diffycultie, m'sieu'."

"Tha' 'z not mannie."

"*Mais,* I thing that don't please you, m'sieu'. I 'ave the fear that Madame Merrifiel' she 'ave the 'ope that M. Davezac he 'ave the willingnezz to change his *ril*-igion. *Mais,* I am compel to tell you— w'at he tell me—rather than change his *ril*-igion he sooner go to hell. Pardon, I am sorrie to tell you that, *mais*—" The small speaker shrugged from ears to elbows.

The host hid his admiration under a cold smile. "Tha' 'z brave, yes," he acknowledged.

"Brave—ah, tha' 'z another troub'—h-all the time fightingg, fightingg, or fran' of somebody fightingg!"

"Ah! but a gen'leman, those time'—! My faith! Père Raphaël, he shall 'ave everything w'at he want. For why he did'n' come with you?"

"M'sieu', he is af-raid to be in debt to you."

" 'Ow he's goin' be in debt to me? Impossib'!"

"He say if you speak well for him to Madame Merrifiel' he is in debt to you the res' of the life, and he don't want see you aggain till any'ow he *commance* to pay you, and he's gone pawnbroken everything w'at he got——"

"Ah!—ah-h!—ah-h-h! My fran', oh-h, w'at that is for?"

"M'sieu', 'tis for—pardon, to tell you that, 'tis a diffycult; tha' 'z a verie daily-cat."

With his eyes helplessly dropped, the host straightened severely

(*78*)

against the high back of his chair. " 'Tis ab-out my son? Ah—go h-on."

"Well, you see, 'Sieur Davezac he hearin' every-*bodie* talk 'bout *that*. And w'en he say he bet any-*bodie*—fight any-*bodie*—w'at say Judge St.-Ange he don't trit his son all right, then every-*bodie* say, 'Oh, yes; the judge he *thing* he trit his son all right, *mais* if the judge know that ris-on his son don't pay those debt'——' "

"Ris-on he don't pay—he don't want!"

"Yes; *mais* they thing 'tis bic-ause yo' son he's fran' of so many poor man, and every time one poor fran' cann' pay his debt' yo' son he pay that with his h-own monie."

The judge shook his drooping head mournfully. "I do not bil-ieve. I never fine one sign of that. If I 'ave see' that, my son he would sleep laz' night in his h-own bed, and me I would sleep in mine. *Mon Dieu!* Père Raphaël, tha' 'z a thing I don' like to talk ab-out, but—w'at I muz find out—'ow that make 'Sieur Davezac take all his thing' pawnshop?"

"Ah, I tell you. He say he goin' find that Jules St.-Ange, goin' lend him those monie, goin' *make* him pay h-all those debt'. Then he make him go at his papa, and say, 'At the end I 'ave *commance*' all right, I goin' to work.' "

The judge looked up sharply, but then sank his head lower than before. "I don't bil-ieve th' 'z a possib' to make. Same time already, me, I am in the debt to 'Sieur Davezac so long my life; if he succeed to finizh, or if he don't succeed to finizh, to me that be h-all the same; he 'ave *commance*'. To *commance*, 'tis enough." His grip trembled on the arms of his chair, but his head came up.

"I thing tha' 'z verie well, m'sieu'," said Père Raphaël, stirring as if to go. A strange voice was distracting both visitor and host with mad though remote and smothered bellowings. The judge, in apology, said that they came from the next house, through the walls.

"I never year it loud like that biffo'. Père Raphaël, I want you tell 'Sieur Davezac—and same time my son I don't want him fine that out—if 'Sieur Davezac he succeed, my son he 'ave planty to pay him back, bic-ause me I shall give my son twice w'at he spend to pay h-all those debt'—never biffo' I di'n' year some noises come through thad wall."

"All right, m'sieu'; I tell him—if I see him. *Mais*, there is one thing: 'Sieur Davezac he say maybee those monie he raise be not enough to pay h-all those debt'; well, any'ow, w'en you see yo' son *commance* to pay, you be satis-*fy;* to commance, 'tis enough. *Mais* me, I——"

With a shrug the speaker rose, and the judge stood up very straight.

"Père Raphaël, no; tha' 'z all w'at I can say—no! For 'Sieur Davezac to commance *'tis* enough, yes; but for my son—and still, my God! with my son I be glad be recon-*cile'*—for him to commance, 'tis too late; he muz' finizh." The speaker's tone, though grieved, was kind, and the raising of his voice was solely to divert his visitor from the noises that continued to search through the partition wall. "Come at home here aggain this evening, will you? If that troub' with my son pass, or if it be worse, all the same I be wanting you bad—fellow-sufferer those sore h-eye'—to play me some card'."

The visitor promised to come, and bowed low for thanks, but both were giving all their heed to the hot altercation that searched through the solid masonry and was bringing the judge undisguised distress. Père Raphaël had faced toward the front door, the judge following and trying to flood the air with his own speech, when there came from the gambler's house a sound as of some one falling, and outcries in several voices. Then there was a jangle of the St.-Ange door-bell. The ready Caroline flew to the door, and Madame Merrifield and Tante sprang in, casting wild glances behind them.

"There!" cried the hostess, with a sister's indignation in every inch of her bonnet and draperies. "Lis-ten! Look! Come there and look, you! You what cannod take advize! Oh, you what, sinze appointed jodge, got no time to be a father!"

The judge caught one outside glimpse and turned away with a groan. In the midst of a multiplying crowd the towering form of Parson Jones, between a burly red ruffian on one side and Jules St.-Ange on the other, was being hurried away, swaying bloody-headed, across the Rue Royale. The three men vanished into the cross street.

"He fine his money gone," cried one child to another. "Dey say one niggah take it; dey gone hunt him up!"

"Caroline, my 'at and shoe'! exclaimed the judge, and would have torn the shade from his eyes, but the sister prevented him. A better thought came. "Père Raphaël"—he tried to peer this way and that

—"Père Raphaël, go you, tell my son—ah, my God! where is that Père Raphaël?"

"Gone already!" joyously cried Caroline. "Lef' at de fus' beginnin'!" She turned to Florestine and Abigail, who stood clinging to each other, Florestine as pale and grief-broken as though she had been Abigail, and Abigail as strangely full of a new intrepidity as if she were Florestine. "You see him go, bofe 'n you, didn' you? You didn'? He go by de po'te-cochère; yass, suh; crossin' tow'd de riveh, in Toulouse Street, like he gwine head 'em off."

"Go you, Caroline," said the judge, and Florestine spoke the same word, straightening from Abby's clasp. "Go, make quick! You shall fine him!"

But as the young mistress pushed her maid from the room, she added privately: "Fine Miché Jules! Jules! Jules! Fine Miché Jules!"

The judge turned to Madame Merrifield. "Yo' pardon! 'Twas not to give you *that* troub' that those heaven' make you our prisoner; for you I 'ave a different news." Abby moved away, and he spoke on in a murmur. "Père Raphaël, as you 'ave seen——"

The lady received the information with due dignity and thanks, and presently turned to her daughter. "Come, my dear, the overflow has passed off. Put on your things and let us——"

Abigail was beseeching Tante to allow Florestine to go home with her, and when Madame Merrifield urged it the petition was granted.

"Here tha' 'z no place for her ad the presend," said the sister aside to her brother, with tremulous energy.

"Ah, verie good!" was his reply. "For me, I goin' make my son fine out I *am* a judge!" And the moment he was alone he rang for a man-servant and sent him on an errand that filled the slave's face with consternation.

Madame Merrifield's tall house, in which, this afternoon, she was taking some of the sleep owing to her from the night, stood flush with the sidewalk, with its garden on one side, at the corner of two streets. Through its oleanders and myrtles and its high wooden fence of graceful openwork one got a broken view of the rude Place Congo, in a part of which a great multitude were gathered on the board seats of Cayetano's amphitheatre to see his buffalo-and-tiger fight.

Abigail and Florestine were in the garden. The sounds and glimpses they caught in their embowered hiding would have yielded few clear meanings, but Caroline, outside the double gate, went and came, describing and explaining. *That?* That was the up-river men jeering at the Latins. And *that?* That was the Latins snarling back at the *Américains.* Oh, there would be bloody trouble if the show did not come off soon! *That?* That was the *Américains* singing. Yes, the tune was a hymn, the maid admitted to Abigail, "But you can dess thaynk Gawd you cayn't make out de words."

Once she came excitedly saying she had seen, seated in the throng, at inaccessible distances and apart, Colossus and Baptiste. She hurried back in hope to discover Jules, the parson, or Dimitry; but as she vanished Dimitry came along, scanning every window of the house, and quite overlooking the garden until Florestine stepped from cover to the half-open gate. He strode in a step or two, lifted his hat, and with the glow of an aide-de-camp used it to point to the Place Congo.

"Mademoiselle, I cannot stop. I am cloze be'ind the track of 'Sieur St.-Ange. Some-*bodie* pig' the pocket of that Posson Jone', and Posson Jone' and 'Sieur St.-Ange they are pazz at that bull-fight to fine if 'tis his niggah."

"Butt had pawn-*shop!* 'Sieur Davezac, w'at you 'ave make ad that pawn-*shop?*"

The young man straightened with joy. "By those prayer' of my saint, thad monie is raise'! 'Tis now only to fine 'Sieur St.-Ange and give it him. You 'ave the one moiety me I 'ave the other." He backed off.

"Wait, 'Sieur Davezac, wait! My faith! if Posson Jone' don't fine *his* monie, Jules sure to give *those* monie to Posson Jone'!"

Dimitry paused agape while he took in the probability. "Mademoiselle, verie well. I give him that moiety only w'en I see you give him the other."

"But, 'Sieur Davezac, another thing! Père Raphaël, he's come yonder and the judge say 'h-all right.'"

The suitor flamed with wonder and gratitude. "Hah! now to fedge that Jules St.-Ange!" He sped away.

The longest day in the life of Judge St.-Ange drew to its end.
Again the lamplighter passed. His yellow lights twinkled after him
from corner to corner. Over the darkened shops, and here and there
between them, the balconied windows of one parlor after another
grew luminous inside their curtains. Only those of the St.-Ange
house remained dark. Tinkling into their melancholy dusk with
lighted lamps, two servants in turn had been sent tinkling out of it
again by the solitary judge. "Thad darknezz," he kindly told the
second one, "assuage' those sore h-eye'."

But now came Caroline. Behind her followed the earlier two; each
of the three bore tall, globed lamps, and at their side walked his
sister.

"My brother," she said, "it is the Sabbath." And as the servants
left the lamps and retired, she added, "Ah, have we not darkness
enough, with all those lamp' we can light?"

His inquiry admitted the fact. "Florestine—she is rit-urn'?"

"Florestine she is rit-urn', yes; but better you leave her there
w'ere she wild to be al-lone—in her room. St.-Ange, thad Florestine
her soul—like mine—is in torment for thad boy, yo' son, my de'
brother, oud there in the street."

"He is not in the street, my sister."

The sister clutched her brother's arm in tragic affright, and all
at once he lost his self-command, and exclaimed, "My son!—my
span'threef!—vagabond!—robber of strenger'!"

"W'ere he is, St.-Ange? Ah, my God! w'at you 'ave done?"

"If that pol-ice 'ave done w'at I sen' them to do, he is in the
calaboose."

With a moan as if she were stabbed, the sister sank into a chair
and hid her face. The judge rose and pulled a bell-cord, and she
hurried out. Before he could speak to the servant who responded, the
door-bell rang imperiously.

"Go, you; that 'ave the soun' of M. Davezac. If yes—or if Père
Raphaël—tell him come in. Anybody bis-ide, I cann' see them to-
night—bic-ause those sore h-eye'. Ah, my God!" he added to himself, "I wizh I 'ave not promize' to play those card'!"

M. Davezac entered with a head as high as if he came with a demand for surrender. What could it mean? At an austere distance he

bowed low. Yet the judge made himself almost jovial. "Aha! ad the end you are there for that rip-lye, eh?"

"Rip-lye, m'sieu'?"

"Ah, thad news you wizh me to inform you from Madame Merrifiel'. Sinze several hour' 'tis waiting, thad news. But I like *that*, your dillybration; you will perchanze have the patienze if first I h-ask you some news—of my son."

"M'sieu', 'tis for that I am biffo' you. I h-owe you one debt——"

" 'Sieur Davezac, no. My God! if my son was a li'l' mo' like you——"

"If he was a li'l' mo' like me, m'sieu', he would be sleeping to-night in the calaboose, yes."

"My God! young man, you 'ave save' my son from the calaboose?"

"I 'ave save' who' I can, but yo' good neighbo' of the negs door——"

"Miguel and Joe?"

"They are in the calaboose."

"And Baptiste?"

"In the calaboose."

"And Posson Jone'?"

"In the calaboose."

"And that Collosse of Rhode'?"

"The devil only know'!"

"And Jules?"

"M'sieu', yo' son is ad yo' door."

The father half left his chair, but a painful thought forced him back again. "Young man, young man, you 'ave lent monie to my son—to ruin him worze than biffo'?"

"Lend monie—my faith! I beg him till I sweat!—I beg him till I swear!—I beg him till I cry!—no use! I cannod make him to borrow me. All he say, 'My conscien'! my honor! Pay *my* debt' with *yo'* monie? Ampossib'!"

Again the judge half left his chair, but again he restrained himself. "And my son he is yond' at my door to talk to me ab-out paying those——"

"No, m'sieu'; he's there to ged that Posson Jone' let out from calaboose."

"Hah!" The judge was disappointed. "But any'ow, tha' 'z well;

I never intan' Posson Jone' to be put in calaboose. Only Jules he ought come mo' sooner!"

"No, m'sieu', no use to come mo' sooner, till Posson Jone' he 'ave time to sleep off thad lemonade. And w'iles he's doing that we try to fine his ole niggah—my soul! we are nearly *parizh'* with hunting thad black *imbécile*."

The judge, his ear quickened by his yearning, suddenly started for the door and as he went its bell softly jingled. But when he opened it, there stood, not his son, but Père Raphaël. If M. Davezac had believed himself caught in a trap set for him he could not have stared with more disconcertion. Suddenly, with scarcely a decent salutation to the newcomer, he said to the judge, "I'll go and fedge yo' son."

But with a kind gesture Père Raphaël detained him, while addressing the judge. "Yo' son? He's not there. But yet he's coming. Only, he rim-ember one other plaze to look for that *domestique* he's hunting, and he say tell M. Davezac wait till he come."

"Good!" cried the judge, in pure gladness. "And to pazz the time whiles waiting—card'! Card', Père Raphaël! like this morning arrange'. And the game a three-cornered till Jules come and make it a four!"

Père Raphaël hesitated. "If monsieur," he said, "will pardon me not uncovering the head?—biccause I"—his throat seemed still to be ailing—"I 'ave leave' be'ind me that shed for those sore h-eye'."

"Ah, you shall take mine!" cried the host. But that kind of loan was not one for a lender to insist upon, and they sat down to the game as they were. While they were in it to the elbows the door-bell sounded again and Jules St.-Ange presently stood before them. Father and son said a cautiously kind good-evening. The others bowed.

"*Con*-tinue, messieurs," begged the young man, "ah, *con*-tinue the game. I am come only——"

"Ah, we know," said the judge; "but tha' 'z not a *nécessaire* presently. Come, you shall play, my boy. There is yo' chair, there are yo' counter', waiting sinze the big-gening. Come!"

"Ah, no, papa. I like to play you thad game, messieurs, yes; and, beside', I like to win me some monie. To-night tha' 'z the firs' time I ever got use for monie; *mais*, 'ow I'm goin' to win me anything if

all that time I dunno if I'm goin' ged that paper for Posson Jone'
to pazz out? Ah, no!"

"For w'at thad Posson Jone' is in calaboose, my son?"

"Papa, he is there for a verie strange; he is lock' for his ril-
igion."

"My son! for his ril-igion?"

" 'Tis for preaching the specious providence! I know, Père
Raphaël, for you that would be a sin, to preach that in the church;
but Posson Jone' he di'n' preach that in the church; he preach' it
ad thad bull-ring. He thing it is right ad that bull-ring; well, then,
ad that bull-ring it is right. Ah, if he 'ave the 'abit to thing that is
right, well, he cann' he'p *that*; 'tis his 'abit."

"Assuredlee," murmured Père Raphaël.

"Me, I don't care about those 'abit'," cried the prodigal, with
sudden warmth, "if a man stick to his ril-igion and pay his debt'!"

"Ah!" cried the judge, in a glow.

"An' if he can fight like he preach'!" exclaimed M. Davezac.

"Ah, bah!" laughed the judge. "Posson Jone' he fight w'en they
try to stop him pritching?"

"*Mais certainement*," said Jules, "in that whole city there is not a
priest to fight like that Posson Jone'—exceb' "—he saluted defer-
entially—"that be Père Raphaël. Bic-ause, my faith! I bil-ieve he
fight juz' as good if he 'ave been sober. And same time *crying*—to
pay his debt'!"

"Jules, my boy," the judge pointed to an escritoire—"write me
there for Posson Jone' to pazz from that calaboose so soon he want'."

"Also Baptiste, papa?" asked Jules, as he labored with the pen.

"Yes, likewise pud that—'also the mulatto boy Baptiste.' Give it
me—and the pen."

Presently the pass was in the son's breast pocket, and the four
took up the cards. From the first Père Raphaël had played with a
nerve that challenged the judge's admiration, and now at once began to lead the betting with a gentle and taciturn intrepidity.
Dimitry followed with equal daring, the judge and his son laughed
and kept their caution, and Jules dragged in the constant and startling losses of the reckless pair. It seemed but a hop, skip, and jump
from the time they began until these two rose with an air of res-
ignation.

"Ah!" cried the host, "finish-*ing?* Me, I am loser al-*so,* but that luck boun' to turn. We are juz' commance'."

M. Davezac shrugged amusedly and spread his hands downward. "To commance 'tis enough; I 'ave precisely los' all I've got there with *me.*"

"Me the same," coughed Père Raphaël.

First one and then the other drew forth a wallet and laid its paper contents uncounted before Jules. The prodigal rose, made them into one wad, and with a gracious bow thrust them into the same pocket that held the parson's release. The father rose last, and stood in unconfessed but passionate suspense.

"Well, messieurs," said Jules, saluting as he backed away, "you will egscuse that hurry, with my fran' in that calaboose, and——"

"Jules," responded the judge, following toward the drawing-room door, while Père Raphaël and Davezac drew away in opposite directions, "you don't need to go if you——" He felt a touch on his arm; his sister stood beside him.

"Jules," she interposed, "if you 'ave there already not quite enough to pud you out of debt——"

"Tante—papa"—the son drew forth his gains—"I win that in yo' 'ouse, and from fran'. You thing that be honorab' to pay that to shopkipper? My faith, that is a secred!" He looked around to appeal the point to Père Raphaël, but the hooded figure had vanished, and Davezac stood between him and his kindred, heaving with indignation. "M'sieu' St.-Ange!" said Dimitry.

Jules smiled fondly. "M'sieu' Davezac?"

"You know w'at I would say, me, if that was not yo' 'ouse here?"

" 'Tis not my 'ouse. W'at that is you would say?"

"I would say, take that monie and pay those debt', or fight me under those live-oak', Bayou St. Jean, to-morrow sun-*rise!*"

The prodigal smiled on. "I meet you there. My faith! tha' 'z the first time I ever got use for monie, and then you thing I'm goin' teck it and pay my *debt'?* Ah, m'sieu', I be sorry to fighd you for that, but—'tis a matt' of conscien'!"

The speaker's last glimpse of the company as he left them showed the judge turning fiercely upon Davezac, and his aunt heatedly arraigning her brother. Surely he would not have shut himself out had he seen his father, at the instant of the door's closing, saved from a fall only by the arms of Tante and Florestine as the latter darted into the room, or had he heard himself imperatively called by the weeping girl.

The judge recovered himself, lifted the shade from his eyes, painfully blinked around the room, and spoke with dignity. "M'sieu' Davezac—Père Raphaël——"

But not even Tante or Florestine remained to reply. Only Caroline responded: "Miché Dabzac an' Père Raphaël done gone, miché. Yass, suh, by de po'te-cochère." A statement, like history, only partly true.

Once more the market-houses sparkled with candles, resounded with cheerful discords. Out on Bayou Road, in the sky that over-arched Suburb St. Jean, the Sabbath night faded into day. Under one of the bayou's vast oaks stood Caroline, casting frightened eyes everywhere and speaking warily to some one out of sight. "Dis bound to be de place," she said; "yondeh de schooneh; but no pahson, an' no Miché Jules. Lawd, sen' 'em quick! Look' to me like ow dough done cook' when I see de jedge an' po' ole momselle leave de house afo' day, but when dey tu'n' off to look up Father Pierre I praise' G— Good Lawd, yondeh come Miché Dabzac!"

"Hi-ide!" stealthily called her hidden confederate, but Dimitry had seen her.

"Mawnin', Miché Dabzac," the maid pertly saluted, "mawnin', suh."

With a stately frown he signed to her to speak more quietly, and she obeyed, though with a show of amusement.

"D' ain't nobody here 'cep' you an' me, an' us all done ruin' now, anyhow, 'less 'n I can waylay Pahson Jone' an' 'suade him fo' to not let Miché Jules give him dat ah monie. Dass all Miss Flo'stine 'ould eveh sen' me out here faw at dis scan'lous hour."

"Then go you back. Tell her he shall not give it, I shall privvent him!"

"Lawd, miché, but s'posin' he done gi'n it to him already."

"He shall give it him back. Go you at home; tha' 'z not the place for you here. My faith! *militraise*, I bil-ieve you are there only to fine that villain Baptiste."

"I swear I ain't! I ain't see' dat fool sence de middle o' de night, when he set off ag'in to try to scare up Pahson Jone' ole niggeh."

"Go you at home, Caroline."

"Miché Dabzac, I see' Miss Abby sence I see' you las'."

The maid backed enticingly toward the trunk of the oak; the young man followed.

"Yass, suh; las' evenin', when y' all gone, Père Raphaël an' all, Miss Flo'stine writ me a pass an' slipp' me out fo' to run tell Miss Abby an' her ma how Miché Jules 'fuse to pay his debt', an' w'at pass mo'oveh 'twix' him an' you———"

"Ah, ah! she 'ave no ri-ight!"

"Hol' on! hol' on! De Lawd move' her to do it. I fine 'em confessin' dey conscience to one 'notheh, Madame Mayfiel' a-sobbin' 'caze she been to Catholic church, and Miss Abby 'caze o' de way we raise dat ah monie; an' when I tell 'em o' dis yeh las' pickle you done got us in———"

"Me? me? me?"

"Oh, yass, suh; yass, suh; yass, suh! When you tell Miché Jules he got to pay or fight, ain't he dess djuty-bound to fight and to not pay, fo' to p'otec' his honoh? You dess ax Miss Flo'stine!"

"Ah, bah! He can pay firz' and fight after."

The maid started with surprise, but then laughed. "My sakes! miché, he wouldn' think o' dat in fi-ive years. And when I told dem po' ladies what you done, dey dess drap' 'pon one 'notheh an' cry like dey heart—Lawd! yondeh Madame Mayfiel' now!"

"Diable! go you at home!"

"Too late; she done spied me. Oh, now we is gone done it to de las' lick! Here she come to stop de djuel, an' fine nobody 'cep' we two togetheh! Fo' Gawd's sake! ef you got yo' djuelin'-tools hid away anywhuz round here, run fetch 'em out an' parade 'em all you kin!

"Mawnin', Madame Mayfiel'. Lawd! you out here alone?"

"Oh, Caroline, where is my daughter? Where is Abigail? And why does Mr. Davezac avoid me?"

"Lawd! Madame Mayfiel', he think 'tis Miché Jules comin', an' he dess gone git his djuelin'-tools."

The young man reappeared. He bowed superbly to Mrs. Merrifield, but glared on Caroline. "*Misérable!* Who has stole me those sword' from the hole of thad tree?"

"Swords!" gasped the frightened lady, at which the youth bowed again and then stiffened high.

"Madame, if that is by yo' command——"

Her brows lifted with distress. "No, sir, no, no! I've overstepped, but I haven't stolen—oh, who can tell me where is my daughter?"

"Lawd A'mighty!" cried Caroline, "ain't she home in bed?"

"Bed? We've neither of us touched one! At daylight I left her and went to market——"

The alarmed Davezac pressed close. "You leff her?"

"She begged me to go! It was to find you! Oh, sir, I'll buy off the pawnbroker if only you'll not fight until we've got everything back into the judge's house!"

"But yo' daughteh! yo' daughteh! when you have ritturn'?"

"I found her note. She'd seen Father Pierre passing, called him in and told him all! And she's gone with him, writing me that I'd understand! But I don't, and I can't, and I'm afraid something dreadful has——"

"Ah, madame, with Father Pierre, no! They 'ave gone perchanze ad the judge. I'll go there and——"

He sprang to go, but at the second stride halted squarely before the small, cowled figure of Père Raphaël, who had issued from a clump of bushes holding out to him the missing swords. "You are forgettingg?"

"Yes! I was forgettingg!"

"Or maybee you don't want to fighd some mo', and finding egscuze to leave?"

The young man snatched the swords and swelled for a fitting retort from a Creole gentleman to a priest of his faith; but before he could find it Mrs. Merrifield and Caroline rushed in between them, panting in fright and shame, "The judge! the judge and his sister!"

The judge and his sister arrived at high speed, she with her hair in her eyes, he with his green shade on one ear. "Florestine!" they called. "Florestine, she's not here? Where is Florestine? Ah, Madame Merrifiel', Florestine is gone with Jules! Jules have rob' the 'ouse and gone with Florestine!"

But the distracted mother scarcely heard them, for yet another pair came after them in close pursuit, and with a moan of joy she sprang from the group into the arms of Abigail beside Father

Pierre, while Caroline tearfully cried to the judge and his sister, "Momselle Flo'stine all right, mawsteh! She safe, mist'ess! She *all right!* I swah to Gawd she all right! You kin ax Père Rapha'—o-o-oh, Lawd, but dis *is* de Lawd's own doin's! Yondeh Miché Jules and de piney-wood' pahson!"

Amid these preoccupations Father Pierre, hurriedly drawn aside by Père Raphaël, received from that small informant swift assertions that visibly amazed him, and propositions to which he nevertheless eagerly consented. As Jules, the parson, and Baptiste came into view engrossed in the welcome sight of the *Isabella* schooner, Father Pierre waved back the couples about him. "We are too mannie, ladies and gen'lemen. Back, iv you please—and even you, judge. Père Raphaël and me we are sue-ficient."

Père Raphaël was already moving toward Jules and the parson, and Father Pierre followed. At the vessel's side Parson Jones paused to pledge Jules a lifelong affection. Grouped with the ladies and Davezac the judge was holding himself well in hand; but when he witnessed the love and admiration his boy had won from a stranger and the remotest of aliens, his *sine qua non* crumbled at last, and to the bounding joy of all behind him, "Father Pierre!" he warily called, "a word, a word, not more! Say to Père Raphaël he can tell my son if he *say* he goin' pay those debt' with those monie everything be all right. To commance, 'tis enough!"

With a gay nod Father Pierre motioned him off and pressed nearer Père Raphaël. Before they could come close, Jules, following the schooner as with limp sails she moved along the shore to the poling of her crew—but all that is of earlier record: how his card-table winnings were offered the parson and declined; how Colossus reappeared and what he did; how Jules swore, laughed, and wept, and how, as the schooner finally bore away his God-sent friend, he stood and gazed after its fading topmasts.

While he so stood, his father, oblivious of all bystanders, the green shade lost and "those sore h-eye'" forgotten, stood and gazed on him with a sympathy as keen and evident as his yearning suspense; and if the observance of these emotions intensified the sympathy and suspense of every one, what words shall tell their raptures when they saw Jules at length turn and say, "Baptiste, you know what I goin' do wid dis monie?"

"*Non*, miché."

"Well, you can strike me dead if I don't goin' to pay all my debts."

He began a little song, if you remember; but while its opening measure was still on his tongue, at the first townward bend of the path, the whole glad flock of his seekers, with the judge at their front, stopped his way.

"Papa!" exclaimed the joyous prodigal.

"My son!" cried the father. "An egschange! a fair egschange! Yo' absolution for mine!"

So they came into each other's arms. Yet in the next breath they were half apart again. "But Florestine?" they cried in one breath, "ah, where—" Both voices were silenced by Jules's amazement at something happening behind his father, and the judge, turning, stared, with his son, upon Père Raphaël frantically clasping and kissing—*kissing*, do you realize it?—kissing and embracing Tante, Abigail, Mrs. Merrifield and even Caroline. But cowl and eye-shade had been crowded off the face and head, and these were the face and head of Florestine.

"Forgive you, my child?" the aunt was exclaiming. "Ah, betteh you h-ask somebody betteh than me; for, me, I only fine that out, that robb'rie, when, too late, I commance' to make the same thing myseff."

"To commance," sighed the happy girl to Father Pierre as they all turned homeward together, " 'tis enough. Me, the same like Jules, I am discourage' to be wicked any mo', those Providence get al-ong so well without."

MADAME DELPHINE

Chapter I

AN OLD HOUSE

A FEW steps from the St. Charles Hotel, in New Orleans, brings you to and across Canal Street, the central avenue of the city, and to that corner where the flower-women sit at the inner and outer edges of the arcaded sidewalk, and make the air sweet with their fragrant merchandise. The crowd—and if it is near the time of the carnival it will be great—will follow Canal Street.

But you turn, instead, into the quiet, narrow way which a lover of Creole antiquity, in fondness for a romantic past, is still prone to call the Rue Royale. You will pass a few restaurants, a few auction-rooms, a few furniture warehouses, and will hardly realize that you have left behind you the activity and clatter of a city of merchants before you find yourself in a region of architectural decrepitude, where an ancient and foreign-seeming domestic life, in second stories, overhangs the ruins of a former commercial prosperity, and upon every thing has settled down a long sabbath of decay. The vehicles in the street are few in number, and are merely passing through; the stores are shrunken into shops; you see here and there, like a patch of bright mould, the stall of that significant fungus, the Chinaman. Many great doors are shut and clamped and grown gray with cobweb; many street windows are nailed up; half the balconies are begrimed and rust-eaten, and many of the humid arches and alleys which characterize the older Franco-Spanish piles of stuccoed brick betray a squalor almost oriental.

Yet beauty lingers here. To say nothing of the picturesque, sometimes you get sight of comfort, sometimes of opulence, through the unlatched wicket in some porte-cochère—red-painted brick pavement, foliage of dark palm or pale banana, marble or granite masonry and blooming parterres; or through a chink between some pair of heavy batten window-shutters, opened with an almost reptile wariness, your eye gets a glimpse of lace and brocade upholstery, silver and bronze, and much similar rich antiquity.

The faces of the inmates are in keeping; of the passengers in the street a sad proportion are dingy and shabby; but just when these are putting you off your guard, there will pass you a woman—more likely two or three—of patrician beauty.

Now, if you will go far enough down this old street, you will see, as you approach its intersection with ——. Names in that region elude one like ghosts.

However, as you begin to find the way a trifle more open, you will not fail to notice on the right-hand side, about midway of the square, a small, low, brick house of a story and a half, set out upon the sidewalk, as weather-beaten and mute as an aged beggar fallen asleep. Its corrugated roof of dull red tiles, sloping down toward you with an inward curve, is overgrown with weeds, and in the fall of the year is gay with the yellow plumes of the golden-rod. You can almost touch with your cane the low edge of the broad, overhanging eaves. The batten shutters at door and window, with hinges like those of a postern, are shut with a grip that makes one's knuckles and nails feel lacerated. Save in the brick-work itself there is not a cranny. You would say the house has the lockjaw. There are two doors, and to each a single chipped and battered marble step. Continuing on down the sidewalk, on a line with the house, is a garden masked from view by a high, close board-fence. You may see the tops of its fruit-trees—pomegranate, peach, banana, fig, pear, and particularly one large orange, close by the fence, that must be very old.

The residents over the narrow way, who live in a three-story house, originally of much pretension, but from whose front door hard times have removed almost all vestiges of paint, will tell you:

"Yass, de 'ouse is in'abit; 'tis live in."

And this is likely to be all the information you get—not that they would not tell, but they cannot grasp the idea that you wish to know—until, possibly, just as you are turning to depart, your informant, in a single word and with the most evident non-appreciation of its value, drops the simple key to the whole matter:

"Dey's quadroons."

He may then be aroused to mention the better appearance of the place in former years, when the houses of this region generally stood farther apart, and that garden comprised the whole square.

Here dwelt, sixty years ago and more, one Delphine Carraze; or,

as she was commonly designated by the few who knew her, Madame Delphine. That she owned her home, and that it had been given her by the then deceased companion of her days of beauty, were facts so generally admitted as to be, even as far back as that sixty years ago, no longer a subject of gossip. She was never pointed out by the denizens of the quarter as a character, nor her house as a "feature." It would have passed all Creole powers of guessing to divine what you could find worthy of inquiry concerning a retired quadroon woman; and not the least puzzled of all would have been the timid and restive Madame Delphine herself.

Chapter II

MADAME DELPHINE

DURING the first quarter of the present century, the free quadroon caste of New Orleans was in its golden age. Earlier generations— sprung, upon the one hand, from the merry gallants of a French colonial military service which had grown gross by affiliation with Spanish-American frontier life, and, upon the other hand, from comely Ethiopians culled out of the less Negroidal types of African live goods, and bought at the ship's side with vestiges of quills and cowries and copper wire still in their headdresses—these earlier generations, with scars of battle or private rencontre still on the fathers, and of servitude on the manumitted mothers, afforded a mere hint of the splendor that was to result from a survival of the fairest through seventy-five years devoted to the elimination of the black pigment and the cultivation of hyperian excellence and nymphean grace and beauty. Nor, if we turn to the present, is the evidence much stronger which is offered by the *gens de couleur* whom you may see in the quadroon quarter this afternoon, with "Ichabod" legible on their murky foreheads through a vain smearing of toilet powder, dragging their chairs down to the narrow gateway of their close-fenced gardens, and staring shrinkingly at you as you pass, like a nest of yellow kittens.

But as the present century was in its second and third decades, the *quadroones* (for we must contrive a feminine spelling to define the strict limits of the caste as then established) came forth in splendor. Old travelers spare no terms to tell their praises, their faultlessness of feature, their perfection of form, their varied styles of beauty—for there were even pure Caucasian blondes among them —their fascinating manners, their sparkling vivacity, their chaste and pretty wit, their grace in the dance, their modest propriety, their taste and elegance in dress. In the gentlest and most poetic sense they were indeed the sirens of this land, where it seemed "always afternoon"—a momentary triumph of an Arcadian over a Christian civilization, so beautiful and so seductive that it became the subject of special chapters by writers of the day more original than correct as social philosophers.

The balls that were got up for them by the male *sang-pur* were to that day what the carnival is to the present. Society balls given the same nights proved failures through the coincidence. The magnates of government—municipal, state, federal—those of the army, of the learned professions and of the clubs—in short, the white male aristocracy in everything save the ecclesiastical desk—were there. Tickets were high-priced to insure the exclusion of the vulgar. No distinguished stranger was allowed to miss them. They were beautiful! They were clad in silken extenuations from the throat to the feet, and wore, withal, a pathos in their charm that gave them a family likeness to innocence.

Madame Delphine, were you not a stranger, could have told you all about it; though hardly, I suppose, without tears.

But at the time of which we would speak (1821–22) her day of splendor was set, and her husband—let us call him so for her sake—was long dead. He was an American, and, if we take her word for it, a man of noble heart and extremely handsome; but this is knowledge which we can do without.

Even in those days the house was always shut, and Madame Delphine's chief occupation and end in life seemed to be to keep well locked up indoors. She was an excellent person, the neighbors said —a very worthy person; and they were, maybe, nearer correct than they knew. They rarely saw her save when she went to or returned from church; a small, rather tired-looking, dark quadroone of very good features and a gentle thoughtfulness of expression which would take long to describe: call it a widow's look.

In speaking of Madame Delphine's house, mention should have been made of a gate in the fence on the Royal Street sidewalk. It is gone now, and was out of use then, being fastened once for all by an iron staple clasping the cross-bar and driven into the post.

Which leads us to speak of another person.

Chapter III

CAPITAINE LEMAITRE

HE WAS one of those men that might be any age—thirty, forty, forty-five; there was no telling from his face what was years and what was only weather. His countenance was of a grave and quiet, but also luminous, sort, which was instantly admired and ever afterward remembered, as was also the fineness of his hair and the blueness of his eyes. Those pronounced him youngest who scrutinized his face the closest. But waiving the discussion of age, he was odd, though not with the oddness that he who had reared him had striven to produce.

He had not been brought up by mother or father. He had lost both in infancy, and had fallen to the care of a rugged old military grandpa of the colonial school, whose unceasing endeavor had been to make "his boy" as savage and ferocious a holder of unimpeachable social rank as it became a pure-blooded French Creole to be who would trace his pedigree back to the god Mars.

"Remember, my boy," was the adjuration received by him as regularly as his waking cup of black coffee, "that none of your family line ever kept the laws of any government or creed." And if it was well that he should bear this in mind, it was well to reiterate it persistently, for, from the nurse's arms, the boy wore a look, not of docility so much as of gentle, *judicial* benevolence. The domestics of the old man's house used to shed tears of laughter to see that look on the face of a babe. His rude guardian addressed himself to the modification of this facial expression; it had not enough of majesty in it, for instance, or of large dare-deviltry; but with care these could be made to come.

And, true enough, at twenty-one (in Ursin Lemaitre), the labors of his grandfather were an apparent success. He was not rugged, nor was he loud-spoken, as his venerable trainer would have liked to present him to society; but he was as serenely terrible as a well-aimed rifle, and the old man looked upon his results with pride. He had cultivated him up to that pitch where he scorned to practice any vice, or any virtue, that did not include the principle of self-assertion. A few touches only were wanting here and there to achieve perfection, when suddenly the old man died. Yet it was his proud satisfaction, before he finally lay down, to see Ursin a favored companion and the peer, both in courtesy and pride, of those polished gentlemen famous in history, the brothers Lafitte.

The two Lafittes were, at the time young Lemaitre reached his majority (say 1808 or 1812), only merchant-blacksmiths, so to speak, a term intended to convey the idea of blacksmiths who never soiled their hands, who were men of capital, stood a little higher than the clergy, and moved in society among its autocrats. But they were full of possibilities, men of action, and men, too, of thought, with already a pronounced disbelief in the custom-house. In these days of big carnivals they would have been patented as the dukes of Little Manchac and Barataria.

Young Ursin Lemaitre (in full the name was Lemaitre-Vigne-vielle) had not only the hearty friendship of these good people, but also a natural turn for accounts; and as his two friends were looking about them with an enterprising eye, it easily resulted that he presently connected himself with the blacksmithing profession. Not exactly at the forge in the Lafittes' famous smithy, among the African Samsons, who, with their shining black bodies bared to the waist, made the Rue St. Pierre ring with the stroke of their hammers; but as a—there was no occasion to mince the word in those days—smuggler.

Smuggler—patriot—where was the difference? Beyond the ken of a community to which the enforcement of the revenue laws had long been merely so much out of every man's pocket and dish, into the all-devouring treasury of Spain. At this date they had come under a kinder yoke, and to a treasury that at least echoed when the customs were dropped into it; but the change was still new. What could a man be more than Capitaine Lemaitre was—the soul of honor, the pink of courtesy, with the courage of the lion, and the magnanimity of the elephant; frank—the very exchequer of truth! Nay, go higher still: his paper was good in Toulouse Street. To the gossips in the gaming-clubs he was the culminating proof that smuggling was one of the sublimer virtues.

Years went by. Events transpired which have their place in history. Under a government which the community by and by saw was conducted in their interest, smuggling began to lose its respectability and to grow disreputable, hazardous, and debased. In certain onslaughts made upon them by officers of the law, some of the smugglers became murderers. The business became unprofitable for a time until the enterprising Lafittes—thinkers—bethought them of a corrective—"privateering."

Thereupon the United States Government set a price upon their heads. Later yet it became known that these outlawed pirates had been offered money and rank by Great Britain if they would join her standard, then hovering about the water-approaches to their native city, and that they had spurned the bribe; wherefore their heads were ruled out of the market, and, meeting and treating with Andrew Jackson, they were received as lovers of their country, and as compatriots fought in the battle of New Orleans at the head of their fearless men, and—here tradition takes up the tale—were never seen afterward.

Capitaine Lemaitre was not among the killed or wounded, but he was among the missing.

Chapter IV

THREE FRIENDS

THE roundest and happiest-looking priest in the city of New Orleans was a little man fondly known among his people as Père Jerome. He was a Creole and a member of one of the city's leading families. His dwelling was a little frame cottage, standing on high pillars just inside a tall, close fence, and reached by a narrow outdoor stair from the green batten gate. It was well surrounded by crape-myrtles, and communicated behind by a descending stair and a plank-walk with the rear entrance of the chapel over whose worshippers he daily spread his hands in benediction. The name of the street—ah! there is where light is wanting. Save the Cathedral and the Ursulines, there is very little of record concerning churches at that time, though they were springing up here and there. All there is certainty of is that Père Jerome's frame chapel was some little newborn "down-town" thing, that may have survived the passage of years, or may have escaped "Paxton's Directory" "so as by fire." His parlor was dingy and carpetless; one could smell distinctly there the vow of poverty. His bedchamber was bare and clean, and the bed in it narrow and hard; but between the two was a dining-room that would tempt a laugh to the lips of any who looked in. The table was small, but stout, and all the furniture of the room substantial, made of fine wood, and carved just enough to give the notion of wrinkling pleasantry. His mother's and sister's doing, Père Jerome would explain; they would not permit this apartment—or department—to suffer. Therein, as well as in the parlor, there was odor, but of a more epicurean sort, that explained interestingly the Père Jerome's rotundity and rosy smile.

In this room, and about this miniature round table, used sometimes to sit with Père Jerome two friends to whom he was deeply attached—one, Evariste Varrillat, a playmate from early childhood, now his brother-in-law; the other, Jean Thompson, a companion from youngest manhood, and both, like the little priest himself, the regretful rememberers of a fourth comrade who was a comrade no more. Like Père Jerome, they had come, through years, to the thick of life's conflict—the priest's brother-in-law a physician, the other an attorney, and brother-in-law to the lonely wanderer—yet they loved to huddle around this small board, and be boys again in heart while men in mind. Neither one nor another was leader. In earlier days they had always yielded to him who no longer met with them a certain chieftainship, and they still thought of him and talked of him, and, in their conjectures, groped after him, as one of whom they continued to expect greater things than of themselves.

They sat one day drawn thus close together, sipping and theorizing, speculating upon the nature of things in an easy, bold, sophomoric way, the conversation for the most part being in French, the native tongue of the doctor and priest, and spoken with facility by Jean Thompson the lawyer, who was half *Américain;* but running sometimes into English and sometimes into mild laughter. Mention had been made of the absentee.

Père Jerome advanced an idea something like this:

"It is impossible for any finite mind to fix the degree of criminality of any human act or of any human life. The Infinite One alone can know how much of our sin is chargeable to us, and how much to our brothers or our fathers. We all participate in one another's sins. There is a community of responsibility attaching to every misdeed. No human since Adam—nay, nor Adam himself—ever sinned entirely to himself. And so I never am called upon to contemplate a crime or a criminal but I feel my conscience pointing at me as one of the accessories."

"In a word," said Evariste Varrillat, the physician, "you think we are partly to blame for the omission of many of your Paternosters, eh?"

Father Jerome smiled.

"No; a man cannot plead so in his own defence; our first father tried that, but the plea was not allowed. But, now, there is our absent friend. I tell you truly this whole community ought to be recognized as partners in his moral errors. Among another people, reared under wiser care and with better companions, how different might he not have been! How can *we* speak of him as a law-breaker who might have saved him from that name?" Here the speaker turned to Jean Thompson, and changed his speech to English. "A lady sez to me to-day: 'Père Jerome, 'ow dat is a dreadfool dat 'e gone at de coas' of Cuba to be one corsair! Ain't it?' 'Ah, madame,' I sez, ' 'tis a terrible! I 'ope de good God will fo'give me an' you fo' dat!' "

Jean Thompson answered quickly:

"You should not have let her say that."

"*Mais*, fo' w'y?"

"Why, because, if you are partly responsible, you ought so much the more to do what you can to shield his reputation. You should have said"—the attorney changed to French—" 'He is no pirate; he has merely taken out letters of marque and reprisal under the flag of the republic of Carthagena!' "

"Ah, bah!" exclaimed Doctor Varrillat, and both he and his brother-in-law, the priest, laughed.

"Why not?" demanded Thompson.

"Oh!" said the physician, with a shrug, "say id thad way iv you wand."

Then, suddenly becoming serious, he was about to add something else, when Père Jerome spoke.

"I will tell you what I could have said. I could have said: 'Madame, yes; 'tis a terrible fo' him. He stum'le in de dark; but dat good God will mek it a *mo' terrible* fo' dat man oohever he is, w'at put 'at light out!' "

"But how do you know he is a pirate?" demanded Thompson, aggressively.

"How do we know?" said the little priest, returning to French. "Ah! there is no other explanation of the ninety-and-nine stories that come to us, from every port where ships arrive from the north coast of Cuba, of a commander of pirates there who is a marvel of courtesy and gentility"—*

"And whose name is Lafitte," said the obstinate attorney.

"And who, nevertheless, is not Lafitte," insisted Père Jerome.

"Daz troo, Jean," said Doctor Varrillat. "We hall know daz troo."

Père Jerome leaned forward over the board and spoke, with an air of secrecy, in French.

"You have heard of the ship which came into port here last Monday. You have heard that she was boarded by pirates, and that the captain of the ship himself drove them off."

"An incredible story," said Thompson.

"But not so incredible as the truth. I have it from a passenger. There was on the ship a young girl who was very beautiful. She came on deck, where the corsair stood, about to issue his orders, and, more beautiful than ever in the desperation of the moment, confronted him with a small missal spread open, and, her finger on the Apostles' Creed, commanded him to read. He read it, uncovering his head as he read, then stood gazing on her face, which did not quail; and then with a low bow, said: 'Give me this book and I will do your bidding.' She gave him the book and bade him leave the ship, and he left it unmolested."

Père Jerome looked from the physician to the attorney and back again, once or twice with his dimpled smile.

"But he speaks English, they say," said Jean Thompson.

"He has, no doubt, learned it since he left us," said the priest.

"But this ship-master, too, says his men called him Lafitte."

"Lafitte? No. Do you not see? It is your brother-in-law, Jean Thompson! It is your wife's brother! Not Lafitte, but" (softly) "Lemaitre! Lemaitre! Capitaine Ursin Lemaitre!"

The two guests looked at each other with a growing drollery on either face, and presently broke into a laugh.

"Ah!" said the doctor, as the three rose up, "you juz kip dad cog-an'-bull fo' yo' negs summon."

Père Jerome's eyes lighted up—

"I goin' to do it!"

---

* See gazettes of the period.

"I tell you," said Evariste, turning upon him with sudden gravity, "iv dad is troo, I tell you w'ad is sure-sure! Ursin Lemaitre din kyare nut'n fo' doze creed; *he fall in love!*"

Then, with a smile, turning to Jean Thompson, and back again to Père Jerome:

"But anny'ow you tell it in dad summon dad 'e kyare fo' dad creed."

Père Jerome sat up late that night, writing a letter. The remarkable effects upon a certain mind, effects which we shall presently find him attributing solely to the influences of surrounding nature, may find for some a more sufficient explanation in the fact that this letter was but one of a series, and that in the rover of doubted identity and incredible eccentricity Père Jerome had a regular correspondent.

Chapter V

THE CAP FITS

About two months after the conversation just given, and therefore somewhere about the Christmas holidays of the year 1821, Père Jerome delighted the congregation of his little chapel with the announcement that he had appointed to preach a sermon in French on the following Sabbath—not there, but in the cathedral.

He was much beloved. Notwithstanding that among the clergy there were two or three who shook their heads and raised their eyebrows, and said he would be at least as orthodox if he did not make quite so much of the Bible and quite so little of the dogmas, yet "the common people heard him gladly." When told, one day, of the unfavorable whispers, he smiled a little and answered his informant—whom he knew to be one of the whisperers himself—laying a hand kindly upon his shoulder:

"Father Murphy"—or whatever the name was—"your words comfort me."

"How is that?"

"Because—'*Væ quum benedixerint mihi homines!*' " *

The appointed morning, when it came, was one of those exquisite days in which there is such a universal harmony, that worship rises from the heart like a spring.

* "Woe unto me when all men speak well of me!"

"Truly," said Père Jerome to the companion who was to assist him in the mass, "this is a Sabbath day which we do not have to make holy, but only to *keep* so."

Maybe it was one of the secrets of Père Jerome's success as a preacher, that he took more thought as to how he should feel, than as to what he should say.

The cathedral of those days was called a very plain old pile, boasting neither beauty nor riches; but to Père Jerome it was very lovely; and before its homely altar, not homely to him, in the performance of those solemn offices, symbols of Heaven's mightiest truths, in the hearing of the organ's harmonies, and the yet more eloquent interunion of human voices in the choir, in overlooking the worshipping throng which knelt under the soft, chromatic lights, and in breathing the sacrificial odors of the chancel, he found a deep and solemn joy; and yet I guess the finest thought of his soul the while was one that came thrice and again:

"Be not deceived, Père Jerome, because saintliness of feeling is easy here; you are the same priest who overslept this morning, and over-ate yesterday, and will, in some way, easily go wrong to-morrow and the day after."

He took it with him when—the *Veni Creator* sung—he went into the pulpit. Of the sermon he preached, tradition has preserved for us only a few brief sayings, but they are strong and sweet.

"My friends," he said—this was near the beginning—"the angry words of God's book are very merciful—they are meant to drive us home; but the tender words, my friends, they are sometimes terrible! Notice these, the tenderest words of the tenderest prayer that ever came from the lips of a blessed martyr—the dying words of the holy Saint Stephen, 'Lord, lay not this sin to their charge.' Is there nothing dreadful in that? Read it thus: 'Lord, lay not this sin to *their* charge.' Not to the charge of them who stoned him? To whose charge then? Go ask the holy Saint Paul. Three years afterward, praying in the temple at Jerusalem, he answered that question: 'I stood by and consented.' He answered for himself only; but the Day must come when all that wicked council that sent Saint Stephen away to be stoned, and all that city of Jerusalem, must hold up the hand and say: 'We, also, Lord—we stood by.' Ah! friends, under the simpler meaning of that dying saint's prayer for the pardon of his murderers is hidden the terrible truth that we all have a share in one another's sins."

Thus Père Jerome touched his key-note. All that time has spared us beside may be given in a few sentences.

"Ah!" he cried once, "if it were merely my own sins that I had to answer for, I might hold up my head before the rest of mankind; but no, no, my friends—we cannot look each other in the face, for each has helped the other to sin. Oh, where is there any room, in this world of common disgrace, for pride? Even if we had no common hope, a common despair ought to bind us together and forever silence the voice of scorn!"

And again, this:

"Even in the promise to Noë, not again to destroy the race with a flood, there is a whisper of solemn warning. The moral account of the antediluvians was closed off and the balance brought down in the year of the deluge; but the account of those who come after runs on and on, and the blessed bow of promise itself warns us that God will not stop it till the Judgment Day! O God, I thank thee that that day must come at last, when thou wilt destroy the world, and stop the interest on my account!"

It was about at this point that Père Jerome noticed, more particularly than he had done before, sitting among the worshippers near him, a small, sad-faced woman, of pleasing features, but dark and faded, who gave him profound attention. With her was another in better dress, seemingly a girl still in her teens, though her face and neck were scrupulously concealed by a heavy veil, and her hands, which were small, by gloves.

"Quadroones," thought he, with a stir of deep pity.

Once, as he uttered some stirring word, he saw the mother and daughter (if such they were), while they still bent their gaze upon him, clasp each other's hand fervently in the daughter's lap. It was at these words:

"My friends, there are thousands of people in the city of New Orleans to whom society gives the ten commandments of God with all the *nots* rubbed out! Ah! good gentlemen! if God sends the poor weakling to purgatory for leaving the right path, where ought some of you to go who strew it with thorns and briers!"

The movement of the pair was only seen because he watched for it. He glanced that way again as he said:

"O God, be very gentle with those children who would be nearer heaven this day had they never had a father and mother, but had got their religious training from such a sky and earth as we have in Louisiana this holy morning! Ah! my friends, nature is a big-print catechism!"

The mother and daughter leaned a little farther forward, and exchanged the same spasmodic hand-pressure as before. The mother's eyes were full of tears.

"I once knew a man," continued the little priest, glancing to a side aisle where he had noticed Evariste and Jean sitting against each other, "who was carefully taught, from infancy to manhood, this single only principle of life: defiance. Not justice, not righteousness, not even gain; but defiance: defiance to God, defiance to man, defiance to nature, defiance to reason; defiance and defiance and defiance."

"He is going to tell it!" murmured Evariste to Jean.

"This man," continued Père Jerome, "became a smuggler and at last a pirate in the Gulf of Mexico. Lord, lay not that sin to his charge alone! But a strange thing followed. Being in command of men of a sort that to control required to be kept at the austerest distance, he now found himself separated from the human world and thrown into the solemn companionship with the sea, with the air, with the storm, the calm, the heavens by day, the heavens by night. My friends, that was the first time in his life that he ever found himself in really good company.

"Now, this man had a great aptness for accounts. He had kept them—had rendered them. There was beauty, to him, in a correct, balanced, and closed account. An account unsatisfied was a deformity. The result is plain. That man, looking out night after night upon the grand and holy spectacle of the starry deep above and the watery deep below, was sure to find himself, sooner or later, mastered by the conviction that the great Author of this majestic creation keeps account of it; and one night there came to him, like a spirit walking on the sea, the awful, silent question: 'My account with God—how does it stand?' Ah! friends, that is a question which the book of nature does not answer.

(*107*)

"Did I say the book of nature is a catechism? Yes. But, after it answers the first question with 'God,' nothing but questions follow; and so, one day, this man gave a ship full of merchandise for one little book which answered those questions. God help him to understand it! and God help you, monsieur, and you, madame, sitting here in your *smuggled clothes,* to beat upon the breast with me and cry, 'I, too, Lord—I, too, stood by and consented.' "

Père Jerome had not intended these for his closing words; but just there, straight away before his sight and almost at the farthest door, a man rose slowly from his seat and regarded him steadily with a kind, bronzed, sedate face, and the sermon, as if by a sign of command, was ended. While the *Credo* was being chanted he was still there; but when, a moment after its close, the eye of Père Jerome returned in that direction, his place was empty.

As the little priest, his labor done and his vestments changed, was turning into the Rue Royale and leaving the cathedral out of sight, he just had time to understand that two women were purposely allowing him to overtake them, when the one nearer him spoke in the Creole patois, saying, with some timid haste:

"Good-morning, Père—Père Jerome; Père Jerome, we thank the good God for that sermon."

"Then, so do I," said the little man. They were the same two that he had noticed when he was preaching. The younger one bowed silently; she was a beautiful figure, but the slight effort of Père Jerome's kind eyes to see through the veil was vain. He would presently have passed on, but the one who had spoken before said:

"I thought you lived in the Rue des Ursulines."

"Yes; I am going this way to see a sick person."

The woman looked up at him with an expression of mingled confidence and timidity.

"It must be a blessed thing to be so useful as to be needed by the good God," she said.

Père Jerome smiled:

"God does not need me to look after his sick; but he allows me to do it, just as you let your little boy in frocks carry in chips." He might have added that he loved to do it, quite as much.

It was plain the woman had somewhat to ask, and was trying to get courage to ask it.

"You have a little boy?" asked the priest.

"No, I have only my daughter"; she indicated the girl at her side. Then she began to say something else, stopped, and with much nervousness asked:

"Père Jerome, what was the name of that man?"

"His name?" said the priest. "You wish to know his name?"

"Yes, monsieur" (or *miché*, as she spoke it); "it was such a beautiful story." The speaker's companion looked another way.

"His name," said Father Jerome—"some say one name and some another. Some think it was Jean Lafitte, the famous; you have heard of him? And do you go to my church, Madame——?"

"No, miché; not in the past; but from this time, yes. My name" —she choked a little, and yet it evidently gave her pleasure to offer this mark of confidence—"is Madame Delphine—Delphine Carraze."

Chapter VI

A CRY OF DISTRESS

Père Jerome's smile and exclamation, as some days later he entered his parlor in response to the announcement of a visitor, were indicative of hearty greeting rather than surprise.

"Madame Delphine!"

Yet surprise could hardly have been altogether absent, for though another Sunday had not yet come around, the slim, smallish figure sitting in a corner, looking very much alone, and clad in dark attire, which seemed to have been washed a trifle too often, was Delphine Carraze on her second visit. And this, he was confident, was over and above an attendance in the confessional, where he was sure he had recognized her voice.

She rose bashfully and gave her hand, then looked to the floor, and began a faltering speech, with a swallowing motion in the throat, smiled weakly and commenced again, speaking, as before, in a gentle, low note, frequently lifting up and casting down her eyes, while shadows of anxiety and smiles of apology chased each other rapidly across her face. She was trying to ask his advice.

"Sit down," said he; and when they had taken seats she resumed, with downcast eyes:

"You know—probably I should have said this in the confessional, but"—

"No matter, Madame Delphine; I understand; you did not want an oracle, perhaps; you want a friend."

She lifted her eyes, shining with tears, and dropped them again.

"I"—she ceased. "I have done a"—she dropped her head and shook it despondingly—"a cruel thing." The tears rolled from her eyes as she turned away her face.

Père Jerome remained silent, and presently she turned again, with the evident intention of speaking at length.

"It began nineteen years ago—by"—her eyes, which she had lifted, fell lower than ever, her brow and neck were suffused with blushes, and she murmured—"I fell in love."

She said no more, and by and by Père Jerome replied:

"Well, Madame Delphine, to love is the right of every soul. I believe in love. If your love was pure and lawful I am sure your angel guardian smiled upon you; and if it was not, I cannot say you have nothing to answer for, and yet I think God may have said: 'She is a quadroone; all the rights of her womanhood trampled in the mire, sin made easy to her—almost compulsory—charge it to account of whom it may concern.'"

"No, no!" said Madame Delphine, looking up quickly, "some of it might fall upon"— Her eyes fell, and she commenced biting her lips and nervously pinching little folds in her skirt. "He was good—as good as the law would let him be—better, indeed, for he left me property, which really the strict law does not allow. He loved our little daughter very much. He wrote to his mother and sisters, owning all his error and asking them to take the child and bring her up. I sent her to them when he died, which was soon after, and did not see my child for sixteen years. But we wrote to each other all the time, and she loved me. And then—at last"— Madame Delphine ceased speaking, but went on diligently with her agitated fingers, turning down foolish hems lengthwise of her lap.

"At last your mother-heart conquered," said Père Jerome.

She nodded.

"The sisters married, the mother died; I saw that even where she was she did not escape the reproach of her birth and blood, and when she asked me to let her come"— The speaker's brimming eyes rose an instant. "I know it was wicked, but—I said, come."

The tears dripped through her hands upon her dress.

"Was it she who was with you last Sunday?"

"Yes."

"And now you do not know what to do with her?"

"*Ah! c'est ça oui!*—that is it."

"Does she look like you, Madame Delphine?"

"Oh, thank God, no! you would never believe she was my daughter; she is white and beautiful!"

"You thank God for that which is your main difficulty, Madame Delphine."

"Alas! yes."

Père Jerome laid his palms tightly across his knees with his arms bowed out, and fixed his eyes upon the ground, pondering.

"I suppose she is a sweet, good daughter?" said he, glancing at Madame Delphine, without changing his attitude.

Her answer was to raise her eyes rapturously.

"Which gives us the dilemma in its fullest force," said the priest, speaking as if to the floor. "She has no more place than if she had dropped upon a strange planet." He suddenly looked up with a brightness which almost as quickly passed away, and then he looked down again. His happy thought was the cloister; but he instantly said to himself: "They cannot have overlooked that choice, except intentionally—which they have a right to do." He could do nothing but shake his head.

"And suppose you should suddenly die," he said; he wanted to get at once to the worst.

The woman made a quick gesture, and buried her head in her handkerchief, with the stifled cry:

"Oh, Olive, my daughter!"

"Well, Madame Delphine," said Père Jerome, more buoyantly, "one thing is sure: we *must* find a way out of this trouble."

"Ah!" she exclaimed, looking heavenward, "if it might be!"

"But it must be!" said the priest.

"But how shall it be?" asked the desponding woman.

"Ah!" said Père Jerome, with a shrug, "God knows."

"Yes," said the quadroone, with a quick sparkle in her gentle eye; "and I know, if God would tell anybody, He would tell you!"

The priest smiled and rose.

"Do you think so? Well, leave me to think of it. I will ask Him."

"And He will tell you!" she replied. "And He will bless you!" She rose and gave her hand. As she withdrew it she smiled. "I had such a strange dream," she said, backing toward the door.

"Yes?"

"Yes. I got my troubles all mixed up with your sermon. I dreamed I made that pirate the guardian of my daughter."

Père Jerome smiled also, and shrugged.

"To you, Madame Delphine, as you are placed, every white man in this country, on land or on water, is a pirate, and of all pirates, I think that one is, without doubt, the best."

"Without doubt," echoed Madame Delphine, wearily, still withdrawing backward. Père Jerome stepped forward and opened the door.

The shadow of some one approaching it from without fell upon the threshold, and a man entered, dressed in dark blue cottonade, lifting from his head a fine Pánama hat, and from a broad, smooth brow, fair where the hat had covered it, and dark below, gently stroking back his very soft, brown locks. Madame Delphine slightly started aside, while Père Jerome reached silently, but eagerly, forward, grasped a larger hand than his own, and motioned its owner to a seat. Madame Delphine's eyes ventured no higher than to discover that the shoes of the visitor were of white duck.

"Well, Père Jerome," she said, in a hurried undertone, "I am just going to say Hail Marys all the time till you find that out for me!"

"Well, I hope that will be soon, Madame Carraze. Good-day, Madame Carraze."

And as she departed, the priest turned to the newcomer and extended both hands, saying, in the same familiar dialect in which he had been addressing the quadroone:

"Well-a-day, old playmate! After so many years!"

They sat down side by side, like husband and wife, the priest playing with the other's hand, and talked of times and seasons past, often mentioning Evariste and often Jean.

Madame Delphine stopped short halfway home and returned to Père Jerome's. His entry door was wide open and the parlor door ajar. She passed through the one and with downcast eyes was standing at the other, her hand lifted to knock, when the door was drawn open and the white duck shoes passed out. She saw, besides, this time the blue cottonade suit.

"Yes," the voice of Père Jerome was saying, as his face appeared in the door—"Ah! Madame"—

"I lef' my para*sol*," said Madame Delphine, in English.

There was this quiet evidence of a defiant spirit hidden somewhere down under her general timidity, that, against a fierce conventional prohibition, she wore a bonnet instead of the turban of her caste, and carried a parasol.

Père Jerome turned and brought it.

He made a motion in the direction in which the late visitor had disappeared.

"Madame Delphine, you saw dat man?"

"Not his face."

"You couldn' billieve me iv I tell you w'at dat man pur*pose* to do!"

"Is dad so, Père Jerome?"

"He's goin' to hopen a bank!"

"Ah!" said Madame Delphine, seeing she was expected to be astonished.

Père Jerome evidently longed to tell something that was best kept secret; he repressed the impulse, but his heart had to say something. He threw forward one hand and looking pleasantly at Madame Delphine, with his lips dropped apart, clenched his extended hand and, thrusting it toward the ground, said in a solemn undertone:

"He is God's own banker, Madame Delphine."

Chapter VII

MICHÉ VIGNEVIELLE

MADAME DELPHINE sold one of the corner lots of her property. She had almost no revenue, and now and then a piece had to go. As a consequence of the sale, she had a few large bank-notes sewed up in her petticoat, and one day—maybe a fortnight after her tearful interview with Père Jerome—she found it necessary to get one of these changed into small money. She was in the Rue Toulouse, looking from one side to the other for a bank which was not in that street at all, when she noticed a small sign hanging above a door, bearing the name "Vignevielle." She looked in. Père Jerome had told her (when she had gone to him to ask where she should apply for change) that if she could only wait a few days, there would be a new concern opened in Toulouse Street—it really seemed as if Vignevielle was the name, if she could judge; it looked to be, and it was, a private banker's—"U. L. Vignevielle's," according to a larger inscription which met her eyes as she ventured in. Behind the counter, exchanging some last words with a busy-mannered man outside, who, in withdrawing, seemed bent on running over Madame Delphine, stood the man in blue cottonade, whom she had met in Père Jerome's doorway. Now, for the first time, she saw his face, its strong, grave, human kindness shining softly on each and every bronzed feature. The recognition was mutual. He took pains to speak first, saying, in a reassuring tone, and in the language he had last heard her use:

" 'Ow I kin serve you, madame?"

"Iv you pliz, to mague dad bill change, miché."

She pulled from her pocket a wad of dark cotton handkerchief, from which she began to untie the imprisoned note. Madame Delphine had an uncommonly sweet voice, and it seemed so to strike Monsieur Vignevielle. He spoke to her once or twice more, as he waited on her, each time in English, as though he enjoyed the humble melody of its tone, and presently, as she turned to go, he said:

"Madame Carraze!"

She started a little, but bethought herself instantly that he had heard her name in Père Jerome's parlor. The good father might even have said a few words about her after her first departure; he had such an overflowing heart. "Madame Carraze," said Monsieur Vignevielle, "doze kine of note wad you *'an'* me juz now is bein' contrefit. You muz tek kyah from doze kine of note. You see"— He drew from his cash-drawer a note resembling the one he had just changed for her, and proceeded to point out certain tests of genuineness. The counterfeit, he said, was so and so.

"Bud," she exclaimed, with much dismay, "dad was de manner of my bill! Id muz be—led me see dad bill wad I give you—if you pliz, miché."

Monsieur Vignevielle turned to engage in conversation with an employé and a new visitor, and gave no sign of hearing Madame Delphine's voice. She asked a second time, with like result, lingered timidly, and as he turned to give his attention to a third visitor, reiterated:

"Miché Vignevielle, I wizh you pliz led"—

"Madame Carraze," he said, turning so suddenly as to make the frightened little woman start, but extending his palm with a show of frankness, and assuming a look of benignant patience, " 'ow I kin fine doze note now, mongs' all de rez? Iv you pliz nod to mague me doze troub'."

The dimmest shadow of a smile seemed only to give his words a more kindly authoritative import, and as he turned away again with a manner suggestive of finality, Madame Delphine found no choice but to depart. But she went away loving the ground beneath the feet of Monsieur U. L. Vignevielle.

"Oh, Père Jerome!" she exclaimed in the corrupt French of her caste, meeting the little father on the street a few days later, "you told the truth that day in your parlor. *Mo conné li à c't heure.* I know him now; he is just what you call him."

"Why do you not make him *your* banker, also, Madame Delphine?"

"I have done so this very day!" she replied, with more happiness in her eyes than Père Jerome had ever before seen there.

"Madame Delphine," he said, his own eyes sparkling, "make *him* your daughter's guardian; for myself, being a priest, it would not be best; but ask him; I believe he will not refuse you."

Madame Delphine's face grew still brighter as he spoke.

"It was in my mind," she said.

Yet to the timorous Madame Delphine many trifles became, one after another, an impediment to the making of this proposal, and many weeks elapsed before further delay was positively without excuse. But at length, one day in May, 1822, in a small private office behind Monsieur Vignevielle's banking-room—he sitting beside a table, and she, more timid and demure than ever, having just taken a chair by the door—she said, trying, with a little bashful laugh, to make the matter seem unimportant, and yet with some tremor of voice: "Miché Vignevielle, I bin maguing my will." (Having commenced their acquaintance in English, they spoke nothing else.)

" 'Tis a good idy," responded the banker.

"I kin mague you de troub' to kib dad will fo' me, Miché Vigne-vielle?"

"Yez."

She looked up with grateful reassurance; but her eyes dropped again as she said:

"Miché Vignevielle"— Here she choked, and began her peculiar motion of laying folds in the skirt of her dress, with trembling fingers. She lifted her eyes, and as they met the look of deep and placid kindness that was in his face, some courage returned, and she said:

"Miché."

"Wad you wand?" asked he, gently.

"If it arrive to me to die"—

"Yez?"

Her words were scarcely audible:

"I wand you teg kyah my lill' girl."

"You 'ave one lill' gal, Madame Carraze?"

She nodded with her face down.

"An' you godd some mo' chillen?"

"No."

"I nevva know dad, Madame Carraze. She's a lill' small gal?"

Mothers forget their daughters' stature. Madame Delphine said:

"Yez."

For a few moments neither spoke, and then Monsieur Vignevielle said:

"I will do dad."

"Lag she been you' h-own?" asked the mother, suffering from her own boldness.

"She's a good lill' chile, eh?"

"Miché, she's a lill' hangel!" exclaimed Madame Delphine, with a look of distress.

"Yez; I teg kyah 'v 'er, lag my h-own. I mague you dad promise."

"But"— There was something still in the way, Madame Delphine seemed to think.

The banker waited in silence.

"I suppose you will want to see my lill' girl?"

He smiled; for she looked at him as if she would implore him to decline.

"Oh, I tek you' word fo' hall dad, Madame Carraze. It mague no differend wad she loog lag; I don' want see 'er."

Madame Delphine's parting smile—she went very shortly—was gratitude beyond speech.

Monsieur Vignevielle returned to the seat he had left, and resumed a newspaper—the *Louisiana Gazette* in all probability—which he had laid down upon Madame Delphine's entrance. His eyes fell upon a paragraph which had previously escaped his notice. There they rested. Either he read it over and over unwearyingly, or he was lost in thought. Jean Thompson entered.

"Now," said Mr. Thompson, in a suppressed tone, bending a little across the table, and laying one palm upon a package of papers which lay in the other, "it is completed. You could retire from your business any day inside of six hours without loss to anybody." (Both here and elsewhere, let it be understood that where good English is given the words were spoken in good French.)

Monsieur Vignevielle raised his eyes and extended the newspaper to the attorney, who received it and read the paragraph. Its substance was that a certain vessel of the navy had returned from a cruise in the Gulf of Mexico and Straits of Florida, where she had done valuable service against the pirates—having, for instance, destroyed in one fortnight in January last twelve pirate vessels afloat, two on the stocks, and three establishments ashore.

"United States brig *Porpoise*," repeated Jean Thompson. "Do you know her?"

"We are acquainted," said Monsieur Vignevielle.

Chapter VIII

SHE

A QUIET footstep, a grave new presence on financial sidewalks, a neat garb slightly out of date, a gently strong and kindly pensive face, a silent bow, a new sign in the Rue Toulouse, a lone figure with a cane, walking in meditation in the evening light under the willows of Canal Marigny, a long-darkened window relighted in the Rue Conti—these were all; a fall of dew would scarce have been more quiet than was the return of Ursin Lemaitre-Vignevielle to the precincts of his birth and early life.

But we hardly give the event its right name. It was Capitaine Lemaitre who had disappeared; it was Monsieur Vignevielle who had come back. The pleasures, the haunts, the companions that had once held out their charms to the impetuous youth, offered no enticements to Madame Delphine's banker. There is this to be said even for the pride his grandfather had taught him, that it had always held him above low indulgences; and though he had dallied with kings, queens, and knaves through all the mazes of Faro, Rondeau, and Craps, he had done it loftily; but now he maintained a peaceful estrangement from all. Evariste and Jean, themselves, found him only by seeking.

"It is the right way," he said to Père Jerome, the day we saw him there. "Ursin Lemaitre is dead. I have buried him. He left a will. I am his executor."

"He is crazy," said his lawyer brother-in-law, impatiently.

"On the contr-y," replied the little priest, " 'e 'as come ad hisse'f."

Evariste spoke.

"Look at his face, Jean. Men with that kind of face are the last to go crazy."

"You have not proved that," replied Jean, with an attorney's obstinacy. "You should have heard him talk the other day about that newspaper paragraph. 'I have taken Ursin Lemaitre's head; I have it with me; I claim the reward, but I desire to commute it to citizenship.' He is crazy."

Of course Jean Thompson did not believe what he said; but he said it, and, in his vexation, repeated it, on the banquettes and at the clubs; and presently it took the shape of a sly rumor, that the returned rover was a trifle snarled in his top-hamper.

This whisper was helped into circulation by many trivial eccentricities of manner, and by the unaccountable oddness of some of his transactions in business.

"My dear sir!" cried his astounded lawyer, one day, "you are not running a charitable institution!"

"How do you know?" said Monsieur Vignevielle. There the conversation ceased.

"Why do you not found hospitals and asylums at once," asked the attorney, at another time, with a vexed laugh, "and get the credit of it?"

"And make the end worse than the beginning," said the banker, with a gentle smile, turning away to a desk of books.

"Bah!" muttered Jean Thompson.

Monsieur Vignevielle betrayed one very bad symptom. Wherever he went he seemed looking for somebody. It may have been perceptible only to those who were sufficiently interested in him to study his movements; but those who saw it once saw it always. He never passed an open door or gate but he glanced in! and often, where it stood but slightly ajar, you might see him give it a gentle push with his hand or cane. It was very singular.

He walked much alone after dark. The *guichinangoes* (garroters, we might say), at those times the city's particular terror by night, never crossed his path. He was one of those men for whom danger appears to stand aside.

One beautiful summer night, when all nature seemed hushed in ecstasy, the last blush gone that told of the sun's parting, Monsieur Vignevielle, in the course of one of those contemplative, uncompanioned walks which it was his habit to take, came slowly along the more open portion of the Rue Royale, with a step which was soft without intention, occasionally touching the end of his stout cane gently to the ground and looking upward among his old acquaintances, the stars.

It was one of those southern nights under whose spell all the sterner energies of the mind cloak themselves and lie down in bivouac, and the fancy and the imagination, that cannot sleep, slip their fetters and escape, beckoned away from behind every flowering bush and sweet-smelling tree, and every stretch of lonely, half-lighted walk, by the genius of poetry. The air stirred softly now and then, and was still again, as if the breezes lifted their expectant pinions and lowered them once more, awaiting the rising of the moon in a silence which fell upon the fields, the roads, the gardens, the walls, and the suburban and half-suburban streets, like a pause in worship. And anon she rose.

Monsieur Vignevielle's steps were bent toward the more central part of the town, and he was presently passing along a high, close, board-fence, on the right-hand side of the way, when, just within this enclosure, and almost overhead, in the dark boughs of a large orange-tree, a mocking-bird began the first low flute-notes of his all-night song. It may have been only the nearness of the songster that attracted the passer's attention, but he paused and looked up.

And then he remarked something more—that the air where he had stopped was filled with the overpowering sweetness of the night-jasmine. He looked around; it could only be inside the fence. There was a gate just there. Would he push it, as his wont was? The grass was growing about it in a thick turf, as though the entrance had not been used for years. An iron staple clasped the cross-bar, and was driven deep into the gate-post. But now an eye that had been in the blacksmithing business—an eye which had later received high training as an eye for fastenings—fell upon that staple, and saw at a glance that the wood had shrunk from it, and it had sprung from its hold, though without falling out. The strange habit asserted itself; he laid his large hand upon the cross-bar; the turf at the base yielded, and the tall gate was drawn partly open.

At that moment, as at the moment whenever he drew or pushed a door or gate, or looked in at a window, he was thinking of one, the image of whose face and form had never left his inner vision since the day it had met him in his life's path and turned him face about from the way of destruction.

The bird ceased. The cause of the interruption, standing within the opening, saw before him, much obscured by its own numerous shadows, a broad, ill-kept, many-flowered garden, among whose untrimmed rose-trees and tangled vines, and often, also, in its old walks of pounded shell, the coco-grass and crab-grass had spread riotously, and sturdy weeds stood up in bloom. He stepped in and drew the gate to after him. There, very near by, was the clump of jasmine, whose ravishing odor had tempted him. It stood just beyond a brightly moonlit path, which turned from him in a curve toward the residence, a little distance to the right, and escaped the view at a point where it seemed more than likely a door of the house might open upon it. While he still looked, there fell upon his ear, from around that curve, a light footstep on the broken shells—one only, and then all was for a moment still again. Had he mistaken? No. The same soft click was repeated nearer by, a pale glimpse of robes came through the tangle, and then, plainly to view, appeared an outline—a presence—a form—a spirit—a girl!

From throat to instep she was as white as Cynthia. Something

(*120*)

above the medium height, slender, lithe, her abundant hair rolling in dark, rich waves back from her brows and down from her crown, and falling in two heavy plaits beyond her round, broadly girt waist and full to her knees, a few escaping locks eddying lightly on her graceful neck and her temples—her arms, half hid in a snowy mist of sleeve, let down to guide her spotless skirts free from the dewy touch of the grass—straight down the path she came!

Will she stop? Will she turn aside? Will she espy the dark form in the deep shade of the orange, and, with one piercing scream, wheel and vanish? She draws near. She approaches the jasmine; she raises her arms, the sleeves falling like a vapor down to the shoulders; rises upon tiptoe, and plucks a spray. O Memory! Can it be? *Can it be?* Is this his quest, or is it lunacy? The ground seems to Monsieur Vignevielle the unsteady sea, and he to stand once more on a deck. And she? As she is now, if she but turn toward the orange, the whole glory of the moon will shine upon her face. His heart stands still; he is waiting for her to do that. She reaches up again; this time a bunch for her mother. That neck and throat! Now she fastens a spray in her hair. The mocking-bird cannot withhold; he breaks into song—she turns—she turns her face—it is she, it is she! Madame Delphine's daughter is the girl he met on the ship.

Chapter IX

OLIVE

SHE was just passing seventeen—that beautiful year when the heart of the maiden still beats quickly with the surprise of her new dominion, while with gentle dignity her brow accepts the holy coronation of womanhood. The forehead and temples beneath her loosely bound hair were fair without paleness, and meek without languor. She had the soft, lack-lustre beauty of the South; no ruddiness of coral, no waxen white, no pink of shell; no heavenly blue in the glance; but a face that seemed, in all its other beauties, only a tender accompaniment for the large, brown, melting eyes, where the openness of child-nature mingled dreamily with the sweet mysteries of maiden thought. We say no color of shell on face or throat; but this was no deficiency, that which took its place being the warm, transparent tint of sculptured ivory.

This side doorway which led from Madame Delphine's house into her garden was overarched partly by an old remnant of vine-covered lattice, and partly by a crape-myrtle, against whose small, polished trunk leaned a rustic seat. Here Madame Delphine and Olive loved to sit when the twilights were balmy or the moon was bright.

"*Chérie*," said Madame Delphine on one of those evenings, "why do you dream so much?"

She spoke in the patois most natural to her, and which her daughter had easily learned.

The girl turned her face to her mother, and smiled, then dropped her glance to the hands in her own lap, which were listlessly handling the end of a ribbon. The mother looked at her with fond solicitude. Her dress was white again; this was but one night since that in which Monsieur Vignevielle had seen her at the bush of night-jasmine. He had not been discovered, but had gone away, shutting the gate, and leaving it as he had found it.

Her head was uncovered. Its plaited masses, quite black in the moonlight, hung down and coiled upon the bench, by her side. Her chaste drapery was of that revived classic order which the world of fashion was again laying aside to reassume the mediæval bondage of the staylace; for New Orleans was behind the fashionable world, and Madame Delphine and her daughter were behind New Orleans. A delicate scarf, pale blue, of lightly netted worsted, fell from either shoulder down beside her hands. The look that was bent upon her changed perforce to one of gentle admiration. She seemed the goddess of the garden.

Olive glanced up. Madame Delphine was not prepared for the movement, and on that account repeated her question:

"What are you thinking about?"

The dreamer took the hand that was laid upon hers between her own palms, bowed her head, and gave them a soft kiss.

The mother submitted. Wherefore, in the silence which followed, a daughter's conscience felt the burden of having withheld an answer, and Olive presently said, as the pair sat looking up into the sky:

"I was thinking of Père Jerome's sermon."

Madame Delphine had feared so. Olive had lived on it ever since the day it was preached. The poor mother was almost ready to re-pent having ever afforded her the opportunity of hearing it. Meat and drink had become of secondary value to her daughter; she fed upon the sermon.

Olive felt her mother's thought and knew that her mother knew her own; but now that she had confessed, she would ask a question:

"Do you think, *maman*, that Père Jerome knows it was I who gave that missal?"

"No," said Madame Delphine, "I am sure he does not."

Another question came more timidly:

"Do—do you think he knows *him?*"

"Yes, I do. He said in his sermon he did."

Both remained for a long time very still, watching the moon glid-ing in and through among the small dark and white clouds. At last the daughter spoke again.

"I wish I was Père—I wish I was as good as Père Jerome."

"My child," said Madame Delphine, her tone betraying a painful summoning of strength to say what she had lacked the courage to utter—"my child, I pray the good God you will not let your heart go after one whom you may never see in this world!"

The maiden turned her glance, and their eyes met. She cast her arms about her mother's neck, laid her cheek upon it for a moment, and then, feeling the maternal tear, lifted her lips, and, kissing her, saïd:

"I will not! I will not!"

But the voice was one, not of willing consent, but of desperate resolution.

"It would be useless, anyhow," said the mother, laying her arm around her daughter's waist.

Olive repeated the kiss, prolonging it passionately.

"I have nobody but you," murmured the girl; "I am a poor quadroone!"

She threw back her plaited hair for a third embrace, when a sound in the shrubbery startled them.

"*Qui ci ça?*" called Madame Delphine, in a frightened voice, as the two stood up, holding to each other.

No answer.

"It was only the dropping of a twig," she whispered, after a long holding of the breath. But they went into the house and barred it everywhere.

It was no longer pleasant to sit up. They retired, and in course of time, but not soon, they fell asleep, holding each other very tight, and fearing, even in their dreams, to hear another twig fall.

Chapter X

BIRDS

MONSIEUR VIGNEVIELLE looked in at no more doors or windows; but if the disappearance of this symptom was a favorable sign, others came to notice which were especially bad—for instance, wakefulness. At well-nigh any hour of the night, the city guard, which itself dared not patrol singly, would meet him on his slow, un-molested, sky-gazing walk.

"Seems to enjoy it," said Jean Thompson; "the worst sort of evidence. If he showed distress of mind, it would not be so bad; but his calmness—ugly feature."

The attorney had held his ground so long that he began really to believe it was tenable.

By day, it is true, Monsieur Vignevielle was at his post in his quiet "bank." Yet here, day by day, he was the source of more and more vivid astonishment to those who held preconceived notions of a banker's calling. As a banker, at least, he was certainly out of bal-ance; while as a promenader, it seemed to those who watched him that his ruling idea had now veered about, and that of late he was ever on the quiet alert, not to find, but to evade, somebody.

"Olive, my child," whispered Madame Delphine one morning, as the pair were kneeling side by side on the tiled floor of the church, "yonder is Miché Vignevielle! If you will only look at once—he is just passing a little in— Ah, much too slow again; he stepped out by the side-door."

The mother thought it a strange providence that Monsieur Vigne-vielle should always be disappearing whenever Olive was with her.

One early dawn, Madame Delphine, with a small empty basket on her arm, stepped out upon the banquette in front of her house, shut and fastened the door very softly, and stole out in the direction whence you could faintly catch, in the stillness of the daybreak, the songs of the Gascon butchers and the pounding of their meat-axes on the stalls of the distant market-house. She was going to see if she could find some birds for Olive—the child's appetite was so poor; and, as she was out, she would drop an early prayer at the cathedral. Faith and works.

"One must venture something, sometimes, in the cause of religion," thought she, as she started timorously on her way. But she had not gone a dozen steps before she repented her temerity. There was some one behind her.

There should not be any thing terrible in a footstep merely because it is masculine; but Madame Delphine's mind was not prepared to consider that. A terrible secret was haunting her. Yesterday morning she had found a shoe-track in the garden. She had not disclosed the discovery to Olive, but she had hardly closed her eyes the whole night.

The step behind her now might be the fall of that very shoe. She quickened her pace, but did not leave the sound behind. She hurried forward almost at a run; yet it was still there—no farther, no nearer. Two frights were upon her at once—one for herself, another for Olive, left alone in the house; but she had but the one prayer—"God protect my child!" After a fearful time she reached a place of safety, the cathedral. There, panting, she knelt long enough to know the pursuit was, at least, suspended, and then arose, hoping and praying all the saints that she might find the way clear for her return in all haste to Olive.

She approached a different door from that by which she had entered, her eyes in all directions and her heart in her throat.

"Madame Carraze."

She started wildly and almost screamed, though the voice was soft and mild. Monsieur Vignevielle came slowly forward from the shade of the wall. They met beside a bench, upon which she dropped her basket.

"Ah, Miché Vignevielle, I thang de good God to mid you!"

"Is dad so, Madame Carraze? Fo' w'y dad is?"

"A man was chase me all dad way since my 'ouse!"

"Yes, madame, I sawed him."

"You sawed 'im? Oo it was?"

" 'Twas only one man wad is a foolizh. De people say he's crezzie. *Mais*, he don' goin' to meg you no 'arm."

"But I was scare' fo' my lill' girl."

"Noboddie don' goin' trouble you' lill' gal, Madame Carraze."

Madame Delphine looked up into the speaker's strangely kind and patient eyes, and drew sweet reassurance from them.

"Madame," said Monsieur Vignevielle, "wad pud you hout so hearly dis morning?"

She told him her errand. She asked if he thought she would find any thing.

"Yez," he said, "it was possible—a few lill' *bécassines-de-mer*, ou somezin' ligue. But fo' w'y you' lill' gal lose doze hapetide?"

"Ah, miché"—Madame Delphine might have tried a thousand times again without ever succeeding half so well in lifting the curtain upon the whole, sweet, tender, old, old-fashioned truth—"ah, miché, she wone tell me!"

"Bud, anny'ow, madame, wad you thing?"

"Miché," she replied, looking up again with a tear standing in either eye, and then looking down once more as she began to speak, "I thing—I thing she's lonesome."

"You thing?"

She nodded.

"Ah! Madame Carraze," he said, partly extending his hand, "you see? 'Tis impossible to mague you' owze shud so tighd to priv-en dad. Madame, I med one mizteg."

"Ah, *non*, miché!"

"Yez. There har nod one poss'bil'ty fo' me to be dad guardian of you' daughteh!"

Madame Delphine started with surprise and alarm.

"There is ondly one wad can be," he continued.

"But oo, miché?"

"God."

"Ah, Miché Vignevielle"— She looked at him appealingly.

"I don' goin' to dizzerd you, Madame Carraze," he said.

She lifted her eyes. They filled. She shook her head, a tear fell, she bit her lip, smiled, and suddenly dropped her face into both hands, sat down upon the bench and wept until she shook.

"You dunno wad I mean, Madame Carraze?"

She did not know.

"I mean dad guardian of you' daughteh godd to fine 'er now one 'uzban'; an' noboddie are hable to do dad egceb de good God 'imsev. But, madame, I tell you wad I do."

She rose up. He continued:

"Go h-open you' owze; I fin' you' daughteh dad 'uzban'."

Madame Delphine was a helpless, timid thing; but her eyes showed she was about to resent this offer. Monsieur Vignevielle put forth his hand—it touched her shoulder—and said, kindly still, and without eagerness:

"One w'ite man, madame: 'tis prattycabble. I *know* 'tis prattycabble. One w'ite jantleman, madame. You can truz me. I goin' fedge 'im. H-ondly you go h-open you' owze."

Madame Delphine looked down, twining her handkerchief among her fingers.

He repeated his proposition.

"You will come firz' by you'se'f?" she asked.

"Iv you wand."

She lifted up once more her eye of faith. That was her answer.

"Come," he said, gently, "I wan' sen' some bird ad you' lill' gal."

And they went away, Madame Delphine's spirit grown so exaltedly bold that she said as they went, though a violent blush followed her words:

"Miché Vignevielle, I thing Père Jerome mighd be ab'e to tell you someboddie."

Chapter XI

FACE TO FACE

MADAME DELPHINE found her house neither burned nor rifled.

"*Ah! ma piti sans popa!* Ah! my little fatherless one!" Her faded bonnet fell back between her shoulders, hanging on by the strings, and her dropped basket, with its "few lill' *bécassines-de-mer*" dangling from the handle, rolled out its okra and soup-joint upon the floor. "*Ma piti!* kiss!—kiss!—kiss!"

"But is it good news you have, or bad?" cried the girl, a fourth or fifth time.

"*Dieu sait, ma chère; mo pas conné!*—God knows, my darling; I cannot tell!"

The mother dropped into a chair, covered her face with her apron, and burst into tears, then looked up with an effort to smile, and wept afresh.

"What have you been doing?" asked the daughter, in a long-drawn, fondling tone. She leaned forward and unfastened her mother's bonnet-strings. "Why do you cry?"

"For nothing at all, my darling; for nothing—I am such a fool."

The girl's eyes filled. The mother looked up into her face and said:

"No, it is nothing, nothing, only that"—turning her head from side to side with a slow, emotional emphasis, "Miché Vignevielle is the best—*best* man on the good Lord's earth!"

Olive drew a chair close to her mother, sat down and took the little yellow hands into her own white lap, and looked tenderly into her eyes. Madame Delphine felt herself yielding; she must make a show of telling something:

"He sent you those birds!"

The girl drew her face back a little. The little woman turned away, trying in vain to hide her tearful smile, and they laughed together, Olive mingling a daughter's fond kiss with her laughter.

"There is something else," she said, "and you shall tell me."

"Yes," replied Madame Delphine, "only let me get composed."

But she did not get so. Later in the morning she came to Olive with the timid yet startling proposal that they would do what they could to brighten up the long-neglected front room. Olive was mystified and troubled, but consented, and thereupon the mother's spirits rose.

The work began, and presently ensued all the thumping, the trundling, the lifting and letting down, the raising and swallowing of dust, and the smells of turpentine, brass, pumice and woollen rags that go to characterize a housekeeper's *émeute;* and still, as the work progressed, Madame Delphine's heart grew light, and her little black eyes sparkled.

"We like a clean parlor, my daughter, even though no one is ever coming to see us, eh?" she said, as entering the apartment she at last sat down, late in the afternoon. She had put on her best attire.

Olive was not there to reply. The mother called but got no answer. She rose with an uneasy heart, and met her a few steps beyond the door that opened into the garden, in a path which came up from an old latticed bower. Olive was approaching slowly, her face pale and wild. There was an agony of hostile dismay in the look, and the trembling and appealing tone with which, taking the frightened mother's cheeks between her palms, she said:

"*Ah! ma mère, qui vini 'ci ce soir?*—Who is coming here this evening?"

"Why, my dear child, I was just saying, we like a clean"—

But the daughter was desperate:

"Oh, tell me, my mother, *who* is coming?"

"My darling, it is our blessed friend, Miché Vignevielle!"

"To see me?" cried the girl.

"Yes."

"Oh; my mother, what have you done?"

"Why, Olive, my child," exclaimed the little mother, bursting into tears, "do you forget it is Miché Vignevielle who has promised to protect you when I die?"

The daughter had turned away, and entered the door; but she faced around again, and extending her arms toward her mother, cried:

"How can—he is a white man—I am a poor"—

"Ah! *chérie,*" replied Madame Delphine, seizing the outstretched hands, "it is there—it is there that he shows himself the best man alive! He sees that difficulty; he proposes to meet it; he says he will find you a suitor!"

Olive freed her hands violently, motioned her mother back, and stood proudly drawn up, flashing an indignation too great for speech; but the next moment she had uttered a cry, and was sobbing on the floor.

The mother knelt beside her and threw an arm about her shoulders.

"Oh, my sweet daughter, you must not cry! I did not want to tell you at all! I did not want to tell you! It isn't fair for you to cry so hard. Miché Vignevielle says you shall have the one you wish, or none at all, Olive, or none at all."

"None at all! none at all! None, none, none!"

"No, no, Olive," said the mother, "none at all. He brings none with him to-night, and shall bring none with him hereafter."

Olive rose suddenly, silently declined her mother's aid, and went alone to their chamber in the half-story.

Madame Delphine wandered drearily from door to window, from window to door, and presently into the newly furnished front room which now seemed dismal beyond degree. There was a great Argand lamp in one corner. How she had labored that day to prepare it for evening illumination! A little beyond it, on the wall, hung a crucifix. She knelt under it, with her eyes fixed upon it, and thus silently remained until its outline was indistinguishable in the deepening shadows of evening.

She arose. A few minutes later, as she was trying to light the lamp, an approaching step on the sidewalk seemed to pause. Her heart stood still. She softly laid the phosphorus-box out of her hands. A shoe grated softly on the stone step, and Madame Delphine, her heart beating in great thuds, without waiting for a knock, opened the door, bowed low, and exclaimed in a soft perturbed voice:

"Miché Vignevielle!"

He entered, hat in hand, and with that almost noiseless tread which we have noticed. She gave him a chair and closed the door; then hastened, with words of apology, back to her task of lighting the lamp. But her hands paused in their work again—Olive's step was on the stairs; then it came off the stairs; then it was in the next room, and then there was the whisper of soft robes, a breath of gentle perfume, and a snowy figure in the door. She was dressed for the evening.

"*Maman?*"

Madame Delphine was struggling desperately with the lamp, and at that moment it responded with a tiny bead of light.

"I am here, my daughter."

She hastened to the door, and Olive, all unaware of a third presence, lifted her white arms, laid them about her mother's neck, and, ignoring her effort to speak, wrested a fervent kiss from her lips. The crystal of the lamp sent out a faint gleam; it grew; it spread on every side; the ceiling, the walls lighted up; the crucifix, the furniture of the room came back into shape.

"*Maman!*" cried Olive, with a tremor of consternation.

"It is Miché Vignevielle, my daughter"—

The gloom melted swiftly away before the eyes of the startled maiden, a dark form stood out against the farther wall, and the light, expanding to the full, shone clearly upon the unmoving figure and quiet face of Capitaine Lemaitre.

Chapter XII

THE MOTHER BIRD

ONE afternoon, some three weeks after Capitaine Lemaitre had called on Madame Delphine, the priest started to make a pastoral call and had hardly left the gate of his cottage, when a person, overtaking him, plucked his gown:

"Père Jerome"—

He turned.

The face that met his was so changed with excitement and distress that for an instant he did not recognize it.

"Why, Madame Delphine"—

"Oh, Père Jerome! I wan' see you so bad, so bad! *Mo oulé dit quiç'ose*—I godd some' to tell you."

The two languages might be more successful than one, she seemed to think.

"We had better go back to my parlor," said the priest, in their native tongue.

They returned.

Madame Delphine's very step was altered—nervous and inelastic. She swung one arm as she walked, and brandished a turkey-tail fan.

"I was glad, yass, to kedge you," she said, as they mounted the front, outdoor stair; following her speech with a slight, unmusical laugh, and fanning herself with unconscious fury.

"*Fé chaud,*" she remarked again, taking the chair he offered and continuing to ply the fan.

Père Jerome laid his hat upon a chest of drawers, sat down opposite her, and said, as he wiped his kindly face:

"Well, Madame Carraze?"

Gentle as the tone was, she started, ceased fanning, lowered the fan to her knee, and commenced smoothing its feathers.

"Père Jerome"— She gnawed her lip and shook her head.

"Well?"

She burst into tears.

The priest rose and loosed the curtain of one of the windows. He did it slowly—as slowly as he could, and, as he came back, she lifted her face with sudden energy, and exclaimed:

"Oh, Père Jerome, de law is brogue! de law is brogue! I brogue it! 'Twas me! 'Twas me!"

The tears gushed out again, but she shut her lips very tight, and dumbly turned away her face. Père Jerome waited a little before replying; then he said, very gently:

"I suppose dad muss 'ave been by accyden', Madame Delphine?"

The little father felt a wish—one which he often had when weeping women were before him—that he were an angel instead of a man, long enough to press the tearful cheek upon his breast, and assure the weeper God would not let the lawyers and judges hurt her. He allowed a few moments more to pass, and then asked:

"*N'est-ce-pas*, Madame Delphine? Daz ze way, ain't it?"

"No, Père Jerome, no. My daughter—oh, Père Jerome, I bethroath my lill' girl—to a w'ite man!" And immediately Madame Delphine commenced savagely drawing a thread in the fabric of her skirt with one trembling hand, while she drove the fan with the other. "Dey goin' git marry."

On the priest's face came a look of pained surprise. He slowly said:

"Is dad possib', Madame Delphine?"

"Yass," she replied, at first without lifting her eyes; and then again, "Yass," looking full upon him through her tears, "yass, 'tis tru'."

He rose and walked once across the room, returned, and said, in the Creole dialect:

"Is he a good man—without doubt?"

"De bez in God's world!" replied Madame Delphine, with a rapturous smile.

"My poor, dear friend," said the priest, "I am afraid you are being deceived by somebody."

There was the pride of an unswerving faith in the triumphant tone and smile with which she replied, raising and slowly shaking her head:

"Ah-h, no-o-o, miché! Ah-h, no, no! Not by Ursin Lemaitre-Vignevielle!"

Père Jerome was confounded. He turned again, and, with his hands at his back and his eyes cast down, slowly paced the floor.

"He *is* a good man," he said, by and by, as if he thought aloud. At length he halted before the woman.

"Madame Delphine"—

The distressed glance with which she had been following his steps was lifted to his eyes.

"Suppose dad should be true w'at doze peop' say 'bout Ursin."

"*Qui ci ça?* What is that?" asked the quadroone, stopping her fan.

"Some peop' say Ursin is crezzie."

"Ah, Père Jerome!" She leaped to her feet as if he had smitten her, and putting his words away with an outstretched arm and wide-open palm, suddenly lifted hands and eyes to heaven, and cried: "I wizh to God—*I wizh to God*—de whole worl' was crezzie dad same way!" She sank, trembling, into her chair. "Oh, no, no," she continued, shaking her head, " 'tis not Miché Vignevielle w'at's crezzie." Her eyes lighted with sudden fierceness. " 'Tis dad *law!* Dad *law* is crezzie! Dad law is a fool!"

A priest of less heart-wisdom might have replied that the law is —the law; but Père Jerome saw that Madame Delphine was expecting this very response. Wherefore he said, with gentleness:

"Madame Delphine, a priest is not a bailiff, but a physician. How can I help you?"

A grateful light shone a moment in her eyes, yet there remained a piteous hostility in the tone in which she demanded:

"*Mais, pou'quoi yé fé cette méchanique là?*—What business had they to make that contraption?"

His answer was a shrug with his palms extended and a short, disclamatory "Ah." He started to resume his walk, but turned to her again and said:

"Why did they make that law? Well, they made it to keep the two races separate."

Madame Delphine startled the speaker with a loud, harsh, angry laugh. Fire came from her eyes and her lip curled with scorn.

"Then they made a lie, Père Jerome! Separate! No-o-o! They do not want to keep us separated; no, no! But they *do* want to keep us despised!" She laid her hand on her heart, and frowned upward with physical pain. "But, very well! from which race do they want to keep my daughter separate? She is seven parts white! The law did not stop her from being that; and now, when she wants to be a white man's good and honest wife, shall that law stop her? Oh, no!" She rose up. "No; I will tell you what that law is made for. It is made to—punish—my—child—for—not—choosing—her—father! Père Jerome—my God, what a law!" She dropped back into her seat. The tears came in a flood, which she made no attempt to restrain.

"No," she began again—and here she broke into English—"fo' me I don' kyare; but, Père Jerome—'tis fo' dat I came to tell you —dey *shall not* punizh my daughter!" She was on her feet again, smiting her heaving bosom with the fan. "She shall marrie oo she want!"

Père Jerome had heard her out, not interrupting by so much as a motion of the hand. Now his decision was made, and he touched her softly with the ends of his fingers.

"Madame Delphine, I want you to go at 'ome. Go at 'ome."

"Wad you goin' mague?" she asked.

"Nottin'. But go at 'ome. Kip quite; don' put you'se'f sig. I goin' see Ursin. We trah to figs dat law fo' you."

"You kin figs dad!" she cried, with a gleam of joy.

"We goin' to try, Madame Delphine. Adieu!"

He offered his hand. She seized and kissed it thrice, covering it with tears, at the same time lifting up her eyes to his and murmuring:

"De bez man God evva mague!"

At the door she turned to offer a more conventional good-by; but he was following her out, bareheaded. At the gate they paused an instant, and then parted with a simple adieu, she going home and he returning for his hat, and starting again upon his interrupted business.

Before he came back to his own house, he stopped at the lodgings of Monsieur Vignevielle, but did not find him in.

"Indeed," the servant at the door said, "he said he might not return for some days or weeks."

So Père Jerome, much wondering, made a second detour toward the residence of one of Monsieur Vignevielle's employés.

"Yes," said the clerk, "his instructions are to hold the business, as far as practicable, in suspense, during his absence. Every thing is in another name." And then he whispered:

"Officers of the Government looking for him. Information got from some of the prisoners taken months ago by the United States brig *Porpoise*. But"—a still softer whisper—"have no fear; they will never find him: Jean Thompson and Evariste Varrillat have hid him away too well for that."

Chapter XIII

TRIBULATION

THE Saturday following was a very beautiful day. In the morning a light fall of rain had passed across the town, and all the afternoon you could see signs, here and there upon the horizon, of other showers. The ground was dry again, while the breeze was cool and sweet, smelling of wet foliage and bringing sunshine and shade in frequent and very pleasing alternation.

There was a walk in Père Jerome's little garden, of which we have not spoken, off on the right side of the cottage, with his chamber window at one end, a few old and twisted, but blossom-laden, crape-myrtles on either hand, now and then a rose of some unpretending variety and some bunches of rue, and at the other end a shrine, in whose blue niche stood a small figure of Mary, with folded hands and uplifted eyes. No other window looked down upon the spot, and its seclusion was often a great comfort to Père Jerome.

Up and down this path, but a few steps in its entire length, the priest was walking, taking the air for a few moments after a prolonged sitting in the confessional. Penitents had been numerous this afternoon. He was thinking of Ursin. The officers of the Government had not found him, nor had Père Jerome seen him; yet he believed they had, in a certain indirect way, devised a simple project by which they could at any time "figs dad law," providing only that these Government officials would give over their search; for, though he had not seen the fugitive, Madame Delphine had seen him, and had been the vehicle of communication between them. There was an orange-tree, where a mocking-bird was wont to sing and a girl in white to walk, that the detectives wot not of. The law was to be "figs" by the departure of the three frequenters of the jasmine-scented garden in one ship to France, where the law offered no obstacles.

It seemed moderately certain to those in search of Monsieur Vignevielle (and it was true) that Jean and Evariste were his harborers; but for all that the hunt, even for clews, was vain. The little banking establishment had not been disturbed. Jean Thompson had told the searchers certain facts about it, and about its gentle proprietor as well, that persuaded them to make no move against the concern, if the same relations did not even induce a relaxation of their efforts for his personal discovery.

Père Jerome was walking to and fro, with his hands behind him, pondering these matters. He had paused a moment at the end of the walk farthest from his window, and was looking around upon the sky, when, turning, he beheld a closely veiled female figure standing at the other end, and knew instantly that it was Olive.

She came forward quickly and with evident eagerness.

"I came to confession," she said, breathing hurriedly, the excitement in her eyes shining through her veil, "but I find I am too late."

"There is no too late or too early for that; I am always ready," said the priest. "But how is your mother?"

"Ah!"—

Her voice failed.

"More trouble?"

"Ah, sir, I have *made* trouble. Oh, Père Jerome, I am bringing so much trouble upon my poor mother!"

Père Jerome moved slowly toward the house, with his eyes cast down, the veiled girl at his side.

"It is not your fault," he presently said. And after another pause:

"I thought it was all arranged."

He looked up and could see, even through the veil, her crimson blush.

"Oh, no," she replied, in a low, despairing voice, dropping her face.

"What is the difficulty?" asked the priest, stopping in the angle of the path, where it turned toward the front of the house.

She averted her face, and began picking the thin scales of bark from a crape-myrtle.

"Madame Thompson and her husband were at our house this morning. *He* had told Monsieur Thompson all about it. They were very kind to me at first, but they tried"— She was weeping.

"What did they try to do?" asked the priest.

"They tried to make me believe he is insane."

She succeeded in passing her handkerchief up under her veil.

"And I suppose then your poor mother grew angry, eh?"

"Yes; and they became much more so, and said if we did not write, or send a writing, to *him*, within twenty-four hours, breaking the"—

"Engagement," said Père Jerome.

"They would give him up to the Government. Oh, Père Jerome, what shall I do? It is killing my mother!"

She bowed her head and sobbed.

"Where is your mother now?"

"She has gone to see Monsieur Jean Thompson. She says she has a plan that will match them all. I do not know what it is. I begged her not to go; but oh, sir, *she is* crazy—and I am no better."

"My poor child," said Père Jerome, "what you seem to want is not absolution, but relief from persecution."

"Oh, father, I have committed mortal sin—I am guilty of pride and anger."

"Nevertheless," said the priest, starting toward his front gate, "we will put off your confession. Let it go until to-morrow morning; you will find me in my box just before mass; I will hear you then. My child, I know that in your heart, now, you begrudge the time it would take; and that is right. There are moments when we are not in place even on penitential knees. It is so with you now. We must find your mother. Go you at once to your house; if she is there, comfort her as best you can, and *keep her in, if possible,* until I come. If she is not there, stay; leave me to find her; one of you, at least, must be where I can get word to you promptly. God comfort and uphold you. I hope you may find her at home; tell her, for me, not to fear"—he lifted the gate-latch—"that she and her daughter are of more value than many sparrows; that God's priest sends her that word from Him. Tell her to fix her trust in the great Husband of the Church, and she shall yet see her child receiving the grace-giving sacrament of matrimony. Go; I shall, in a few minutes, be on my way to Jean Thompson's, and shall find her, either there or wherever she is. Go; they shall not oppress you. Adieu!"

A moment or two later he was in the street himself.

Chapter XIV

BY AN OATH

PÈRE JEROME, pausing on a street corner in the last hour of sunlight, had wiped his brow and taken his cane down from under his arm to start again, when somebody, coming noiselessly from he knew not where, asked, so suddenly as to startle him:

"*Miché, commin yé pellé la rie ici?*—How do they call this street here?"

It was by the bonnet and dress, disordered though they were, rather than by the haggard face which looked distractedly around, that he recognized the woman to whom he replied in her own patois:

"It is the Rue Burgundy. Where are you going, Madame Delphine?"

She almost leaped from the ground.

"Oh, Père Jerome! *mo pas conné*—I dunno. You know w'ere's dad 'ouse of Miché Jean Tomkin? *Mo courri 'ci, mo courri là*—*mo pas capabe li trouvé*. I go (run) here—there—I cannot find it," she gesticulated.

"I am going there myself," said he; "but why do you want to see Jean Thompson, Madame Delphine?"

"I *'blige'* to see 'im!" she replied, jerking herself half around away, one foot planted forward with an air of excited preoccupation; "I godd some' to tell 'im wad I *'blige'* to tell 'im!"

"Madame Delphine"—

"Oh! Père Jerome, fo' de love of de good God, show me dad way to de 'ouse of Jean Tomkin!"

Her distressed smile implored pardon for her rudeness.

"What are you going to tell him?" asked the priest.

"Oh, Père Jerome"—in the Creole patois again—"I am going to put an end to all this trouble—only I pray you do not ask me about it now; every minute is precious!"

He could not withstand her look of entreaty.

"Come," he said, and they went.

Jean Thompson and Doctor Varrillat lived opposite each other on the Bayou road, a little way beyond the town limits as then prescribed. Each had his large, white-columned, four-sided house among the magnolias—his huge live-oak overshadowing either corner of the darkly shaded garden, his broad, brick walk leading down to the tall, brick-pillared gate, his square of bright, red pavement on the turf-covered sidewalk, and his railed platform spanning the draining-ditch, with a pair of green benches, one on each edge, facing each other crosswise of the gutter. There, any sunset hour, you were sure to find the householder sitting beside his cool-robed matron, two or three slave nurses in white turbans standing at hand, and an excited throng of fair children, nearly all of a size.

Sometimes, at a beckon or call, the parents on one side of the way would join those on the other, and the children and nurses of both families would be given the liberty of the opposite platform and an ice-cream fund! Generally the parents chose the Thompson platform, its outlook being more toward the sunset.

Such happened to be the arrangement this afternoon. The two husbands sat on one bench and their wives on the other, both pairs very quiet, waiting respectfully for the day to die, and exchanging only occasional comments on matters of light moment as they passed through the memory. During one term of silence Madame Varrillat, a pale, thin-faced, but cheerful-looking lady, touched Madame Thompson, a person of two and a half times her weight, on her extensive and snowy bare elbow, directing her attention obliquely up and across the road.

About a hundred yards distant, in the direction of the river, was a long, pleasantly shaded green strip of turf, destined in time for a sidewalk. It had a deep ditch on the nearer side, and a fence of rough cypress palisades on the farther, and these were overhung, on the one hand, by a row of bitter-orange-trees inside the enclosure, and, on the other, by a line of slanting china-trees along the outer edge of the ditch. Down this cool avenue two figures were approaching side by side. They had first attracted Madame Varrillat's notice by the bright play of sunbeams which, as they walked, fell upon them in soft, golden flashes through the chinks between the palisades.

Madame Thompson elevated a pair of glasses which were no detraction from her very good looks, and remarked, with the serenity of a reconnoitring general:

"*Père Jerome et cette milatraise.*"

All eyes were bent toward them.

"She walks like a man," said Madame Varrillat, in the language with which the conversation had opened.

"No," said the physician, "like a woman in a state of high nervous excitement."

Jean Thompson kept his eyes on the woman, and said:

"She must not forget to walk like a woman in the State of Louisiana"—as near as the pun can be translated. The company laughed. Jean Thompson looked at his wife, whose applause he prized, and she answered by an asseverative toss of the head, leaning back and contriving, with some effort, to get her arms folded. Her laugh was musical and low, but enough to make the folded arms shake gently up and down.

"Père Jerome is talking to her," said one. The priest was at that moment endeavoring, in the interest of peace, to say a good word for the four people who sat watching his approach. It was in the old strain:

"Blame them one part, Madame Delphine, and their fathers, mothers, brothers, and fellow-citizens the other ninety-nine."

But to every thing she had the one amiable answer which Père Jerome ignored:

"I am going to arrange it to satisfy everybody, all together. *Tout à fait.*"

"They are coming here," said Madame Varrillat, half articulately.

"Well, of course," murmured another; and the four rose up, smil-

ing courteously, the doctor and attorney advancing and shaking
hands with the priest.

No—Père Jerome thanked them—he could not sit down.

"This, I believe you know, Jean, is Madame Delphine"—

The quadroone courtesied.

"A friend of mine," he added, smiling kindly upon her, and turning, with something imperative in his eye, to the group. "She says
she has an important private matter to communicate."

"To me?" asked Jean Thompson.

"To all of you; so I will— Good-evening." He responded nothing
to the expressions of regret, but turned to Madame Delphine. She
murmured something.

"Ah! yes, certainly." He addressed the company: "She wishes
me to speak for her veracity; it is unimpeachable. Well, good-
evening." He shook hands and departed.

The four resumed their seats, and turned their eyes upon the
standing figure.

"Have you something to say to us?" asked Jean Thompson,
frowning at her law-defying bonnet.

"*Oui,*" replied the woman, shrinking to one side, and laying hold
of one of the benches, "*mo oulé di' tou' ç'ose*"—I want to tell every
thing. "*Miché Vignevielle la plis bon homme di moune*"—the best
man in the world; "*mo pas capabe li fé tracas*"—I cannot give him
trouble. "*Mo pas capabe, non; m'olé di' tous ç'ose.*" She attempted
to fan herself, her face turned away from the attorney, and her eyes
rested on the ground.

"Take a seat," said Doctor Varrillat, with some suddenness,
starting from his place and gently guiding her sinking form into
the corner of the bench. The ladies rose up; somebody had to stand;
the two races could not both sit down at once—at least not in that
public manner.

"Your salts," said the physician to his wife. She handed the
vial. Madame Delphine stood up again.

"We will all go inside," said Madame Thompson, and they passed
through the gate and up the walk, mounted the steps, and entered
the deep, cool drawing-room.

Madame Thompson herself bade the quadroone be seated.

"Well?" said Jean Thompson, as the rest took chairs.

"*C'est drole*—it's funny"—said Madame Delphine, with a piteous effort to smile, "that nobody thought of it. It is so plain. You have only to look and see. I mean about Olive." She loosed a button in the front of her dress and passed her hand into her bosom. "And yet, Olive herself never thought of it. She does not know a word."

The hand came out holding a miniature. Madame Varrillat passed it to Jean Thompson.

"*Ouala so popa*," said Madame Delphine. "That is her father."

It went from one to another, exciting admiration and murmured praise.

"She is the image of him," said Madame Thompson, in an austere undertone, returning it to her husband.

Doctor Varrillat was watching Madame Delphine. She was very pale. She had passed a trembling hand into a pocket of her skirt, and now drew out another picture, in a case the counterpart of the first. He reached out for it, and she handed it to him. He looked at it a moment, when his eyes suddenly lighted up and he passed it to the attorney.

"*Et là*"—Madame Delphine's utterance failed—"*et là ouala sa moman*. That is her mother."

The three others instantly gathered around Jean Thompson's chair. They were much impressed.

"It is true beyond a doubt!" muttered Madame Thompson.

Madame Varrillat looked at her with astonishment.

"The proof is right there in the faces," said Madame Thompson.

"Yes! yes!" said Madame Delphine, excitedly; "the proof is there! You do not want any better! I am willing to swear to it! But you want no better proof! That is all anybody could want! My God! you cannot help but see it!"

Her manner was wild.

Jean Thompson looked at her sternly.

"Nevertheless you say you are willing to take your solemn oath to this."

"Certainly"—

"You will have to do it."

"Certainly, Miché Thompson, *of course* I shall; you will make out the paper and I will swear before God that it is true! Only"—

turning to the ladies—"do not tell Olive; she will never believe it. It will break her heart! It"—

A servant came and spoke privately to Madame Thompson, who rose quickly and went to the hall. Madame Delphine continued, rising unconsciously:

"You see, I have had her with me from a baby. She knows no better. He brought her to me only two months old. Her mother had died in the ship, coming out here. He did not come straight from home here. His people never knew he was married!"

The speaker looked around suddenly with a startled glance. There was a noise of excited speaking in the hall.

"It is not true, Madame Thompson!" cried a girl's voice.

Madame Delphine's look became one of wildest distress and alarm, and she opened her lips in a vain attempt to utter some request, when Olive appeared a moment in the door, and then flew into her arms.

"My mother! my mother! my mother!"

Madame Thompson, with tears in her eyes, tenderly drew them apart and let Madame Delphine down into her chair, while Olive threw herself upon her knees, continuing to cry:

"Oh, my mother! Say you are my mother!"

Madame Delphine looked an instant into the upturned face, and then turned her own away, with a long, low cry of pain, looked again, and laying both hands upon the suppliant's head, said:

"*Oh, chère piti à moin, to pa' ma fie!*—Oh, my darling little one, you are not my daughter!"— Her eyes closed, and her head sank back; the two gentlemen sprang to her assistance, and laid her upon a sofa unconscious.

When they brought her to herself, Olive was kneeling at her head silently weeping.

"*Maman, chère maman!*" said the girl softly, kissing her lips.

"*Ma courri c'ez moin*—I will go home"—said the mother, drearily.

"You will go home with me," said Madame Varrillat, with great kindness of manner—"just across the street here; I will take care of you till you feel better. And Olive will stay here with Madame Thompson. You will be only the width of the street apart."

But Madame Delphine would go nowhere but to her home. Olive

she would not allow to go with her. Then they wanted to send a servant or two to sleep in the house with her for aid and protection; but all she would accept was the transient service of a messenger to invite two of her kinspeople—man and wife—to come and make their dwelling with her.

In course of time these two—a poor, timid, helpless pair—fell heir to the premises. Their children had it after them; but, whether in those hands or these, the house had its habits and continued in them; and to this day the neighbors, as has already been said, rightly explain its close-sealed, uninhabited look by the all-sufficient statement that the inmates "is quadroons."

Chapter XV

KYRIE ELEISON

THE second Saturday afternoon following was hot and calm. The lamp burning before the tabernacle in Père Jerome's little church might have hung with as motionless a flame in the window behind. The lilies of St. Joseph's wand, shining in one of the half-opened panes, were not more completely at rest than the leaves on tree and vine without, suspended in the slumbering air. Almost as still, down under the organ-gallery, with a single band of light falling athwart his box from a small door which stood ajar, sat the little priest, behind the lattice of the confessional, silently wiping away the sweat that beaded on his brow and rolled down his face. At distant intervals the shadow of some one entering softly through the door would obscure, for a moment, the band of light, and an aged crone, or a little boy, or some gentle presence that the listening confessor had known only by the voice for many years, would kneel a few moments beside his waiting ear, in prayer for blessing and in review of those slips and errors which prove us all akin.

The day had been long and fatiguing. First, early mass; a hasty meal; then a business call upon the archbishop in the interest of some projected charity; then back to his cottage, and so to the banking-house of "Vignevielle," in the Rue Toulouse. There all was open, bright, and reassured, its master virtually, though not actually, present. The search was over and the seekers gone, personally wiser than they would tell, and officially reporting that (to the best of their knowledge and belief, based on evidence, and especially on the assurances of an unexceptionable eye-witness, to wit, Monsieur Vignevielle, banker) Capitaine Lemaitre was dead and buried. At noon there had been a wedding in the little church. Its scenes lingered before Père Jerome's vision now—the kneeling pair: the bridegroom, rich in all the excellences of man, strength and kindness slumbering interlocked in every part and feature; the bride, a saintly weariness on her pale face, her awesome eyes lifted in adoration upon the image of the Saviour; the small knots of friends behind: Madame Thompson, large, fair, self-contained; Jean Thompson, with the affidavit of Madame Delphine showing through his tightly buttoned coat; the physician and his wife, sharing one expression of amiable consent; and last—yet first—one small, shrinking female figure, here at one side, in faded robes and dingy bonnet. She sat as motionless as stone, yet wore a look of apprehension, and in the small, restless black eyes which peered out from the pinched and wasted face, betrayed the peacelessness of a harrowed mind; and neither the recollection of bride, nor of groom, nor of potential friends behind, nor the occupation of the present hour, could shut out from the tired priest the image of that woman, or the sound of his own low words of invitation to her, given as the company left the church—"Come to confession this afternoon."

By and by a long time passed without the approach of any step, or any glancing of light or shadow, save for the occasional progress from station to station of some one over on the right who was noiselessly going the way of the cross. Yet Père Jerome tarried.

"She will surely come," he said to himself; "she promised she would come."

A moment later, his sense, quickened by the prolonged silence, caught a subtle evidence or two of approach, and the next moment a penitent knelt noiselessly at the window of his box, and the whisper came tremblingly, in the voice he had waited to hear:

"*Bénissez-moin, mo' Père, pa'ce que mo péché.*" (Bless me, father, for I have sinned.)

He gave his blessing.

"*Ainsi soit-il*—Amen," murmured the penitent, and then, in the soft accents of the Creole patois, continued:

" 'I confess to Almighty God, to the blessed Mary, ever Virgin, to blessed Michael the Archangel, to blessed John the Baptist, to the holy Apostles Peter and Paul, and to all the saints, that I have sinned exceedingly in thought, word, and deed, *through my fault, through my fault, through my most grievous fault.*' I confessed on Saturday, three weeks ago, and received absolution, and I have performed the penance enjoined. Since then"— There she stopped.

There was a soft stir, as if she sank slowly down, and another as if she rose up again, and in a moment she said:

"Olive *is* my child. The picture I showed to Jean Thompson is the half-sister of my daughter's father, dead before my child was born. She is the image of her and of him; but, O God! Thou knowest! Oh, Olive, my own daughter!"

She ceased, and was still. Père Jerome waited, but no sound came. He looked through the window. She was kneeling, with her forehead resting on her arms—motionless.

He repeated the words of absolution. Still she did not stir.

"My daughter," he said, "go to thy home in peace." But she did not move.

He rose hastily, stepped from the box, raised her in his arms, and called her by name:

"Madame Delphine!" Her head fell back in his elbow; for an instant there was life in the eyes—it glimmered—it vanished, and tears gushed from his own and fell upon the gentle face of the dead, as he looked up to heaven and cried:

"Lord, lay not this sin to her charge!"

BELLES DEMOISELLES PLANTATION

$\mathcal{T}$HE original grantee was Count ——, assume the name to be De Charleu; the old Creoles never forgive a public mention. He was the French king's commissary. One day, called to France to explain the lucky accident of the commissariat having burned down with his account-books inside, he left his wife, a Choctaw Comptesse, behind.

Arrived at court, his excuses were accepted, and that tract granted him where afterwards stood Belles Demoiselles Plantation. A man cannot remember every thing! In a fit of forgetfulness he married a French gentlewoman, rich and beautiful, and "brought her out." However, "All's well that ends well"; a famine had been in the colony, and the Choctaw Comptesse had starved, leaving nought but a half-caste orphan family lurking on the edge of the settlement, bearing our French gentlewoman's own new name, and being mentioned in Monsieur's will.

And the new Comptesse—she tarried but a twelvemonth, left Monsieur a lovely son, and departed, led out of this vain world by the swamp-fever.

From this son sprang the proud Creole family of De Charleu. It rose straight up, up, up, generation after generation, tall, branchless, slender, palm-like; and finally, in the time of which I am to tell, flowered with all the rare beauty of a century-plant, in Artemise, Innocente, Felicité, the twins Marie and Martha, Leontine and little Septima; the seven beautiful daughters for whom their home had been fitly named Belles Demoiselles.

The Count's grant had once been a long Pointe, round which the Mississippi used to whirl, and seethe, and foam, that it was horrid to behold. Big whirlpools would open and wheel about in the savage eddies under the low bank, and close up again, and others open, and spin, and disappear. Great circles of muddy surface would boil up from hundreds of feet below, and gloss over, and seem to float away —sink, come back again under water, and with only a soft hiss surge up again, and again drift off, and vanish. Every few minutes the loamy bank would tip down a great load of earth upon its besieger, and fall back a foot—sometimes a yard—and the writhing river would press after, until at last the Pointe was quite swallowed up, and the great river glided by in a majestic curve, and asked no more; the bank stood fast, the "caving" became a forgotten misfortune, and the diminished grant was a long, sweeping, willowy bend, rustling with miles of sugar-cane.

Coming up the Mississippi in the sailing craft of those early days, about the time one first could descry the white spires of the old St. Louis Cathedral, you would be pretty sure to spy, just over to your right under the levee, Belles Demoiselles Mansion, with its broad veranda and red painted cypress roof, peering over the embankment, like a bird in the nest, half hid by the avenue of willows which one of the departed De Charleus—he that married a Marot—had planted on the levee's crown.

The house stood unusually near the river, facing eastward, and standing four-square, with an immense veranda about its sides, and a flight of steps in front spreading broadly downward, as we open arms to a child. From the veranda nine miles of river were seen; and in their compass, near at hand, the shady garden full of rare and beautiful flowers; farther away broad fields of cane and rice, and the distant quarters of the slaves, and on the horizon everywhere a dark belt of cypress forest.

The master was old Colonel De Charleu—Jean Albert Henri Joseph De Charleu-Marot, and "Colonel" by the grace of the first American governor. Monsieur—he would not speak to any one who called him "Colonel"—was a hoary-headed patriarch. His step was firm, his form erect, his intellect strong and clear, his countenance classic, serene, dignified, commanding, his manners courtly, his voice musical—fascinating. He had had his vices—all his life; but had borne them, as his race do, with a serenity of conscience and a cleanness of mouth that left no outward blemish on the surface of the gentleman. He had gambled in Royal Street, drank hard in Orleans Street, run his adversary through in the dueling-ground at Slaughter-house Point, and danced and quarreled at the St. Philippe Street Theatre quadroon balls. Even now, with all his courtesy and bounty, and a hospitality which seemed to be enter-

taining angels, he was bitter-proud and penurious, and deep down in his hard-finished heart loved nothing but himself, his name, and his motherless children. But these!—their ravishing beauty was all but excuse enough for the unbounded idolatry of their father. Against these seven goddesses he never rebelled. Had they even required him to defraud old De Carlos—

I can hardly say.

Old De Carlos was his extremely distant relative on the Choctaw side. With this single exception, the narrow thread-like line of descent from the Indian wife, diminished to a mere strand by injudicious alliances, and deaths in the gutters of old New Orleans, was extinct. The name, by Spanish contact, had become De Carlos; but this one surviving bearer of it was known to all, and known only, as Injin Charlie.

One thing I never knew a Creole to do. He will not utterly go back on the ties of blood, no matter what sort of knots those ties may be. For one reason, he is never ashamed of his or his father's sins; and for another—he will tell you—he is "all heart!"

So the different heirs of the De Charleu estate had always strictly regarded the rights and interests of the De Carloses, especially their ownership of a block of dilapidated buildings in a part of the city, which had once been very poor property, but was beginning to be valuable. This block had much more than maintained the last De Carlos through a long and lazy lifetime, and, as his household consisted only of himself, and an aged and crippled Negress, the inference was irresistible that he "had money." Old Charlie, though by *alias* an "Injin," was plainly a dark white man, about as old as Colonel De Charleu, sunk in the bliss of deep ignorance, shrewd, deaf, and, by repute at least, unmerciful.

The Colonel and he always conversed in English. This rare accomplishment, which the former had learned from his Scotch wife —the latter from up-river traders—they found an admirable medium of communication, answering, better than French could, a similar purpose to that of the stick which we fasten to the bit of one horse and breast-gear of another, whereby each keeps his distance. Once in a while, too, by way of jest, English found its way among the ladies of Belles Demoiselles, always signifying that their sire was about to have business with old Charlie.

Now a long-standing wish to buy out Charlie troubled the Colonel. He had no desire to oust him unfairly; he was proud of being always fair; yet he did long to engross the whole estate under one title. Out of his luxurious idleness he had conceived this desire, and thought little of so slight an obstacle as being already somewhat in debt to old Charlie for money borrowed, and for which Belles Demoiselles was, of course, good, ten times over. Lots, buildings, rents, all, might as well be his, he thought, to give, keep, or destroy. "Had he but the old man's heritage. Ah! he might bring that into existence which his *belles demoiselles* had been begging for, 'since many years'; a home—and such a home—in the gay city. Here he should tear down this row of cottages, and make his garden wall; there that long rope-walk should give place to vine-covered arbors; the bakery yonder should make way for a costly conservatory; that wine ware-house should come down, and the mansion go up. It should be the finest in the State. Men should never pass it, but they should say— 'the palace of the De Charleus; a family of grand descent, a people of elegance and bounty, a line as old as France, a fine old man, and seven daughters as beautiful as happy; whoever dare attempt to marry there must leave his own name behind him!'

"The house should be of stones fitly set, brought down in ships from the land of '*les Yankees*,' and it should have an airy belvedere, with a gilded image tiptoeing and shining on its peak, and from it you should see, far across the gleaming folds of the river, the red roof of Belles Demoiselles, the country-seat. At the big stone gate there should be a porter's lodge, and it should be a privilege even to see the ground."

Truly they were a family fine enough, and fancy-free enough to have fine wishes, yet happy enough where they were, to have had no wish but to live there always.

To those, who, by whatever fortune, wandered into the garden of Belles Demoiselles some summer afternoon as the sky was red-dening towards evening, it was lovely to see the family gathered out upon the tiled pavement at the foot of the broad front steps, gayly chatting and jesting, with that ripple of laughter that comes so pleasingly from a bevy of girls. The father would be found seated in their midst, the centre of attention and compliment, witness, arbiter, umpire, critic, by his beautiful children's unanimous appointment, but the single vassal, too, of seven absolute sovereigns.

Now they would draw their chairs near together in eager discus-sion of some new step in the dance, or the adjustment of some rich adornment. Now they would start about him with excited comments to see the eldest fix a bunch of violets in his button-hole. Now the twins would move down a walk after some unusual flower, and be greeted on their return with the high-pitched notes of delighted feminine surprise.

As evening came on they would draw more quietly about their

paternal centre. Often their chairs were forsaken, and they grouped themselves on the lower steps, one above another, and surrendered themselves to the tender influences of the approaching night. At such an hour the passer on the river, already attracted by the dark figures of the broad-roofed mansion, and its woody garden standing against the glowing sunset, would hear the voices of the hidden group rise from the spot in the soft harmonies of an evening song; swelling clearer and clearer as the thrill of music warmed them into feeling, and presently joined by the deeper tones of the father's voice; then, as the daylight passed quite away, all would be still, and he would know that the beautiful home had gathered its nestlings under its wings.

And yet, for mere vagary, it pleased them not to be pleased.

"Arti!" called one sister to another in the broad hall, one morning—mock amazement in her distended eyes—"something is goin' to took place!"

"*Comm-e-n-t?*"—long-drawn perplexity.

"Papa is goin' to town!"

The news passed up-stairs.

"Inno!"—one to another meeting in a doorway—"something is goin' to took place!"

"*Qu'est-ce-que c'est!*"—vain attempt at gruffness.

"Papa is goin' to town!"

The unusual tidings were true. It was afternoon of the same day that the Colonel tossed his horse's bridle to his groom, and stepped up to old Charlie, who was sitting on his bench under a China-tree, his head, as was his fashion, bound in a Madras handkerchief. The "old man" was plainly under the effect of spirits, and smiled a deferential salutation without trusting himself to his feet.

"Eh, well Charlie!"—the Colonel raised his voice to suit his kinsman's deafness—"how is those times with my friend Charlie?"

"Eh?" said Charlie, distractedly.

"Is that goin' well with my friend Charlie?"

"In de house—call her"—making a pretence of rising.

"*Non, non!* I don't want"—the speaker paused to breathe—"ow is collection?"

"Oh!" said Charlie, "every day he make me more poorer!"

(*152*)

"What do you hask for it?" asked the planter indifferently, designating the house by a wave of his whip.

"Ask for w'at?" said Injin Charlie.

"De *house!* What you ask for it?"

"I don't believe," said Charlie.

"What you would *take* for it!" cried the planter.

"Wait for w'at?"

"What you would *take* for the whole block?"

"I don't want to sell him!"

"I'll give you *ten thousand dollah* for it."

"Ten t'ousand dollah for dis house? Oh, no, dat is no price. He is blame good old house—dat old house." (Old Charlie and the Colonel never swore in presence of each other.) "Forty years dat old house didn't had to be paint! I easy can get fifty t'ousand dollah for dat old house."

"Fifty thousand picayunes; yes," said the Colonel.

"She's a good house. Can make plenty money," pursued the deaf man.

"That's what make you so rich, eh, Charlie?"

"*Non*, I don't make nothing. Too blame clever, me, dat's de troub'. She's a good house—make money fast like a steamboat— make a barrel full in a week! Me, I lose money all de days. Too blame clever."

"Charlie!"

"Eh?"

"Tell me what you'll take."

"Make? I don't make *nothing*. Too blame clever."

"What will you *take?*"

"Oh! I got enough already—half drunk now."

"What will you take for the 'ouse?"

"You want to buy her?"

"I don't know"—(shrug)—"may*be*—if you sell it cheap."

"She's a bully old house."

There was a long silence. By and by old Charlie commenced—

"Old Injin Charlie is a low-down dog."

"*C'est vrai, oui!*" retorted the Colonel in an undertone.

"He's got Injin blood in him."

The Colonel nodded assent.

"But he's got some blame good blood, too, ain't it?"

The Colonel nodded impatiently.

"*Bien!* Old Charlie's Injin blood says, 'Sell de house, Charlie, you blame old fool!' *Mais*, old Charlie's good blood says, 'Charlie! if you sell dat old house, Charlie, you low-down old dog, Charlie, what de Compte De Charleu make for you grace-gran'-muzzer, de dev' can eat you, Charlie, I don't care.' "

"But you'll sell it anyhow, won't you, old man?"

"No!" And the *no* rumbled off in muttered oaths like thunder out on the Gulf. The incensed old Colonel wheeled and started off.

"Curl!" (Colonel) said Charlie, standing up unsteadily.

The planter turned with an inquiring frown.

"I'll trade with you!" said Charlie.

The Colonel was tempted. " 'Ow'l you trade?" he asked.

"My house for yours!"

The old Colonel turned pale with anger. He walked very quickly back, and came close up to his kinsman.

"Charlie!" he said.

"Injin Charlie"—with a tipsy nod.

But by this time self-control was returning. "Sell Belles Demoiselles to you?" he said in a high key, and then laughed "Ho, ho, ho!" and rode away.

A cloud, but not a dark one, overshadowed the spirits of Belles Demoiselles' plantation. The old master, whose beaming presence had always made him a shining Saturn, spinning and sparkling within the bright circle of his daughters, fell into musing fits, started out of frowning reveries, walked often by himself, and heard business from his overseer fretfully.

No wonder. The daughters knew his closeness in trade, and attributed to it his failure to negotiate for the Old Charlie buildings —so to call them. They began to depreciate Belles Demoiselles. If a north wind blew, it was too cold to ride. If a shower had fallen, it was too muddy to drive. In the morning the garden was wet. In the evening the grasshopper was a burden. *Ennui* was turned into capital; every headache was interpreted a premonition of ague; and when the native exuberance of a flock of ladies without a want or a care burst out in laughter in the father's face, they spread their French eyes, rolled up their little hands, and with rigid wrists and mock vehemence vowed and vowed again that they only laughed at their misery, and should pine to death unless they could move to the sweet city. "Oh! the theatre! Oh! Orleans Street! Oh! the masquerade! the Place d'Armes! the ball!" and they would call upon Heaven with French irreverence, and fall into each other's arms, and whirl down the hall singing a waltz, end with a grand collision and fall, and, their eyes streaming merriment, lay the blame on the slippery floor, that would some day be the death of the whole seven.

Three times more the fond father, thus goaded, managed, by accident—business accident—to see old Charlie and increase his offer; but in vain. He finally went to him formally.

"Eh?" said the deaf and distant relative. "For what you want him, eh? Why you don't stay where you halways be 'appy? Dis is a blame old rat-hole—good for old Injin Charlie—da's all. Why you don't stay where you be halways 'appy? Why you don't buy somewheres else?"

"That's none of your business," snapped the planter. Truth was, his reasons were unsatisfactory even to himself.

A sullen silence followed. Then Charlie spoke:

"Well, now, look here; I sell you old Charlie's house."

"*Bien!* and the whole block," said the Colonel.

"Hold on," said Charlie. "I sell you de 'ouse and de block. Den I go and git drunk, and go to sleep; de dev' comes along and says, 'Charlie! old Charlie, you blame low-down old dog, wake up! What you doin' here? Where's de 'ouse what Monsieur le Compte give your grace-gran-muzzer? Don't you see dat fine gentyman, De Charleu, done gone and tore him down and make him over new, you blame old fool, Charlie, you low-down old Injin dog!'"

"I'll give you forty thousand dollars," said the Colonel.

"For de 'ouse?"

"For all."

The deaf man shook his head.

"Forty-five!" said the Colonel.

"What a lie? For what you tell me 'What a lie?' I don't tell you no lie."

"*Non, non!* I give you *forty-five!*" shouted the Colonel.

Charlie shook his head again.

"Fifty!"

He shook it again.

The figures rose and rose to—

"Seventy-five!"

The answer was an invitation to go away and let the owner alone, as he was, in certain specified respects, the vilest of living creatures, and no company for a fine gentyman.

The "fine gentyman" longed to blaspheme—but before old Charlie!—in the name of pride, how could he? He mounted and started away.

"Tell you what I'll make wid you," said Charlie.

The other, guessing aright, turned back without dismounting, smiling.

"How much Belles Demoiselles hoes me now?" asked the deaf one.

"One hundred and eighty thousand dollars," said the Colonel, firmly.

"Yass," said Charlie. "I don't want Belles Demoiselles."

The old Colonel's quiet laugh intimated it made no difference either way.

"But me," continued Charlie, "me—I'm got le Compte De Charleu's blood in me, any'ow—a litt' bit, any'ow, ain't it?"

The Colonel nodded that it was.

"*Bien!* If I go out of dis place and don't go to Belles Demoiselles, de peoples will say—dey will say, "Old Charlie he been all doze time tell a blame *lie!* He ain't no kin to his old grace-gran-muzzer, not a blame bit! He don't got nary drop of De Charleu blood to save his blame low-down old Injin soul! No, sare! What I want wid money, den? No, sare! My place for yours!"

He turned to go into the house, just too soon to see the Colonel make an ugly whisk at him with his riding-whip. Then the Colonel, too, moved off.

Two or three times over, as he ambled homeward, laughter broke through his annoyance, as he recalled old Charlie's family pride and the presumption of his offer. Yet each time he could but think better of—not the offer to swap, but the preposterous ancestral loyalty. It was so much better than he could have expected from his "low-down" relative, and not unlike his own whim withal—the proposition which went with it was forgiven.

This last defeat bore so harshly on the master of Belles Demoiselles, that the daughters, reading chagrin in his face, began to repent. They loved their father as daughters can, and when they saw their pretended dejection harassing him seriously they restrained their complaints, displayed more than ordinary tenderness, and heroically and ostentatiously concluded there was no place like Belles Demoiselles. But the new mood touched him more than the old, and only refined his discontent. Here was a man, rich without the care of riches, free from any real trouble, happiness as native to his house as perfume to his garden, deliberately, as it were with premeditated malice, taking joy by the shoulder and bidding her be gone to town, whither he might easily have followed, only that the very same ancestral nonsense that kept Injin Charlie from selling the old place for twice its value prevented him from choosing any other spot for a city home.

But by and by the charm of nature and the merry hearts around him prevailed; the fit of exalted sulks passed off, and after a while the year flared up at Christmas, flickered, and went out.

New Year came and passed; the beautiful garden of Belles Demoiselles put on its spring attire; the seven fair sisters moved from rose to rose; the cloud of discontent had warmed into invisible vapor in the rich sunlight of family affection, and on the common memory the only scar of last year's wound was old Charlie's sheer impertinence in crossing the caprice of the De Charleus. The cup of gladness seemed to fill with the filling of the river.

How high that river was! Its tremendous current rolled and tumbled and spun along, hustling the long funeral flotillas of drift—and how near shore it came! Men were out day and night, watching the levee. On windy nights even the old Colonel took part, and grew light-hearted with occupation and excitement, as every minute the river threw a white arm over the levee's top, as though it would vault over. But all held fast, and, as the summer drifted in, the water sunk down into its banks and looked quite incapable of harm.

On a summer afternoon of uncommon mildness, old Colonel Jean Albert Henri Joseph De Charleu-Marot, being in a mood for reverie, slipped the custody of his feminine rulers and sought the crown of the levee, where it was his wont to promenade. Presently he sat upon a stone bench—a favorite seat. Before him lay his broadspread fields; near by, his lordly mansion; and being still—perhaps by female contact—somewhat sentimental, he fell to musing on his past. It was hardly worthy to be proud of. All its morning was reddened with mad frolic, and far toward the meridian it was marred with elegant rioting. Pride had kept him well-nigh useless, and despised the honors won by valor; gaming had dimmed prosperity; death had taken his heavenly wife; voluptuous ease had mortgaged his lands; and yet his house still stood, his sweet-smelling fields were still fruitful, his name was fame enough; and yonder and yonder, among the trees and flowers, like angels walking in Eden, were the seven goddesses of his only worship.

Just then a slight sound behind him brought him to his feet. He cast his eyes anxiously to the outer edge of the little strip of bank between the levee's base and the river. There was nothing visible. He paused, with his ear toward the water, his face full of frightened expectation. Ha! There came a single plashing sound, like some great beast slipping into the river, and little waves in a wide semicircle came out from under the bank and spread over the water!

"My God!"

He plunged down the levee and bounded through the low weeds to the edge of the bank. It was sheer, and the water about four feet below. He did not stand quite on the edge, but fell upon his knees a couple of yards away, wringing his hands, moaning and weeping, and staring through his watery eyes at a fine, long crevice just discernible under the matted grass, and curving outward on either hand toward the river.

"My God!" he sobbed aloud; "my God!" and even while he called, his God answered: the tough Bermuda grass stretched and snapped, the crevice slowly became a gape, and softly, gradually, with no sound but the closing of the water at last, a ton or more of earth settled into the boiling eddy and disappeared.

At the same instant a pulse of the breeze brought from the garden behind, the joyous, thoughtless laughter of the fair mistresses of Belle Demoiselles.

The old Colonel sprang up and clambered over the levee. Then forcing himself to a more composed movement, he hastened into the house and ordered his horse.

"Tell my children to make merry while I am gone," he left word. "I shall be back to-night," and the horse's hoofs clattered down a by-road leading to the city.

"Charlie," said the planter, riding up to a window, from which the old man's nightcap was thrust out, "what you say, Charlie— my house for yours, eh, Charlie—what you say?"

"Ello!" said Charlie; "from where you come from dis time of to-night?"

"I come from the Exchange in St. Louis Street." (A small fraction of the truth.)

"What you want?" said matter-of-fact Charlie.

"I come to trade."

The low-down relative drew the worsted off his ears. "Oh! yass," he said with an uncertain air.

"Well, old man Charlie, what you say: my house for yours— like you said—eh, Charlie?"

"I dunno," said Charlie; "it's nearly mine now. Why you don't stay dare youse'f?"

(*159*)

"Because I don't want!" said the Colonel savagely. "Is dat reason enough for you? You better take me in de notion, old man, I tell you—yes!"

Charlie never winced; but how his answer delighted the Colonel! Quoth Charlie:

"I don't care—I take him!—*mais*, possession give right off."

"Not the whole plantation, Charlie; only"—

"I don't care," said Charlie; "we easy can fix dat. *Mais*, what for you don't want to keep him? I don't want him. You better keep him."

"Don't you try to make no fool of me, old man," cried the planter.

"Oh, no!" said the other. "Oh, no! but you make a fool of yourself, ain't it?"

The dumbfounded Colonel stared; Charlie went on:

"Yass! Belles Demoiselles is more wort' dan tree block like dis one. I pass by dare since two weeks. Oh, pritty Belles Demoiselles! De cane was wave in de wind, de garden smell like a bouquet, de white-cap was jump up and down on de river; seven *belles demoiselles* was ridin' on horses. 'Pritty, pritty, pritty!' says old Charlie. Ah! *Monsieur le père*, 'ow 'appy, 'appy, 'appy!

"Yass!" he continued—the Colonel still staring—"le Compte De Charleu have two familie. One was low-down Choctaw, one was high up *noblesse*. He gave the low-down Choctaw dis old rat-hole; he give Belles Demoiselles to you gran-fozzer; and now you don't be *satisfait*. What I'll do wid Belles Demoiselles? She'll break me in two years, yass. And what you'll do wid old Charlie's house, eh? You'll tear her down and make you'se'f a blame old fool. I rather wouldn't trade!"

The planter caught a big breathful of anger, but Charlie went straight on:

"I rather wouldn't, *mais* I will do it for you;—just the same, like Monsieur le Compte would say, 'Charlie, you old fool, I want to shange houses wid you.'"

So long as the Colonel suspected irony he was angry, but as Charlie seemed, after all, to be certainly in earnest, he began to feel conscience-stricken. He was by no means a tender man, but his lately discovered misfortune had unhinged him, and this strange, undeserved, disinterested family fealty on the part of Charlie

touched his heart. And should he still try to lead him into the pitfall he had dug? He hesitated;—no, he would show him the place by broad daylight, and if he chose to overlook the "caving bank," it would be his own fault;—a trade's a trade.

"Come," said the planter, "come at my house to-night; to-morrow we look at the place before breakfast, and finish the trade."

"For what?" said Charlie.

"Oh, because I got to come in town in the morning."

"I don't want," said Charlie. "How I'm goin' to come dere?"

"I git you a horse at the liberty stable."

"Well—anyhow—I don't care—I'll go." And they went.

When they had ridden a long time, and were on the road darkened by hedges of Cherokee rose, the Colonel called behind him to the "low-down" scion:

"Keep the road, old man."

"Eh?"

"Keep the road."

"Oh, yes; all right; I keep my word; we don't goin' to play no tricks, eh?"

But the Colonel seemed not to hear. His ungenerous design was beginning to be hateful to him. Not only old Charlie's unprovoked goodness was prevailing; the eulogy on Belles Demoiselles had stirred the depths of an intense love for his beautiful home. True, if he held to it, the caving of the bank, at its present fearful speed, would let the house into the river within three months; but were it not better to lose it so, than sell his birthright? Again—coming back to the first thought—to betray his own blood! It was only Injin Charlie; but had not the De Charleu blood just spoken out in him? Unconsciously he groaned.

After a time they struck a path approaching the plantation in the rear, and a little after, passing from behind a clump of live-oaks, they came in sight of the villa. It looked so like a gem, shining through its dark grove, so like a great glow-worm in the dense foliage, so significant of luxury and gaiety, that the poor master, from an overflowing heart, groaned again.

"What?" asked Charlie.

The Colonel only drew his rein, and, dismounting mechanically, contemplated the sight before him. The high, arched doors and windows were thrown wide to the summer air; from every opening the bright light of numerous candelabra darted out upon the sparkling foliage of magnolia and bay, and here and there in the spacious verandas a colored lantern swayed in the gentle breeze. A sound of revel fell on the ear, the music of harps; and across one window, brighter than the rest, flitted, once or twice, the shadows of dancers. But oh! the shadows flitting across the heart of the fair mansion's master!

"Old Charlie," said he, gazing fondly at his house, "you and me is both old, eh?"

"Yaas," said the stolid Charlie.

"And we has both been bad enough in our time, eh, Charlie?"

Charlie, surprised at the tender tone, repeated "Yaas."

"And you and me is mighty close?"

"Blame close, yaas."

"But you never know me to cheat, old man!"

"No"—impassively.

"And do you think I would cheat you now?"

"I dunno," said Charlie. "I don't believe."

"Well, old man, old man"—his voice began to quiver—"I sha'n't cheat you now. My God!—old man, I tell you—you better not make the trade!"

"Because for what?" asked Charlie in plain anger; but both looked quickly toward the house! The Colonel tossed his hands wildly in the air, rushed forward a step or two, and giving one fearful scream of agony and fright, fell forward on his face in the path. Old Charlie stood transfixed with horror. Belles Demoiselles, the realm of maiden beauty, the home of merriment, the house of dancing, all in the tremor and glow of pleasure, suddenly sunk, with one short, wild wail of terror—sunk, sunk, down, down, down, into the merciless, unfathomable flood of the Mississippi.

Twelve long months were midnight to the mind of the childless father; when they were only half gone, he took his bed; and every day, and every night, old Charlie, the "low-down," the "fool," watched him tenderly, tended him lovingly, for the sake of his name, his misfortunes, and his broken heart. No woman's step crossed the floor of the sick-chamber, whose western dormer windows over-peered the dingy architecture of old Charlie's block; Charlie and a skilled physician, the one all interest, the other all gentleness, hope, and patience—these only entered by the door; but by the window came in a sweet-scented evergreen vine, transplanted from the caving bank of Belles Demoiselles. It caught the rays of sunset in its flowery net and let them softly in upon the sick man's bed; gathered the glancing beams of the moon at midnight, and often wakened the sleeper to look, with his mindless eyes, upon their pretty silver fragments strewn upon the floor.

By and by there seemed—there was—a twinkling dawn of returning reason. Slowly, peacefully, with an increase unseen from day to day, the light of reason came into the eyes, and speech became coherent; but withal there came a failing of the wrecked body, and the doctor said that Monsieur was both better and worse.

One evening, as Charlie sat by the vine-clad window with his fireless pipe in his hand, the old Colonel's eyes fell full upon his own, and rested there.

"Charl—," he said with an effort, and his delighted nurse hastened to the bedside and bowed his best ear. There was an unsuccessful effort or two, and then he whispered, smiling with sweet sadness—

"We didn't trade."

The truth, in this case, was a secondary matter to Charlie; the main point was to give a pleasing answer. So he nodded his head decidedly, as who should say—"Oh yes, we did, it was a bona-fide swap!" but when he saw the smile vanish, he tried the other expedient and shook his head with still more vigor, to signify that they had not so much as approached a bargain; and the smile returned.

Charlie wanted to see the vine recognized. He stepped backward to the window with a broad smile, shook the foliage, nodded and looked smart.

"I know," said the Colonel, with beaming eyes, "—many weeks."

The next day—

"Charl—"

The best ear went down.

"Send for a priest."

The priest came, and was alone with him a whole afternoon.

When he left, the patient was very haggard and exhausted, but smiled and would not suffer the crucifix to be removed from his breast.

One more morning came. Just before dawn Charlie, lying on a pallet in the room, thought he was called, and came to the bedside.

"Old man," whispered the failing invalid, "is it caving yet?"

Charlie nodded.

"It won't pay you out."

"Oh, dat makes not'ing," said Charlie. Two big tears rolled down his brown face. "Dat makes not'in."

The Colonel whispered once more:

"*Mes belles demoiselles!* in paradise;—in the garden—I shall be with them at sunrise"; and so it was.

MADAME DÉLICIEUSE

Just adjoining the old Café de Poésie on the corner, stood the little one-story, yellow-washed tenement of Dr. Mossy, with its two glass doors protected by batten shutters, and its low, weed-grown tile roof sloping out over the sidewalk. You were very likely to find the Doctor in, for he was a great student and rather negligent of his business—as business. He was a small, sedate, Creole gentleman of thirty or more, with a young-old face and manner that provoked instant admiration. He would receive you—be you who you may—in a mild, candid manner, looking into your face with his deep blue eyes, and reassuring you with a modest, amiable smile, very sweet and rare on a man's mouth.

To be frank, the Doctor's little establishment was dusty and disorderly—very. It was curious to see the jars, and jars, and jars. In them were serpents and hideous fishes and precious specimens of many sorts. There were stuffed birds on broken perches; and dried lizards, and eels, and little alligators, and old skulls with their crowns sawed off, and ten thousand odd scraps of writing-paper strewn with crumbs of lonely lunches, and interspersed with long-lost spatulas and rust-eaten lancets.

All New Orleans, at least all Creole New Orleans, knew, and yet did not know, the dear little Doctor. So gentle, so kind, so skilful, so patient, so lenient; so careless of the rich and so attentive to the poor; a man, all in all, such as, should you once love him, you would love him forever. So very learned, too, but with apparently no idea of how to *show himself* to his social profit—two features much more smiled at than respected, not to say admired, by a people remote from the seats of learning, and spending most of their esteem upon animal heroisms and exterior display.

"Alas!" said his wealthy acquaintances, "what a pity; when he might as well be rich."

"Yes, his father has plenty."

"Certainly, and gives it freely. But intends his son shall see none of it."

"His son? You dare not so much as mention him."

"Well, well, how strange! But they can never agree—not even upon their name. Is not that droll?—a man named General Villivicencio, and his son, Dr. Mossy!"

"Oh, that is nothing; it is only that the Doctor drops the *de Villivicencio*."

"Drops the *de Villivicencio?* but I think the *de Villivicencio* drops him, ho, ho, ho—*diable!*"

Next to the residence of good Dr. Mossy towered the narrow, red-brick-front mansion of young Madame Délicieuse, firm friend at once and always of those two antipodes, General Villivicencio and

Dr. Mossy. Its dark, covered carriage-way was ever rumbling, and, with nightfall, its drawing-rooms always sent forth a luxurious light from the lace-curtained windows of the second-story balconies.

It was one of the sights of the Rue Royale to see by night its tall, narrow outline reaching high up toward the stars, with all its windows aglow.

The Madame had had some tastes of human experience; had been betrothed at sixteen (to a man she did not love, "being at that time a fool," as she said); one summer day at noon had been a bride, and at sundown—a widow. Accidental discharge of the tipsy bridegroom's own pistol. Pass it by! It left but one lasting effect on her, a special detestation of quarrels and weapons.

The little maidens whom poor parentage has doomed to sit upon street door-sills and nurse their infant brothers have a game of "choosing" the beautiful ladies who sweep by along the pavement; but in Rue Royale there was no choosing; every little damsel must own Madame Délicieuse or nobody, and as that richly adorned and regal favorite of old General Villivicencio came along they would lift their big, bold eyes away up to her face and pour forth their admiration in a universal—"Ah-h-h-h!"

But, mark you, she was good Madame Délicieuse as well as fair Madame Délicieuse: her principles, however, not constructed in the austere Anglo-Saxon style, exactly (what need, with the lattice of the confessional not a stone's-throw off?). Her kind offices and beneficent schemes were almost as famous as General Villivicencio's splendid alms; if she could at times do what the infantile Washington said he could not, why, no doubt she and her friends generally looked upon it as a mere question of enterprise.

She had charms, too, of intellect—albeit not such a sinner against time and place as to be an "educated woman"—charms that, even in a plainer person, would have brought down the half of New Orleans upon one knee, with both hands on the left side. *She* had the *whole* city at her feet, and, with the fine tact which was the perfection of her character, kept it there contented. Madame was, in short, one of the kind that gracefully wrest from society the prerogative of doing as they please, and had gone even to such extravagant lengths as driving out in the *Américain* faubourg, learning the English tongue, talking national politics, and similar freaks whereby she provoked the unbounded worship of her less audacious lady friends. In the centre of the cluster of Creole beauties which everywhere gathered about her, and, most of all, in those incomparable companies which assembled in her own splendid drawing-rooms, she was always queen lily. *Her* house, *her* drawing-rooms, etc.; for the little brown aunt who lived with her was a mere piece of curious furniture.

There was this notable charm about Madame Délicieuse, she improved by comparison. She never looked so grand as when, hanging on General Villivicencio's arm at some gorgeous ball, these two bore down on you like a royal barge lashed to a ship-of-the-line. She never looked so like her sweet name, as when she seated her prettiest lady adorers close around her, and got them all a-laughing.

Of the two balconies which overhung the banquette on the front of the Délicieuse house, one was a small affair, and the other a deeper and broader one, from which Madame and her ladies were wont upon gala days to wave handkerchiefs and cast flowers to the friends in the processions. There they gathered one Eighth of January morning to see the military display. It was a bright blue day, and the group that quite filled the balcony had laid wrappings aside, as all flower-buds are apt to do on such Creole January days, and shone resplendent in spring attire.

The sight-seers passing below looked up by hundreds and smiled at the ladies' eager twitter, as, flirting in humming-bird fashion from one subject to another, they laughed away the half-hours waiting for the pageant. By and by they fell a-listening, for Madame Délicieuse had begun a narrative concerning Dr. Mossy. She sat somewhat above her listeners, her elbow on the arm of her chair, and her plump white hand waving now and then in graceful gesture, they silently attending with eyes full of laughter and lips starting apart.

"*Vous savez,*" she said (they conversed in French of course), "you know it is now long that Dr. Mossy and his father have been in disaccord. Indeed, when have they not differed? For, when Mossy was but a little boy, his father thought it hard that he was not a rowdy. He switched him once because he would not play with his toy gun and drum. He was not *so* high when his father wished to send him to Paris to enter the French army; but he would not go. We used to play often together on the banquette—for I am not so very many years younger than he, no indeed—and, if I wanted some fun, I had only to pull his hair and run into the house; he would cry, and monsieur papa would come out with his hand spread open and"—

Madame gave her hand a malicious little sweep, and joined heartily in the laugh which followed.

"That was when they lived over the way. But wait! you shall see; I have something. This evening the General"—

The houses of Rue Royale gave a start and rattled their windows. In the long, irregular line of balconies the beauty of the city rose up. Then the houses jumped again and the windows rattled; Madame steps inside the window and gives a message which the housemaid smiles at in receiving. As she turns the houses shake again, and now again; and now there comes a distant strain of trumpets, and by and by the drums and bayonets and clattering hoofs, and plumes and dancing banners; far down the long street stretch out the shining ranks of gallant men, and the fluttering, over-leaning swarms of ladies shower down their sweet favors and wave their countless welcomes.

In the front, towering above his captains, rides General Villivicencio, veteran of 1814–15, and, with the gracious pomp of the old-time gentleman, lifts his cocked hat, and bows, and bows.

Madame Délicieuse's balcony was a perfect maze of waving kerchiefs. The General looked up for the woman of all women; she was not there. But he remembered the other balcony, the smaller one, and cast his glance onward to it. There he saw Madame and one other person only. A small blue-eyed, broad-browed, scholarly-looking man whom the arch lady had lured from his pen by means of a mock professional summons, and who now stood beside her, a smile of pleasure playing on his lips and about his eyes.

"*Vite!*" said Madame, as the father's eyes met the son's. Dr. Mossy lifted his arm and cast a bouquet of roses. A girl in the crowd bounded forward, caught it in the air, and, blushing, handed it to the plumed giant. He bowed low, first to the girl, then to the balcony above; and then, with a responsive smile, tossed up two splendid kisses, one to Madame, and one, it seemed—

"For what was that cheer?"

(*169*)

"Why, did you not see? General Villivicencio cast a kiss to his son."

The staff of General Villivicencio were a faithful few who had not bowed the knee to any abomination of the *Américains*, nor sworn deceitfully to any species of compromise; their beloved city was presently to pass into the throes of an election, and this band, heroically unconscious of their feebleness, putting their trust in "reactions" and like delusions, resolved to make one more stand for the traditions of their fathers. It was concerning this that Madame Délicieuse was incidentally about to speak when interrupted by the boom of cannon; they had promised to meet at her house that evening.

They met. With very little discussion or delay (for their minds were made up beforehand), it was decided to announce in the French-English newspaper that, at a meeting of leading citizens, it had been thought consonant with the public interest to place before the people the name of General Hercule Mossy de Villivicencio. No explanation was considered necessary. All had been done in strict accordance with time-honored customs, and if any one did not know it it was his own fault. No eulogium was to follow, no editorial indorsement. The two announcements were destined to stand next morning, one on the English side and one on the French, in severe simplicity, to be greeted with profound gratification by a few old gentlemen in blue cottonade, and by roars of laughter from a rampant majority.

As the junto were departing, sparkling Madame Délicieuse detained the General at the head of the stairs that descended into the tiled carriage-way, to wish she was a man, that she might vote for him.

"But, General," she said, "had I not a beautiful bouquet of ladies on my balcony this morning?"

The General replied, with majestic gallantry, that "it was as magnificent as could be expected with the central rose wanting." And so Madame was disappointed, for she was trying to force the General to mention his son. "I will bear this no longer; he shall not rest," she had said to her little aunt, "until he has either kissed his son or quarreled with him." To which the aunt had answered that, "*coûte que coûte,* she need not cry about it"; nor did she. Though the General's compliment had foiled her thrust, she answered gayly to the effect that enough was enough; "but, ah! General," dropping her voice to an undertone, "if you had heard what some of those rosebuds said of you!"

The old General pricked up like a country beau. Madame laughed to herself, "Monsieur Peacock, I have thee"; but aloud she said gravely:

"Come into the drawing-room, if you please, and seat yourself. You must be greatly fatigued."

The friends who waited below overheard the invitation.

"*Au revoir, Général,*" said they.

"*Au revoir, messieurs,*" he answered, and followed the lady.

"General," said she, as if her heart were overflowing, "you have been spoken against. Please sit down."

"Is that true, Madame?"

"Yes, General."

She sank into a luxurious chair.

"A lady said to-day—but you will be angry with me, General."

"With you, Madame? That is not possible."

"I do not love to make revelations, General; but when a noble friend is evil spoken of"—she leaned her brow upon her thumb and forefinger, and looked pensively at her slipper's toe peeping out at the edge of her skirt on the rich carpet—"one's heart gets very big."

"Madame, you are an angel! But what said she, Madame?"

"Well, General, I have to tell you the whole truth, if you will not be angry. We were all speaking at once of handsome men. She said to me: 'Well, Madame Délicieuse, you may say what you will of General Villivicencio, and I suppose it is true; but everybody knows'—pardon me, General, but just so she said—'all the world knows he treats his son very badly.'"

"It is not true," said the General.

"If I wasn't angry!" said Madame, making a pretty fist. " 'How can that be?' I said. 'Well,' she said, 'mamma says he has been angry with his son for fifteen years.' 'But what did his son do?' I said. 'Nothing,' said she. '*Ma foi,*' I said, 'me, I too would be angry if my son had done nothing for fifteen years'—ho, ho, ho!"

"It is not true," said the General.

The old General cleared his throat, and smiled as by compulsion.

"You know, General," said Madame, looking distressed, "it was nothing to joke about, but I had to say so, because I did not know what your son had done, nor did I wish to hear any thing against one who has the honor to call you his father."

She paused a moment to let the flattery take effect, and then proceeded:

"But then another lady said to me; she said, 'For shame, Clarisse, to laugh at good Dr. Mossy; nobody—neither General Villivicencio, neither any other, has a right to be angry against that noble, gentle, kind, brave' "—

"Brave!" said the General, with a touch of irony.

"So she said," answered Madame Délicieuse, "and I asked her, 'how brave?' 'Brave?' she said, 'why, braver than *any soldier*, in tending the small-pox, the cholera, the fevers, and all those horrible things. Me, I saw his father once run from a snake; I think *he* wouldn't fight the small-pox—my faith!' she said, 'they say that Dr. Mossy does all that and never wears a scapular!—and does it nine hundred and ninety-nine times in a thousand for nothing! *Is* that brave, Madame Délicieuse, or is it not?'—And, General—what could I say?"

Madame dropped her palms on either side of her spreading robes and waited pleadingly for an answer. There was no sound but the drumming of the General's fingers on his sword-hilt. Madame resumed:

"I said, 'I do not deny that Mossy is a noble gentleman';—I had to say that, had I not, General?"

"Certainly, Madame," said the General, "my son is a gentleman, yes."

" 'But,' I said, 'he should not make monsieur his father angry.' "

"True," said the General, eagerly.

"But that lady said: 'Monsieur his father makes himself angry,' she said. 'Do you know, Madame, why his father is angry so long?' Another lady says, 'I know!' 'For what?' said I. 'Because he refused to become a soldier; mamma told me that.' 'It cannot be!' I said."

The General flushed. Madame saw it, but relentlessly continued:

" '*Mais oui*,' said that lady. 'What!' I said, 'think you General

Villivicencio will not rather be the very man most certain to respect a son who has the courage to be his own master? Oh, what does he want with a poor fool of a son who will do only as he says? You think he will love him less for healing instead of killing? Mesdemoiselles, you do not know that noble soldier!' "

The noble soldier glowed, and bowed his acknowledgments in a dubious, half remonstrative way, as if Madame might be producing material for her next confession, as, indeed, she diligently was doing; but she went straight on once more, as a surgeon would.

"But that other lady said: 'No, Madame, no, ladies; but I am going to tell you why Monsieur the General is angry with his son.' 'Very well, why?'— 'Why? It is just—because—he is—a little man!' "

General Villivicencio stood straight up.

"Ah! *mon ami*," cried the lady, rising excitedly, "I have wounded you and made you angry, with my silly revelations. Pardon me, my friend. Those were foolish girls, and, anyhow, they admired you. They said you looked glorious—grand—at the head of the procession."

Now, all at once, the General felt the tremendous fatigues of the day; there was a wild, swimming, whirling sensation in his head that forced him to let his eyelids sink down; yet, just there, in the midst of his painful bewilderment, he realized with ecstatic complacency that the most martial-looking man in Louisiana was standing in his spurs with the hand of Louisiana's queenliest woman laid tenderly on his arm.

"I am a wretched tattler!" said she.

"Ah! no, Madame, you are my dearest friend, yes."

"Well, anyhow, I called them fools. 'Ah! innocent creatures,' I said, 'think you a man of his sense and goodness, giving his thousands to the sick and afflicted, will cease to love his only son because he is not big like a horse or quarrelsome like a dog? No, ladies, there is a great reason which none of you know.' 'Well, well,' they cried, 'tell it; he has need of a very good reason; tell it now.' 'My ladies,' I said, 'I must not'—for, General, for all the world I knew not a reason why you should be angry against your son; you know, General, you have never told me."

The beauty again laid her hand on his arm and gazed, with round-eyed simplicity, into his sombre countenance. For an instant her witchery had almost conquered.

"Nay, Madame, some day I shall tell you; I have more than one burden *here*. But let me ask you to be seated, for I have a question, also, for you, which I have longed to ask. It lies heavily upon my heart; I must ask it now. A matter of so great importance"—

Madame's little brown aunt gave a faint cough from a dim corner of the room.

" 'Tis a beautiful night," she remarked, and stepped out on the balcony.

Then the General asked his question. It was a very long question, or, maybe, repeated twice or thrice; for it was fully ten minutes before he moved out of the room, saying good-evening.

Ah! old General Villivicencio. The most martial-looking man in Louisiana! But what would the people, the people who cheered in the morning, have said, to see the fair Queen Délicieuse at the top of the stair, sweetly bowing you down into the starlight—humbled, crestfallen, rejected!

The campaign opened. The Villivicencio ticket was read in French and English with the very different sentiments already noted. In the Exchange, about the courts, among the "banks," there was lively talking concerning its intrinsic excellence and extrinsic chances. The young gentlemen who stood about the doors of the so-called "coffee-houses" talked with a frantic energy alarming to any stranger, and just when you would have expected to see them jump and bite large mouthfuls out of each other's face, they would turn and enter the door, talking on in the same furious manner, and, walking up to the bar, click their glasses to the success of the Villivicencio ticket. Sundry swarthy and wrinkled remnants of an earlier generation were still more enthusiastic. There was to be a happy renaissance; a purging out of Yankee ideas; a blessed home-coming of those good old Bourbon morals and manners which Yankee notions had expatriated. In the cheerfulness of their anticipations they even went the length of throwing their feet high in air, thus indicating how the Villivicencio ticket was going to give "doze *Américains*" the kick under the nose.

In the three or four weeks which followed, the General gathered a surfeit of adulation, notwithstanding which he was constantly and with pain imagining a confused chatter of ladies, and when he shut his eyes with annoyance, there was Madame Délicieuse standing, and saying, "I knew not a reason why you should be angry against your son," gazing in his face with hardened simplicity, and then— that last scene on the stairs wherein he seemed still to be descending, down, down.

Madame herself was keeping good her resolution.

"Now or never," she said, "a reconciliation or a quarrel."

When the General, to keep up appearances, called again, she so moved him with an account of certain kindly speeches of her own invention, which she imputed to Dr. Mossy, that he promised to call and see his son; "perhaps"; "pretty soon"; "probably."

Dr. Mossy, sitting one February morning among his specimens and books of reference, finishing a thrilling chapter on the cuticle, too absorbed to hear a door open, suddenly realized that something was in his light, and, looking up, beheld General Villivicencio standing over him. Breathing a pleased sigh, he put down his pen, and, rising on tiptoe, laid his hand upon his father's shoulder, and lifting his lips like a little wife, kissed him.

"Be seated, papa," he said, offering his own chair, and perching on the desk.

The General took it, and, clearing his throat, gazed around upon the jars and jars with their little Adams and Eves in zoölogical gardens.

"Is all going well, papa?" finally asked Dr. Mossy.

"Yes."

Then there was a long pause.

" 'Tis a beautiful day," said the son.

"Very beautiful," rejoined the father.

"I thought there would have been a rain, but it has cleared off," said the son.

"Yes," responded the father, and drummed on the desk.

"Does it appear to be turning cool?" asked the son.

"No; it does not appear to be turning cool at all," was the answer.

"H'm 'm!" said Dr. Mossy.

"Hem!" said General Villivicencio.

Dr. Mossy, not realizing his own action, stole a glance at his manuscript.

"I am interrupting you," said the General, quickly, and rose.

"No, no! pardon me; be seated; it gives me great pleasure to—I did not know what I was doing. It is the work with which I fill my leisure moments."

So the General settled down again, and father and son sat very close to each other—in a bodily sense; spiritually they were many miles apart. The General's finger-ends, softly tapping the desk, had the sound of far-away drums.

"The city—it is healthy?" asked the General.

"Did you ask me if"—said the little Doctor, starting and looking up.

"The city—it has not much sickness at present?" repeated the father.

"No, yes—not much," said Mossy, and, with utter unconsciousness, leaned down upon his elbow and supplied an omitted word to the manuscript.

The General was on his feet as if by the touch of a spring.

"I must go!"

"Ah! no, papa," said the son.

"But, yes, I must."

"But wait, papa, I had just now something to speak of"—

"Well?" said the General, standing with his hand on the door, and with rather a dark countenance.

Dr. Mossy touched his fingers to his forehead, trying to remember.

"I fear I have—ah! I rejoice to see your name before the public, dear papa, and at the head of the ticket."

The General's displeasure sank down like an eagle's feathers. He smiled thankfully, and bowed.

"My friends compelled me," he said.

"They think you will be elected?"

"They will not doubt it. But what think you, my son?"

Now the son had a conviction which it would have been madness to express, so he only said:

"They could not elect one more faithful."

The General bowed solemnly.

"Perhaps the people will think so; my friends believe they will."

"Your friends who have used your name should help you as much as they can, papa," said the Doctor. "Myself, I should like to assist you, papa, if I could."

"A-bah!" said the pleased father, incredulously.

"But, yes," said the son.

A thrill of delight filled the General's frame. *This* was like a son.

"Thank you, my son! I thank you much. Ah, Mossy, my dear boy, you make me happy!"

"But," added Mossy, realizing with a tremor how far he had gone, "I see not how it is possible."

The General's chin dropped.

"Not being a public man," continued the Doctor; "unless, indeed, my pen—you might enlist my pen."

He paused with a smile of bashful inquiry. The General stood aghast for a moment, and then caught the idea.

"Certainly! cer-tain-ly! ha, ha, ha!"—backing out of the door—"certainly! Ah! Mossy, you are right, to be sure; to make a complete world we must have swords *and* pens. Well, my son, *au revoir*; no, I cannot stay—I will return. I hasten to tell my friends that the pen of Dr. Mossy is on our side! Adieu, dear son."

Standing outside on the banquette he bowed—not to Dr. Mossy, but to the balcony of the big red-brick front—a most sunshiny smile, and departed.

The very next morning, as if fate had ordered it, the Villivicencio ticket was attacked—ambushed, as it were, from behind the *Américain* newspaper. The onslaught was—at least General Villivicencio said it was—absolutely ruffianly. Never had all the lofty courtesies and formalities of chivalric contest been so completely ignored. Poison balls—at least personal epithets—were used. The General himself was called "antiquated!" The friends who had nominated him, they were positively sneered at; dubbed "fossils," "old ladies," and their caucus termed "irresponsible"—thunder and lightning! gentlemen of honor to be termed "not responsible!" It was asserted that the nomination was made secretly, in a private house, by two or three unauthorized harum-scarums (that touched the very bone) who had with more caution than propriety withheld their names. The article was headed, "The Crayfish-eaters' Ticket." It con-

(*177*)

tinued further to say that, had not the publication of this ticket been regarded as a dull hoax, it would not have been suffered to pass for two weeks unchallenged, and that it was now high time the universal wish should be realized in its withdrawal.

Among the earliest readers of this production was the young Madame. She first enjoyed a quiet gleeful smile over it, and then called:

"Ninide, here, take this down to Dr. Mossy—stop." She marked the communication heavily with her gold pencil. "No answer; he need not return it."

About the same hour, and in a neighboring street, one of the "not responsibles" knocked on the Villivicencio castle gate. The General invited him into his bedroom. With a short and strictly profane harangue the visitor produced the offensive newspaper, and was about to begin reading, when one of those loud nasal blasts, so peculiar to the Gaul, resounded at the gate, and another "not responsible" entered, more excited, if possible, than the first. Several minutes were spent in exchanging fierce sentiments and slapping the palm of the left hand rapidly with the back of the right. Presently there was a pause for breath.

"Alphonse, proceed to read," said the General, sitting up in bed.

"De Crayfish-eaters' Ticket"—began Alphonse; but a third rapping at the gate interrupted him, and a third "irresponsible" re-enforced their number, talking loudly and wildly to the waiting-man as he came up the hall.

Finally, Alphonse read the article. Little by little the incensed gentlemen gave it a hearing, now two words and now three, interrupting it to rip out long, rasping maledictions, and wag their forefingers at each other as they strode ferociously about the apartment.

As Alphonse reached the close, and dashed the paper to the floor, the whole quartet, in terrific unison, cried for the blood of the editor.

But hereupon the General spoke with authority.

"No, messieurs," he said, buttoning his dressing-gown, savagely, "you shall not fight him. I forbid it—you shall not!"

"But," cried the three at once, "one of us must fight, and you—you cannot; if *you* fight our cause is lost! The candidate must not fight."

"Hah-h! messieurs," cried the hero, beating his breast and lifting his eyes, "*grace au ciel*. I have a son. Yes, my beloved friends, a son who shall call the villain out and make him pay for his impudence with blood, or eat his words in to-morrow morning's paper. Heaven be thanked that gave me a son for this occasion! I shall see him at once—as soon as I can dress."

"We will go with you."

"No, gentlemen, let me see my son alone. I can meet you at Maspero's in two hours. Adieu, my dear friends."

He was resolved.

"*Au revoir*," said the dear friends.

Shortly after, cane in hand, General Villivicencio moved with an ireful stride up the banquette of Rue Royale. Just as he passed the red-brick front one of the batten shutters opened the faintest bit, and a certain pair of lovely eyes looked after him, without any of that round simplicity which we have before discovered in them. As he half turned to knock at his son's door he glanced at this very shutter, but it was as tightly closed as though the house were an enchanted palace.

Dr. Mossy's door, on the contrary, swung ajar when he knocked, and the General entered.

"Well, my son, have you seen that newspaper? No, I think not. I *see* you have not, since your cheeks are not red with shame and anger."

Dr. Mossy looked up with astonishment from the desk where he sat writing.

"What is that, papa?"

"My faith! Mossy, is it possible you have not heard of the attack upon me, which has surprised and exasperated the city this morning?"

"No," said Dr. Mossy, with still greater surprise, and laying his hand on the arm of his chair.

His father put on a dying look. "My soul!" At that moment his glance fell upon the paper which had been sent in by Madame Délicieuse. "But, Mossy, my son," he screamed, "*there* it is!" striking it rapidly with one finger—"there! there! there! read it! It calls me 'not responsible!' 'not responsible' it calls me! Read! read!"

"But, papa," said the quiet little Doctor, rising, and accepting the crumpled paper thrust at him, "I have read this. If this is it, well, then, already I am preparing to respond to it."

The General seized him violently, and, spreading a suffocating kiss on his face, sealed it with an affectionate oath.

"Ah, Mossy, my boy, you are glorious! You had begun already to write! You are glorious! Read to me what you have written, my son."

The Doctor took up a bit of manuscript, and resuming his chair, began:

"MESSRS. EDITORS: On your journal of this morning"—

"Eh! how! you have not written it in English, is it, son?"

"But, yes, papa."

" 'Tis a vile tongue," said the General; "but, if it is necessary—proceed."

"MESSRS. EDITORS: On your journal of this morning is published an editorial article upon the Villivicencio ticket, which is plentiful and abundant with mistakes. Who is the author or writer of the above said editorial article your correspondent does at present ignore, but doubts not he is one who, hasty to form an opinion, will yet, however, make his assent to the correction of some errors and mistakes which"—

"Bah!" cried the General.

Dr. Mossy looked up, blushing crimson.

"Bah!" cried the General, still more forcibly. *"Bêtise!"*

"How?" asked the gentle son.

" 'Tis all nonsent!" cried the General, bursting into English. "Hall you 'ave to say is: ' *'Sieurs Editeurs!* I want you s'all give de nem of de indignan' scoundrel who meck some lies on you' paper about *mon père et ses amis!'* "

"Ah-h!" said Dr. Mossy, in a tone of derision and anger.

His father gazed at him in mute astonishment. He stood beside his disorderly little desk, his small form drawn up, a hand thrust into his breast, and that look of invincibility in his eyes such as blue eyes sometimes surprise us with.

"You want me to fight," he said.

"My faith!" gasped the General, loosening in all his joints. "I believe—you may cut me in pieces if I do not believe you were going to reason it out in the newspaper! Fight? If I want you to fight? Upon my soul, I believe you do not want to fight!"

"No," said Mossy.

"My God!" whispered the General. His heart seemed to break.

"Yes," said the steadily gazing Doctor, his lips trembling as he opened them. "Yes, your God. I am afraid"—

"Afraid!" gasped the General.

"Yes," rang out the Doctor, "afraid; afraid! God forbid that I should not be afraid. But I will tell you what I do not fear—I do not fear to call your affairs of honor—murder!"

"My son!" cried the father.

"I retract," cried the son; "consider it unsaid. I will never reproach my father."

"It is well," said the father. "I was wrong. It is my quarrel. I go to settle it myself."

Dr. Mossy moved quickly between his father and the door. General Villivicencio stood before him utterly bowed down.

"What will you?" sadly demanded the old man.

"Papa," said the son, with much tenderness, "I cannot permit you. Fifteen years we were strangers, and yesterday were friends. You must not leave me so. I will even settle this quarrel for you. You must let me. I am pledged to your service."

The peace-loving little doctor did not mean "to settle," but "to adjust." He felt in an instant that he was misunderstood; yet, as quiet people are apt to do, though not wishing to deceive, he let the misinterpretation stand. In his embarrassment he did not know with absolute certainty what he should do himself.

The father's face—he thought of but one way to settle a quarrel —began instantly to brighten. "I would myself do it," he said, apologetically, "but my friends forbid it."

"And so do I," said the Doctor, "but I will go myself now, and will not return until all is finished. Give me the paper."

"My son, I do not wish to compel you."

There was something acid in the Doctor's smile as he answered:

"No; but give me the paper, if you please."

The General handed it.

"Papa," said the son, "you must wait here for my return."

(*181*)

"But I have an appointment at Maspero's at"—

"I will call and make excuse for you," said the son.

"Well," consented the almost happy father, "go, my son; I will stay. But if some of your sick shall call?"

"Sit quiet," said the son. "They will think no one is here." And the General noticed that the dust lay so thick on the panes that a person outside would have to put his face close to the glass to see within.

In the course of half an hour the Doctor had reached the newspaper office, thrice addressed himself to the wrong person, finally found the courteous editor, and easily convinced him that his father had been imposed upon; but when Dr. Mossy went farther, and asked which one of the talented editorial staff had written the article:

"You see, Doctor," said the editor—"just step into my private office a moment."

They went in together. The next minute saw Dr. Mossy departing hurriedly from the place, while the editor complacently resumed his pen, assured that he would not return.

General Villivicencio sat and waited among the serpents and innocents. His spirits began to droop again. Revolving Mossy's words, he could not escape the fear that possibly, after all, his son might compromise the Villivicencio honor in the interests of peace. Not that he preferred to put his son's life in jeopardy; he would not object to an adjustment, provided the enemy should beg for it. But if not, whom would his son select to perform those friendly offices indispensable in polite quarrels? Some half-priest, half-woman? Some spectacled book-worm? He suffered.

The monotony of his passive task was relieved by one or two callers who had the sagacity (or bad manners) to peer through the dirty glass, and then open the door, to whom, half rising from his chair, he answered, with a polite smile, that the Doctor was out, nor could he say how long he might be absent. Still the time dragged painfully, and he began at length to wonder why Mossy did not return.

There came a rap at the glass door different from all the raps that had forerun it—a fearless, but gentle, dignified, graceful rap; and the General, before he looked round, felt in all his veins that it came from the young Madame. Yes, there was her glorious outline thrown sidewise upon the glass. He hastened and threw open the door, bending low at the same instant, and extending his hand.

She extended hers also, but not to take his. With a calm dexterity that took the General's breath, she reached between him and the door, and closed it.

"What is the matter?" anxiously asked the General—for her face, in spite of its smile, was severe.

"General," she began, ignoring his inquiry—and, with all her Creole bows, smiles, and insinuating phrases, the severity of her countenance but partially waned—"I came to see my physician—your son. Ah! General, when I find you reconciled to your son, it makes me think I am in heaven. You will let me say so? You will not be offended with the old playmate of your son?"

She gave him no time to answer.

"He is out, I think, is he not? But I am glad of it. It gives us occasion to rejoice together over his many merits. For you know, General, in all the years of your estrangement, Mossy had no friend like myself. I am proud to tell you so now; is it not so?"

The General was so taken aback that, when he had thanked her in a mechanical way, he could say nothing else. She seemed to fall for a little while into a sad meditation that embarrassed him beyond measure. But as he opened his mouth to speak, she resumed:

"Nobody knew him so well as I; though I, poor me, I could not altogether understand him; for look you, General, he was—what do you think?—*a great man!*—nothing else."

"How?" asked the General, not knowing what else to respond.

"You never dreamed of that, eh?" continued the lady. "But, of course not; nobody did but me. Some of those *Américains*, I suppose, knew it; but who would ever ask them? Here in Royal Street, in New Orleans, where we people know nothing and care nothing but for meat, drink, and pleasure, he was only Dr. Mossy, who gave pills. My faith! General, no wonder you were disappointed in your son, for you thought the same. Ah! yes, you did! But why did you not ask me, his old playmate? I knew better. I could have told you how your little son stood head and shoulders above the crowd. I could have told you some things too wonderful to believe. I could have told you that his name was known and honored in the scientific schools of Paris, of London, of Germany! Yes! I could have shown you"—she warmed as she proceeded—"I could have shown you letters (I begged them of him), written as between brother and brother, from the foremost men of science and discovery!"

She stood up, her eyes flashing with excitement.

"But why did you never tell me?" cried the General.

"He never would allow me—but you—why did you not ask me? I will tell you; you were too proud to mention your son. But he had pride to match yours—ha!—achieving all—every thing—with an assumed name! 'Let me tell your father,' I implored him; but—'let him find me out,' he said, and you never found him out. Ah! there he was fine. He would not, he said, though only for your sake, re-enter your affections as any thing more or less than just—your son. Ha!"

And so she wer' on. Twenty times the old General was astonished anew, twenty times was angry or alarmed enough to cry out, but twenty times she would not be interrupted. Once he attempted to laugh, but again her hand commanded silence.

"Behold, monsieur, all these dusty specimens, these revolting fragments. How have you blushed to know that our idle people laugh in their sleeves at these things! How have you blushed—and you his father! But why did you not ask me? I could have told you: 'Sir, your son is not an apothecary; not one of these ugly things but has helped him on in the glorious path of discovery; discovery, General—your son—known in Europe as a scientific discoverer!' Ah-h! the blind people say, 'How is that, that General Villivicencio should be dissatisfied with his son? He is a good man, and a good doctor, only a little careless, that's all.' But *you* were more blind still, for you shut your eyes tight like this; when, had you searched for his virtues as you did for his faults, you, too, might have known before it was too late what nobility, what beauty, what strength, were in the character of your poor, poor son!"

"Just Heaven! Madame, you shall not speak of my son as of one dead and buried! But, if you have some bad news"—

"Your son took your quarrel on his hands, eh?"

"I believe so—I think"—

"Well; I saw him an hour ago in search of your slanderer!"

"He must find him!" said the General, plucking up.

"But if the search is already over," slowly responded Madame.

The father looked one instant in her face, then rose with an exclamation:

"Where is my son? What has happened? Do you think I am a child, to be trifled with—a horse to be teased? Tell me of my son!"

Madame was stricken with genuine anguish.

"Take your chair," she begged; "wait; listen; take your chair."

"Never!" cried the General; "I am going to find my son—my God! Madame, you have *locked this door!* What are you, that you should treat me so? Give me, this instant"—

"Oh! Monsieur, I beseech you to take your chair, and I will tell you all. You can do nothing now. Listen! suppose you should rush out and find that your son had played the coward at last! Sit down and"—

"Ah! Madame, this is play!" cried the distracted man.

"But no; it is not play. Sit down; I want to ask you something."

He sank down and she stood over him, anguish and triumph strangely mingled in her beautiful face.

"General, tell me true; did you not force this quarrel into your son's hand? I *know* he would not choose to have it. Did you not do it to test his courage, because all these fifteen years you have made yourself a fool with the fear that he became a student only to escape being a soldier? Did you not?"

Her eyes looked him through and through.

"And if I did?" demanded he with faint defiance.

"Yes! and if he has made dreadful haste and proved his courage?" asked she.

"Well, then"—the General straightened up triumphantly—"then he is my son!"

He beat the desk.

"And heir to your wealth, for example?"

"Certainly."

The lady bowed in solemn mockery.

"It will make him a magnificent funeral!"

The father bounded up and stood speechless, trembling from head to foot. Madame looked straight in his eye.

"Your son has met the writer of that article."

"Where?" the old man's lips tried to ask.

"Suddenly, unexpectedly, in a passage-way."

"My God! and the villain"—

"Lives!" cried Madame.

He rushed to the door, forgetting that it was locked.

"Give me that key!" he cried, wrenched at the knob, turned away bewildered, turned again toward it, and again away; and at every step and turn he cried, "Oh! my son, my son! I have killed my son! Oh! Mossy, my son, my little boy! Oh! my son, my son!"

Madame buried her face in her hands and sobbed aloud. Then the father hushed his cries and stood for a moment before her.

"Give me the key, Clarisse, let me go."

She rose and laid her face on his shoulder.

"What is it, Clarisse?" asked he.

"Your son and I were ten years betrothed."

"Oh, my child!"

"Because, being disinherited, he would not be my husband."

"Alas! would to God I had known it! Oh! Mossy, my son."

"Oh! monsieur," cried the lady, clasping her hands, "forgive me —mourn no more—your son is unharmed! *I* wrote the article—I am your recanting slanderer! Your son is hunting for me now. I told my aunt to misdirect him. I slipped by him unseen in the carriage-way."

The wild old General, having already staggered back and rushed forward again, would have seized her in his arms, had not the little Doctor himself at that instant violently rattled the door and shook his finger at them playfully as he peered through the glass.

"Behold!" said Madame, attempting a smile: "open to your son; here is the key."

She sank into a chair.

Father and son leaped into each other's arms; then turned to Madame:

"Ah! thou lovely mischief-maker"—

She had fainted away.

"Ah! well, keep out of the way, if you please, papa," said Dr. Mossy, as Madame presently reopened her eyes; "no wonder you fainted; you have finished some hard work—see; here; so; Clarisse, dear, take this."

Father and son stood side by side, tenderly regarding her as she revived.

"Now, papa, you may kiss her; she is quite herself again, already."

"My daughter!" said the stately General; "this—is my son's ransom; and, with this—I withdraw the Villivicencio ticket."

"You shall not," exclaimed the laughing lady, throwing her arms about his neck.

"But, yes!" he insisted; "my faith! you will at least allow me to remove my dead from the field."

"But, certainly," said the son; "see, Clarisse, here is Madame, your aunt, asking us all into the house. Let us go."

The group passed out into the Rue Royale, Dr. Mossy shutting the door behind them. The sky was blue, the air was soft and balmy, and on the sweet south breeze, to which the old General bared his grateful brow, floated a ravishing odor of—

"Ah! what is it?" the veteran asked of the younger pair, seeing the little aunt glance at them with a playful smile.

Madame Délicieuse, for almost the first time in her life, and Dr. Mossy for the thousandth—blushed.

It was the odor of orange-blossoms.

CAFÉ DES EXILÉS

THAT which in 1835—I think he said thirty-five—was a reality in the Rue Burgundy—I think he said Burgundy—is now but a reminiscence. Yet so vividly was its story told me, that at this moment the old Café des Exilés appears before my eye, floating in the clouds of reverie, and I doubt not I see it just as it was in the old times.

An antiquated story-and-a-half Creole cottage sitting right down on the banquette, as do the Choctaw squaws who sell bay and sassafras and life-everlasting, with a high, close board-fence shutting out of view the diminutive garden on the southern side. An ancient willow droops over the roof of round tiles, and partly hides the discolored stucco, which keeps dropping off into the garden as though the old café was stripping for the plunge into oblivion—disrobing for its execution. I see, well up in the angle of the broad side gable, shaded by its rude awning of clapboards, as the eyes of an old dame are shaded by her wrinkled hand, the window of Pauline. Oh for the image of the maiden, were it but for one moment, leaning out of the casement to hang her mocking-bird and looking down into the garden—where, above the barrier of old boards, I see the top of the fig-tree, the pale green clump of bananas, the tall palmetto with its jagged crown, Pauline's own two orange-trees holding up their hands toward the window, heavy with the promises of

(*188*)

autumn; the broad, crimson mass of the many-stemmed oleander, and the crisp boughs of the pomegranate loaded with freckled apples, and with here and there a lingering scarlet blossom.

The Café des Exilés, to use a figure, flowered, bore fruit, and dropped it long ago—or rather Time and Fate, like some uncursed Adam and Eve, came side by side and cut away its clusters, as we sever the golden burden of the banana from its stem; then, like a banana which has borne its fruit, it was razed to the ground and made way for a newer, brighter growth. I believe it would set every tooth on edge should I go by there now—now that I have heard the story—and see the old site covered by the "Shoofly Coffee-house." Pleasanter far to close my eyes and call to view the unpretentious portals of the old café, with her children—for such those exiles seem to me—dragging their rocking-chairs out, and sitting in their wonted group under the long, out-reaching eaves which shaded the banquette of the Rue Burgundy.

It was in 1835 that the Café des Exilés was, as one might say, in full blossom. Old M. D'Hemecourt, father of Pauline and host of the café, himself a refugee from San Domingo, was the cause—at least the human cause—of its opening. As its white-curtained, glazed doors expanded, emitting a little puff of his own cigarette smoke, it was like the bursting of catalpa blossoms, and the exiles came like bees, pushing into the tiny room to sip its rich variety of tropical sirups, its lemonades, its orangeades, its orgeats, its barley-waters, and its outlandish wines, while they talked of dear home—that is to say, of Barbadoes, of Martinique, of San Domingo, and of Cuba.

There were Pedro and Benigno, and Fernandez and Francisco, and Benito. Benito was a tall, swarthy man, with immense gray moustachios, and hair as harsh as tropical grass and gray as ashes. When he could spare his cigarette from his lips, he would tell you in a cavernous voice, and with a wrinkled smile, that he was "a-t-thorty-seveng."

There was Martinez of San Domingo, yellow as a canary, always sitting with one leg curled under him, and holding the back of his head in his knitted fingers against the back of his rocking-chair. Father, mother, brother, sisters, all, had been massacred in the struggle of '21 and '22; he alone was left to tell the tale, and told it often, with that strange, infantile insensibility to the solemnity of his bereavement so peculiar to Latin people.

But, besides these, and many who need no mention, there were two in particular, around whom all the story of the Café des Exilés, of old M. D'Hemecourt and of Pauline, turns as on a double centre. First, Manuel Mazaro, whose small, restless eyes were as black and bright as those of a mouse, whose light talk became his dark girlish face, and whose redundant locks curled so prettily and so wonderfully black under the fine white brim of his jaunty Panama. He had the hands of a woman, save that the nails were stained with the smoke of cigarettes. He could play the guitar delightfully, and wore his knife down behind his coat-collar.

The second was "Major" Galahad Shaughnessy. I imagine I can see him, in his white duck, brass-buttoned roundabout, with his sabreless belt peeping out beneath, all his boyishness in his sea-blue eyes, leaning lightly against the door-post of the Café des Exilés as a child leans against his mother, running his fingers over a basketful of fragrant limes, and watching his chance to strike some solemn Creole under the fifth rib with a good old Irish joke.

Old D'Hemecourt drew him close to his bosom. The Spanish Creoles were, as the old man termed it, both cold and hot, but never warm. Major Shaughnessy was warm, and it was no uncommon thing to find those two apart from the others, talking in an undertone, and playing at *confidantes* like two school-girls. The kind old man was at this time drifting close up to his sixtieth year. There was much he could tell of San Domingo, whither he had been carried from Martinique in his childhood, whence he had become a refugee to Cuba, and thence to New Orleans in the flight of 1809.

It fell one day to Manuel Mazaro's lot to discover, by sauntering within earshot, that to Galahad Shaughnessy only, of all the children of the Café des Exilés, the good host spoke long and confidentially concerning his daughter. The words, half heard and magnified like objects seen in a fog, meaning Manuel Mazaro knew not what, but made portentous by his suspicious nature, were but the old man's recital of the grinding he had got between the millstones of his poverty and his pride, in trying so long to sustain, for little Pauline's sake, that attitude before society which earns respect from a surface-viewing world. It was while he was telling this that Manuel Mazaro drew near; the old man paused in an embarrassed way; the Major, sitting sidewise in his chair, lifted his cheek from its resting-place on his elbow; and Mazaro, after standing an awkward moment, turned away with such an inward feeling as one may guess would arise in a heart full of Cuban blood, not unmixed with Indian.

As he moved off, M. D'Hemecourt resumed: that in a last extremity he had opened, partly from dire want, partly for very love to homeless souls, the Café des Exilés. He had hoped that, as strong drink and high words were to be alike unknown to it, it might not prejudice sensible people; but it had. He had no doubt they said among themselves, "She is an excellent and beautiful girl and deserving all respect"; and respect they accorded, but their *respects* they never came to pay.

"A café is a café," said the old gentleman. "It is nod possib' to ezcapc him, aldough de Café des Exilés is differen' from de rez."

"It's different from the Café des Réfugiés," suggested the Irishman.

"Differen' as possib'," replied M. D'Hemecourt. He looked about upon the walls. The shelves were luscious with ranks of cooling sirups which he alone knew how to make. The expression of his face changed from sadness to a gentle pride, which spoke without words, saying—and let our story pause a moment to hear it say:

"If any poor exile, from any island where guavas or mangoes or plantains grow, wants a draught which will make him see his home among the coco-palms, behold the Café des Exilés ready to take the poor child up and give him the breast! And if gold or silver he has them not, why Heaven and Santa Maria, and Saint Christopher bless him! It makes no difference. Here is a rocking-chair, here a cigarette, and here a light from the host's own tinder. He will pay when he can."

As this easily pardoned pride said, so it often occurred; and if the newly come exile said his father was a Spaniard—"Come!" old M. D'Hemecourt would cry; "another glass; it is an innocent drink; my mother was a Castilian." But, if the exile said his mother was a Frenchwoman, the glasses would be forthcoming all the same, for "My father," the old man would say, "was a Frenchman of Martinique, with blood as pure as that wine and a heart as sweet as this

(*191*)

honey; come, a glass of orgeat"; and he would bring it himself in a quart tumbler.

Now, there are jealousies and jealousies. There are people who rise up quickly and kill, and there are others who turn their hot thoughts over silently in their minds as a brooding bird turns her eggs in the nest. Thus did Manuel Mazaro, and took it ill that Galahad should see a vision in the temple while he and all the brethren tarried without. Pauline had been to the Café des Exilés in some degree what the image of the Virgin was to their churches at home; and for her father to whisper her name to one and not to another was, it seemed to Mazaro, as if the old man, were he a sacristan, should say to some single worshipper, "Here, you may have this madonna; I make it a present to you." Or, if such was not the handsome young Cuban's feeling, such, at least, was the disguise his jealousy put on. If Pauline was to be handed down from her niche, why, then, farewell Café des Exilés. She was its preserving influence, she made the place holy; she was the burning candles on the altar. Surely the reader will pardon the pen that lingers in the mention of her.

And yet I know not how to describe the forbearing, unspoken tenderness with which all these exiles regarded the maiden. In the balmy afternoons, as I have said, they gathered about their mother's knee, that is to say, upon the banquette outside the door. There, lolling back in their rocking-chairs, they would pass the evening hours with oft-repeated tales of home; and the moon would come out and glide among the clouds like a silver barge among islands wrapped in mist, and they loved the silently gliding orb with a sort of worship, because from her soaring height she looked down at the same moment upon them and upon their homes in the far Antilles. It was somewhat thus that they looked upon Pauline as she seemed to them held up halfway to heaven, they knew not how. Ah! those who have been pilgrims; who have wandered out beyond harbor and light; whom fate hath led in lonely paths strewn with thorns and briers not of their own sowing; who, homeless in a land of homes, see windows gleaming and doors ajar, but not for them—it is they who well understand what the worship is that cries to any daughter of our dear mother Eve whose footsteps chance may draw across the path, the silent, beseeching cry, "Stay a little instant that I may look upon you. Oh, woman, beautifier of the earth! Stay till I recall the face of my sister; stay yet a moment while I look from afar, with helpless-hanging hands, upon the softness of thy cheek, upon the folded coils of thy shining hair; and my spirit shall fall down and say those prayers which I may never again—God knoweth—say at home."

She was seldom seen; but sometimes, when the lounging exiles would be sitting in their afternoon circle under the eaves, and some old man would tell his tale of fire and blood and capture and escape, and the heads would lean forward from the chair-backs and a great stillness would follow the ending of the story, old M. D'Hemecourt would all at once speak up and say, laying his hands upon the narrator's knee, "Comrade, your throat is dry, here are fresh limes; let my dear child herself come and mix you a lemonade." Then the neighbors over the way, sitting about their doors, would by and by softly say, "See, see! there is Pauline!" and all the exiles would rise from their rocking-chairs, take off their hats and stand as men stand in church, while Pauline came out like the moon from a cloud, descended the three steps of the café door, and stood with waiter and glass, a new Rebecca with her pitcher, before the swarthy wanderer.

What tales that would have been tear-compelling, nay, heart-rending, had they not been palpable inventions, the pretty, woman-ish Mazaro from time to time poured forth, in the ever ungratified hope that the goddess might come down with a draught of nectar for him, it profiteth not to recount; but I should fail to show a family feature of the Café des Exilés did I omit to say that these make-believe adventures were heard with every mark of respect and credence; while, on the other hand, they were never attempted in the presence of the Irishman. He would have moved an eyebrow, or made some barely audible sound, or dropped some seemingly innocent word, and the whole company, spite of themselves, would have smiled. Wherefore, it may be doubted whether at any time the curly-haired young Cuban had that playful affection for his Celtic comrade, which a habit of giving little velvet taps to Galahad's cheek made a show of.

Such was the Café des Exilés, such its inmates, such its guests, when certain apparently trivial events began to fall around it as germs of blight fall upon corn, and to bring about that end which cometh to all things.

The little seed of jealousy, dropped into the heart of Manuel Mazaro, we have already taken into account.

Galahad Shaughnessy began to be specially active in organizing a society of Spanish Americans, the design of which, as set forth in its manuscript constitution, was to provide proper funeral honors to such of their membership as might be overtaken by death; and, whenever it was practicable, to send their ashes to their native land. Next to Galahad in this movement was an elegant old Mexican physician, Dr. ——— (his name escapes me), whom the Café des Exilés sometimes took upon her lap—that is to say door-step—but whose favorite resort was the old Café des Réfugiés in the Rue Royale (Royal Street, as it was beginning to be called). Manuel Mazaro was made secretary.

It was for some reason thought judicious for the society to hold its meetings in various places, now here, now there; but the most frequent rendezvous was the Café des Exilés; it was quiet; those Spanish Creoles, however they may afterward cackle, like to lay their plans noiselessly, like a hen in a barn. There was a very general confidence in this old institution, a kind of inward assurance that "mother wouldn't tell"; though, after all, what great secrets could there be connected with a mere burial society?

Before the hour of meeting, the Café des Exilés always sent away her children and closed her door. Presently they would commence returning, one by one, as a flock of wild fowl will do, that has been startled up from its accustomed haunt. Frequenters of the Café des Réfugiés also would appear. A small gate in the close garden-fence let them into a room behind the café proper, and by and by the apartment would be full of dark-visaged men conversing in the low, courteous tone common to their race. The shutters of doors and windows were closed and the chinks stopped with cotton; some people are so jealous of observation.

On a certain night after one of these meetings had dispersed in its peculiar way, the members retiring two by two at intervals, Manuel Mazaro and M. D'Hemecourt were left alone, sitting close together in the dimly lighted room, the former speaking, the other, with no pleasant countenance, attending. It seemed to the young Cuban a proper precaution—he was made of precautions—to speak in English. His voice was barely audible.

"——sayce to me, 'Manuel, she t-theeng I want-n to marry hore.' Señor, you shouth 'ave see' him laugh!"

M. D'Hemecourt lifted up his head, and laid his hand upon the young man's arm.

"Manuel Mazaro," he began, "iv dad w'ad you say is nod"—

The Cuban interrupted.

"If is no' t-thrue you will keel Manuel Mazaro?—a' r-r-right-a!"

"No," said the tender old man, "no, bud h-I am positeef dad de Madjor will shood you."

Mazaro nodded, and lifted one finger for attention.

"—— sayce to me, 'Manuel, you goin' tell-a Señor D'Hemecourt, I fin'-a you some nigh' an' cut-a you' heart ou'.' An' I sayce to heem-a, 'Boat-a if Señor D'Hemecourt he fin'-in' ou' frone Pauline' "—

"*Silence!*" fiercely cried the old man. "My God! 'Sieur Mazaro, neider you, neider somebody helse s'all h'use de nem of me daughter. It is nod possib' dad you s'all spick him! I cannot pearmid thad."

While the old man was speaking these vehement words, the Cuban was emphatically nodding approval.

"Co-rect-a, co-rect-a, señor," he replied. "Señor, you' r-r-right-a; escuse-a me, señor, escuse-a me. Señor D'Hemecourt, Mayor Shaughness', when he talkin' wi' me he usin' hore-a name o the t-thime-a!"

"My fren'," said M. D'Hemecourt, rising and speaking with labored control, "I muz tell you good-nighd. You 'ave sooprise me a verry gred deal. I s'all *in*vestigade doze ting; an', Manuel Mazaro, h-I am a hole man; bud I will requez you, iv dad wad you say is nod de true, my God! not to h-ever ritturn again ad de Café des Exilés."

Mazaro smiled and nodded. His host opened the door into the garden, and, as the young man stepped out, noticed even then how handsome was his face and figure, and how the odor of the night-jasmine was filling the air with an almost insupportable sweetness. The Cuban paused a moment, as if to speak, but checked himself, lifted his girlish face, and looked up to where the daggers of the palmetto-tree were crossed upon the face of the moon, dropped his glance, touched his Panama, and silently followed by the bare-headed old man, drew open the little garden-gate, looked cautiously out, said good-night, and stepped into the street.

As M. D'Hemecourt returned to the door through which he had come, he uttered an ejaculation of astonishment. Pauline stood before him. She spoke hurriedly in French.

"Papa, papa, it is not true."

"No, my child," he responded, "I am sure it is not true; I am sure it is all false; but why do I find you out of bed so late, little bird? The night is nearly gone."

He laid his hand upon her cheek.

"Ah, papa, I cannot deceive you. I thought Manuel would tell you something of this kind, and I listened."

The father's face immediately betrayed a new and deeper distress.

"Pauline, my child," he said with tremulous voice, "if Manuel's story is all false, in the name of Heaven how could you think he was going to tell it?"

He unconsciously clasped his hands. The good child had one trait which she could not have inherited from her father; she was quick-witted and discerning; yet now she stood confounded.

"Speak, my child," cried the alarmed old man; "speak! let me live, and not die."

"Oh, papa," she cried, "I do not know!"

The old man groaned.

"Papa, papa," she cried again, "I felt it; I know not how; something told me."

"Alas!" exclaimed the old man, "if it was your conscience!"

"No, no, no, papa," cried Pauline, "but I was afraid of Manuel Mazaro, and I think he hates him—and I think he will hurt him in any way he can—and I *know* he will even try to kill him. Oh! my God!"

She struck her hands together above her head, and burst into a flood of tears. Her father looked upon her with such sad sternness as his tender nature was capable of. He laid hold of one of her arms to draw a hand from the face whither both hands had gone.

"You know something else," he said; "you know that the Major loves you, or you think so: is it not true?"

She dropped both hands, and, lifting her streaming eyes that had nothing to hide straight to his, suddenly said:

"I would give worlds to think so!" and sunk upon the floor.

He was melted and convinced in one instant.

"Oh, my child, my child," he cried, trying to lift her. "Oh, my poor little Pauline, your papa is not angry. Rise, my little one; so; kiss me; Heaven bless thee. Pauline, treasure, what shall I do with thee? Where shall I hide thee?"

"You have my counsel already, papa."

"Yes, my child, and you were right. The Café des Exilés never should have been opened. It is no place for you; no place at all."

"Let us leave it," said Pauline.

"Ah! Pauline, I would close it to-morrow if I could, but now it is too late; I cannot."

"Why?" asked Pauline pleadingly.

She had cast an arm about his neck. Her tears sparkled with a smile.

"My daughter, I cannot tell you; you must go now to bed; good-night—or good-morning; God keep you!"

"Well, then, papa," she said, "have no fear; you need not hide me; I have my prayer-book, and my altar, and my garden, and my window; my garden is my fenced city, and my window my watch-tower; do you see?"

"Ah! Pauline," responded the father, "but I have been letting the enemy in and out at pleasure."

"Good-night," she answered, and kissed him three times on either cheek; "the blessed Virgin will take care of us; good-night; *he* never said those things; not he; good-night."

The next evening Galahad Shaughnessy and Manuel Mazaro met at that "very different" place, the Café des Réfugiés. There was much free talk going on about Texan annexation, about chances of war with Mexico, about San Domingan affairs, about Cuba and many et-ceteras. Galahad was in his usual gay mood. He strode about among a mixed company of *Louisianais*, Cubans, and *Améri-cains*, keeping them in a great laugh with his account of one of Ole Bull's concerts, and how he had there extorted an invitation from M. and Mme. Devoti to attend one of their famous children's fancy dress balls.

"Halloo!" said he as Mazaro approached, "heer's the etheerial Angelica herself. Look-ut heer, sissy, why ar'n't ye in the maternal arms of the Café des Exilés?"

Mazaro smiled amiably and sat down. A moment after, the Irishman, stepping away from his companions, stood before the young Cuban, and asked, with a quiet business air:

"D'ye want to see me, Mazaro?"

The Cuban nodded, and they went aside. Mazaro, in a few quick words, looking at his pretty foot the while, told the other on no account to go near the Café des Exilés, as there were two men hanging about there, evidently watching for him, and—

"Wut's the use o' that?" asked Galahad; "I say, wut's the use o' that?"

Major Shaughnessy's habit of repeating part of his words arose from another, of interrupting any person who might be speaking.

"They must know—I say they must know that whenever I'm nowhurs else I'm heer. What do they want?"

Mazaro made a gesture, signifying caution and secrecy, and smiled, as if to say, "You ought to know."

"Aha!" said the Irishman softly. "Why don't they come here?"

"Z-afrai'," said Mazaro; "d'they frai' to do an'teen een d-these-a crowth."

"That's so," said the Irishman; "I say, that's so. If I don't feel very much like go-un, I'll not go; I say, I'll not go. We've no business to-night, eh, Mazaro?"

"No, señor."

A second evening was much the same, Mazaro repeating his warning. But when, on the third evening, the Irishman again repeated his willingness to stay away from the Café des Exilés unless he should feel strongly impelled to go, it was with the mental reservation that he did feel very much in that humor, and, unknown to Mazaro, should thither repair, if only to see whether some of those deep old fellows were not contriving a practical joke.

"Mazaro," said he, "I'm go-un around the caurnur a bit; I want ye to wait heer till I come back. I say I want ye to wait heer till I come back; I'll be gone about three-quarters of an hour."

Mazaro assented. He saw with satisfaction the Irishman start in a direction opposite that in which lay the Café des Exilés, tarried fifteen or twenty minutes, and then, thinking he could step around to the Café des Exilés and return before the expiration of the allotted time, hurried out.

Meanwhile that peaceful habitation sat in the moonlight with her children about her feet. The company outside the door was somewhat thinner than common. M. D'Hemecourt was not among them, but was sitting in the room behind the café. The long table which the burial society used at their meetings extended across the apartment, and a lamp had been placed upon it. M. D'Hemecourt sat by the lamp. Opposite him was a chair, which seemed awaiting an expected occupant. Beside the old man sat Pauline. They were talking in cautious undertones, and in French.

"No," she seemed to insist; "we do not know that he refuses to come. We only know that Manuel says so."

The father shook his head sadly. "When has he ever stayed away three nights together before?" he asked. "No, my child; it is intentional. Manuel urges him to come, but he only sends poor excuses."

"But," said the girl, shading her face from the lamp and speaking with some suddenness, "why have you not sent word to him by some other person?"

M. D'Hemecourt looked up at his daughter a moment, and then smiled at his own simplicity.

"Ah!" he said. "Certainly; and that is what I will—run away, Pauline. There is Manuel, now, ahead of time!"

A step was heard inside the café. The maiden, though she knew the step was not Mazaro's, rose hastily, opened the nearest door, and disappeared. She had barely closed it behind her when Galahad Shaughnessy entered the apartment.

M'Hemecourt rose up, both surprised and confused.

"Good-evening, Munsher D'Himecourt," said the Irishman. "Munsher D'Himecourt, I know it's against rules—I say, I know it's against rules to come in here, but"—smiling—"I want to have a private wurd with ye. I say, I want to have a private wurd with ye."

In the closet of bottles the maiden smiled triumphantly. She also wiped the dew from her forehead, for the place was very close and warm.

With her father was no triumph. In him sadness and doubt were so mingled with anger that he dared not lift his eyes, but gazed at the knot in the wood of the table, which looked like a caterpillar curled up. Mazaro, he concluded, had really asked the Major to come.

"Mazaro tol' you?" he asked.

"Yes," answered the Irishman. "Mazaro told me I was watched, and asked"—

"Madjor," unluckily interrupted the old man, suddenly looking up and speaking with subdued fervor, "for w'y—iv Mazaro tol' you —for w'y you din come more sooner? Dad is one 'eavy charge again' you."

"Didn't Mazaro tell ye why I didn't come?" asked the other, beginning to be puzzled at his host's meaning.

"Yez," replied M. D'Hemecourt, "bud one brev zhenteman should not be afraid of"—

The young man stopped him with a quiet laugh. "Munsher D'Himecourt," said he, "I'm nor afraid of any two men living—I say I'm nor afraid of any two men living, and certainly not of the two that's bean a-watchin' me lately, if they're the two I think they are."

M. D'Hemecourt flushed in a way quite incomprehensible to the speaker, who nevertheless continued:

"It was the charges," he said, with some slyness in his smile. "They *are* heavy, as ye say, and that's the very reason—I say that's the very reason why I stayed away, ye see, eh? I say that's the very reason I stayed away."

Then, indeed, there was a dew for the maiden to wipe from her brow, unconscious that every word that was being said bore a different significance in the mind of each of the three. The old man was agitated.

"Bud, sir," he began, shaking his head and lifting his hand.

"Bless yer soul, Munsher D'Himecourt," interrupted the Irishman. "Wut's the use o' grapplin' two cut-throats, when"—

"Madjor Shaughnessy!" cried M. D'Hemecourt, losing all self-control. "H-I am nod a cud-troad, Madjor Shaughnessy, h-an I 'ave a r-r-righd to wadge you."

The Major rose from his chair.

"What d'ye mean?" he asked vacantly, and then: "Look-ut here, Munsher D'Himecourt, one of uz is crazy. I say one"—

"No, sar-r-r!" cried the other, rising and clenching his trembling fist. "H-I am nod crezzy. I 'ave de righd to wadge dad man wad mague rimark aboud me dotter."

"I never did no such a thing."

"You did."

"I never did no such a thing."

"Bud you 'ave jus hacknowledge'—"

"I never did no such a *thing*, I tell ye, and the man that's told ye so is a liur."

"Ah-h-h-h!" said the old man, wagging his finger. "Ah-h-h-h! You call Manuel Mazaro one liar?"

The Irishman laughed out.

"Well, I should say so!"

He motioned the old man into his chair, and both sat down again.

"Why, Munsher D'Himecourt, Mazaro's been keepin' me away from heer with a yarn about two Spaniards watchin' for me. That's what I came in to ask ye about. My dear sur, do ye s'pose I wud talk about the goddess—I mean, yer daughter—to the likes o' Mazaro— I say to the likes o' Mazaro?"

To say the old man was at sea would be too feeble an expression— he was in the trough of the sea, with a hurricane of doubts and fears whirling around him. Somebody had told a lie, and he, having struck upon its sunken surface, was dazed and stunned. He opened his lips to say he knew not what, when his ear caught the voice of Manuel Mazaro, replying to the greeting of some of his comrades outside the front door.

"He is comin'!" cried the old man. "Mague you'sev hide, Madjor; do not led 'im kedge you, *mon Dieu!*"

The Irishman smiled.

"The little yellow wretch!" said he quietly, his blue eyes dancing. "I'm goin' to catch *him*."

A certain hidden hearer instantly made up her mind to rush out between the two young men and be a heroine.

"*Non, non!*" exclaimed M. D'Hemecourt excitedly. "Nod in de Café des Exilés—nod now, Madjor. Go in dad door, hif you pliz,

Madjor. You will heer 'im w'at he 'ave to say. Mague you'sev de troub'. Nod dad door—diz one."

The Major laughed again and started toward the door indicated, but in an instant stopped.

"I can't go in theyre," he said. "That's yer daughter's room."

"*Oui, oui, mais!*" cried the other softly, but Mazaro's step was near.

"I'll just slip in heer," and the amused Shaughnessy tripped lightly to the closet door, drew it open in spite of a momentary resistance from within which he had no time to notice, stepped into a small recess full of shelves and bottles, shut the door, and stood

face to face—the broad moonlight shining upon her through a small, high-grated opening on one side—with Pauline. At the same instant the voice of the young Cuban sounded in the room.

Pauline was in a great tremor. She made as if she would have opened the door and fled, but the Irishman gave a gesture of earnest protest and reassurance. The reopened door might make the back parlor of the Café des Exilés a scene of blood. Thinking of this, what could she do? She stayed.

"You goth a heap-a thro-vle, señor," said Manuel Mazaro, taking the seat so lately vacated. He had patted M. D'Hemecourt tenderly on the back and the old gentleman had flinched; hence the remark, to which there was no reply.

"Was a bee crowth a' the *Café the Réfugiés,*" continued the young man.

"Bud, w'ere dad Madjor Shaughnessy?" demanded M. D'Hemecourt, with the little sternness he could command.

"Mayor Shaughness'—yez-a; was there; boat-a," with a disparaging smile and shake of the head, "*he* woon-a come-a to you, señor, oh! no."

The old man smiled bitterly.

"*Non?*" he asked.

"Oh, no, señor!" Mazaro drew his chair closer. "Señor"; he paused—"eez a-vary bath-a fore-a you' thaughter, eh?"

"W'at?" asked the host, snapping like a tormented dog.

"D-theze talkin' 'bou'," answered the young man; "d-theze coffee-howces noth a goo' plaze-a fore hore, eh?"

The Irishman and the maiden looked into each other's eyes an instant, as people will do when listening; but Pauline's immediately fell, and when Mazaro's words were understood, her blushes became visible even by moonlight.

"He's r-right!" emphatically whispered Galahad.

She attempted to draw back a step, but found herself against the shelves. M. D'Hemecourt had not answered. Mazaro spoke again.

"Boat-a you canno' help-a, eh? I know, 'out-a she gettin' marry, eh?"

Pauline trembled. Her father summoned all his force and rose as if to ask his questioner to leave him; but the handsome Cuban motioned him down with a gesture that seemed to beg for only a moment more.

"Señor, if a-was one man whath lo-va you' thaughter, all is possiblee to lo-va."

Pauline, nervously braiding some bits of wire which she had unconsciously taken from a shelf, glanced up—against her will—into the eyes of Galahad. They were looking so steadily down upon her that with a great leap of the heart for joy she closed her own and half turned away. But Mazaro had not ceased.

"All is possiblee to lo-va, señor, you shouth-a let marry hore an' tak'n 'way frone d'these plaze, señor."

"Manuel Mazaro," said M. D'Hemecourt, again rising, "you 'ave say enough."

"No, no, señor; no, no; I want tell-a you—*is* a-one man—*whath lo-va* you' thaughter; an' I *knowce* him!"

Was there no cause for quarrel, after all? Could it be that Mazaro was about to speak for Galahad? The old man asked in his simplicity:

"Madjor Shaughnessy?"

Mazaro smiled mockingly.

"Mayor Shaughness'," he said; "oh, no; not Mayor Shaughness'!"

Pauline could stay no longer; escape she must, though it be in Manuel Mazaro's very face. Turning again and looking up into Galahad's face in a great fright, she opened her lips to speak, but—

"Mayor Shaughness'," continued the Cuban; "*he* nev'r-a lo-va you' thaughter."

Galahad was putting the maiden back from the door with his hand.

"Pauline," he said, "it's a lie!"

"An', señor," pursued the Cuban, "if a was possiblee you' thaughter to lo-va heem, a-wouth-a be worse-a kine in worlt; but, señor, *I*"—

M. D'Hemecourt made a majestic sign for silence. He had resumed his chair, but he rose up once more, took the Cuban's hat from the table and tendered it to him.

"Manuel Mazaro, you 'ave"—

"Señor, I goin' tell you"—

"Manuel Mazaro, you"—

"Boat-a, señor"—

"Bud, Manuel Maz"—

"Señor, escuse-a me"—

"Huzh!" cried the old man. "Manuel Mazaro, you 'ave desceive' me! You 'ave *mocque* me, Manu"—

"Señor," cried Mazaro, "I swear-a to you that all-a what I sayin' ees-a"—

He stopped aghast. Galahad and Pauline stood before him.

"Is what?" asked the blue-eyed man, with a look of quiet delight on his face, such as Mazaro instantly remembered to have seen on it one night when Galahad was being shot at in the Sucking Calf Restaurant in St. Peter Street.

The table was between them, but Mazaro's hand went upward toward the back of his coat-collar.

"Ah, ah!" cried the Irishman, shaking his head with a broader smile and thrusting his hand threateningly into his breast; "don't ye do that! just finish yer speech."

"Was-a notthin'," said the Cuban, trying to smile back.

"Yer a liur," said Galahad.

"No," said Mazaro, still endeavoring to smile through his agony; "z-was on'y tellin' Señor D'Hemecourt someteen z-was t-thrue."

"And I tell ye," said Galahad, "ye'r a liur, and to be so kind an' get yersel' to the front stoop, as I'm desiruz o' kickin' ye before the crowd."

"Madjor!" cried D'Hemecourt—

"Go," said Galahad, advancing a step toward the Cuban.

Had Manuel Mazaro wished to personate the prince of darkness, his beautiful face had the correct expression for it. He slowly turned, opened the door into the café, sent one glowering look behind, and disappeared.

Pauline laid her hand upon her lover's arm.

"Madjor," began her father.

"Oh, Madjor and Madjor," said the Irishman; "Munsher D'Himecourt, just say 'Madjor, heer's a gude wife fur ye,' and I'll let the little serpent go."

Thereupon, sure enough, both M. D'Hemecourt and his daughter, rushing together, did what I have been hoping all along, for the reader's sake, they would have dispensed with; they burst into tears; whereupon the Major, with his Irish appreciation of the ludicrous, turned away to hide his smirk and began good-humoredly to scratch himself first on the temple and then on the thigh.

Mazaro passed silently through the group about the door-steps, and not many minutes afterward, Galahad Shaughnessy, having taken a place among the exiles, rose with the remark that the old gentleman would doubtless be willing to tell them good-night. Good-night was accordingly said, the Café des Exilés closed her windows, then her doors, winked a moment or two through the cracks in the shutters and then went fast asleep.

The Mexican physician, at Galahad's request, told Mazaro that at the next meeting of the burial society he might and must occupy his accustomed seat without fear of molestation; and he did so.

The meeting took place some seven days after the affair in the back parlor, and on the same ground. Business being finished, Galahad, who presided, stood up, looking, in his white duck suit among his darkly clad companions, like a white sheep among black ones, and begged leave to order "dlasses" from the front room. I say among black sheep; yet, I suppose, than that double row of languid, effeminate faces, one would have been taxed to find a more harmless-looking company. The glasses were brought and filled.

"Gentlemen," said Galahad, "comrades, this may be the last time we ever meet together an unbroken body."

Martinez of San Domingo, he of the horrible experience, nodded with a lurking smile, curled a leg under him and clasped his fingers behind his head.

"Who knows," continued the speaker, "but Señor Benito, though strong and sound and har'ly thirty-seven"—here all smiled—"may be taken ill to-morrow?"

Martinez smiled across to the tall, gray Benito on Galahad's left, and he, in turn, smilingly showed to the company a thin, white line of teeth between his moustachios like distant reefs.

"Who knows," the young Irishman proceeded to inquire, "I say, who knows but Pedro, theyre, may be struck wid a fever?"

Pedro, a short, compact man of thoroughly mixed blood, and with an eyebrow cut away, whose surname no one knew, smiled his acknowledgments.

"Who knows?" resumed Galahad, when those who understood English had explained in Spanish to those who did not, "but they may soon need the services not only of our good doctor heer, but of our society; and that Fernandez and Benigno, and Gonzales and Dominguez, may not be chosen to see, on that very schooner lying at the Picayune Tier just now, their beloved remains and so forth safely delivered into the hands and lands of their people. I say, who knows bur it may be so!"

The company bowed graciously as who should say, "Well-turned phrases, señor—well-turned."

"And *amigos*, if so be that such is their approoching fate, I will say"— He lifted his glass, and the rest did the same.

"I say, I will say to them, Creoles, countrymen, and lovers, boun voyadge an' good luck to ye's."

For several moments there was much translating, bowing, and murmured acknowledgments; Mazaro said: "*Bueno!*" and all around among the long double rank of moustachioed lips amiable teeth were gleaming, some white, some brown, some yellow, like bones in the grass.

"And now, gentlemen," Galahad recommenced, "fellow-exiles, once more. Munsher D'Himecourt, it was yer practice, until lately, to reward a good talker with a dlass from the hands o' yer daughter." (*Si, si!*) "I'm bur a poor speaker." (*Si, si, señor, z-a-fine-a kin'-a can be; si!*) "However, I'll ask ye, not knowun bur it may be the last time we all meet together, if ye will not let the goddess of the Café des Exilés grace our company with her presence for just about one minute?" (*Yez-a, señor; si; yez-a; oui.*)

Every head was turned toward the old man, nodding the echoed request.

"Ye see, friends," said Galahad in a true Irish whisper, as M. D'Hemecourt left the apartment, "her poseetion has been a-growin' more and more embarrassin' daily, and the operaytions of our society were likely to make it wurse in the future; wherefore I have lately taken steps—I say I tuke steps this morn to relieve the old gentleman's distresses and his daughter's"—

He paused. M. D'Hemecourt entered with Pauline, and the exiles all rose up. Ah!—but why say again she was lovely?

Galahad stepped forward to meet her, took her hand, led her to the head of the board, and turning to the company, said:

"Friends and fellow-patriots, Misthress Shaughnessy."

There was no outburst of astonishment—only the same old bowing, smiling, and murmuring of compliment. Galahad turned with a puzzled look to M. D'Hemecourt, and guessed the truth. In the joy of an old man's heart he had already that afternoon told the truth to each and every man separately, as a secret too deep for them to reveal, but too sweet for him to keep. The Major and Pauline were man and wife.

The last laugh that was ever heard in the Café des Exilés sounded softly through the room.

"Lads," said the Irishman. "Fill yer dlasses. Here's to the Café des Exilés, God bless her!"

And the meeting slowly adjourned.

Two days later, signs and rumors of sickness began to find place about the Café des Réfugiés, and the Mexican physician made three calls in one day. It was said by the people around that the tall Cuban gentleman named Benito was very sick in one of the back rooms. A similar frequency of the same physician's calls was noticed about the Café des Exilés.

"The man with one eyebrow," said the neighbors, "is sick. Pauline left the house yesterday to make room for him."

"Ah! is it possible?"

"Yes, it is really true; she and her husband. She took her mocking-bird with her; he carried it; he came back alone."

On the next afternoon the children about the Café des Réfugiés enjoyed the spectacle of the invalid Cuban moved on a trestle to the Café des Exilés, although he did not look so deathly sick as they could have liked to see him, and on the fourth morning the doors of the Café des Exilés remained closed. A black-bordered funeral notice, veiled with crape, announced that the great Caller-home of exiles had served his summons upon Don Pedro Hernandez (surname borrowed for the occasion), and Don Carlos Mendez y Benito.

The hour for the funeral was fixed at four P.M. It never took place. Down at the Picayune Tier on the river bank there was, about two o'clock that same day, a slight commotion, and those who stood aimlessly about a small, neat schooner, said she was "seized." At four there suddenly appeared before the Café des Exilés a squad of men with silver crescents on their breasts—police officers. The old cottage sat silent with closed doors, the crape hanging heavily over the funeral notice like a widow's veil, the little unseen garden sending up odors from its hidden censers, and the old weeping-willow bending over all.

"Nobody here?" asks the leader.

The crowd which has gathered stares without answering.

As quietly and peaceably as possible the officers pry open the door. They enter, and the crowd pushes in after. There are the two coffins, looking very heavy and solid, lying in state but unguarded.

The crowd draws a breath of astonishment. "Are they going to wrench the tops off with hatchet and chisel?"

Rap, rap, rap; wrench, rap, wrench. Ah! the cases come open.

"Well kept?" asks the leader flippantly.

"Oh, yes," is the reply. And then all laugh.

One of the lookers-on pushes up and gets a glimpse within.

"What is it?" ask the other idlers.

He tells one quietly.

"What did he say?" ask the rest, one of another.

"He says they are not dead men, but new muskets"—

"Here, clear out!" cries an officer, and the loiterers fall back and by and by straggle off.

The exiles? What became of them, do you ask? Why, nothing; they were not troubled, but they never all came together again. Said a chief-of-police to Major Shaughnessy years afterward:

"Major, there was only one thing that kept your expedition from succeeding—you were too sly about it. Had you come out flat and said what you were doing, we'd never a-said a word to you. But that little fellow gave us the wink, and then we had to stop you."

And was no one punished? Alas! one was. Poor, pretty, curly-headed traitorous Mazaro! He was drawn out of Carondelet Canal —cold, dead! And when his wounds were counted—they were just the number of the Café des Exilés' children, less Galahad. But the mother—that is, the old café—did not see it; she had gone up the night before in a chariot of fire.

In the files of the old *Picayune* and *Price-Current* of 1837 may be seen the mention of Galahad Shaughnessy among the merchants—"our enterprising and accomplished fellow-townsman," and all that. But old M. D'Hemecourt's name is cut in marble, and his citizenship is in "a city whose maker and builder is God."

Only yesterday I dined with the Shaughnessys—fine old couple and handsome. Their children sat about them and entertained me most pleasantly. But there isn't one can tell a tale as their father can—'twas he told me this one, though here and there my enthusiasm may have taken liberties. He knows the history of every old house in the French Quarter; or, if he happens not to know a true one, he can make one up as he goes along.

'SIEUR GEORGE

*I*N THE heart of New Orleans stands a large four-story brick building, that has so stood for about three-quarters of a century. Its rooms are rented to a class of persons occupying them simply for lack of activity to find better and cheaper quarters elsewhere. With its gray stucco peeling off in broad patches, it has a solemn look of gentility in rags, and stands, or, as it were, hangs, about the corner of two ancient streets, like a faded fop who pretends to be looking for employment.

Under its main archway is a dingy apothecary-shop. On one street is the bazaar of a *modiste en robes et chapeaux* and other humble shops; on the other, the immense batten doors with gratings over the lintels, barred and bolted with masses of cobwebbed iron, like the door of a donjon, are overhung by a creaking sign (left by the sheriff), on which is faintly discernible the mention of wines and liquors. A peep through one of the shops reveals a square court within, hung with many lines of wet clothes, its sides hugged by rotten staircases that seem vainly trying to clamber out of the rubbish.

The neighborhood is one long since given up to fifth-rate shops, whose masters and mistresses display such enticing mottoes as "*Au gagne petit!*" Innumerable children swarm about, and, by some charm of the place, are not run over, but obstruct the sidewalks playing their clamorous games.

The building is a thing of many windows, where passably good-looking women appear and disappear, clad in cotton gowns, water-

ing little outside shelves of flowers and cacti, or hanging canaries' cages. Their husbands are keepers in wine-warehouses, rent-collectors for the agents of old Frenchmen who have been laid up to dry in Paris, custom-house supernumeraries and court-clerks' deputies (for your second-rate Creole is a great seeker for little offices). A decaying cornice hangs over, dropping bits of mortar on passers below, like a boy at a boarding-house.

The landlord is one Kookoo, an ancient Creole of doubtful purity of blood, who in his landlordly old age takes all suggestions of repairs as personal insults. He was but a stripling when his father left him this inheritance, and has grown old and wrinkled and brown, a sort of periodically animate mummy, in the business. He smokes cascarilla, wears velveteen, and is as punctual as an executioner.

To Kookoo's venerable property a certain old man used for many years to come every evening, stumbling through the groups of prattling children who frolicked about in the early moonlight—whose name no one knew, but whom all the neighbors designated by the title of 'Sieur George. It was his wont to be seen taking a straight— too straight—course toward his home, never careening to right or left, but now forcing himself slowly forward, as though there were a high gale in front, and now scudding briskly ahead at a ridiculous little dog-trot, as if there were a tornado behind. He would go up the main staircase very carefully, sometimes stopping halfway up for thirty or forty minutes' doze, but getting to the landing eventually, and tramping into his room in the second story, with no little elation to find it still there. Were it not for these slight symptoms of potations, he was such a one as you would pick out of a thousand for a miser. A year or two ago he suddenly disappeared.

A great many years ago, when the old house was still new, a young man with no baggage save a small hair-trunk came and took the room I have mentioned and another adjoining. He supposed he might stay fifty days—and he stayed fifty years and over. This was a very fashionable neighborhood, and he kept the rooms on that account month after month.

But when he had been here about a year something happened to him, so it was rumored, that greatly changed the tenor of his life; and from that time on there began to appear in him and to accumulate upon each other in a manner which became the profound study of Kookoo, the symptoms of a decay, whose cause baffled the land-lord's limited powers of conjecture for well-nigh half a century. Hints of a duel, of a reason warped, of disinheritance, and many other unauthorized rumors, fluttered up and floated off, while he became recluse, and, some say, began incidentally to betray the un-manly habit which we have already noticed. His neighbors would have continued neighborly had he allowed them, but he never let himself be understood, and *les Américains* are very droll anyhow; so, as they could do nothing else, they cut him.

So exclusive he became that (though it may have been for econ-omy) he never admitted even a housemaid, but kept his apartments himself. Only the merry serenaders, who in those times used to sing under the balconies, would now and then give him a crumb of their feast for pure fun's sake; and after a while, because they could not find out his full name, called him, at hazard, George—but always prefixing Monsieur. Afterward, when he began to be careless in his dress, and the fashion of serenading had passed away, the commoner people dared to shorten the title to " 'Sieur George."

Many seasons came and went. The city changed like a growing boy; gentility and fashion went up-town, but 'Sieur George still re-tained his rooms. Every one knew him slightly, and bowed, but no one seemed to know him well, unless it were a brace or so of those convivial fellows in regulation-blue at little Fort St. Charles. He often came home late, with one of these on either arm, all singing different tunes and stopping at every twenty steps to tell secrets. But by and by the fort was demolished, church and government property melted down under the warm demand for building-lots, the city spread like a ringworm—and one day 'Sieur George steps out of the old house in full regimentals!

The Creole neighbors rush bareheaded into the middle of the street, as though there were an earthquake or a chimney on fire. What to do or say or think they do not know; they are at their wits' ends, therefore well-nigh happy. However, there is a German blacksmith's shop near by, and they watch to see what *Jacob* will do. Jacob steps into the street with every eye upon him; he approaches Mon-sieur—he addresses to him a few remarks—they shake hands—they engage in some conversation—Monsieur places his hand on his sword!—now Monsieur passes.

The populace crowd around the blacksmith, children clap their hands softly and jump up and down on tiptoes of expectation— 'Sieur George is going to the war in Mexico!

"Ah!" says a little girl in the throng, " 'Sieur George's two rooms will be empty; I find that very droll."

The landlord—this same Kookoo—is in the group. He hurls himself into the house and up the stairs. "Fifteen years pass since he have been in those room!" He arrives at the door—it is shut— "It is lock!"

In short, further investigation revealed that a youngish lady in black, who had been seen by several neighbors to enter the house, but had not, of course, been suspected of such remarkable intentions, had, in company with a middle-aged slave-woman, taken these two rooms, and now, at the slightly opened door, proffered a month's rent in advance. What could a landlord do but smile? Yet there was a pretext left; "the rooms must need repairs?"—"No, sir; he could look in and see." Joy! he looked in. All was neatness. The floor unbroken, the walls cracked but a little, and the cracks closed with new plaster, no doubt by the jealous hand of 'Sieur George himself. Kookoo's eyes swept sharply round the two apartments. The furniture was all there. Moreover, there was Monsieur's little hair-trunk. He should not soon forget that trunk. One day, fifteen years or more before, he had taken hold of that trunk to assist Monsieur to arrange his apartment, and Monsieur had drawn his fist back and cried to him to "drop it!" *Mais!* there it was, looking very suspicious in Kookoo's eyes, and the lady's domestic, as tidy as a yellow-bird, went and sat on it. Could that trunk contain treasure? It might, for Madame wanted to shut the door, and, in fact, did so.

The lady was quite handsome—had been more so, but was still young—spoke the beautiful language, and kept, in the inner room, her discreet and taciturn mulattress, a tall, straight woman, with a fierce eye, but called by the young Creoles of the neighborhood "confound' good lookin'."

Among *les Américains,* where the new neighbor always expects to be called upon by the older residents, this lady might have made friends in spite of being as reserved as 'Sieur George; but the reverse being the Creole custom, and she being well pleased to keep her own company, chose mystery rather than society.

(*213*)

The poor landlord was sorely troubled; it must not be that any thing *de trop* take place in his house. He watched the two rooms narrowly, but without result, save to find that Madame plied her needle for pay, spent her money for little else besides harpstrings, and took good care of the little trunk of Monsieur. This espionage was a good turn to the mistress and maid, for when Kookoo announced that all was proper, no more was said by outsiders. Their landlord never got but one question answered by the middle-aged maid:

"Madame, he feared, was a litt' bit embarrass' *pour* money, eh?"

"*Non;* Mademoiselle (Mademoiselle, you notice!) had some property, but did not want to eat it up."

Sometimes lady-friends came, in very elegant private carriages, to see her, and one or two seemed to beg her—but in vain—to go away with them; but these gradually dropped off, until lady and servant were alone in the world. And so years, and the Mexican war, went by.

The volunteers came home; peace reigned, and the city went on spreading up and down the land; but 'Sieur George did not return. It overran the country like coco-grass. Fields, roads, woodlands, that were once 'Sieur George's places of retreat from mankind, were covered all over with little one-story houses in the "Old Third," and fine residences and gardens up in "Lafayette." Streets went slicing like a butcher's knife, through old colonial estates, whose first masters never dreamed of the city reaching them—and 'Sieur George was still away. The four-story brick got old and ugly, and the surroundings dim and dreamy. Theatres, processions, dry-goods stores, government establishments, banks, hotels, and all spirit of enterprise were gone to Canal Street and beyond, and the very beggars were gone with them. The little trunk got very old and bald, and still its owner lingered; still the lady, somewhat the worse for lapse of time, looked from the balcony-window in the brief southern twilights, and the maid every morning shook a worn rug or two over the dangerous-looking railing; and yet neither had made friends or enemies.

The two rooms, from having been stingily kept at first, were needing repairs half the time, and the occupants were often moving, now into one, now back into the other; yet the hair-trunk was seen only by glimpses, the landlord, to his infinite chagrin, always being a little too late in offering his services, the women, whether it was light or heavy, having already moved it. He thought it significant.

Late one day of a most bitter winter—that season when, to the ecstatic amazement of a whole city-full of children, snow covered the streets ankle-deep—there came a soft tap on the corridor-door of this pair of rooms. The lady opened it, and beheld a tall, lank, iron-gray man, a total stranger, standing behind—Monsieur George! Both men were weather-beaten, scarred, and tattered. Across 'Sieur George's crown, leaving a long, bare streak through his white hair, was the souvenir of a Mexican sabre.

The landlord had accompanied them to the door: it was a magnificent opportunity. Mademoiselle asked them all in, and tried to furnish a seat to each; but failing, 'Sieur George went straight across the room and *sat on the hair-trunk*. The action was so conspicuous, the landlord laid it up in his penetrative mind.

'Sieur George was quiet, or, as it appeared, quieted. The mulattress stood near him, and to her he addressed, in an undertone, most of the little he said, leaving Mademoiselle to his companion. The stranger was a warm talker, and seemed to please the lady from the first; but if he pleased, nothing else did. Kookoo, intensely curious, sought some pretext for staying, but found none. They were, altogether, an uncongenial company. The lady seemed to think Kookoo had no business there; 'Sieur George seemed to think the same concerning his companion; and the few words between Mademoiselle and 'Sieur George were cool enough. The maid appeared nearly satisfied, but could not avoid casting an anxious eye at times upon her mistress. Naturally the visit was short.

The next day but one, the two gentlemen came again in better attire. 'Sieur George evidently disliked his companion, yet would not rid himself of him. The stranger was a gesticulating, stagy fellow, much Monsieur's junior, an incessant talker in Creole-French, always excited on small matters and unable to appreciate a great one. Once, as they were leaving, Kookoo—accidents will happen—was under the stairs. As they began to descend the tall man was speaking; "—better to bury it"—the startled landlord heard him say, and held his breath, thinking of the trunk; but no more was uttered.

A week later they came again.

A week later they came again.

A week later they came yet again!

The landlord's eyes began to open. There must be a courtship in progress. It was very plain now why 'Sieur George had wished not to be accompanied by the tall gentleman; but since his visits had become regular and frequent, it was equally plain why he did not get rid of him;—because it would not look well to be going and coming too often alone. Maybe it was only this tender passion that the tall man had thought "better to bury." Lately there often came sounds of gay conversation from the first of the two rooms, which had been turned into a parlor; and as, week after week, the friends

came down-stairs, the tall man was always in high spirits and anxious to embrace 'Sieur George, who—"sly dog," thought the landlord—would try to look grave, and only smiled in an embarrassed way. "Ah! Monsieur, you tink to be varry conning; *mais* you not so conning as Kookoo, no"; and the inquisitive little man would shake his head and smile, and shake his head again, as a man has a perfect right to do under the conviction that he has been for twenty years baffled by a riddle and is learning to read it at last; he had guessed what was in 'Sieur George's head, he would by and by guess what was in the trunk.

A few months passed quickly away, and it became apparent to every eye in or about the ancient mansion that the landlord's guess was not so bad; in fact, that Mademoiselle was to be married.

On a certain rainy spring afternoon, a single hired hack drove up to the main entrance of the old house, and after some little bustle and the gathering of a crowd of damp children about the big doorway, 'Sieur George, muffled in a newly repaired overcoat, jumped out and went up-stairs. A moment later he reappeared, leading Mademoiselle, wreathed and veiled, down the stairway. Very fair was Mademoiselle still. Her beauty was mature—fully ripe—maybe a little too much so, but only a little; and as she came down with the ravishing odor of bridal flowers floating about her, she seemed the garlanded victim of a pagan sacrifice. The mulattress in holiday gear followed behind.

The landlord owed a duty to the community. He arrested the maid on the last step: "Your mistress, she goin' *pour marier* 'Sieur George? It make me glad, glad, glad!"

"Marry 'Sieur George? *Non*, monsieur."

"*Non?* Not marrie 'Sieur George? *Mais comment?*"

"She's going to marry the tall gentleman."

"*Diable!* ze long gentyman!"— With his hands upon his forehead, he watched the carriage trundle away. It passed out of sight through the rain; he turned to enter the house, and all at once tottered under the weight of a tremendous thought—they had left the trunk! He hurled himself up-stairs as he had done seven years before, but again—"Ah, bah!!"—the door was locked, and not a picayune of rent due.

Late that night a small square man, in a wet overcoat, fumbled his way into the damp entrance of the house, stumbled up the cracking stairs, unlocked, after many languid efforts, the door of the two rooms, and falling over the hair-trunk, slept until the morning sunbeams climbed over the balcony and in at the window, and shone full on the back of his head. Old Kookoo, passing the door just then, was surprised to find it slightly ajar—pushed it open silently, and saw, within, 'Sieur George in the act of rising from his knees beside the mysterious trunk! He had come back to be once more the tenant of the two rooms.

'Sieur George, for the second time, was a changed man—changed from bad to worse; from being retired and reticent, he had come, by reason of advancing years, or mayhap that which had left the terrible scar on his face, to be garrulous. When, once in a while, employment sought him (for he never sought employment), whatever remuneration he received went its way for something that left him dingy and threadbare. He now made a lively acquaintance with his landlord, as, indeed, with every soul in the neighborhood, and told all his adventures in Mexican prisons and Cuban cities; including full details of the hardships and perils experienced jointly with the "long gentleman" who had married Mademoiselle, and who was no Mexican or Cuban, but a genuine Louisianian.

"It was he that fancied me," he said, "not I him; but once he had fallen in love with me I hadn't the force to cast him off. How Madame ever should have liked him was one of those woman's freaks that a man mustn't expect to understand. He was no more fit for her than rags are fit for a queen; and I could have choked his head off the night he hugged me round the neck and told me what a suicide she had committed. But other fine women are committing that same folly every day, only they don't wait until they're thirty-four or five to do it.— 'Why don't I like him?' Well, for one reason, he's a drunkard!" Here Kookoo, whose imperfect knowledge of English prevented his intelligent reception of the story, would laugh as if the joke came in just at this point.

However, with all Monsieur's prattle, he never dropped a word about the man he had been before he went away; and the great hair-trunk puzzle was still the same puzzle, growing greater every day.

Thus the two rooms had been the scene of some events quite queer, if not really strange; but the queerest that ever they presented, I guess, was 'Sieur George coming in there one day, crying like a little child, and bearing in his arms an infant—a girl—the lovely offspring of the drunkard whom he so detested, and poor, robbed, spirit-broken and now dead Madame. He took good care of the orphan, for orphan she was very soon. The long gentleman was pulled out of the Old Basin one morning, and 'Sieur George identified the body at the Trémé station. He never hired a nurse—the father had sold the lady's maid quite out of sight; so he brought her through all the little ills and around all the sharp corners of baby-life and childhood, without a human hand to help him, until one evening, having persistently shut his eyes to it for weeks and months, like one trying to sleep in the sunshine, he awoke to the realization that she was a woman. It was a smoky one in November, the first cool day of autumn. The sunset was dimmed by the smoke of burning prairies, the air was full of the ashes of grass and reeds, ragged urchins were lugging home sticks of cordwood, and when a bit of coal fell from a cart in front of Kookoo's old house, a child was boxed half across the street and robbed of the booty by a *blanchisseuse de fin* from over the way.

The old man came home quite steady. He mounted the stairs smartly without stopping to rest, went with a step unusually light and quiet to his chamber and sat by the window opening upon the rusty balcony.

It was a small room, sadly changed from what it had been in old times; but then so was 'Sieur George. Close and dark it was, the walls stained with dampness and the ceiling full of bald places that showed the lathing. The furniture was cheap and meagre, including conspicuously the small, curious-looking hair-trunk. The floor was of wide slabs fastened down with spikes, and sloping up and down in one or two broad undulations, as if they had drifted far enough down the current of time to feel the tide-swell.

However, the floor was clean, the bed well made, the cypress table in place, and the musty smell of the walls partly neutralized by a geranium on the window-sill.

He so coming in and sitting down, an unseen person called from the room adjoining (of which, also, he was still the rentee), to know if he were he, and being answered in the affirmative, said, "Papa George, guess who was here to-day?"

"Kookoo, for the rent?"

"Yes, but he will not come back."

"No? why not?"

"Because you will not pay him."

"No? and why not?"

"Because I have paid him."

"Impossible! where did you get the money?"

"Cannot guess?—Mother Nativity."

"What, not for embroidery?"

"No? and why not? *Mais oui!*"—saying which, and with a pleasant laugh, the speaker entered the room. She was a girl of sixteen or
thereabout, very beautiful, with very black hair and eyes. A face
and form more entirely out of place you could not have found in the
whole city. She sat herself at his feet, and, with her interlocked
hands upon his knee, and her face, full of childish innocence mingled with womanly wisdom, turned to his, appeared for a time to
take principal part in a conversation which, of course, could not be
overheard in the corridor outside.

Whatever was said, she presently rose, he opened his arms, and

she sat on his knee and kissed him. This done, there was a silence,
both smiling pensively and gazing out over the rotten balcony into
the street. After a while she started up, saying something about the
change of weather, and, slipping away, thrust a match between the
bars of the grate. The old man turned about to the fire, and she
from her little room brought a low sewing-chair and sat beside him,
laying her head on his knee, and he stroking her brow with his brown
palm.

And then, in an altered—a low, sad tone—he began a monotonous recital.

Thus they sat, he talking very steadily and she listening, until all the neighborhood was wrapped in slumber—all the neighbors, but not Kookoo.

Kookoo in his old age had become a great eavesdropper; his ear and eye took turns at the key-hole that night, for he tells things that were not intended for outside hearers. He heard the girl sobbing, and the old man saying, "But you must go now. You cannot stay with me safely or decently, much as I wish it. The Lord only knows how I'm to bear it, or where you're to go; but He's your Lord, child, and He'll make a place for you. I was your grandfather's death; I frittered your poor, dead mother's fortune away: let that be the last damage I do.

"I have always meant every thing for the best," he added half in soliloquy.

From all Kookoo could gather, he must have been telling her the very story just recounted. She had dropped quite to the floor, hiding her face in her hands, and was saying between her sobs, "I cannot go, Papa George; oh, Papa George, I cannot go!"

Just then 'Sieur George, having kept a good resolution all day, was encouraged by the orphan's pitiful tones to contemplate the most senseless act he ever attempted to commit. He said to the sobbing girl that she was not of his blood; that she was nothing to him by natural ties; that his covenant was with her grandsire to care for his offspring; and though it had been poorly kept, it might be breaking it worse than ever to turn her out upon ever so kind a world.

"I have tried to be good to you all these years. When I took you, a wee little baby, I took you for better or worse. I intended to do well by you all your childhood-days, and to do best at last. I thought surely we should be living well by this time, and you could choose from a world full of homes and a world full of friends.

"I don't see how I missed it!" Here he paused a moment in meditation, and presently resumed with some suddenness:

"I thought that education, far better than Mother Nativity has given you, should have afforded your sweet charms a noble setting; that good mothers and sisters would be wanting to count you into their families, and that the blossom of a happy womanhood would open perfect and full of sweetness.

"I would have given my life for it. I did give it, such as it was; but it was a very poor concern, I know—my life—and not enough to buy any good thing.

"I have had a thought of something, but I'm afraid to tell it. It didn't come to me to-day or yesterday; it has beset me a long time—for months."

The girl gazed into the embers, listening intensely.

"And oh! dearie, if I could only get you to think the same way, you might stay with me then."

"How long?" she asked, without stirring.

"Oh, as long as Heaven should let us. But there is only one chance," he said, as it were feeling his way, "only one way for us to stay together. Do you understand me?"

She looked up at the old man with a glance of painful inquiry.

"If you could be—my wife, dearie?"

She uttered a low, distressful cry, and, gliding swiftly into her room, for the first time in her young life turned the key between them.

And the old man sat and wept.

Then Kookoo, peering through the key-hole, saw that they had been looking into the little trunk. The lid was up, but the back was toward the door, and he could see no more than if it had been closed.

He stooped and stared into the aperture until his dry old knees were ready to crack. It seemed as if 'Sieur George was stone, only stone couldn't weep like that.

Every separate bone in his neck was hot with pain. He would have given ten dollars—ten sweet dollars!—to have seen 'Sieur George get up and turn that trunk around.

There! 'Sieur George rose up—what a face!

He started toward the bed, and as he came to the trunk he paused, looked at it, muttered something about "ruin," and something about "fortune," kicked the lid down and threw himself across the bed.

Small profit to old Kookoo that he went to his own couch; sleep was not for the little landlord. For well-nigh half a century he had suspected his tenant of having a treasure hidden in his house, and to-night he had heard his own admission that in the little trunk was a fortune. Kookoo had never felt so poor in all his days before. He felt a Creole's anger, too, that a tenant should be the holder of wealth while his landlord suffered poverty.

And he knew very well, too, did Kookoo, what the tenant would do. If he did not know what he kept in the trunk, he knew what he kept behind it, and he knew he would take enough of it to-night to make him sleep soundly.

No one would ever have supposed Kookoo capable of a crime. He was too fearfully impressed with the extra-hazardous risks of dishonesty; he was old, too, and weak, and, besides all, intensely a coward. Nevertheless, while it was yet two or three hours before daybreak, the sleep-forsaken little man arose, shuffled into his garments, and in his stocking-feet sought the corridor leading to 'Sieur George's apartment. The November night, as it often does in that region, had grown warm and clear; the stars were sparkling like diamonds pendent in the deep blue heavens, and at every window and lattice and cranny the broad, bright moon poured down its glittering beams upon the hoary-headed thief, as he crept along the mouldering galleries and down the ancient corridor that led to 'Sieur George's chamber.

'Sieur George's door, though ever so slowly opened, protested with a loud creak. The landlord, wet with cold sweat from head to foot, and shaking till the floor trembled, paused for several minutes, and then entered the moon-lit apartment. The tenant, lying as if he had not moved, was sleeping heavily. And now the poor coward trembled so, that to kneel before the trunk, without falling, he did not know how. Twice, thrice, he was near tumbling headlong. He became as cold as ice. But the sleeper stirred, and the thought of losing his opportunity strung his nerves up in an instant. He went softly down upon his knees, laid his hands upon the lid, lifted it, and let in the intense moonlight. The trunk was full, full, crowded down and running over full, of the tickets of the Havana Lottery!

A little after daybreak, Kookoo from his window saw the orphan, pausing on the corner. She stood for a moment, and then drove into the dense fog which had floated in from the river, and disappeared. He never saw her again.

But her Lord is taking care of her. Once only she has seen 'Sieur George. She had been in the belvedere of the house which she now calls home, looking down upon the outspread city. Far away south-ward and westward the great river glistened in the sunset. Along its sweeping bends the chimneys of a smoking commerce, the maga-zines of surplus wealth, the gardens of the opulent, the steeples of a hundred sanctuaries and thousands on thousands of mansions and hovels covered the fertile birthright arpents which 'Sieur George, in his fifty years' stay, had seen tricked away from dull colonial Esaus by their blue-eyed brethren of the North. Nearer by she looked upon the forlornly silent region of lowly dwellings, neglected by legislation and shunned by all lovers of comfort, that once had been the smiling fields of her own grandsire's broad plantation; and but a little way off, trudging across the marshy commons, her eye caught sight of 'Sieur George following the sunset out upon the prairies to find a night's rest in the high grass.

She turned at once, gathered the skirt of her pink calico uni-form, and, watching her steps through her tears, descended the steep winding-stair to her frequent kneeling-place under the fragrant candles of the chapel-altar in Mother Nativity's asylum.

'Sieur George is houseless. He cannot find the orphan. Mother Nativity seems to know nothing of her. If he could find her now, and could get from her the use of ten dollars for but three days, he knows a combination which would repair all the past; it could not fail, he—thinks. But he cannot find her, and the letters he writes—all containing the one scheme—disappear in the mail-box, and there's an end.